THE
DEPTHS
WITHIN

PART 1

Printed in Australia
First published July 2023
This edition first published 2024

Cover design by Melinda Childs
Internal design by Jessica Chaplin

Paperback ISBN 978-1-7637529-0-0
eBook ISBN 978-1-6637529-1-7

More great titles can be found by visiting www.matthewcirsonauthor.com.au

A catalogue record for this work is available from the National Library of Australia

THE
DEPTHS
WITHIN

PART 1

MATTHEW CIRSON

50% of author's proceeds from the sale of this book will be donated to "Soldier On," to assist with the health and mental wellbeing of current and ex-serving ADF personnel.

MICHAEL

The eastern world, it is explodin',
Violence flarin', bullets loadin',
You're old enough to kill but not for votin',
You don't believe in war, but what's that gun you're totin',
And even the Jordan River has bodies floatin',
But you tell me over and over and over again, my friend,
Ah, you don't believe we're on the eve of destruction.

Barry McGuire – *Eve of Destruction* (1965)

It was another typical morning for Michael Baker; he had woken up alone and broken his fast in sweet solitude. The boy had cleaned himself, brushed his teeth with the disgusting 'Close Up' mouth wash and toothpaste in one, with red gel instead of white. He remembered the first time he had ever used it; the sight of the red liquid pouring out of his mouth and trickling down the drain had almost made him faint. He had rinsed and rinsed while he sporadically checked the inside of his mouth, the red gums, and his bright white teeth in the dusty mirror of the only bathroom for twenty minutes. Until his father beat him for using too much of the tank water.

He often thought of his father during his long, daily walk to the Chinchilla sawmill that his father managed. His head slanted forward as he watched his engineering boots trudge down the freshly graded dirt road. He watched the dust erupt in a furious flurry each time he swung his foot a little too low and mused at how the wind slowly whisked it away to eventually dissipate and vanish, as though it had never existed. Sometimes he wished he could do the same.

Tony Baker was a large man who stood over six foot with massive, mauler hands and large, hairy arms. He wore his temper like his hair, so short that you could barely hide a blade of grass beneath its longest point. Tony had served with the Royal Australian Army in the Second World War as a sapper and saw extensive combat in the South Pacific. Along with his brothers in arms, they had traversed the Kokoda Trail and had eventually, with great loss, routed the Japanese from their holes and thrown them back, inch by inch. That is all that Tony would ever tell Michael or Jack, his older brother, his voice slurring, heavy with drink. His eyes red with intoxication, half-closed, failing to focus. Yet even the boy could see there was so much more; he could see it in his eyes. He saw it in the way he drank, the way the big man hit him for running in the house or for not completing his chores. Once the target of his rage had been laid down on the ground, they were left to wither under the look of fury and disgust as he stared down at either of his two children or, worse yet, his wife.

Michael kicked a pebble off the road and watched it vanish into the gidgee bushes that scattered the fire trail. He thought to a time when he was no older than six or seven and had rushed to his father's side, when he had pushed through the rear screen door at their residence in the north-east country of Chinchilla, Queensland. Happy to share with his father that he had been watching a documentary on the Second World War. Tony had faltered for what had only seemed like a split second as he processed the words that came from the smiling mouth of his youngest child. The big man glanced down at his darling son and dropped his jacket onto the back of one of the worn, timber dining room chairs which surrounded the Baker family's undersized dining room table like the 'Kings Guard' of a fictional tale. He walked to the fridge door without a word, opened it and removed his first Fosters long neck. Tony tore the lid from its perch around the brown glass rim with his monstrous hand and stood while he stared down at his son, whose smile still had not faltered. As he tipped his head back and poured the brown, stinking liquid into his mouth, Michael still saw one eye staring down at him, unblinking, unwavering. It wasn't until his mother had walked into the room did Tony open his mouth.

'The boy tells me he's been watching the war.'

His mother smiled briefly at her husband and continued to simmer the mince that was browning in the old cast iron pan above the wood fire stove. 'You know he loves watching those things; he swore he saw you once to—'

For a large man, Tony Baker had always been greasy quick; this was but one of the times that Michael could remember the sheer speed of the man. He brought the back of his right hand across his wife's face in an effortless movement that sent Grace Baker sprawling to the floor, along with the mince and the pitted old iron pan. The clap that rang out as the backside of his father's hand drove into the soft cheek of his mother's face stuck with the boy for years, along with the crash that the old cast iron pan made as it slammed into the hardwood floor, hard enough to mark it. The mince for her husband's meal still sizzled while it covered the kitchen floor from the stove to the back door.

Grace raised her hand to caress her quickly reddening cheek. With a grimace, she propped herself up with her other hand. 'Tony?' She whimpered as she looked up at her husband.

Tony stood over her with a look of absolute disgust on his face; Michael remembered the feeling of relief that his father's attention wasn't on himself when his temper had exploded. He tilted his head back for another swig of beer and continued to stare at Grace in the same manner. 'I work my fuckin' ass off day after day.' He raised one of his huge hands to point at Michael, 'and you let this fat shit sit on his, to watch what I did in my past?'

Grace whimpered again and mumbled an apology. However, she still had not broken her eye contact at this stage.

'You get him working, Grace. I'm not carrying him forever, and I'm not hearing about those days again; I thought I married a woman with sense.'

Grace broke her eye contact with her husband and turned her face to the ground. Her long dark hair tumbled around her neck and shoulders, so long it touched the floor in places. Her ears shone red with her own anger or shame; the boy never knew which. At some point, Tony had realised that his son still stood there. He stomped over to him and grabbed Michael by the scruff of the neck, lifting him from the ground to swing by his side. He felt the rough feel of his father's hand, the power in his arm and the strange sensation of weightlessness.

'Clean this shit up,' Tony barked as he stomped his way to the rear door of their dwelling, the same door he had entered some two minutes before. Michael remembered his thoughts that perhaps the night wouldn't have been so memorable if only he hadn't opened his big mouth. Tony pushed the screen door open with his son's forehead and roughly threw him onto the grass to the left of the path; Michael was at least thankful that he wasn't thrown on the concrete.

'Sit down!' his father exclaimed as his bulk disappeared into the darkness. Michael remembered sobbing at this stage; succumbing to the cool of the night air and the dampness of the lawn beneath him. He recalled the hard decision to run back inside to the safety of the house and of his mother or to stay and obey. He remembered the following thought, which still chilled him: *Is it truly safe with Mum?*

She had been reduced to a whimpering mess due to her son's happiness to see his father, for his weakness. It was at this point Tony's large, unforgettable shape had emerged from the darkness of the Bakers backyard. In one hand, he held his old axe; in the other, a large dead gum branch. The big man's heavy footfalls echoed softly as his weight drove his boots into the soft ground. The lighter point of the dead branch in his hand scratched at the ground behind him as he moved, as if trying to grasp some strong surface to save itself from the man's iron grip. Tony embedded the axe head into the soft grass and threw the dead gum branch to the ground in front of his son.

'Now, make yourself useful and cut up this branch to keep your family warm tonight.'

'D-Dad,' Michael had started, but it was a mistake. He didn't learn quickly in those days; that was the second time he had failed to keep his mouth shut. The next instant, he had found himself sprawled on the ground, clutching his face and staring at the grass. The inside of his head erupted with the ringing from his ear, and his chest heaved uncontrollably now with the sobs he could not contain.

'You fuckin' want another one?' Tony growled beneath his breath, his hand still cocked, 'Get going or sleep out here tonight; I couldn't give a shit either way.' Tony, at that point, straightened up and stretched his back; he turned without a further word and pulled the rusting screen door open and disappeared back into the kitchen. The screen door clapped a few times against its frame as it swung back on its hinges. Michael, still down in the grass, continued to sob. When he heard some more soft padding on the grass behind him. In the moonlight, he made out the colossal frame of his older brother, Jack slowly made his way along the side of the house. He stopped about five feet away from his younger brother and leaned up against the cladding with a grim look. Jack always looked grim. For a boy of early adolescence, he had a remarkably deep voice. It was easy to see that sooner rather than later, the elder brother was going to outgrow his father and outweigh him. Still, Jack was no idiot, and he knew what side his bread was buttered on and how to keep it that way. He avoided Tony like the plague.

'Better get to it; you'll get it worse if he gets another beer into him and you haven't started.' His voice was truly deep; he had to keep his words low at this point so their boom wouldn't attract their father.

'Can't you help me?' Michael had asked, still on the ground. He continued to sob and cupped his red, stinging cheek. His eyes fixated on the axe head buried in the ground, its handle like the hull of an alien ship marooned in foreign soil.

'You started this; you sleep in the bed you've made for yourself. If I help you, I'll get it worse.' Jack shifted his weight from the wall and slowly stood back under his own power. He crossed his arms and frowned; his jaw muscles worked. 'You'll get hit again. Maybe not today, but you'll learn to handle it.' He brought one of his own large hands up to his head and scratched at his scalp. His bicep bulged as his fingers moved to ease the itch. Jack could have broken the branch to kindling with his bare hands, but he still wasn't going to help his brother. 'You're the one that got Mum hit anyway, so why would I help you?' Jack swung his huge arm back down to his side and turned his already monstrous frame to disappear back into the darkness of the Baker's lot.

'Jack,' Michael sobbed after him, but there was no answer apart from the soft padding of his large feet burying themselves into the soft grass as he trudged away and disappeared into the darkness as his father had before.

Michael clambered to his feet. His cheek still stung from the blow his father had laid down upon him. He held his hand out to grasp the axe handle; it settled upon the cold, hard dark timber that jutted out of the ground. The boy used his weight to free the steel head from its mooring, yet either the boy was too light, or the soft ground sucked to the pitted surface of the axe. He clutched it with trembling hands while tears freely poured from his small eyes and ran down his cheeks, one pale white, the other an inflamed red. Grunting between sobs, he slowly worked the axe head loose, then struggled to drag it over to the dead gum branch that still lay in wait for him. He placed one of his hands further up the shaft, kept the other low, and heaved.

Michael felt as if he were the mythical David in an attempt to lift Goliath's sword. A boy less than ten, who had shown no signs in following his father's build, as Jack had at such a young age. Crying out as he heaved again, Michael managed to lift the axe head a foot off the ground. He held the wavering axe head above the branch, his back already afire with strain, and let it fall. There was a dull thud as the heavy, pitted steel head fell onto the branch, bounced, and then fell to the grass. The indent the dull steel made in the timber was barely visible. Michael cried out in frustration; tears still stung his eyes. However, he arched his back as he strained once more to raise the axe up again. He lifted the steel as high as he could, this time a foot and a half above the ground. He squared his feet and lunged as the blade fell through the air to hit the branch five inches to the right of the original dent. The blade glanced as it connected and left a smaller indent than the first.

Inside the Baker's kitchen, he heard the muffled conversation, very short and unaffectionate. There was dull click and static with garbled noises, then eventually, soft tones fluttered into the boy's ears from the Kelvinator radio that endured its lonely life on the window-sill of the kitchen. It was the first time that the boy had heard this song. The muffled, static plagued tunes were difficult to hear clearly, but they were clear enough to understand the song.

'*Then, in 1915, my country said, son, it's time you stopped rambling; there's work to be done.*' Michael heaved the heavy axe head into the air again, his back stiff with an ache that had spread to his legs and arms; this was only the third swing. '*So, they gave me a tin hat, and they gave me a gun, and they marched me away to the war.*'

It took Michael what seemed like two hours in the cold to eventually break the dead gum branch into six pieces. Inside, he heard his mother cleaning the kitchen, the meal that he was yet to eat, more than likely trashed or consumed by his own father. He listened to the entirety of the song, and with each new verse, the words seemed to burn themselves into his brain. They called to him, nursed him, yet at the same time bludgeoned him worse than any hit from his father. As he heaved the dull steel into the air and let it take its treacherous fall, the words in his head echoed on and on.

'*And the band played Waltzing Matilda as the ships pulled away from the quay.*'

His hands were a bloody mess by the time he had finished. The dried timber didn't seem as cold and smooth as when he had first started, and his back screamed in agony.

'*And amidst all the tears, the flag-waving and cheers.*' He leaned the axe, its blood-streaked handle, up against the side of the clad house and picked up the few pieces of dead gum branch. He remembered how his hand had left a bloody print when he pulled open the rusting screen door and ambled into the house. '*We sailed off for Gallipoli*'

His father was seated in his accustomed chair at the head of the dining table, begrudgingly mauling his way through the mince that had been placed before him. His expression was that of disgust; he had a chunk of hard bread in his hands, which he used to sop up some of the juices from the oily mince. As the boy hobbled passed him, the big man lifted his gaze and saw the timber in his hands, and a furrowed expression came over his face.

'Boy,' the large man called without turning as he jammed a piece of the sopping bread into his mouth and chewed loudly. Michael, who had noticed that his brother and mother were absent, stopped and turned to look at his father. His eyes still stung from the tears that had continuously wet his cheeks throughout the ordeal.

'That's a gum branch,' the big man barked as he sopped up more juice from his place with the remaining chunk of hard, stale bread. He jammed it into his mouth once again as the excess oil ran down his dirty cheek to his chin, where it massed at the lowest point and finally fell to make a stain on his blue, chambray work shirt, which would remain till this day.

'I cut it for you,' Michael's almost inaudible voice quivered. 'Like you said.'

Tony carried on like he hadn't heard. 'Gum smokes when it's burned,' he barked as he pushed the plate in front of him away from his setting, signalling that he was finished with the meal. He pushed back the timber chair from the table; the legs groaned under his weight and echoed a low screech as they ground against the hardwood floor. Tony raised to his full height and snatched the timber chunks from his son's trembling, bleeding hands. They were all chipped and whittled from his untrained axe swings. The big man strode to the door that Michael had entered from, pushed it open and hurled the timber outside. 'You'll smoke the whole house out, you idiot. Gum branch, fair dinkum.' He shook his head. 'Get cleaned up and go to bed.' With that, Tony brushed past his bleeding, dirty son. He reefed another Fosters from the fridge and passed by Michael once more before he stormed outside. The screen door slapped against its frame as it swung shut in Michael's face. It was shortly after that, the tears started to flow once more in the boy's frustration.

Michael was now twelve, the same age that Jack had been back then. He was still nowhere near the height and weight of his older brother. He was five feet tall and weighed one hundred and fifty pounds soaking wet. Whereas Jack was now a monstrous seven feet and weighed a freakish three hundred and sixty pounds. The boy continued his journey down the fire trail from the Baker residence to the mill while he pondered the memory. He reminisced mainly about his mother and father. Grace Baker had come to him in his bed later that evening and had begged him not to blame his father. She had said that when Tony went overseas he was a beautiful man who only cared for her; he promised her they would marry on his return. He would whisk her away to a faraway paradise that she could only dream of. However, when he returned, the happy young man wasn't really there anymore. It couldn't be said that the big man didn't have a sense of humour; unfortunately, neither could it be it said that he slept peacefully and that his return home was without incident. Soon he started drinking, and it helped at first. He slept easier, and he was more relaxed, but as time went on, he needed to drink more and more to forget. The woman had pleaded with her son that night to never mention those days to him again, as it was wrong of her to let him watch that show.

The boy didn't see how it was her fault; he recalled the black and white faces of the young men boarding the ships to head overseas to glory. They were young; they were smiling, near invincible as the sheer thrill of the adventure that stood before them was visible in their eyes. But the boy could never remember his father with the same glint in his eye, the same boyish charm. The drinking had gotten worse over the last years. More often than not, he wouldn't return home and would either fall down drunk at the Chinchilla Hotel or collapse on the Darcy's porch swing.

The Darcy family owned the property adjacent to the Baker's lot. Paul, the head of the family, worked under Tony at the sawmill. Michael had taken a liking to Paul as he often removed the old man from the house; more importantly, he referred to Michael by the name Mick.

'Mick,' he said to himself, smiling as he rounded the final bend of his journey. As the fire trail widened and the scrub fell further away from the edges of the track, beaten back to submission from the years of constant use. His engineers' boots paced down the trail and continued to kick up dust on every third or fourth step. His hands jammed deep into the pockets of his jeans as he looked down at his own blue chambray shirt. 'Mick' was embroidered above the chest pocket on the left hand side. He preferred Mick to Michael. However, Darcy seemed to be the only one who referred to him by that name. As the mill came into view, the whistle powered by the steam of the boiler hollered its dreadful tune to the world and signalled the start of shift. The boy pulled his hands from his pocket and ran the last two hundred yards to the open gates of the Chinchilla sawmill.

RANKIN

The pub's atmosphere was dark, dank and fairly quiet. Just the way he liked it. The limited rays of light which struggled to push through the dirty windows had completely lost the entirety of their strength by the time their weak, trembling fingers had caressed the filthy, ash littered bar top. Stale smoke lingered in the air and slowly listed from side to side. Perturbed by the breath of the only man at the bar and the faint movements of the ceiling fan, which struggled to make a rotation a minute. Still, anything helped in this damned heat. The darkness of the bar was struck by the sheer brilliance of a sulphur match. Shadows of lonely stools stood like giants on the pale and cracked drywall, while the glow of the orange light flickered and danced to give the walls the appearance that they were alive.

The only man in the pub held the burning match close to his face and lit the cigarette pressed between his cracked lips. As sudden as the match light had disturbed the darkness, the man was plunged back into it as he extinguished the open flame with the first exhale of his fresh cigarette. He tossed the black, twisted stem of the match into the ashtray in front of him; he watched as the timber stem bounced out of the glass container and skittered across the bar top. It nestled against more cigarette ash, which had likewise failed to land in its target area. He held the smouldering butt in his hand, his eyes transfixed on the burning cherry, how each strand of tobacco slowly broke down, consumed by the fire which gave it life. In many ways, the man could see how life was the epitome of a cigarette. It began in the brilliant flourish of fire and light and ended in the ashes of what its past had been. Nothing left but a wasted shell, discarded into the wind as its last embers guttered, left alone to die.

In the ten months that Rankin Bartlett had served in South Vietnam, he had seen enough death. He had spent too many days walking through the jungle while each gnarled tree he passed cast shadows that moved like the Vietcong. The heat bearing down, slowly breaking him down. With each step, the precious water that was left in his body would run down his forehead or neck to further darken the saturated greens that he wore. His sandy blonde hair seemed to be forever pressed to his face under his camouflage bucket hat. He had had enough of patrol; he had had enough. This shit country, this shit land, and the people that didn't even want the westerners here. He raised the cigarette to his lips and took a long drag. He watched as the cherry bore down the paper shaft of the cigarette, edging closer to the brown butt and its death. Since he arrived last November, Rankin's life consisted of the endless cycle of sleeping, eating and patrol work. 8RAR had missed the major action. They had missed the bloody events of Tet and had begun to see the loss of the morale within their own troops, as well as the Americans. The North Vietnamese Army were on the trail South, the Vietcong were everywhere, one never knew who was who and whether they wanted you dead until you were.

He had seen too many of his friends either killed or mortally wounded in his ten months of service. Although his friends and brothers slain in the field by conventional methods still rung in his memory, it was those that had come to unexpected ends that haunted him. The man scoffed to himself, and a faint smile crept across the sweat-streaked, pale face. Of all the thoughts that ran through his head, who would've thought that a young man of twenty-one could think the way he did now? To compare the deaths of his brothers in arms and their nature to whether they were conventional or not. As he brought his smoke up for another drag, the smile vanished, and his eyes focused on the flaring cherry once more. The truth is, none of them were conventional, and none were peaceful. Men didn't just curl up and die without a fight; there was always pain attached. He crushed the wasted butt of the cigarette out in the overcrowded ashtray as the barman reappeared. A short, hate-filled Vietnamese man, donned only in shorts, with a filthy tea towel hung over his shoulder. He prattled something in his native tongue to Rankin while he flapped his arms. The barman could complain as much as he wanted as, in the end, the Australian was his only patron.

'Whiskey,' Rankin croaked. He never met the barman's eyes; he was still focused on the crushed cigarette butt. The embers that fought to stay lit, the last of its fuel, nearly burned out. As the dirty glass was placed in front of him and the whiskey sloshed over the sides, Rankin thought back to his early days. The patrols were hard, Operation Hammersly was harder still, but the monotony of the patrols and the sleepless nights were always broken by the thirty-six-hour recreation passes. His close friends, Max, Will and Gary, who had travelled together first from Sydney to Enoggera after their conscription, then finally to this shithole. They served in the same platoon, drank together, and bunked together. They fought together, and it had been together that they had found this dank shithole of a bar. 'Phuoc Mai,' which had translated loosely to 'Future Blessings,' was down an alleyway of a side street in Southern Saigon. It was away from the bustle of the city centre, which was always overcrowded with Yanks. Upon reflection, Rankin surmised it was more the name of the place that had attracted the four brothers to it than anything. Always the larrikin, Gary had pronounced the name of the establishment, 'Fuck Me.'

Since the naming, every rec pass had been spent leaning on the dirty bar top, drinking the lousy whiskey and talking about ventures back home. They goaded each other to who was apt to spend the night shacked up with a pretty Vietnamese girl and what they were willing to pay. All four had, at one time or another, taken their turn with a girl of the night. He would have liked to have said women, but frankly, they were not old enough to be called so. They had handed over their money, they had walked into the low-lit room, which stank of sweat and stale cum, had their way and left. For three of them, the excitement had not been entirely there, each for their own reasons. Will had complained about the waste of money. Max had complained about the lack of effort his girl (who would have been lucky to have been fourteen) had used to finish him. Rankin, on the other hand, simply was not attracted to Asian women. Nonetheless, every time the look sparkled in Gary's eye, he began to peel the label off the brown bottle of the beer he had just finished, Rankin would oblige him and accompany his friend to the city centre, so they could both relieve their stress.

It had been some months now since Gary's death. He was the first of them to go; at least he went doing what he enjoyed. Of all the girls he had to pick, he picked a young girl with a look of fight in her eyes. Excited by the notion of having a girl who would do more than just lay there and stare blankly at him while he pushed himself into her, Gary couldn't resist. He had turned to Rankin, who rubbed his chin while he tried to decide between a girl with a flat chest and a girl with a hair lip, and had laughed.

'I'll be here all night with this one mate. Once you've finished, I'll probably need you to come and give me a hand.' With that, he left the viewing room of the brothel and had vanished behind the deep red velvet curtains that led to the girl's rooms. Rankin remembered his laugh as it trailed off down the hall. It has been said that the problem with the Vietcong and the problem with this country is that a westerner never knew who was for or against them. This girl, with the fight in her eyes, had sewn single-edged razor blades inside of herself so that they faced inwards. The idea was that when a man entered her, he would glide past the blades unharmed, but when he tried to pull out, the blades would catch his shaft. The harder the man pulled back, the deeper the blades would cut.

The screams of pain and the swearing alerted Rankin to the event. He had left the hair lipped girl naked on the bed and rushed to his friend's aid. Other westerners emerged into the corridor, some men he knew, most he didn't. All of them wore the same puzzled expression. One American, a big stupid ox of a man with a shaved head and muscular arms, laughed at how Australians couldn't handle their women. When Rankin had finally reached the end of the corridor, still naked as his manhood waved around semi-proud, the shouts had stopped. As he burst through the door, the thought occurred to him that maybe the girl with the look in her eyes had just given him the ride of his life. In the low light, he could see that Gary was still on top of her, yet neither of the figures moved. He saw that his friend's hands were clamped loosely around her throat. Her face was bloody, and one of her eyes had been closed permanently by his friend's fist. The eye that remained open was blank; the look of fight that had once shone out of it like the fires of a freshly lit cigarette was ashen now.

As Rankin dragged his friend off the bed, Gary's manhood remained inside of her. The blood continued to drain quickly from the remains of his member. While the colour drained from his face, his limbs began to shake as the shock set in. As Rankin called for help, he tried to staunch the bleeding by clamping a snow white pillow to his friend's groin while he looked over his shoulder to the light that shone in through the corridor. By the time anyone had bothered to attend the calls, the shakes from Gary's limbs had ceased. The snow white pillow was red with the life that had flowed out of him, and his eyes were still. He recalled the thought that had entered his mind as he had entered the room, 'the ride of his life.'

As the Military Police came and assessed what had happened, Rankin decided the time had come to finally get dressed. He turned his back on his friend and walked stark naked back down the hallway. To his surprise, the hair lipped girl still laid on the bed, her breasts swayed in the low light, and she dragged on a cigarette. Rankin's hands had begun to show the slightest tremor as he bent to retrieve his pants from under the chair which stood next to the bed.

'Are you read–y now?' The girl said as she parted her legs . Rankin stared at her for what seemed like an eternity. Finally, something inside of him broke, and he lashed out. He drove his fist into her face so many times he couldn't remember; all he focused on was the crest of her disfigured lip.

'I'll make sure no one wants to fuck you now, bitch.' Rankin roared as he brought his hand down again and again. That little stunt had earned him a week in the stockade. It seems that beating a female civilian half to death while the Military Police were up the hall was probably not the smartest decision he had ever made.

That was the last time Rankin had paid for sex, and he didn't even get any. Max and Will had never brought up the situation; things like this seemed to spread like wild fire. It had gone right through the American ranks and had begun now to make its way back through to 8RAR. The common joke was that even though the whore was six-foot-deep, Gary was still fucking her from his own casket as he presumably flew back to Enoggera. The sad part was that it was the truth; the South Vietnamese hadn't even bothered to remove Gary's cock from inside her. They were both bagged, tagged and disposed of. Just another unconventional death. Rankin couldn't even beat off to the Playboys in camp anymore. Every time his own shaft began to stiffen, he imagined the razors cut into the sides, the spurt of blood gushing as the pressure inside his bulging member was released, and not in a good way.

Gary's last ride had occurred in January, only two or so months into their tour of duty. It had taken the three remaining brothers in arms some time to get over it, yet it wasn't long before they would have someone else to mourn. The next month, 8RAR took part in Operation Hammersly. Rankin's platoon was whisked to Long Hai from their base in Phuoc Tuy by American Huey's. Rankin recalled the chopper that he rode on; it was the same that took him from the HMAS Sydney to the Silver City when he first arrived. 'The Black Dread' was etched in white letters on its dark hull; he remembered the power of the rotors beating the air down onto him. The powerful roar of its engine and the Yank pilot, Simpson, was probably the only American that Rankin had met and liked.

As the Australians piled into the Black Dread, Simpson drawled something over the radio to his co-pilot and began to unstrap himself. Rankin, the closest to the pilot, had shrugged as Simpson clambered out of the cabin while the rotors still churned overhead. Due to the sound that the Huey's enormous motor and rotors put out, talking without a headset was near impossible. Simpson made a gesture to the Australian that he needed to take a piss and began to walk away. Suddenly he stopped, turned back to look at Rankin, who still leaned in the open cargo bay of the Huey as he watched him. The American returned and considered him; he leaned in close and shouted in the Australian's ear, 'Just don't leave without me.' Without a second look, he turned and walked off to relieve himself. The dry humour was a welcome change from the rest of the Americans that Rankin had encountered. The proud fools who rushed into conflict, some of which were still spaced out on LSD, created carnage and mayhem wherever they went. They talked down to the Aussies like they were inferior, like they were the force who handled all the heavy work. Although Rankin disliked most Americans, he loved their Huey's.

As the Black Dread powered up, Rankin watched the grass wave and bow down to the air that rushed over it. The huge metal beast soared into the air, its engine roared as the surroundings of Phuoc Tuy became visible. He saw the mass of tents, the solid frames of the command bunkers, half dug into the ground. Sandbags were piled up against the part of the structures which remained above the soil. He saw the perimeter etched out, the tin roofs of the machine gun stations and the small faces of the men that manned their posts. The poor bastards that sweltered in the heat under the tin that shielded them and, more importantly, the M60s from the sporadic yet powerful downpours of rain.

Rankin scratched his arm as he watched the command base disappear from view. Replaced at first by the wasted jungle, which was chewed away by fire and Agent Orange, which he expected was the reason why his left forearm was red with rash. Yet as the Black Dread cut through the air, the jungle became thicker until all he saw was an impenetrable mess of canopy and hills. He saw the other Huey's trailed behind the Dread, in the line of formation that the Americans generally always used. The right side gunner shifted in his seat; the barrel of the M2 fifty calibre swayed with him as he moved. As Simpson began to pick up both altitude and speed, the wind buffeted the cabin and gushed in through the open bay doors. The green canopy swirled underneath them, a blur of slightly differing shades. The heat of the day began to wash away, and his sweat-soaked greens felt cool against his pale skin. His sandy blonde hair flowed around his face as the wind continued to push through the open doors. He leaned his head up against the wall of the cabin and drifted in a daydream, his mind whisked from Sydney to Gary, then to his other friends and how in some weeks they'd be back in 'Fuck Me's' where they would enjoy more whisky. They would shoot the breeze in the small, stifling pub, away from the Yanks, with only each other's company to be concerned with. He closed his eyes and allowed sleep to come over him. When the nights were as hot as the days, and the mosquitos were so prolific in the dark, sleep did not come easy. A soldier needed to take it when he could. The rolling, soft rocking motion the Dread took in the air soothed him.

The big fifty boomed in rapid succession, and Rankin sprung awake, nearly falling straight out of the cabin. Simpson had the Huey moving starboard low to the ground. The grass beneath them shuddered and fought to stay upright as the rotors pushed air over them. Out of the bay doors, he saw four small men run into the trees. The fifty continued to roar in quick succession; water and dirt flew up in large shoots around the men as they fled the Dread. Two of the men were thrown sideways as the enormous projectiles pummelled into them. Red mist lingered in the air where they had been and almost shielded the escape of the last VC as they disappeared into the trees. The fifty fell silent; Simpson shook his head and pointed in the same direction. He yelled into the headset's receiver at the gunner, and the fifty took up its pounding again.

The jungle was thick, and every step was calculated. A man needed to watch their footing while manoeuvring their rifles as they wove through the vines and branches. The fifties, on the other hand, were monsters; Rankin watched as the M2's barrel spat fire and the large brass, artillery like cases spilled out from underneath the big machines frame. The jungle seemed to ripple with every pulsing round that went into it. Chunks of timber could be seen exploding from the centres of trees, bushes trembled, and smaller saplings fell under the wrath of the weapon. Satisfied, Simpson spun the dark hull of the beast around so the cabin faced the direction the men entered the jungle and settled the skids on the soft grass. The Australians piled out of the dark hull, hunched over as they slowly made their way towards the tree line. Rankin was third back, only a shit-kicker; he was not a man to give orders, only to take them. He held his SLR close to his chest, the timber handle and foregrip already warm and sweating in the humidity. The back of his shirt clung heavily to his back, pressed to his skin by the heavy pack that he carried. Behind him, the Black Dread powered up once more and took off in the direction it had come from, returning to Phuoc Tuy for more Australian Diggers.

In front of him, he saw Max, the largest of the four brothers, as he came to a halt next to one of the fallen Viet Cong. His eyes remained on the jungle in front of him; the mess next to him was no longer a threat. As Rankin settled at the tree line some five feet to the right of Max, he stole a glimpse of the fallen Viet Cong. The two men were the size of boys; they were dressed in rags and donned woven bamboo hats, which were now strewn across their faces. One of the men had caught one of the big fifties in his lower hip; the bullet had smashed his lower frame. Chunks of bone and guts were spread across the grass; in the distance, the sound of the Dread had faded to a low thud. Apart from the slight breeze that rustled the leaves and the odd sound of wildlife, the six men had plunged into complete silence. The platoon leader, Corporal John Rixon, took a split second to search the two dispatched Viet Cong. As they had no pockets, he didn't waste much time; he removed the magazines from the Chinese AKs that lay beside them and threw them into the scrub. They were here to move into striking distance against a fortified position that the Vietnamese held; it was the Australian's task to storm the bunkers in three days' time. The Dread had dropped them some ten miles from the bunkers, and they were to move in quietly to assess the situation. Then they would hunker down until the time for the attack came and strike from concealed positions in the darkness. A leaf taken straight out of the book of the Viet Cong.

As they began the trek into the jungle, they spread themselves out twenty feet between men to avoid multiple casualties from a single machine gun spurt. Rankin saw the chunks of timber from the Dread's side gun. What he had found surprising was that he was now at least a hundred feet inside the tree line. The clearing and Landing Zone could no longer be seen, yet there were still great big holes in trees that were evidently fresh. It was no wonder the small men back there were thrown by the impact. As the lead man, Will rounded a large tree, his head whipped to the right, and he began to swing his rifle around, but realisation hit his face, and he relaxed. Will turned to Rixon and motioned for him to look in the spot that he had just stumbled on and continued his pace forward into the thick scrub. Rixon likewise poked his head around the large tree, and a grimace came over his face; he looked to Rankin and made a similar gesture of warning. They were now a hundred and fifty-odd feet into the thick jungle. At around chest height for Rankin, there was a decent bullet hole cut into the trunk of the tree.

Behind it, one of the two Viet Cong that had made it into the tree line lay beheaded. The side gunner's bullet had made it this far into the scrub through a considerable tree and had managed to decapitate the VC behind it. Thank God for Simpson, thank God for the Dread.

As Rankin turned to warn Daniels, who was around twenty feet behind him, screams rang out forty feet in front of him. Rankin turned sharply and raised his rifle to his shoulder in his expectation to see a VC charge, but there was nothing. He saw Rixon hurry forward and noticed that he didn't bother to conceal himself or keep himself low as he slung his SLR. Rankin followed suit; if Rixon was running to the one who was screaming, then it had to be Will who was hit. He took off in pursuit and left the beheaded VC behind him when in front of him, Rixon raised a clenched fist.

'STOP!'

He froze and went to a knee instinctively as he concealed himself in the thick scrub. The screams continued to howl out; now, they were only fifteen feet in front of his position.

'Rixon, is he okay?' Rankin yelled out after Rixon as he became entangled in a personal struggle to maintain cover while succumbing to his curiosity to see what had occurred.

'Does he sound it?' Rixon barked back before he swore under his breath; he sounded fairly concerned. 'Come on up, but move slow, Punjis.'

The final word explained everything to Rankin, 'Punjis.' The VC would dig holes three feet deep and embed sharpened bamboo spears into the bottom of the depths. Then they would carefully cover the opening of the pit with sticks and leaves to conceal the fact that there was a hole under the mess. Rankin made his way forward; this operation seemed to be off to a good start, a hundred and fifty feet into the jungle and one man down already. The screams had begun to dissipate by the time he made it to their side. Will had indeed fallen into a pit filled with Punji stakes. One such stake had penetrated through his entire right thigh, another had embedded itself into his side just under his ribs, and a third had cut his left calf. His breaths had become erratic as he tried to subdue his screams. Rixon was in front of him; his rifle was to his shoulder as he scanned the area in front.

'Shit. It's okay Will, it's okay. We will get you out of there, man.' Rankin leaned down into the pit to grab one of Will's hands. Will sweated profusely; his skin had gone a pallid grey while his breaths had become even shorter. As soon as Rankin leaned in, he was hit by an aroma of shit and blood. He looked at some of the Punji stakes which had missed his friend altogether and saw faecal matter spread over the sharpened bamboo points. 'It's okay, man, you'll be alright.'

In front of him, Rixon shifted in his position; he swung his rifle slightly to the left and fired three rounds. 'Fuck! Contact! Bartlett up front.' The sound of the SLR echoed through the jungle; in the distance, he could hear leaves rustling from both directions. Behind him, Max and the others were making their way up. In front of them, the VC headed in to take advantage of the situation. As Rankin let go of Will's hand, he saw his friend's eyes close in what could be either pain or shame. He left him and moved to Rixon's left side; he unslung his SLR as he went.

He went to a knee and brought the rifle up to his shoulder, but low so he could see the jungle in front of him. Shadows moved about in front as if taunting; it was difficult to see if it was men or the trees. Rixon fired twice more at the shadows while he yelled to the men behind him to pull Will out of the hole. Rankin scanned the trees, left to right to left again. As he scanned across to Rixon's section, he saw a small-framed man come out from behind a tree. He was dressed only in shorts, mud smeared all over him. In his hands, he carried an old bolt action rifle, which looked as though it was covered in more mud than the man who carried it. Rankin began to raise the SLR to his shoulder when Rixon fired, and a spray of red mist rose from the man's throat before he collapsed.

'Boys, they're coming; get him out of there!' Rankin called behind him. Now he heard Max talk to Will in the pit. Another man, Daniels, was with him. Daniels was the radio operator and was on the horn to Simpson and shouted his request that he come back. The operation was still in its early hours; it wasn't too late to dust Will off, it wouldn't jeopardise the mission. There couldn't be any doubt to the VC that westerners had stumbled across them. They would've known when the fifty opened up. Two more small figures emerged from the shadows in front of them, these ones carried AK-47s and opened fire on the Australians while they ran. Bullets skittered off the ground in front and around Rankin as he raised his SLR to his shoulder. As he opened fire, he heard one bullet whistle past his left ear. The two SLRs opened up on the men as they charged. In five shots, they were both down.

'Get him out of there!' Rixon called back as he took his eyes away from the front. 'How long for Simpson?' he barked at Daniels.

'Five minutes!' he shouted back. Max and Daniels had managed to free Will from the pit, yet he had lost consciousness in the effort.

'In front!' Rankin called as more men moved out of the shadows, firing. Rixon returned his attention to the front; he swore as he did and joined his fire with his subordinates. He dropped two more as Rankin took out another. When the last one had dropped, Rixon removed the half-empty magazine from his rifle and stuffed it down his shirt, then reached behind him for a fresh one. He clambered to his feet as he spoke.

'Let's move back. Bartlett, let us get twenty feet, then follow us;

we're fucked if we stay here.'

At the rear of the Australian force, McDonnel had begun to fire his rifle into the scrub.

'Contact right!' he called. Rankin spun to his right and could see more small-framed men moving out of the shadows; some of these were children. Infantile or not, they had made their decision when they had aimed their weapons at the Australians. Rixon and McDonnel managed to turn the attackers on the right side. Rankin kept an eye on the situation as he turned his head every second or so to glance back out the front into the thickness of the jungle.

Something hit him in the left shoulder. Something heavy and hard, which made him topple off balance and fall to his side. A metal cylinder on a timber handle lay on the ground in front of him. Without hesitation, Rankin latched onto the timber handle and threw it out to the left of him; his shoulder throbbed slightly as he did so. His heart pounded in his chest. 'Grenade!' he screamed as he flung the stick grenade into the shrubs. He put his head to the ground in anticipation and covered his neck with his left hand. The grenade exploded some twenty feet in front of him, and his ears began to ring.

He raised his head. He was still low in the thick scrub. Four men approached his position, two from the left, two in the front; the grenade had flushed them out. He lifted his rifle and fired on the two at his left as he shifted his position to put a large tree between himself and the ones at his front. The first man he hit in the chest, as he did so, his head flung back, his mouth open as he collapsed, the second one on the left began to emit a shrill scream as he began to fire his AK wildly in Rankin's direction. As he trained his SLR on the second one, he saw that it was actually a woman who was shooting at him, and he paused. An AK round impacted the tree he leaned on, which was enough to wake him up. He shot her in the stomach once. She dropped the rifle and hunched over whilst she continued to scream. He shot her again in the face and silenced her forever as he regained his feet and moved onto the two that were to his front. Behind him, he heard Rixon yell at him to pull back while McDonnel still pumped rounds into the trees to the right.

As Rankin leaned out from cover, he took the first of the two frontal attackers. The young man approached and foolishly kept his rifle trained on the wrong side of the tree that Rankin crouched behind. The second had apparently disappeared. With SLR raised, he worked his way around the tree. Each slight movement revealed more and more of the wasteful greenery, the hideous vines that hung like dead limbs. The child stood over the corpse of the screaming woman, his AK by his side. As he raised his eyes to Rankin, who crouched in cover, only his eyes visible over the muzzle of his rifle, tears cut clean courses down his young, grime covered face. Hatred burned in his eyes as, for what felt like minutes, they continued to stare at one another. The child turned to face him and raised his rifle, which had a short gleaming bayonet fixed to the end. As he charged, he howled a cry that burned into Rankin's mind further with each step the child took. He felt as though he was powerless to succumb to the boy until a slight tension on the pressure of his finger had the child soldier fall mere feet in front of him. His upper back was blown to pieces by the round which pierced his heart. Rankin spared the boy a second look before he raised himself to his feet and continued back to his section.

Being careful to go around the Punji pit that had started this whole mess, Rankin moved backward toward the clearing and his brothers. The sweat ran rivers down his face now. However, with the adrenaline that pumped through his veins, he couldn't feel a damn thing. Not even the blood that trickled down his leg; a souvenir from the screaming woman. He kept up his retreat as he walked backwards with his rifle still semi-raised. One young man came around the right of a tree. Rankin put him down quickly with a shot to the centre of his chest, and he fell in a heap; the air rushed out of him as he did so. He walked backwards to cover his own retreat. He knew he would need to change his magazine soon. The SLRs only held twenty rounds, and in the excitement, he had forgotten how many he had fired. A man's head appeared around the base of a tree, and Rankin opened up on him. The SLR fired twice and then nothing.

'Fuck,' he called as he spun around. He tore the magazine from the rifle and let it fall to the ground. As he turned, his foot became caught under a root, and he went down hard. The air went out of him as he fell, yet his foot had managed to work free. As he rolled off his rifle and onto his side, he inserted another magazine into its frame. He racked the charging handle, but the VC was already onto him. The small man fired his AK as he advanced from behind the enormous tree. As the pursuer advanced, Rankin retreated as fast as he could around the base of another large trunk to further conceal himself from view. It would only be a second before the VC would have him. Just as the man's torso came into view, SLR shots fired from behind Rankin, and the man's chest caved in. As he collapsed, he continued to stare at Rankin until the life had left his eyes totally, and he was gone.

Rankin clambered to his feet and checked his rifle. In the distance, the whup, whup, whup of the Black Dread's powerful rotors could be heard.

'Here he comes boys!' Rankin shouted as he ran back to his brothers. McDonnel had moved up in front of Rankin, the rest were well and truly on the way to the clearing. Rankin raced past McDonnel and shouted, 'Twenty, twenty. Alright?' McDonnel nodded as he scanned the forest again. Rankin rounded a tree, spun back to face McDonnel, and called out his name to signal his man to come back.

McDonnel and Rankin covered each other's retreat. By the time they burst through the foliage, the Dread had begun its descent into the clearing. On the starboard side facing them, the gunner was ready on the fifty. Rixon faced the jungle and stood thirty feet from the tree line; Max and Daniels each had one of Will's arms over their shoulders; his head lolled around uselessly. They all clambered back onto the Dread, their tail between their legs. Rixon had donned a headset and was in deep discussion with Simpson as the Dread climbed into the air once more. Rankin glanced at Will. His face was ashen, sweat ran down his face, and his greens were soaked. The wounds on his leg were surrounded by shit and dirt, full of all sorts of foreign material. His stomach turned. At least they got him out quick, he should be okay, he thought as The Dread began to descend again rapidly. There was another clearing below them. As it touched down, Rixon signalled for everyone to get out. The mission was continuing. As he left the Dread, Rankin stole a glance at Will and touched his cheek.

Another match burst into flames. The bright orange, like the fire of the fifty that day, like the red velvet of the curtains. He lit another cigarette and extinguished the flames of the match once more with his exhale and tossed the burned, twisted stem into the ashtray. He threw back the dirty glass and swallowed the entire contents in one gulp.

'Whiskey!' he shouted as he took another drag on the cigarette. Will had made it back to camp alive. They had cleaned his wounds, stitched him up and had given him morphine for the pain. Unfortunately, he had come down with septicaemia, blood poisoning from the shit spread over the Punji Steaks; he was dead within a week.

'WHISKEY!' he barked again as he slammed the glass onto the benchtop. The bartender returned, the hateful look still in his eyes. He poured the Australian another glass and watched as he swallowed the entire contents again in one hit.

'Leave the bottle,' he said as he made eye contact with the bartender for the first time that evening. He hung his head forward, the cigarette still clasped between his lips. He had twenty-four hours left of his rec pass, and he intended to use every second.

MICHAEL

Put a candle in the window
'Cause I feel I've gotta move
Though I'm goin', goin'
I'll be comin' home soon
Long as I can see the light

Creedence Clearwater Revival – *As Long as I can see the Light* (1970)

His father's office had never been a particularly inviting place to the boy. It was a small, dark room with two windows, both of which were always covered with dirty, rotting curtains. There was only ever one source of light, which came from the centre of a ceiling fan, whose days of spinning were long finished. That was about the only relief that Michael had found in that room. That ceiling fan would be on rain, hail or shine in the winter or summer, or if no one was there at all. The slow, methodical clack, clack, clack as the fan ran its never-ending circle over and over again had almost succeeded in driving the boy out of his mind. Michael had often complained about the noise that the fan emitted, how it hindered the schoolwork he attempted to complete on the dirty, matted carpet of his father's office. However, Tony had always ignored the complaints and had allowed the fan to continue.

Clack, Clack, Clack.

The day the fan had finally stopped working, Michael had made the mistake of exclaiming his happiness. Tony gazed up at the fan with one of his old veteran's hands on his chin when Michael had made this mistake. The big man sat down with a quick, angry glance at his son. The boy had realised his mistake instantly and quickly turned his head back down to his novel, Mary Shelley's 'Frankenstein.' An instant later, the clacking of the fan was replaced by the *thwap, thwap, thwap,* of Tony's large work boot, as it tapped against the side of his old worn desk. Michael wasn't a stupid boy, although he made the odd mistake, he was not naïve enough to ask his father to stop. Tony had not relented for the rest of the afternoon, thwap, thwap, thwap. For four hours of otherwise silence. When the time had come for Tony, Michael and Jack to leave the mill, Tony sighed and raised himself from his aging castor chair. As the large man strode to the office door, Michael saw the faintest sign of a limp. The large man favoured his left leg, which gave him the lurching cumbersome demeanour of the Monster in the book he was holding. The boy did well to refrain from laughing, but if Tony Baker had turned to see his son's face, he would have seen a smile from ear to ear.

This memory always astounded Michael. Did his father honestly despise him that much? He had continuously thudded his boot against his desk, to the point of pain, just to inconvenience his son. Although his mother, Grace Baker, had always told Michael that Tony loved them all in his own way, sometimes it was hard to see. The bad definitely outweighed the good.

Michael had made his way to the main mill building from the fire trail, which he walked every morning. He made a quick, 'good day' to Paul Darcy as they passed each other in the main doorway of the mill's operating floor. The boy was slightly happy that he had not seen his brother Jack, who was out of the back of the main building trying to repair a Canadian trolley, which had been half-crushed. This had occurred when an oversized log had twisted when the twelve-foot saw blade had hit a knot the size of Jack's head and, from the sounds of it, three times as hard. Jack disliked repair work. He was a large man now, and he preferred the simple tasks of picking things up and putting them down somewhere else. At that, no one was better. Metal was hard work, to reshape twisted metal took time and patience, which Jack was short on.

His father's office was above the work floor, on its own mezzanine. A cross backed iron staircase led to a small landing and the metal lined, hardwood door which read 'Manager,' with flaking yellow paint. Michael took his time as he mounted the stairs and looked out on the work floor as he went. The sawmill had fifteen workers total, all of them were hard at work. The five-man squad that maintained the saws and the blades were busy oiling pulleys and tightening the odd bolt. The trolley men were adjusting winches and cleaning the tracks, and Darcy was on the Hyster fork truck manoeuvring the giant logs for the day's cut. Michael had no doubt that as soon as the office door was closed again, a few of the men would go back to talking among themselves. For now, all that was audible was the roar of the Hyster's enormous petrol engine as the huge forklift laboured to lift and push the fallen giants. That, along with the fire and coals that crackled and popped to heat the twenty-foot boiler, which stood to the side of the floor, ready to set the huge saws in motion. Michael couldn't care less what they did, as long as it didn't get him trouble.

He mounted the last three steps, his engineer boots clanged off the grated metal staircase. His left hand grasped the flaking handrail as he pulled himself up. He knocked three times on the metal lined door and grasped the cold handle as he waited for his father's approval to enter. One didn't just enter Tony's office if they knew what was good for them. Especially if one was either of the big man's children, hitting employees wasn't the done thing, although it still wasn't out of the question. On the other hand, to hit one's own children, is the pope catholic? There was never a polite 'yes' or 'enter' with Tony, just a loud grunt of acknowledgment. Once the ceremonious grunt was heard, Michael turned the handle as he pushed the heavy door inwards and entered the dark cavern that was his father's office.

Tony sat where Michael expected, behind his worn, old desk. His hulking shape slouched over the paperwork scattered from end to end. A cigarette smouldered in the overflowing ashtray on the left edge of the scratched and ill-used desktop. The spare office chair, which Michael occasionally used, was today occupied by an open briefcase and more piles of paperwork. The motionless fan hung from the centre of the ceiling, as if looking down at the all the papers that it was powerless to disturb. However, something was different this day. The dusty, filth covered light shade that made the ceiling fan's centre cap was dull and yet light still entered the office from a source other than the gaping door. As Michael drew his eyes away from his father, who still had not looked up to acknowledge his son, he noticed that perhaps for the first time in his living memory, the window to the right of his father's desk had its curtains drawn. For once, summer daylight was flooding the office space. The thought crossed Michael's mind that perhaps this could be the beginning of a good day, even though he was bound to spend its entirety lying on the matted, stinking carpet that lined the hardwood flooring of the mezzanine, at least he would be able to enjoy it basking in the sunlight.

Michael entered the room, heaving the door closed behind him. He was mindful not to slam it, which would be sure to tarnish his father's mood and, worse yet, the opportunity to have a good day. Once the latch had clicked home and the door stood closed, Michael went to his small cupboard, which sat adjacent to the door and held his schoolwork. He began to pull J.R.R. Tolkien's *The Lord of the Rings – The Fellowship of the Ring* and work pamphlets from their tidy stack. He lay down in his accustomed discoloured spot in front of his father's desk and opened the novel to a dog-eared page to continue his and Frodo Baggins' journey to Rivendell.

At one point or another, Michael felt he had missed experiencing school life. The local school at Burra Burri, which catered for most of the students in the area from first year to early adolescence in one small classroom, had barred the Baker family and any future children from further attendance when Jack had rammed another student's head through the classrooms only overhead projector. Jack had committed this assault after the said student had made light of Jack's lack of mathematical abilities. Michael had come across this information partly from his mother when he had asked. Although he had discovered what act his brother had actually committed when Jack had threatened Michael with a similar fate when he had asked Jack to help him with his math problems. Jack had made similar threats to the boy in the past, and most times, to some extent, he had followed through. So, when his brother simply told him to rethink his question, Michael had thought twice and found that the possibility of actually having a friend was not as good as what it seemed like in his head. Instead, his new friends were Samwise, Strider and Gandalf, his old friends were Captain Neptune and Huckleberry Finn. In his dreams, he and his friends would either slay their enemies or journey off to some faraway land. Where the boy from the hot and dusty land of Chinchilla would be honoured for gallantry in battle and loved by all for his kindness and his cool intelligence.

His eyes were closed, and a soft smile crept over his face as his daydream washed over him. He lay in his accustomed spot with the book open in front of his face. Slowly he tilted further away as he dreamt the day away and enjoyed the warm bath that the daylight emitted. He hadn't realised how far into sleep he had actually drifted until his father boomed.

'Boy.'

Michael's eyes snapped open, and, in his fright, he threw the book under his father's desk. The pages fluttered as the hardcover book skidded across the carpet and came to a halt against the drywall behind his father. Michael didn't give his father a chance to question his weakness; he leapt to his feet and stood to attention in front of his old worn desk. Like one of the Elven archers from Rivendell, manning the defences of their lost city.

'Sir?' Michael said timidly, noticing that his father was yet to raise his gaze from the papers on his desk. In the last year or so, Tony had been forced to get glasses. All the time he spent brooding in his cavern with only a ten-watt bulb to illuminate the fine print had taken its toll on the big man. In reality, Tony had probably required glasses for ten years or more. Yet, true to his nature, the big man struggled on. The decision was finally made for him by the owner of the Mill, Terry Macress when Tony had signed a quote to supply the Dalby hardware centre for twenty tonnes of the mill's finest cuts for thirty per cent below the mill's bottom-line operational costs. Mr Macress gave Tony the ultimatum: Get his eyes checked and get glasses or pay the difference himself. Tony Baker, a man who hated being humiliated and would never admit to having anything wrong with his vision, had glasses the following week.

'I've been called to Dalby.'

Dalby? Surely this day couldn't get any better?

'Dalby, sir?' Michael asked quietly and respectfully, trying his utmost to hide his excitement. Dalby was at least two hundred miles from the mill, which would mean that Tony would be away for at least a night. 'For how long?'

'How the fuck would I know?' Tony rasped as he raised his eyes to glare at him over the rim of his glasses. Still, he kept his face directed at the paperwork. 'I need to quote on a job, and due to its size,

Macress wants me there.'

A big job, and paid by the company. He might be there a week.

The big man stood up and stretched his back. He took the horn-rimmed glasses from his massive face and tossed them to the desktop. He brought both massive hands to his face and rubbed at his eyes.

'I'll be taking the mill truck and will deliver a load to the Jandowea depot on the way. I want you to tell Jack that he can take the Ford home tonight, but tomorrow he is to take the farm truck.'

The Bakers, although not a rich family by any stretch, owned two vehicles. The Ford was a black 1965 Fairlane 500 with a white vinyl roof. To hear that Jack was allowed to drive it home was out of character for Tony. Still, Michael knew the only reason was because he didn't trust any of the mill's employees to keep their hands off it while he was in Dalby. To say that Tony had three children would not be going too far. The Ford, Jack and the other one, who was he? The name would come to him soon, oh! Michael.

'While you're down there, tell Darcy to load the truck and blow the horn when he's finished. I want to get out of this shithole.' The large man lit another cigarette. The smoke billowed in front of his face, the match smouldering among the other wasted remnants in the littered ashtray.

Michael didn't wait for any further instructions. Christ, if the old man was going to leave when the truck was loaded, he'd load the damn thing himself. Michael swooped to the door and reefed it open in his joy, then was ever so careful not to slam the door once on the other side. He then sailed down the stairs, his boots skipped off the grated metal as he flew. He saw Paul Darcy still on the Hyster as he moved a mangled ironbark log into line for the Canadian trolley to drag it into the twelve feet of spinning death. Michael briskly made his way over to the man, who had noticed the boy making a line for him and had turned the Hyster's engine off. As the boy came near, he opened one of the cab doors and leaned out. Paul was an average height man of a slim build that wore torn jeans every day and the same beat-up Dunlop shoes. He never wore a shirt or a jacket, but a denim vest that exposed his hairy chest. Atop his head, he wore a pale, greyish Stetson that had faded with the years of abuse it had taken from the hot Queensland sun. As the man leaned out of the gigantic forklift, the boy thought he looked like a pirate clinging to the rigging of a tall ship.

'G'day Mick, what's the old man chasing?'

Michael smiled at the nickname. He liked Paul. He had always been nice to him. Michael relayed his father's instructions and expressed that he was anxious to leave.

'No worries, I'll get it done. Gunna miss my drinking buddy tonight, might seem?' The man took the faded Stetson from his head and wiped his balding forehead with a handkerchief.

'Seems so. Do you know where Jack is? I need to tell him something too.'

Darcy informed him that Jack was still out the back working on the mangled Canadian trolley. Michael thanked him and left him to his duties. He didn't want to take up too much of the man's time. In the end, the longer it took for Darcy to load the truck, the longer Tony would remain.

Michael made his way around to where Jack was swearing at the mangled wreck. The boy wasn't afraid to talk to Jack. He wasn't that bad. They had at least one thing in common: They both wanted to avoid their father as much as possible. He thought to himself that at least the news that he brought would cheer Jack up, and perhaps they might enjoy a ride home together in the Ford. The only problem was that Tony said that Jack could only drive the Ford home. After that, he would have to take the farm truck. The farm truck was a 1928 Whippet that resembled a pile of rust on wheels more than an actual car. The only remaining glass in the vehicle was a sorry excuse for a windscreen. Tattered and worn, like the rest of the old truck, the glass was chipped, and a long trail of a crack ran along the driver's side, which ended in a flurry of a spider's web. The cracks interweaved and ran, swirling through each other, to finally join in the epicentre of a giant stone chip. The seat was salvaged out of a 50s Mercury and was too wide for the truck's body altogether. Its fabric was worn, torn in some places by the tools that remained forgotten in the driver's rear pocket when they took their seat. In one place, a spring was visible, its tip clearly protruding through the old fabric where the old foam inner had collapsed around it.

One didn't start the old Whippet by turning a key. You had to earn your ride and labour as you cranked the tired engine over from the handle at its front end. Jack hated that truck. It wasn't so bad to start as it sounded, put the shift in neutral, prime the carb, set the choke and then crank. Although now and then, the old bitch would backfire, and the crank would come swinging back. One time this had happened, and Jack was a little slow in getting out of the way. The iron crank handle hit just below the elbow, and Michael thought for sure that his arm was broken. Jack's arm didn't break, but it left its mark. It marked Jack's arm and his ego. What was the saying? 'Once bitten, twice shy.'

By the time Michael was within earshot of Jack, the older brother had already lost his patience with the mangled trolley. He threw down the lump hammer, spat at the steel wreck and lit a cigarette. As he stood there smoking, a large hand came up to his head and scratched at his scalp. The biceps that bulged now were gargantuan to those that had squirmed on the lad that leaned up against the side of the Baker's house some years ago.

'Hey,' Michael called as he came to a rest, leaning on the wreck of the trolley behind Jack. The older brother turned his head to look down at his younger brother. Jack's face was dirty, yet there were clean lines where the sweat ran down from his hairline. His jaw was square, and his muscles worked as he glared over his wide nose at his brother.

'What?' A man of little words, Jack took after his father. Michael explained his message and expected to see a sign of relief on the hulking man's face. Although Jack was a monster of a man, Tony was still the man of the house, and if he wanted to lay down some hurt, he would. Yet, Jack just stood there working his jaw muscle as Michael spoke and relayed his father's instructions. When he was finished, he looked up at his older brother and shrugged. 'Okay?'

'Fine.' Jack turned away again and tossed his cigarette as he bent down to pick up the lump hammer. The steel head of the hammer would have been near the size of Michael's face, but the older brother picked it up one-handed. He swung it up over his head and brought the hammer down with all of his force to slam it into the twisted frame of the trolley. The trolley's frame was quarter inch steel, and Michael thought the hammer would just bounce. But when the hammer struck, sparks flew from the impact of the two metals, and the thick hard steel moved under the power of his brother's swing. *Shit*, he thought to himself, *he would hit harder than Dad.*

As Jack went back to swinging the hammer into the twisted hulk, Michael asked him one more question.

'Hey, can I come home with you then?' He would much prefer to ride home with Jack than walk, even though it was a nice day. He only walked to and from the mill to escape his father's company. Jack wasn't that bad.

Jack had raised the hammer up above his head and was just about to swing down when Michael had asked the question. He stopped mid-swing and turned his head again to look down at the boy, his jaw muscle working again. He considered the boy for a moment with his brown/black eyes, sweat still running down his sloped forehead.

'Sure,' he said with a smirk and turned back to his work.

Michael left him to it. What a day, what a day indeed. Basking in the warm daylight, the chance to read his book, the old man was going away and the chance to ride in the Ford. Better than any birthday the boy had ever had. He returned to the stairway and ventured again up to the heavy metal lined door, his mood so fine he had to stop himself from just walking in. *Lucky*, he thought, *almost ruined the perfect day*. He knocked three times and heard the accepting grunt. Tony was packing the stacks of paper into his briefcase when the sound of the Hyster's horn rang out. With a snap, the big man slammed the briefcase closed, barked 'about fuckin time,' and pushed past his son.

Michael smiled as he watched the heavy-laden mill truck drive away that mid-morning through the office window. He sat in his father's chair, his feet up on the desktop as he read his book. Thinking to himself, *this will be my life for the next few days, maybe a week? Shit, it could be two weeks, even the old man had said he didn't know.* Sometimes life wasn't too bad. As he read through the forming of the fellowship of the ring, his eyelids drooped.

Maybe I'll sleep for a bit. What could it hurt? The old man wasn't there. Jack was going to drive him home. He looked up and saw the beautiful Fairlane gleamed as it sat in the mill's yard, next to the Hyster's shed. Its twin beam headlamps reflected the sun's beam into his eyes. Michael closed his eyes again and turned his head back to rest on the oak chair's headrest. Just for a bit.

Michael slept in the chair for three hours. He was awoken by the clunk of the mill's twelve-foot saw blade coming to a halt at the end of the day. The boy yawned and stretched his arms over his head. The sun was no longer shining through the office window, but it was still nice and warm in the office. No wonder he had slept for so long.

He rose from his slumber and collected his book from the ground, he must have dropped it as he slept. With years of his father's stern hand behind him, Michael didn't need to be told what to do, he collected all of his belongings and stored them neatly in the small cupboard. Michael was about to open the door and leave the office when he noticed the window still open. *Dad would want it shut.*

The boy returned to the window and clutched at the remains of the curtain. As he dragged the rotting cloth along its hanging rod, he glanced to the Hyster's shed, his arm stopped. His faint smile faltered. The Hyster was nestled in its dock, and loomed there by itself. Next to it was nothing. Jack had left him behind. So much for a perfect day.

RANKIN

'Way down in the background
I can see frustrated souls of cities burnin'
And all across the water, baby
I see weapons barkin' out the sting of death
And up in the clouds, I can imagine UFOs jumpin' themselves
Laughin' they sayin'
Those people so uptight, they sure know how to make a mess.'

The Jimmi Hendrix Experience – *Somewhere* (1968)

As the Black Dread's rotors powered up, Rankin watched once more as dirt and small stones trembled and rushed away. There was always that point when the gushing wind became so fierce that it seemed that every particle gave up its perch at almost the same time. A ring of dust would form around the Dread, like a protective barrier conjured up by a witch doctor, as the enormous hull rose and the occupants felt their guts sink low into their bodies. He had been in this situation countless times, either travelling to and from the 'Silver City' to enjoy his thirty-six-hour rec pass or to fly to some distant makeshift clearing, which still reeked of Detonation Chord. He remembered trees with leaves still as green as life itself, sprawled over the ground. Their exposed core was still moist, as small oddly coloured insects flowed from their pores. Yet this time was different, it had been announced back in April that they would not be replaced when 8RAR's tour of duty ended in October. Perhaps it could be said that some sense existed in the Australian Government, yet they had little enough to send them to Vietnam in the first place. Little enough to go all the way with L.B.J, yet they were home. The four brothers in arms from Sydney had travelled to Enoggera and then to Saigon; three were home already, and the last one would be heading home next week. This was his last patrol.

He took a deep drag on the cigarette perched between his lips. His eyes slits against the powerful gusts of wind that billowed through the gaping cargo bay doors of the Dread. His last patrol. He turned his head from the view of the ever-consuming jungle. His eyes skittered across the faces of the men that he shared the cargo hold with. A few new faces, yet Rixon, McDonnel and Daniels remained from the originals. His friends were replaced with the remnants of another butchered section. As he closed his eyes, he tried to remember his friend's faces, and for what seemed like a split second, he imagined the three of them, perched on the running boards of the Dread, donned in their greens. Will and Gary both with SLRs slung while they smoked. Max, the largest of the four, with his sixty resting across his legs. All of them laughed, their faces reflected their youth and lacked the worries of life. They were, for all intents and purposes, invincible.

Rankin opened his eyes again as he stared at the boys that were propped where he had imagined his friends. The thought skated across his mind like an insult, *if they were invincible, what did that make him?* He tossed the butt out of the gaping cargo bay and attempted to spit after it, but the wind caught it and splattered it up his forearm. 'Lucky,' he muttered below his breath, completely inaudible under the churning rotors.

He shifted his weight, his hand fell to the small of his back to caress his strained muscles. As he kneaded his twinging spine, his fingertips brushed something cool, and he paused. His mind fell to Max, the last of his friends to fall. He frowned as he retrieved the cool metal block from under his belt. The brass was dull, and speckles of mould were noticeable across the curved sections of its edge, yet there was still some sense of elegance to it. Rankin had allowed the finish to get to this state, as to have a brightly polished piece of metal hanging from one's hip and glinting in the sun was a sure way to join the dead. The brass knuckles or 'dusters' had belonged to Max. He had cast them himself back in Sydney with old fired .303 casings. Having neglected to clean the brass before he melted it, the duster's surface was rife with imperfection. He allowed his fingers to fall through the holes, and he closed his fist around its base. Max was a larger man than Rankin, yet the finger holes were only a fraction too large for the soldier's gnarled fingers. The fighting edge ran a pitted and roughly curved shield around the front of his clenched fist, the base secured tightly in his palm. A ghost of a smile crept over Rankin's face. He had seen three men succumb to the dusters since his arrival in Vietnam. None of them seemed to enjoy the feeling of a man's fist lined with brass driving into them. The sound of the heavy fist fall, the sound of the brass laying into the jaw or forehead and the splat of the man hitting the deck shortly after. Not many people could stand up to it, but there was one.

The pitch of the Huey's turbine changed, and the Dread began to descend. It banked to the right and circled an extended perimeter around the make shift landing zone. The side gunner's barrel rose to the attention of the bank, yet there was no movement through the canopy. Once Simpson had completed his circle, he brought the Huey down. His mouth moved nonstop as he relayed some last minute information to Rixon before they all vacated. The ground was littered with sizeable debris, which was common when soldiers rushed to create a makeshift LZ. Although not a hard job, the clearing of trees with det chord left a mess, and Rankin could tell by how Simpson was shaking his head that they would be jumping the last three or four feet from the Dread. Sure enough, Rixon forced eye contact with every man and signalled that they would indeed be jumping. Simpson had the Dread coming down below the canopy. Once again, he felt admiration for the American. He was awed by the man's sense of judgement and ability to understand where the invisible rotors ended. As the trees surrounding them shook in protest, small branches flew from their cover, and finally, they jumped.

Rankin felt the rotors power down on him the instant his feet left the running board. As he landed awkwardly, one hand grasped the splintered trunk of a nearby sapling to steady himself. Simpson had already pulled the Dread above the canopy line and had started his journey back to Phuoc Tuy. The section headed to the tree line, at Rixon's motion, they halted and bunched up on him to listen to his last minute instructions. An average-sized man whose mousey brown hair was completely covered by his service helmet, his face seemingly always covered in dirt and grime. Rankin had served beneath Corporal John Rixon during his entire tour. He was a stern man, but he kept his boys safe. A vision of Will, lying in the Punji pit with shit and blood smeared all over him raced across Rankin's mind. 'Safe enough,' he muttered once more under his breath. The heavy beating of the rotors was gone. It was replaced by the footfalls and snapping branches under the Australian's boots.

Rixon glanced around at his men, his eyes paused momentarily on each like he was doing a mental roll call. He shifted on his feet, allowing one knee to rest on the ground as they all crouched. 'Simpson told me that the Yanks have air support available if we require it. A couple of Douglas A-1's probably armed with Napalm. Let's try and avoid that if possible.'

'Last thing I need is for some cowboy dropping one on my ass on our last patrol,' complained McDonnel, his eyes fixed on Rixon's.

'The only burn I want to go home with is from the sun.'

'Go home to get plenty of friction burn on your pecker. Did you forget the women back home are out of your price range, mate?' Daniel's sparked, this brought laughter from the rest of the squad.

'Alright. Enough,' Rixon barked gruffly. 'I know it's our last patrol, but that doesn't mean that we are out of danger. In case you can't tell, we're in the thick of it again, and only discipline will get us out. Keep it quiet, stay spread out, and if there's contact, keep low, use the jungle as cover.'

'Just get the Yanks to burn the fuckers. Let's go back,' one of the younger replacements – Powers – said. Almost entitled, like he had another engagement to reach.

Rankin laid a hand on his shoulder and squeezed un-affectionately as he pulled him closer. 'We don't want the fucking Yanks anywhere near us. They'll probably burn us alive for leaving them here in this shithole.' Powers, a boy of nineteen, looked up at him and held his silence. Rankin lowered his head so that his hair fell forward over his face while he continued to glare upward at the boy. As Rixon began his lecture once more, Rankin realised that he still had the dusters clasped around his fingers. Sweat had begun to form in the palm of his hand. The boy watched him as he placed the filthy brass casting into the secure place behind his belt. Once it was locked away, their eyes met once more, yet as soon as Rankin's grey, blue eyes fell on the brown of Powers, the boy quickly averted his gaze. Rixon rose to his feet and surveyed the jungle's darkness beyond the tree line. He removed his helmet and ran a filthy hand through his mousey brown hair, which stood up at all sorts of angles, fixed in place with sweat and dirt. He donned his helmet once more and checked his rifle.

'Twenty feet between men. McDonnel on point, Bartlett on the rear. Keep your eyes open for Punji and stay quiet.'

One by one, the men left the clearing. McDonnel went first, trudging heavily through the jungle to the point of making too much noise. Yet once he had put some ground in between himself and the rest of the squad, he slowed his pace and settled his rifle on his hip. Rixon went second. No sooner had he left his perch than McDonnel ceased to be visible from the tree line. The other two replacements followed soon after, each waited their turn, a largish country boy, Bourke, who had replaced Max on the sixty. Then his support man Vickers, Daniels, then Powers followed and finally, Rankin was left to himself. He noticed that Powers had followed closely to Daniels as the radio operator shifted his heavy load. As Rankin got himself to his feet, he heard the boy ask Daniels, 'Why does he hate the Yanks so much?' Rankin didn't react to the question. He wondered if Daniels could even truthfully answer it, as once his three friends had been killed, Rankin kept to himself. He never talked socially to anyone and spent any spare moment in solitude.

As Rankin crept through the mess of trees and vines, his eyes scanned his surroundings. He had checked his SLR before he left the tree line, one up the spout, a full mag below. He felt confident in the power at his side—it had gotten him this far. There was only one more patrol, and he could kiss the beaten-up thing goodbye. He would return home, first to Enoggera, then to Sydney, and would leave this shit country and the Americans behind. He didn't know which he would be happier to be rid of. The humidity, the sweat, the itching rash which had now worked most of its way up his left arm or the Americans, proud, arrogant and violent. He had never hidden his feelings about the Americans, a sly comment here, a filthy look there, but it wasn't just their attitudes that wound Rankin up, it was so much more. That they had followed the Americans here, the whole 'we saved you in the Pacific back in the forties.' It was Max's face, the shock of what had just happened, as the colour drained from his eyes. It was the laughter.

As Rankin rounded the base of a large tree, he noticed that Powers and Daniels were crouched some ten feet in front of him. Rankin took a knee and watched. He couldn't see why they had stopped, yet rather than break the silence, he would sit in ignorance. Some twenty feet beyond them, he noticed through the choking vines and brush that Vickers waved his hand in a beckoning motion. Slowly, they made their way forward. Rankin was the last to come upon them, as he broke through a heavily vined section between two trees, he struggled with his SLR, which had decided to become snagged on almost everything he passed. He saw probably the one thing which he dreaded more than the visions of his dead friends. A small clearing had been cut into the dense scrub, there was a gaping hole in its centre. Rixon was crouched next to it, his head low as he attempted to catch any hint of movement below.

Rankin's shoulders slumped, *out of the frying pan and into the fire.* Rixon motioned for them all to take a knee, his head still low to the tunnel's gaping mouth, a look of pure concentration on his face. He put a finger to his lips to ensure the silence of his men. Soon enough, with a dissatisfied look on his face, he lifted his head and slowly returned to his men, who were crouched in a cluster ten feet away. McDonnel was ahead of them, his back to the tunnel as he watched out in front.

'Need a volunteer,' Rixon whispered as he removed his pack and rummaged through some pockets. 'We need to go in and collapse the entrance.' He pulled out a small rectangular block with a green wrapper and black text on its face. He placed it next to him while he continued to rummage through his pack. 'Whose volunteering?'

Everyone remained silent. A few exchanged glances, but none stepped forward. Rixon rummaged through his pack until he found a small metallic cylinder and some string. He placed the other pieces alongside the green block, and his eyes fell to his men. His eyebrows furrowed. 'Whose volunteering?' The faintest level of a shout in his hushed tones. The men exchanged another glance. Everyone's eyes went from Rixon to another, then back to Rixon. 'Bartlett, you're up. Drop your gear.'

Rankin's shoulders dropped further. There was a murmur of relief from a few of the others. One of the others even had the hide to murmur, 'Thank fuck.' Rankin shot the lot of them a reproachful look and began to shed himself of his equipment. He picked up his SLR once more and began to head over to Rixon, but after a further glimpse at the opening of the tunnel, he swore and threw his rifle down on his pack. There was no way the bulky Lithgow, which had already given him enough trouble with the vines on this short patrol, would be of any use in the small tunnel. The rest of the men had begun to spread themselves around the small clearing to create a solid perimeter. Rixon knelt next to the tunnel's opening once more and beckoned Rankin over.

'Go in about a hundred feet, maybe more. If you come to a junction, stop. We don't want any coming past.' He stopped, looked Rankin in the face and considered, 'Shut your right eye, don't open the fucker until you're in there.' Rankin looked at him puzzled, but at a disgruntled motion of 'hurry up' from Rixon, he obeyed and closed his right eye tight while looking at his leader with the squinted left. 'Once you get to a point where you're happy, fix the C4 under something. Secure it, so it won't move easy.' He pointed at the green block and partially pulled at the adhesive strip of the packaging. 'Once you've done that, jam the detonator into it all the way,' at this, he gestured toward the metallic cylinder with a ring hook at the end. 'Try to jerry-rig up a trip wire. When you come back out, we will make a commotion and try to lure the fuckers out.'

'You reckon there's any in there?' Rankin asked as he began to stow the C4 and the detonator into his pockets.

'Fuckin' oath could hear them. Take it slow. You'll be right. Take this.' Rixon held out his pistol, a Browning Hi-Power. Rankin took it and checked the chamber. He put it on safe and secured it down the back of his pants.

He slung the string around his neck and felt the fibres stick to his sweat covered skin. How he hated humidity. As he lowered himself into the mouth of the tunnel, he took one last look around at the small opening with his open left eye. He took in the faces of each of the young men, some of them still boys. The ashen colour of their skin and the brightness of their eyes. A sneer curled on his lip as his one open eye fell upon Rixon. Rankin held his gaze for a moment, then he lowered himself to a crouch and entered the gaping hole.

Within the first few feet, he lost all vision. His right eye was still closed. The failing light from the open mouth in the tunnel's roof behind him only managed to penetrate five feet into the ever-consuming darkness. Ahead of him, he heard the faint guttural voices of the Vietcong. He had no idea how far they were as no matter how softly he moved his feet, it sounded as though he was slamming the soles of his boots down on the hard-packed earth. As he continued his way down the tunnel, his empty hands occasionally brushed the sides as he searched for a gap to indicate a junction, his mind went back to Max. He wondered if this was all that Max could see now? When someone died, was it just like going to sleep? He thought about how the life slowly left his face, the way it just vanished. At one point, he was there. Max, his friend, his brother in arms, then the next just an empty vessel, a burned out cigarette.

It happened three months ago, on a twenty-four-hour pass to Saigon. Max and Rankin had not returned to 'Fuck Me,' as only the memories of their friends were left there. They had decided to try another establishment in the city centre. Rankin had been opposed to the idea as with the city centre, you were sure to find Americans and trouble, yet Max was adamant. So, as a good friend should, he followed. They had been in the bar for maybe two hours, it was a nice place. Rather than the packed earth floor of 'Fuck Me's', this was lined with polished hardwood panels. The walls and the countertops were clean. The multiple fans which hung overhead turned furiously and reminded Rankin of the rotors of the Dread. As they sat and nattered with small talk over whiskey and beer, the cool air washed over them. The cigarette smoke carried away from one's mouth to be washed over the floor and eradicated from sight. The staff were friendly and called in on every table every few minutes to either clear the ashtray, service one's drinks or light the cigarette clasped in a man's mouth. He didn't know if the Americans had just arrived or if they had been there for hours. All he knew was that one had approached the two Australians and had asked for a cigarette.

Rankin handed the large American a cigarette and continued his small talk with Max. The American interrupted once more and asked now for a lighter. Max turned and looked up at the Yank with half-drunk eyes.

'What next, mate? Do you want him to smoke it for you too?' He downed the last of his whiskey and waved at the waiter for another. He watched as Rankin handed the American the lighter, which sat on the countertop.

The American lit the cigarette, returned the lighter, and stared at Max while he smoked. 'You think you Australians would be thankful that a real Army is here to look over you.' A stupid grin spread over his face.

'You've got your smoke, mate. Time to leave.' Rankin spoke

unamused, but Max wasn't having any of that.

'If it wasn't for you, Yanks, we wouldn't be here.' Max roared as he took the refreshed whiskey glass from the waiter and downing half of it in one gulp.

'If it wasn't for us "Yanks", you would be speaking Japanese about now, right?' The big American leaned in closer. 'You'd think a bit of gratitude would be in order.'

'Fuck off, idiot.' Max roared as he waved a hand dismissively at the American, suddenly losing interest in the conversation. The American smiled broadly, took another drag from the cigarette and dropped the butt into Max's glass.

'Enjoy your drink.' The American began to walk away.

There were so many nights when Rankin thought upon this moment. What would have happened if Max had stayed sitting? Would he still be here? Would he be heading home soon, along with the rest of them? So many questions, but none of it mattered. Max had risen from his seat, the brass knuckles clasped tightly in his right hand. He grabbed the American's right shoulder and spun him. The sound as the brass slammed into the man's forehead was astounding. There was a faint ping of the metal impacting bone. The only thing that was left was for the American to fall over, yet he didn't. The man's head rolled back on his shoulders, and then it came back up again. Blood ran down his face from the gash, but the stupid grin remained, and the solid consciousness was very apparent in his eyes.

The American grabbed Max by the collar of his shirt and drove him into the bar, pushing him through tables of civilians and soldiers alike; people went everywhere. Some women screamed while men shouted, and to Rankin's surprise, the entire bar erupted into a brawl. He expected this every time he walked into 'Fuck Me's' and had never seen it. The dolled-up place, which was the last place he would've expected it, a fight broke out the first night he walked in.

It took the Military Police only a couple of minutes to break it up as some were already there drinking. The fight was broken up without incident, Max had taken a hiding from the American but had given it right back. The brass dusters had split his lip and removed several teeth. The American's stupid grin would be sparser after that night. Max, Rankin and the American were among others to be ejected from the establishment that night. However, none were taken to be court marshalled. The once friendly staff now scowled and swore at them to leave as they swept up broken glass and held broken chair legs out in front of them as if it was their only child.

The real incident had occurred early the next morning. Being ejected from another bar, the two Australians walked down some back alleys to return to the old faithful 'Fuck Me.' They swayed as they walked and shouted in the streets. They did everything that a drunk soldier on leave should. Max sang a poor rendition of a Bob Dylan song at the top of his lungs while he swayed heavily as he walked and had fallen slightly behind Rankin. Suddenly Max had stopped singing. Rankin had at first thought that his friend had simply forgotten the words, but the slurred lyrics were replaced by a wet slapping sound and a gurgle. Rankin slowly turned around, unsteady on his feet and saw the same big, stupid American behind his friend. A hand was over Max's face, and it pulled his head backwards, the other hand plunged a steak knife into Max's throat and chest. The wet slapping was the sound of his friend's bloody neck that clapped with the hilt of the blade as it was driven in all the way. The American's gaze was fixed on Rankin as he continued to drive the knife in. Then finally, he let Max fall, his stupid grin spread wide across his face, only darkness visible through the gaps in his teeth.

'Next time, show some gratitude,' he barked as he walked off, laughing. Rankin had rushed to his friend, trying as he had once done with Gary to stem the bleeding, but he was too far gone. He watched the life leave his friend's eyes just as he had done before, and the real sense hit him of being alone. There was no one left for him to rely on, no one left to talk to nor drink with. He was one hundred per cent on his own.

Although he had been questioned vigorously about the death of his friend, Rankin had not led the authorities anywhere near the American. He had pleaded ignorance and had told them that Max had stopped to have a piss and never showed up at the bar. He had gotten worried and went looking for him, and this was how he found him. Not surprisingly, the officials had never thought to question Rankin's story and were left thinking that it was an act by the Viet Cong. They had become concerned that soldiers were being picked off on the streets of Saigon. Rankin had taken Max's brass knuckles that night and had sewn a leather pouch on the inside of his belt to hide them. Everywhere he went, the dusters went. At first, he kept them clean, but not long after, he allowed the brass to dull. He allowed the green spots of mould to spread over it, attached to his hip and exposed to the elements, it didn't take long for this to occur.

One night a month or so later, Rankin saw the American in Saigon. The big, stupid prick was surrounded by others, all of them laughed and joked. Rankin continued to watch them throughout the night as he lay in wait. He followed them wherever they went, remaining silent and sober, in his solitude, he was never noticed by anyone. Then the moment came, the American went to the bathroom, Rankin didn't waste time and followed him in. The big American stood in a cubical at the end of the room. The smell of shit and piss was thick. Another man was cleaning himself up at the washbasins. Rankin waited for him to leave and then locked the door after him. The American whistled poorly as he urinated, barely attempting to maintain his aim in the bowl. Max had turned the man before he hit him. Rankin made no such mistake this time. He slipped his fingers through the slightly too large holes and clenched his fist. He walked calmly up behind his target and drove his fist as hard as he could into the back of the man's head. His head went forward and impacted with the tiled wall, and began to return to its normal position. As the man reeled with the hit, piss was flung everywhere. Rankin hit him again, and the man went to his knees, so Rankin hit him again. With this blow, he collapsed over the toilet bowl, his arms grasped the sides as he tried to lift himself out. So, Rankin hit him again and again. He continued to hit him until the back of his head was caved in, the man's arms fell limp on the floor, his head in the bowl. Rankin managed to close the cubical door, washed his hands and the brass dusters in the basin and used the hand towel to dry everything off. He then unlocked the door and left the establishment altogether. He spent the rest of his leave at 'Fuck Me's' and never spoke a word of it to anyone.

His hand, which ran along the earth wall, slipped, all of a sudden, there was nothing behind it. Rankin struggled to see but couldn't even make out his hands in front of him. Realising his stupidity, he finally opened his right eye and was amazed at the difference. He had focused so intently on Max that he didn't even know how far he had travelled. The far off voices still yammered away in their guttural tongue. They didn't seem any closer, but as he thought before, he had no way of knowing. The vision that his adapted right eye gave him was substantially better, and he saw that he stood in the middle of a junction. He took a few blind steps back and began to pull out the C4, yet there was nowhere to secure it. He ran his hand all over the surface, it was rough and hard to the touch. He swore under his breath and pulled the Hi-Power out, and clasped it by the barrel. He hammered away in the darkness at the wall.

His stress levels were out of control, and the sound of the hammering was tremendous. It seemed to echo throughout the tunnel, and he knew if the others further down heard him, he wouldn't have much time at all. He jammed his fingers into the cut he made in the wall and figured it would be enough. He fumbled with the fabric wrapping on the explosive and began to push it into the cavity. The sweat coursed down his back, and his heart hammered in his throat. He pulled the detonator out of his pocket and leaned in to place it securely when two strong hands wrapped themselves around his throat.

MICHAEL

It was an absolutely spectacular morning for Michael Baker. One of the best in living memory. Actually, who was kidding themselves here? This was the best in his living memory. The funny thing was that for a boy who generally enjoyed the company of fellow human beings, the reason why Michael had awoken with such a spring in his step this day was that he was home alone. Tony Baker had left to quote a job in Dalby two days ago, Jack Baker was at the mill filling in for their father. His loving mother, Grace, had taken her leave for a morning walk to the neighbouring property to see her friend Penelope Darcy. Although the Darcy lot is adjacent to the Baker's, the round trip generally took Grace most of the morning. The walk only took about half an hour in a round trip, the rest of the time was taken up gossiping about other women in the area, most of which were wives of men that worked at the mill or discussing their immediate families.

Paul and Penny Darcy had two children, the elder of which was a girl of the same age as Michael and a small four-year-old boy named Billy. Michael had only seen Billy once or twice when the Darcy's had visited for dinner. This occasion did not occur often as the Baker's dining room table was scarcely large enough for the Bakers, let alone the two families together. Billy was a small, fair-haired child with freckled cheeks and an innocent face. Michael had never taken too much interest in the youngest Darcy, his attention had always been elsewhere. Namely on Billy's elder sister. Susan was an auburn-haired, fair-faced girl who stood slightly shorter than Michael. Her shy mentality had always intrigued the boy. She lived with such a loving family, Paul Darcy was the best man that Michael knew, he had to be, he was the only one who called him Mick, after all. Yet she never met his eyes, only for a brief flash and then she'd look at her freshly polished church shoes. That simple flash of blue from her eyes was all it really took for his life to be hers. Such a rare flash of brilliance in a world of suffocating darkness. Her hair was a red glow in a world of grayscale, her pale cheeks like the smooth silk of an Arabian Princess's shawl in a desolate wasteland.

Michael thought deeply about Susan as he broke his fast, for a girl of twelve, she was stunning in her beauty. Michael, however, was plain, yet that didn't stop a boy from dreaming. As he struggled down his last piece of stale bread and marmalade, he thought about the future. He dreamt of whisking Susan away from this dreary shithole and moving to Melbourne. Where the life was apt to be so much more interesting than plain old Chinchilla, cooler too. As he washed his face, he felt himself already start to sweat. He returned to the cramped kitchen and drank some water from the family water bottle. He felt a little bit of a thrill as he put the bottle to his lips and felt the cool liquid run down his throat. If anyone was home, he would surely cop a hiding for this. 'You drink outta the bottle!' He pictured Tony Baker's red face bearing down on him. He placed the water bottle back onto the old Kelvinator's shelf and shut the fridge door, as he noticed there was a lack of a note for him stuck to the rusting metal door. The boy considered, no Dad, no Jack, Mum's okay but no Mum. No chores, there had to be a catch somewhere. However, his young mind raced with all the possible ways he could spend this splendid day. He could walk into town and get an ice cream soda, but he didn't have any money. He could go to the Darcy's to see Susan, but then his mum would give him chores to do. Every idea he thought of, his conscience snapped back a retort, rendering the plan to be redundant.

He dragged his feet as he returned to his bedroom and slumped down onto his bed. The springs groaned as the featherweight boy bounced on the worn, stained mattress. He picked up *The Lord of the Rings: The Fellowship of the Ring* and resigned himself to the fact that he would probably spend the day reading this damned book in this house. *It's too bloody hot in here, though*, his mind instantly snapped at him. He was happy enough with the idea of reading the book, but he supposed he was right, it would have been close to a hundred degrees in the house at that stage, and it was only ten in the morning. 'Don't you love living in Queensland?' Half the time, the reason why people spoke slowly up here was because half of their brains had melted out of their thick heads during some stupid day where the sun blazed down hot enough to melt tar.

'I'll go to the creek and read my book there,' Michael proclaimed as he stood up. He paused for a couple of seconds and waited for the snappy retort of his own mind, but nothing came. A smile crept across his face, he bent down and snatched up his book. He vacated the Baker's old house and stepped into the blazing sun.

The heat was abhorrent, he wondered what the mercury would rise to as he started down the path to the boundary. He couldn't imagine Frodo and Strider making their journey in heat like this, but surely heat like this never existed in fiction, it was probably a mild day every day in Hobbiton. Michael squinted his eyes and raised the book in his right hand to cover his face, something was blinding him, something apart from the bloody sun. He glimpsed under the book in his hand and saw his Father's Fairlane 500 sitting in its carport, the paint gleamed, and the sun's reflection beamed off the chrome grille. 'What a beauty.' Tony's favourite child sat in the shade of its carport, majestic, almost as if it knew that it was the favourite of the household. It was better than him. Although that was probably the case, Michael still loved the car, despite the fact he had never enjoyed a ride in its comfort. Michael found himself walking towards the majestic, rolling iron, taking in the vehicle's curves and the way the light shimmered off the excessive chrome linings. 'This thing had near more chrome than steel on it.' Not even a smudge on any of it either, nor a scratch on the deep black paint, which was surprising in itself. The trails that surrounded the Chinchilla sawmill weren't paved and were only graded four times a year. Yet this beauty didn't even have a chip off one of the brightly polished hub caps. 'The king of the road,' Michael mused as his hand went to the driver's door handle and clasped the release. 'It will be locked,' the boy thought to himself as he pulled the latch.

Clack!

The boy nearly fainted at the sound, he thought something had fallen and hit the car, signalling the end of his short life. How would he explain this? But the driver's door swung open towards him, and the smell of well-kept leather trim touched his nostrils. 'I can't believe it,' he whispered. Jack must have left it unlocked. He recalled that his father wasn't the last to drive the majestic beast, otherwise, surely the doors would have been fastened to any intruder. Michael snapped his head over to the tool shed where the families Whippet normally stood, it was empty. Jack had taken the old truck, 'He forgot to lock Dad's car, no one's home, no one knows.' All these thoughts raced through the boy's mind. He swung the door of the beast out further, taking in the aroma of the leather and pristinely shampooed loop carpet.

Michael turned and slid himself in behind the steering wheel, which seemed like it was larger than he was. He squinted his eyes again as the sun reflected off even more chrome surfaces and tried to blind him like an old roo in the headlights. He took in the interior, the timber veneer dash, the chromed stereo, the gleaming 'T' handle shifter. How he wished that he could drive something like this. Michael did know how to drive, the boys had free rein over the twenties Whippet, which was not worth a penny to anyone in this day and age. It was already so severely rusted and dented that a few more between friends could never be a problem. *That's right*, Michael thought to himself. He could drive, but he wouldn't be stupid enough to. He thought about all the different ways his father could kill him, beat his head in, strangulation, crucifixion, as the boy raised his hands to the ignition. When his hand touched the cool metal of the ignition key, everything stopped for him. He couldn't believe it, Jack was being reckless. Not only had he left the car unlocked, but he had also left the key in the ignition. It's probably lucky that Michael had decided to walk over to the car and look into it, if he hadn't, Jack would've paid dearly for his mistake when Tony came home. Jack was a bigger man than Tony, but that seldom mattered when it came to the Fairlane and reckless behaviour. Michael snapped his hand away from the key, still shocked at his brother's senselessness. Then his oldest friend started up again. 'You're home alone.' His mind was his best and oldest friend, but at times like this, it could be his worst enemy. There was no way he was going to turn that car on. He liked living way too much for this. His hand started back toward the key, 'NO!' He screamed to himself, 'I can't do it, I'm going to get myself killed,' his hand edged even closer. Michael shut his eyes.

The sound of the starter motor cut through the silence of the hot Queensland morning. WHIR WHIR, WHIR, WHIR, Click. The car didn't start. 'Thank God, I don't want the car to start, this was a bad idea,' his mind flashed as his right foot pumped the throttle twice.

WHIR, WHIR, WHIR, the motor ticked as the spark caught, and the 302 Engine roared into life, the car shook a little with the power of the engine, and a rush of life came into Michael. He looked at the instrument panel, all the little indicators raced to their locations like good soldiers manning a wall. Michael pressed the accelerator and revved the big Ford engine. The tacho lifted, and the exhaust roared, then coughed and spat as the needle fell back down to sit at an idle. The red glow of the emergency brake, a bright red exclamation point in brackets, shone in his eyes. 'Stop,' he thought to himself, *No one's here,* his mind retorted. He looked at the gas level, the needle partly covered the letter F, and his foot pressed the accelerator again. The taco rose with engine pitch, proclaiming to the world that this Fairlane was indeed the king of the road and who should stop the king from roaming his kingdom.

'I can't,' Michael fretted, that is crossing the line, there is no coming back from this. *No one knows.* Michael placed his friends down, Frodo and Strider. 'It's time for me to have a journey of my own,' he placed the hardcover book down on the soft leather seat beside him. He glanced down, and his left hand had already grasped the 'T' shifter, his thumb pressed the gate release button. His old friend, his conscience had now taken the forefront of his mind, the sensible boy that sobbed 'I shouldn't be doing this, he's going to kill me,' was long gone. *You're home alone, no one's here, no one knows,* that was all that mattered, nothing else.

Michael heaved the shifter back, reverse, neutral and drive. The big car's transmission clunked softly below him, the engine dropped its revs slightly in anticipation. The tiger purred before it struck out at its prey. The blazing emergency warning shone in Michael's eyes, the red illumination drove into his soul, and he wanted it off. He imagined what it must be like to be at the start of a drag strip, the power urging you to go while the red light pinned you to the spot. All the anticipation that forced one to hold themselves back and the beast beneath them.

Michael looked under the steering wheel, there were three pedals just like in the Whippet, so that was right. He looked to the left of him. There was no hand brake lever, he looked to the dash, and once more, there was no lever to be seen. The blazing exclamation point started to hurt his head now, he was suffering. He needed it turned off. He thought back to when he drove the Whippet last. 'You pushed in the clutch.' He stopped. He hadn't pushed the clutch in to start the car. He looked at the T handle. 'It's an automatic.' His head whipped back down to the pedals, and he looked at the smaller third pedal. He lifted his left foot to it and felt the pressure under it. He started to push down as he stared at the fire red warning on the dash. He heard a faint click under the sound of the rumbling and spluttering Ford V8, and he relaxed as the pressure fell away from under his left foot.

As soon as the red light disappeared, the massive car started rolling forward. Michael immediately panicked. He wasn't holding the steering wheel and had his right foot resting on the loop carpet. His eyes snapped up to the windscreen as the heavy vehicle started to roll at a walking pace out from under the carport and made its dead on charge toward the tool shed. Michael snapped his hands to the large wheel and began to swing the heavy car around to the left. He dared not touch the accelerator, as if he tore up the grass, he would be caught. His right foot rested on the brake pedal as the rolling iron trudged up the drive to the main fire trail. *Just to the track and back*, he thought to himself as he passed the boundary gate. 'No one's here, no one knows.' He brought the heavy car to a stop, its enormous body rocked slightly as the power of the beast urged it to go on, but the boy held its reins. As the front Bridgestone tyres of the big Ford hit the graded earth, he heard the sound of dirt shift and grind under the immense weight of the rolling iron.

'I'm not really home anymore anyway,' he considered. 'Where will I go? I can't go anywhere, but I've come this far and haven't crashed. I'll be okay to go a little further.' He turned his head to the right and looked down the long fire trail. There was no one coming, but that was the way to the Darcy's. He saw the road twist and wind and eventually disappear into the gums that bordered the graded road. Yet if he went in that direction, his mum would eventually hear him or see him, and that was suicide in itself. He turned his head to the left, the trail on this side was straighter. The trees didn't border the track as closely, so it would be easier to manoeuvre around if a car did happen to come the other way. Michael reflected that the chances of seeing another car at all were pretty slim. The left led to the mill, and the right led to nothing. If the boy were absent-minded enough to drive passed the mill, he would be seen. But as the only people that lived on this fire trail (to his knowledge) worked at the mill, he would be safe within operating hours. *No one knows.*

Michael closed his eyes and breathed in deeply. He hadn't realised that it was pretty warm in the car due to his own suspense, and sweat now freely ran down his forehead. His hair clung to his head, and his hands were clammy, sweat worked its way in between his white knuckled hands and the vinyl steering wheel. He wound down the driver's window. A sweet breeze kissed his face, it's funny how he thought it was unbearable outside of the car, now, it was as if a winter breeze listed through the gaping window. A shiver ran down the boy's spine, and he took his foot off the brake pedal. The rolling iron moved onto the graded road and began to pick up speed.

MICHAEL

'Day after day, I'm more confused
Yet I look for the light in the pouring rain
You know that's a game that I hate to lose
I'm feelin' the strain, ain't it a shame.
Beginning to think that I'm wastin' time
I don't understand the things I do
The world outside looks so unkind
So I'm countin' on you to carry me through'

Dobie Gray – *Drift Away* (1973)

The pebbles and loose grit ground away and shifted as the monstrous rolling iron made its way down the fire trail toward the sawmill. There was no destination, there was definitely no intention whatsoever to let the motor car make it as far as the mill itself. Michael would bring the beautifully shaped artwork of steel and chrome to a halt and about-face long before the corrugated iron structure of the Chinchilla sawmill came anywhere near sight. At that point, Michael would slink his father's Fairlane 500 back to the Baker's lot before anyone was wiser. Until then, however, he would enjoy the drive and drift away into his own mind. A bit of excitement and reflection seemed about the best way to spend this blistering hot Queensland day. As the Fairlane picked up speed, the outside air rushed in through the gaping driver's window. Each tree that he passed seemed to call to him as they whisked past. The whooshing noise they made followed pace, and soon it sounded as if they were rotors of a helicopter's blades, priming for take-off.

This was fantastic. Michael was twelve years old. He had driven cars before, namely the nineteen twenties Whippet, but this was something else. The smell of the dusty road, combined with the well-maintained leather upholstery, made for an insane sensation for the boy. The deep, throaty burble of the Ford's 302 engine and the almost inaudible whine of the transmission as the gearbox bands spooled up before it released to the following gear took his imagination away. Beneath all of this was the grind of the heavy car's Bridgestone tyres, compacting the ground beneath its immense weight. Michael looked down at his hardcover book on the passenger seat. His friends would be proud of him, the first step of a journey is always the hardest. Frodo's hardest task was to leave the safety of Bag End and the warmth of his friends and acquaintances. Likewise, it was an extraordinary thing for Michael to get over his fear and actually enter the forbidden domain of his father's car. He wasn't running away, but still, this was a bold move, and he had best be careful. He hated to think of the repercussions if anything were to go amiss with Tony Baker's favourite child.

Michael raised his eyes from the book on the leather-trimmed passenger seat and glimpsed the speedometer. Twenty-five Miles Per Hour. The Fairlane was basically only crawling along, and Michael's confidence in his driving ability was increasing. He glanced at the Fairlane's dash, and the glint of the Deluxe radio caught his eye. The only better way to drift away was to tunes, everyone knew that. As he looked back up to the fire trail, he smiled as he leaned over and switched on the radio. At first, there was nothing but static, but Michael adjusted the band. Eventually, a song he hadn't heard for some time started resonating out of the two forward speakers. 'So, they collected the cripples, the wounded and maimed.' The song that had played from the old Kelvinator wireless radio, the day his father forced him to cut up that dead gum branch.

He had often thought about that song. The longer he thought about it, the more unsure he was about how he felt. There were so many instances that Tony Baker had deserved the disdain that Michael had felt for him, yet the more he thought about that song, the more he couldn't help but feel guilty. *'The legless, the armless, the blind and insane. Those proud wounded heroes of Suvla.'* Tony Baker had served as a sapper in the Second World War and came home after they had routed the Japanese from the Kokoda Trail. His mother had told him that his father was such a loving man before the war, but the man they all saw today was nothing like what he had heard.

Michael glanced down to the speedometer, forty MPH. This was better. The big car glided over the dirt and gravel. The odd corrugation in the road didn't seem to bother it, the suspension of the heavy car seemed to take it on the chin and laugh it off. *'And as our ship pulled into circular quay, I looked at the place where me legs used to be.'* Michael had been interested in the war until that day. He could never bring himself to look any further into it after his father had lashed out. If men like Tony Baker were what war created, he hoped that the Second World War would be the last. But that was all a joke, wasn't it? The Vietnam War seemed to be coming to an end now. As he drove the rolling iron down the secluded track, he wondered how many had died there just today. *'And thank Christ there was nobody waiting for me. To grieve and to mourn and to pity.'* Michael knew there were so many people that came back from the war that weren't the same. So many had lost arms and legs. Many lost their lives, but what had Tony lost? Michael frowned as he pondered this. What had his father lost? He didn't seem to be hurt. The only time the boy had seen the large man even limp was when he had inflicted the damage to himself in an attempt to annoy the boy as he read his book.

'And the band played Waltzing Matilda as they carried us down the gangway.' He drank himself to sleep most nights now. He became violent when he drank, and he never went a night at home without drinking. The boy hadn't been able to sleep one night after his father had struck him across the back. He couldn't even remember the reason why his father had lashed out at him at this particular time; there probably wasn't a reason at all. Tony's temper had flared, and Michael, his youngest, was within reach, so POW, he copped it. His back had throbbed and ached all afternoon, and when it came time to go to bed, it hadn't mattered which way he may try and lay, the pain kept him from dreams. The boy was resigned to the fact that this was more than likely going to be a sleepless night and had risen in the dark to take a short walk around the Baker's lot.

Michael had slipped on his boots and dressed himself, and had left through the back door. He had trudged along through the night and through the scrub surrounding the Baker's place. Thoughts of Susan and her fire-like hair, swept through his mind. The girl he had spoken less than five words to in his life. The girl that was his beacon in the dark. He was lost to himself in these brief wonderous thoughts when a noise shattered them and attracted him to the tool shed. Michael had crept soundlessly to the side of the shed. There was someone in there. The hairs on his neck stood up to attention as he slid his hand along the iron wall. He felt the dirt and grime fall away, disturbed from their perpetual hiding place by the boy who wandered.

Michael grasped the edge of the wall with one hand to steady himself as he peered around the corner and through the opening of the darkened shed. The Whippet stood proud in its place, proud enough for a rusted, dilapidated piece of junk. His father sat in the driver's seat. There was broken glass to the left of the old truck's cabin, where an empty Fosters bottle had been discarded. Tony must have come prepared as he raised a full bottle to his mouth and drained near half of the long neck in three giant gulps. As the large man brought the bottle back down to his lap, something started to happen to him. It was hard to tell what was going on, as the man's face was still in darkness, but it was as if the man was convulsing. The boy had battled with the urge to go to his father's aid, but part of him had hoped that he was having a heart attack.

Hopefully, it's the last of the bastard, the thought burned across his mind. The boy stood where he was, stunned at what he was seeing. He had finally realised what was unfolding in front of him, but he couldn't believe it. It couldn't be true. It wasn't until the large man raised his other hand, with a smouldering cigarette butt to his lips and the glow of the tobacco illuminated his face as his father drew back, that he accepted it. His father was crying. He never spoke, just sat there in the cab of the Whippet, drinking, smoking and crying his eyes out. After the man raised the bottle to his mouth and took another giant gulp of the stinking brown liquid, Michael had seen enough. He slunk back to the safety of his house, being very careful not to take the path that led to him being visible from the tool shed. He didn't want to know what would happen if the old man knew he had seen this. It was a scary prospect. The boy had seen his father do a multitude of things and had seen many emotions, but he had never seen the man cry like this.

'*But nobody cheered. They just stood and stared, and they turned all their faces away.*'

The words cut through Michael like a hot knife through butter. A feeling came over the boy that left him feeling small. Very small indeed. It was obvious to him now that Tony had been injured in the war. He thought perhaps that his father had suffered just as much, if not more, than any man who had lost his life or any that had lost a limb. The realisation had slowly dawned, and all the instances of his father hitting him and screaming at him, red-faced as veins bulged out the side of his neck and forehead. Tony had begun to lose the greatest limb of all. He was losing his mind.

He thought back to something his mother had said to Jack as she scolded the elder child for his neglect of his little brother, who only wanted to walk with him to the mill one day. Jack had blatantly refused the offer. He gave no reason, just a firm refusal. To her smallest son's tears, Grace Baker had scolded Jack, then a boy of eleven, for causing the disquiet. Jack had gone to his own defence, proclaiming that he had never touched the boy, which was true in this case. Jack had never shied from hitting his brother. He never hit hard and never hit his face. Just the shock of his own brother hitting him always put Michael into a fit of tears. As the crying boy lay in his mother's arms looking back at his brother, he heard his mother say, 'You don't need to cut a man to make him bleed, Jack.'

Michael supposed the same could be said that you don't need to kill a man to end his life. His father had gone away to war a loving man and had returned a wreck. The faintest drop of a tear welled in his right eye, and he lowered his gaze from the dusty, dirty road to glance at the speedometer once more. Sixty-five MPH. The boy blinked, his eyes were blurred from the tears that had begun to form. He raised his left hand to his eyes and wiped at them, not really believing what he had seen. He opened his eyes again. The speedometer now was edging closer to seventy MPH, Michael had never been this fast before. The Whippet was lucky to do forty-five, but he now screamed along at seventy, and the big Ford felt like it had plenty more to give. Michael sniffed back some snot. Everything was going funny on him now, after the thoughts about his dad. He squeezed the accelerator for a bit more, and the throaty growl of the engine rose to meet his expectations as he lifted his eyes to the windscreen and froze.

An old pickup was backing its way onto the fire trail in front of him, no more than five hundred yards from where he was. At this speed, Michael near let loose of his bowels at the sight of the rapidly growing picture of doom that his eyes were trapped upon. The boy gasped, not knowing what to do and slammed down on the brake pedal. The warm, humble mutters of the engine were drowned out by the scraping and grinding noise of the extremely heavy car trying to stop itself on the loose gravel road. The nose of the Fairlane dipped so low that the boy thought that the bumper would be driven into the ground. *Oh God, please help me stop,* he screamed in his mind as he pressed even harder on the brake pedal. His knuckles near exploded out of the skin as they grasped down so terribly hard on the wheel. The back end of the car felt left out of this whole situation and began to come around to the right hand side to see what the whole commotion was about. Michael tried as hard as he could to steer into the slide, but he was lost to panic. He could see men in the cabin of the pickup, staring blankly as the big Ford listed on the road, all crossed up as it hurtled toward them.

One of the men raised his hands to cover his face. The nose of the Fairlane drifted off the side of the trail, and Michael, in his panic, released the brake pedal. He had only been able to turn the steering wheel a fraction to the right. Suddenly, the sound of grinding gravel and gouging tyres seemed to quiet as the wheels of the now sliding iron began to roll. Michael trumped the throttle slightly, and the car whipped back around. The nose came back about to face the oncoming truck, thankfully no longer pointing at the gum trees that lined the track. The nose came around, but the truck was coming quicker. 'Holy shit,' the boy shivered as he trounced onto the brake pedal again. The heavy rolling iron began to slide once more. The back end now slightly drifted out to the left, its tyres kissed the corrugations of the edge of the graded section as they went. Michael shut his eyes and screamed, waiting for the crunch. The gravel grounded and hissed, spitting at the metal hub caps of the big Ford, as the car finally came to a halt. The engine hiccupped and stuttered as it struggled to draw breath and keep itself from stalling.

Michael opened his eyes. Unbelievably, he had missed the pickup. He thanked the heavens and God himself; he was saved. As he looked himself over and made sure he was fine, he looked at his hands and saw that he still grasped the steering wheel with a two-handed death grip. His knuckles and now the greater portion of the backs of his hands were bone white. He glanced over to the pickup and noticed it was partly off the road, its engine putted away. He finally had time to notice the truck. The faded blue Bedford pickup was now facing the way Tony Baker's crossed up Fairlane 500 had approached. The driver's door stood open, and an ill-looking, lanky man stood in front of the opening, staring at the frozen boy. Michael only needed a brief glimpse to see that the man was filthy. He wore faded blue jeans near black from grime and what looked to be soot. He wore a browned and heavily stained white singlet, burned and frayed from cigarette butts. His hair hung about shoulder length in dirty, scummed up clots that hung from his scalp like rotted saplings from a dying shrub. In his hand, he held a likewise filthy and holey felt hat, which he held in front of his chest for a moment. Then as he bared his rotted teeth in a grimace, he placed the disgrace of a hat on his rotten head.

'Fairdinkum,' the man called as he slapped his leg. 'I thought you were gonna near write me off.' He slammed the truck's door so hard that the aging wrecker shook from the force. Once the door was closed, Michael could see faint writing on the door, 'Tracker's' was all he could make out, the rest was obscured by mud and what looked like shit. The driver's window was still open, and he saw another man in the truck lean over to look out. The dirty man walked over towards the Fairlane, the engine of which had now settled back into its deep thrum. As he neared, he leaned so he could see in through the window and cackled as he properly saw for the first time the frightened boy. 'Well, I'll be fucked!' The man yelled out, 'Kel, get on out here and take a look at what we got.'

The thought crossed Michael's mind that perhaps he had used up every ounce of luck that he had in just missing the Bedford that now there was none left for himself. He did not like the look of this man. Maybe he knew his father, maybe he didn't. Michael didn't care either way, but he didn't want to talk to him. He wanted to go home. Michael's eyes flashed to the 'T' shifter and saw that it was still in drive. His foot was still clamped heavily on the brake. As he started to lift it, the dirty man must have seen his intentions as he leaned in the window quick as an arrow and seized the ignition key. With a click and a metallic slink, the Fairlane died beneath him.

'Not so fast, my little sweetness,' the man chimed as he pulled the keys out of Michael's view and pocketed them. The boy's mouth hung open; he was screwed. The filthy man stood back a bit, not concerned for the boy in the slightest, as he cackled away. 'Kel, come on out, you need to see this.'

At the second call, the passenger door of the old Bedford creaked open, and an obese man a foot shorter than Jack stepped out. This man probably would have outweighed Jack, but it wasn't due to his strength. He had a gut on him that drooped down towards his knees. When he slid out of the truck, it bounced soggily up on its springs. His mouth hung open as he walked over and breathed heavily as he waddled, each step an effort to push his sagging gut forward. His dirty shirt didn't cover all his stomach, what hung out from underneath was red with stretch lines and inflamed.

When he spoke, he did so through his nose. 'I told you it was the Baker's boy,' Kel spluttered as he waddled over to his brother.

'Yes, you did indeed. I knew it was the car, but it was you that saw it was the Baker runt,' the filthy one said as he grinned his rotting smile down at the boy.

'Out of the car runt, we want to look at you.' Kel had made his way to the Fairlane's hood and leaned on its front guard to get a closer look at him.

'I'm sorry,' Michael pleaded, not wanting to leave the safety of the Fairlane, but there was going to be none of that. The driver's door of the Fairlane swung open, the filthy unnamed man's hand on the handle. 'Just let me go.'

'And how would we feel as responsible adults, leaving a minor to drive away in a car like this to kill himself?' Kel snuffed out as the unnamed man dragged Michael from the car, 'How would you feel about that, Matt?'

The grotty man tossed the boy roughly to the shoulder of the road and spat a glob of phlegm and shit on the trail's shoulder. 'Oh, we couldn't have that brother, could we? That would be very...' His grin faded. 'Uh, what was the word you said?'

'Irresponsible, you fucking idiot,' Kel said as he lifted himself from the Fairlane's guard to stand under his own power once more. He shuffled over to his brother Matt and the Baker's runt, who now lay on the fire trail's edge, propped up on both elbows. The fat man slapped the back of his meaty hand against his brother's chest and then held his hand open in front of him. The filthy brother looked down to the open hand, then to his fat offsider, grimaced and reefed the Fairlane's keys out from his blackened pocket.

As he slammed the keys down into the flabby palm of Kel, the fat man said, 'Get lost now, runt, We know Daddy's not home. If you come looking for us, we will come home for Mummy.' The fat one began to snort and splutter as he waddled to the Fairlane and swung his enormous ass into the driver's seat. He wheezed as he pulled the giant door shut. The boy couldn't believe what was happening. They were taking his father's car.

'No, please,' he called. To which he only got more nasally laughter from Kel and mocking cries from Matt. The Fairlane's starter motor whirred twice, and the engine kicked. There was a clunk, clunk as the fat man worked the T shifter and then he cranked the throttle. The V8 screamed in anger, and the rear tyres erupted in a sea of gravel and dirt. The car shot back towards the Baker's lot and sprayed the now bewildered boy with stones and dirt as it went. There was one last laugh from Matt, and then the Bedford followed suit. Michael watched after them as the dust from both of the vehicles billowed up in front of him. The last he saw of them was the middle finger of the grubby man driving the Bedford, whose right arm hung out of the open driver's window.

RANKIN

'She said: 'There is no reason'
And the truth is plain to see
But I wandered through my playing cards,
And would not let her be.
One of Sixteen vestal virgins,
Who were leaving for the coast.
And although my eyes were open
They might just as well have been closed.'

Procol Harum – *A Whiter Shade of Pale* (1967)

As two powerful hands clasped around Rankin's throat, he was pulled away from the wall, and the detonator dropped from his hands. As he was dragged backwards, he violently kicked his legs out. His sweaty palms went straight to the stranger's, which had now completely closed off his airway. In the panic, Rankin continued to claw at the strangling hands, his feet still kicked as they slid across the hard-packed floor of the tunnel. The darkness consuming everything. As he struggled, he felt the Hi-Power work its way out of his belt and skitter across the floor. Mentally, Rankin swore at himself, his mouth open as he gasped for air. The stranger's hands worked and writhed as they tried to hold their grip around his throat. Sweat continued to run down from his hairline and coated every inch of his skin. The strangler's grip was strong but was waning under the ever-increasing viscosity over Rankin's throat. He could hear the heavy breathing as the man behind him laboured to hold him.

Finally, he found some purchase with his right foot, and he pushed with all his might and slammed himself and the stranger back into the tunnel wall. He felt a rush of air past his left ear as his weight pushed against the man's chest. He pulled his head forward against the straining hands, and in the darkness, he drove his head back. The thud was sickening as the two skulls collided. Lights danced in Rankin's eyes. They swirled and swayed against the pitch black of the tunnel in front of him. The hands fell from his throat, and finally, he could breathe. The warm, stale air felt as though it had been as cool as the first southerly in autumn back home. The first sign of relief from the heat, the way it kissed his throat and filled his screaming lungs, a cool shiver ran down his spine.

Rankin spun around. He couldn't give his attacker any more time, he still couldn't see him, but he could sense the man inches from him. He heard him writhe on the ground behind him, he imagined the hands that were choking the life from him a moment ago, clasping his broken nose. Rankin lunged forward and grasped what he felt was the attacker's wrists and pulled. As he tore his arms away from his face, the man under him screamed. The guttural words of the Vietnamese soldiers echoed against the walls. They pounded the Australian's ears as he drove his right hand under the familiar hidden section of his belt, his left hand still fighting with the screaming gook beneath him. He felt his fingers slide through the holes of the cool metal, the gritty feel of its base nestled into his palm. The man beneath him lashed out and screamed so violently now Rankin had no idea where his face was. He struggled with the man's wrist frantically, his ears pounding from the resonating shouts, which sounded as though they would've been heard back in Sydney. Cursing, Rankin swung in a blind fury. He felt his fist glance the man's cheek, and unbelievably, the shouts became more intense.

'Shut the fuck up, you fucking piece of shit,' Rankin roared into the darkness as he drove his fist down again and again.

Somewhere in the frantic swings, he had connected well enough to send the man's shouts back to muffled murmurs of pain. His attacker had fallen limp, not dead but incapacitated enough for the moment. Rankin's hands skimmed the ground as he moved and searched for the detonator that had skittered across the floor at the beginning of the quick tussle. Below him, distantly, he could hear more men shouting, the sound of movement, as he had feared, they were coming. His hand brushed something cool and hard, it spun slightly on the ground, he clasped it and cursed. The Hi-Power was a good find, but not what he needed. He jammed it down the back of his pants with his left hand, the right still clasped the brass knuckles. The sweat coursed rivers down his face and back, he knelt on the tunnel floor, his hands blindly pattered from one end of the uneven surface to the other as he searched. The sense of urgency rose ever so quickly as he could hear the unknown below him get closer by the second. The shuffles and the sounds of small men while they hurried along the tunnel toward him and rapidly ascended from the depths of hell.

'Fuck, fuck, fuck, fuck,' he muttered in a panic. His palms still scanned the rough surface while he shifted his knees alternately slowly, and he made his way down the tunnel toward the C4 in the wall. Suddenly, no more than five feet in front of him, he heard the unmistakable sound of a foot graze the uneven surface of the tunnel. His eyes burned into the darkness, his left hand ripped the Hi-Power from the back of his pants, and he held it out in front of him. The weight of the pistol in his hand was comforting. A sword in the night, defending against the unseen foe. Yet, the tremor in his left hand, the feel of the sweat in between his palm and the notched handle, left him uneasy. His breaths were shallow, as he waited on his knees, the sound had not come again. While below him, the shuffling and shouts were slowly becoming louder. For what seemed like an hour, Rankin kneeled there, the pistol an extension of his arm. In his mind, he fought against himself and the two arguments that brewed within. The longer he waited, the closer the men below would get, against the argument that only fools rush in. The simple fact was, he had already rushed. He had already missed the junction, which allowed the Vietnamese strangler behind him his chance to alert those below. He was out of options. He began to squeeze the Hi-Power's trigger.

The pistol bucked in his hand. The darkness of the tunnel was instantly eradicated by the muzzle flash, although only for a split second. It has been said that a picture can paint a thousand words. What Rankin saw in that split second of firelight was enough to make him want to turn and forget the C4, to get back to the light and the fresh air above. The man was less than a foot away from the muzzle of the pistol. He had a dirk in his hand and had been sneaking ever so slowly toward Rankin when the muzzle flash had illuminated them both. He was a small-framed man with black short-cropped hair. The lines traced across his face indicated his age, which was reinforced by the bags underneath his bulging eyes. Rankin shouted at the sight of the man and fell backwards, the pistol still outstretched. The vision of the burning tunnel and the newcomer was burned into his eyes. The darkness of the tunnel, which consumed everything a moment later, was now overridden by large white circles that hung before him, blinding him to any forward movement. He heard the knife clatter against the earth and a heavy thump. He could hear the man kicking his feet, as Rankin had done just moments before, and a soft wet gurgle in the darkness as he struggled for breath. Rankin had not seen if he had hit the man in the flash of light, but from the sounds, he was satisfied that he didn't need to worry about the dirk in the darkness anymore.

If there had been any doubt to an outsider's presence in the tunnel, the pistol shot had expelled it. As Rankin moved over the struggling, gurgling mess of the Vietnamese soldier, he could hear urgent shouting from below. The constant hammer blows as mass amounts of people headed through the tunnels toward him had increased in volume by far. In a sheer stroke of luck, as Rankin moved over the dying man, he tripped and fell forward. His face drove into the ground, and he felt something small and metallic under his chest digging into him. His eyes widened as he grasped the item and ran his fingers along it to confirm his thoughts. It was the detonator. With a renewed sense of hope, Rankin clambered back over to the wall on his right and secured the brass knuckles in their place on the inside of his belt as he went.

'Come on, come on,' he reassured himself as he ran his hand along the rough wall and searched once more for the junction. Finally, his hand fell away as he moved along with haste. From there, he found the small indent, which was jam-packed with plastic explosives, easily enough. He roughly knew where he was now in relation to the junction, and he went to work quickly. The sounds of the Viet Cong moving through the tunnel were deafening now, and he knew it wouldn't be long until they were on top of him. He found the C4 and pushed the detonator into it. He felt the plastic move in its crevasse as he pushed, and he removed the string from around his neck, which was sopping wet with sweat.

As he fastened the string to its ring pull, he heard hurried shuffling steps from the junction to his left. Without a pause, he pulled the Hi-Power from the small of his back once more and readied himself. He heard their whispers underneath the movements. They were right on top of him. He slid the pistol against the wall and used the roughness as brail to signify the junction as he still couldn't see and leaned into the opening. As he did, the Viet Cong roared in surprise. Their eyes were obviously much better suited to the underground conditions than Rankin's. He fired three times in quick succession and tried to direct the shots to where he had heard the shout. His ears began to ring, it seemed as though the gun was still firing, and the reports bounced back at him repeatedly. He saw three more flashes from the pistol when he fired. The first flash, he saw the two surprised faces, the whites of their eyes, their yellowed teeth. When he fired the second time, he saw that he had hit the one on the left and that the man's head had become a deformed mess, but the other had raised a rifle. With the third shot, he felt confident that he had hit the rifleman and ducked behind the safety of the tunnel wall.

He was now in full retreat. He trailed the string along with him as he began to return to the one who had attempted to strangle him. He clambered over the one he had shot first and noticed that the gurgling had stopped. He felt his legs become wet with something as he dragged himself over. Still, he held the end of the string in one hand and the Hi-Power in the other, he felt his way along until his hand fell on the strangler's boot. He moved his way atop the man and readied himself to tie the string to him when behind him in the corridor came the clatter of automatic rifle fire. In the small confines of the tunnel, it sounded as though the rifle had let loose next to his ear. Rankin spun before the burst had finished and could see the outline of the junction, illuminated by the muzzle flash. He saw bullets' impact on the opposite wall. They were close, and his time was up. He returned his attention to the man he straddled and began to tie the string to his belt when he felt the man shift beneath him and a hot pain seared in his side as something pushed deeper inside him. With a scream of more surprise than pain, Rankin pushed the pistol into the man's gut and fired. The muffled report was followed immediately by sickening screams of pain.

There was shouting behind him now. He could hear the words clearly, pain or not, he had to leave. He left the screaming man once more, the string secured to his belt, and clambered his way back to the opening of the tunnel with what felt like the dropped dirk in his side. As he struggled on, he paused and fired two more shots behind him into the darkness to try and slow his pursuers by at least a second. The illuminating muzzle flashes did not reveal anything more, just the withering shape of the gut shot strangler. The pain in his side was horrendous, combined with the heat and the exhaustion, he felt sick in the guts and retched as he held his pace. Behind him, he could hear more shouting. The screaming strangler was sobbing to someone, they were right there. In front, he could see the faintest hint of light, the edges of the tunnel were becoming clearer, and he could see the small debris that littered the tunnel floor. As the hand with the pistol moved in front of him, he could see the blood up his arm.

'Bartlett!' The voice rang out from the opening ahead. It startled Rankin so much he almost dropped the pistol again. 'If you're alive down there, would you mind hurrying the fuck up?' As soon as Rixon's voice had faded, there was the tell-tale thud as the sixty opened up, the slow methodical rattle, and under it all, he heard the shouts of who he thought was Bourke. Tunnels generally had more than one exit. The commotion that Rankin had caused would have the Viet Cong rising every fifty to a hundred feet for probably half a mile. The light from the mouth of the tunnel became stronger with each step he took. The thought crossed his mind that when he entered the tunnel less than ten minutes ago, the light had only stretched in for five feet. Now it seemed to him that he had seen the hints of the opening for over a hundred feet. Then finally, he saw it, a bright circle of light in the roof of the tunnel some ten feet away.

'Here!' Rankin screamed as he crawled the last few feet into the section of the tunnel below the opening and tried to clamber out.

Two hands grabbed him by the collar of his shirt and dragged him. As he was pulled from the hole like a child out of the womb, the light blinded him. He felt the cool breeze touch his skin, and he instantly felt better, that was until he looked at the others. Powers was staring at him with a look of horror, his mouth ajar. He saw Bourke behind him as he fired the sixty in bursts into the tree line. Rixon laid him down and told him to drink some water. Rankin panted as he obeyed, he opened his mouth to accept the water. His body shook as the cool liquid which ran down his throat and into his gut sucked the heat out of him as it went. The sensation was sweet. He lowered his eyes and looked himself over. When he had entered the tunnel, he had been clean and rosy, now he was covered from head to toe in blood, dirt and mud. The colour of his greens was no longer recognisable from what he had dragged himself through. A small folding pocket knife stuck out from his side, a souvenir from his friend the strangler. Rixon's eyes fell on the blade, and he pulled it out instantly. Rankin gasped in pain and swore at his commander while Rixon poured water over his wound.

'Looks like you'll be al—' from the tunnel opening below, came a terrific roar. The ground trembled beneath their feet. A rush of air and dust shot out of the mouth of the tunnel The heat it brought with it made it feel like the breath of fire from the nostril of a dragon. Rankin watched as it climbed into the air and became lost among the canopy.

'Fucking good job, Bartlett,' Rixon yelled as he clambered back to his kneeling position. 'Can you walk?' he asked his soldier as he considered him.

Rankin raised himself on an elbow and grasped his wound with his hand. He gazed up at Rixon and gave the slightest of nods and held his hand out for his commander to help him to his feet. Rixon raised him up, handed him his pack and SLR and gestured for him to get ready. His commander moved into position in front of Powers, who was still gaping at Rankin.

'We gotta get out of here. That commotion you started below deck has had these fuckers coming from everywhere.' He adjusted his helmet and then wiped his brow. As Rankin secured his pack and checked his SLR, Daniels emerged from the right of the clearing.

'Simpsons coming in, same LZ, bombing run is starting in ten.'

'Fuck, come on, boys, move it. Bourke on point, keep that sixty pounding.'

The section began to move out. As they left the clearing one by one, Rankin noticed that Powers still stared at him. He gestured for Powers to go on as he wanted to hold the rear, but the boy didn't move.

'Come on, move.' Rankin urged and pushed him. The boy blinked as if he had come to a realisation of where he was and why. He got to his feet to move and turned his back to make his way out of the clearing. At that moment, Rankin saw from the corner of his eye a head and torso emerge from the opening of the tunnel. He turned in time to see a filthy Viet Cong, who had blood running down his face, raise his AK and begin to fire. His mouth was open in a sneer of hate, the report of the AK deafening. Without thinking, Rankin raised his SLR and drove two bullets into the man's chest. The force of the shots flung the small man back into the side of the opening, and he collapsed. The AK fired a few more shots as its muzzle was flipped into the air, and then it finally disappeared back into the depths, along with its wielder.

Rankin turned and saw Powers collapse. There were multiple small holes in the back of his greens. As with Rankin's attire, the fabric quickly changed shade, oozing brown and deep red. Powers fell away from him, face down, his SLR pinned beneath him. Rankin called out to the men in front, but received no answer. He couldn't remember who was the last to leave the clearing; was it Daniels or McDonnel? It didn't matter. He needed help. He yelled out again but still no answer. In the distance, he could hear the whup, whup of the Dread's rotors beating the air. He needed to act fast.

Placing his SLR on the ground, Rankin bent down and grabbed Powers by the collar and heaved him up. His head was beginning to pound again, the heat, the exertion, the amount of sweat he had pumped out in a short time. Thank fuck, this was his last patrol. He bent down and hoisted Powers onto his shoulders. He grabbed his SLR by the barrel and hoisted himself and his burden. He began to trudge through the jungle, chasing the pounding of the sixty and the odd rattle of SLRs and AKs. As he worked his way out of the clearing, he heard more shouts from behind him, from below. The explosives had not worked; he had missed the main junction and had only taken out a smaller one. He already knew he had walked past the first intersecting tunnel, as otherwise, how did the strangler get behind him? The whole thing was a waste of time.

A man burst out of the shrubs to the left and ran in the direction of the rest of the section. He didn't even notice Rankin carrying Powers and simply took off towards the LZ. Firing from the hip, Rankin managed to put a round into the running man's back. He did not feel confident about the shot and hoped that he didn't have to make many more like that, sooner or later, his luck would run out. Yet, with about every ten to twenty steps, more and more of the Viet Cong made their way out of the jungle. They seemed to just come out of the trees. They didn't speak, nor did they move urgently, they just appeared. Sometimes they saw Rankin, other times, as with the first, they didn't and made their way to the LZ to join the fight on the rest of the section. The rest of them must have been copping it. The sixty had fallen silent for a short while, in which it seemed like every other member of the section had opened up with their SLRs so as to not let the quiet take control. Throughout it all, Rankin heard bullets whiz as they screamed past them and multiple snickers after stray rounds had glance off rocks and sailed off into the jungle.

At one point, he collapsed under the weight of Powers. He fell awkwardly and hit the wound on his side as he fell. He grimaced with pain and struggled to right himself, but the oncoming whup, whup of the Dread's rotors kept him going. They needed to keep moving. He couldn't hear any huffs of pain or moans from Powers anymore. Rankin didn't want to think about it. The sick wet sensation which was running down his back was bad enough, yet this was the last patrol. They needed to get out, every one of them.

As they neared the clearing, Rankin noticed the bodies. Small men dressed in shorts and rags for shirts. Women, their chests blown open by the fire-driven metal bullets. The look of hate or love, happiness or sadness, gone from their eyes, nothing left, just the shadow of what they were. Their mouths were open, and their yellowed teeth almost snarled up at Rankin as he passed. As two more men appeared out of the trees on Rankin's right, they fired volleys of shots at him. He fired the SLR again from the hip, one man was caught in the leg and went down quickly but continued to fire. The other man he managed to hit in the gut went down and began to scream in agony. The sensation of gut shooting the man in the tunnel shot through Rankin's mind as a sick feeling went through his own. The man that was hit in the leg was still firing at them, bullets snickered of a tree nearby, and the SLR jammed. Rankin swore and threw it to the ground while turning on his heels to run. With both hands now supporting Powers' weight, he trudged with all the speed he could muster toward the clearing and the sound of the sixty. The Dread sounded as though it was nearly on top of them, soon, the fifty calibre would hammer through the trees, and he sure as shit wanted to be visible to them before that happened. As he ran, he heard a sickening sound of thuds on flesh. There seemed to be a rush of air coming out of Powers' mouth, but there was no time. He continued to run flat out. He traversed the uneven jungle floor, hopped over tree roots and turned sideways to slink through the gap of two trunks. Then finally, they were in the clearing.

There were about thirty Vietnamese lying strewn through the fallen trees of the makeshift LZ. The section had managed to beat them across the treacherous opening and set up a firing position. The Vietnamese that headed straight for the sound of the sixty seemed to have all run straight into the opening and became bogged down in the mess of fallen trunks, vast clumps of leaves that hid divots in the ground beneath them. As Rankin stepped into the clearing, the Huey came into sight overhead. Simpson noticed the gap between Rankin and the rest of the section and positioned the door gunner to watch over Rankin as he lowered into the clearing. He looked up and watched the gunner as he sat there on the side of the Black Dread, some twenty-five feet in the air. From his view on the ground, the fifty was still unusually big, especially to hang out of the side of a Huey. The barrel seemed to stretch out the side as far as the rotors went. Simpson waited until Rankin was most of the way into the clearing before he let the Dread down. Rixon had made his way around the front of the Dread and approached Rankin. The two men struggled with Powers across the strewn trees and bodies to reach their ride home. Simpson turned his hand in a 'come on, let's go' motion as he considered his wristwatch. As soon as everyone had piled into the cargo hold of the Dread, Simpson brought the revs up, and they lifted into the air. The sick feeling in Rankin's gut returned for a short second but seemed to disappear in shock the next.

Simpson did not have time to travel horizontally; he needed to gain sheer altitude instantly. They were only a couple of hundred feet into the air when Rankin saw two small planes in the distance, through the opening on the opposite side of the cargo bay, flying extremely quickly and in their exact direction.

'Hold on!' Rixon bellowed over the shrill whine of the Huey's turbo engine. The Douglas A-1 Skyraiders flew directly under the Dread. As they came out the other side, the ground erupted in flames and smoke. A wall of fire rushed through the trees. The landing zone they had just taken off from was enveloped instantly, the bodies that lay there consumed by the beast. The Napalm licked up into the air, and the smoke that billowed from the devil's fire curled all around them. Its fingers reached up and licked at the bottom of the Dread's hull as if in an attempt to pull them down and inward into its ever-consuming flame. Yet as the tendrils listed above the canopy, they were driven into spirals by the power of the Huey's rotors. It seemed as though the fire would consume even life itself. Then two more Sky Raiders flew under the Dread, through the smoke and beyond. Through the haze and darkness, more fires were visible, erupting from the ground in a solid wall. Everything it touched burned to the ground. He could barely take his eyes from what he saw, the hatred in the fire, the hatred in the eyes of the people. This fucking country.

As he settled himself into the wall of the cargo bay, he lit a cigarette and looked about. Powers was lying on his side, away from Rankin. Rixon was next to him with his hand on his head, looking sullen. Rankin leaned over to grab Powers, but Rixon waved him away, giving him a look of disdain and shook his head. Rankin shot him a confused look and leaned over again to grab Powers. He laid a hand on his arm and pulled. Rixon went to stop him again but let him go. Powers' eyes were open, they were dull and lifeless. The holes in the back of his greens were small, but on the front of his chest, the holes were the size of apples. Rankin looked down at Powers, shocked. He didn't think the boy would be in a good way, but he didn't think he would be dead now. As he looked down into the young man's face, he thought of Gary, the lout, the laughter and the girls. He thought of Will, the snide remarks and the alcohol. Then Max, the brawler, the friend, his dislike of Americans. The brothers that were all gone. Those that had taken tickets home to Enoggera, then Sydney already. It was time. Time to return to them, time to leave this fucking country, time to start his life.

MICHAEL

'I see a bad moon a-rising
I see trouble on the way
I see earthquakes and lightnin'
I see bad times today
Don't go 'round tonight
It's bound to take your life
There's a bad moon on the rise.'

Creedence Clearwater Revival – *Bad Moon Rising* (1969)

The worn down soles of Michael's engineer boots pounded the gravel and dirt of the fire trail. With each footfall, the crunching noise was audible over the kettledrum that pounded in his throat. The heat of the day had started beating down on him the moment he was thrown out of his father's car. Yet he had only just started to notice the pools of sweat beginning to form under his armpits, which discoloured the navy-blue work shirt that clung to his body. His head lowered as he ran, and he pumped his arms and legs as he noticed the pebbles and small potholes already forming on the freshly graded track. 'Mick,' the writing embroidered on his blue work shirt, stood proud against the fabric. There wouldn't be much left of good old Mick after this, he thought.

The boy headed down the track towards the sawmill in his father's Fairlane 500 when Matt and Kel, or whoever they were, had taken it upon themselves to rid Michael of the burden that was his father's car.

They had shot back off in the direction of the Baker's lot, which left Michael with a difficult choice. He could go back home and pretend that he had nothing to do with the situation. After all, the keys were already in the ignition when the boy had found himself in the car. It was plausible, yet Michael didn't think that the declaration of 'I don't know' would get him out of a beating when Tony returned. The other option that lay in the direction of home was to go to the Darcy lot and hope like hell that Paul was there. After all, Paul was the one that had given Michael his nickname. Surely their long time family friend would come to his rescue. But Paul was Tony's friend, to tell one was to tell the other, in his mind, he could see the two men either sitting on the Darcy's porch or leaning up the side of the Baker's house with a long neck each, smoking. 'You'd never guess what your boy got up to while you were in Dalby.' The balding Darcy would laugh as his chest hairs bulged through the open gate of his denim vest while the hand that wasn't burdened with his Fosters long neck mopped the sweat from his hairless brow with the soiled handkerchief. Unacceptable. Tony could never find out about this. In the end, this left Michael with only one realistic option: Run the mile that was left of the fire trail and plead with Jack to help him.

Although not an easy option for Michael, his brother was as brutish as Tony ever was, yet no sooner had the Fairlane and the Tracker's Bedford disappeared over the small rise, the boy had taken to the track like a greyhound released from the gate. The only difference being that the boy wasn't racing to get to a hare, he was running for his life.

THUD, THUD, THUD. As the boy's boots hammered the gravel, he thought of his father's fists laying into his body and his legs. In this situation, he didn't think his face was out of the question either. There was a real possibility that Tony would resort to his favourite of all punishments. 'Go and find something for me to hit you with.'

He could picture his father sitting in his accustomed seat at the head of the Baker's dining room table. His face in his hands as he struggled to comprehend what either of his two children had done. Once he had exclaimed those words, the ceremony would begin. It was the task of the children to scour the small block on which they resided to find something suitable for their father to whip across the backs of their thighs. Michael had first gotten the impression that his brother was an idiot from these such ceremonies. While the boy would look for the softest materials at his disposal, his brother had always come back with enormous dead gum branches. The sound of the dead branch whistled through the air as their now drunk father brought it down on the back of Jack's legs with all the strength he could muster. The grimace of pain from the man's eldest son and the cracking of the dead gum as the dried timber let go under the strain. That crack will be my neck after this, the boy reflected.

THUD, THUD, THUD. The mill was coming into sight now, and some hope flooded back into the boy's heart. Yet the kettledrum that was his heart still pounded furiously. Jack would have to be there. As he closed the final distance to the mill, he thought back to the last item that he had presented his father in their final ceremony. Jack, like always, had presented the big man with a large branch. It took his father only two long swings on his brother's thighs for the branch to give way. Michael, on the other hand, had brought his father a few blades of grass. 'Go nuts,' he remembered saying. Christ, he must have been out of his mind.

Tony had just looked at the blades of grass, then finally, after a long pause, he looked at his son, smiling. 'Fuck that, I have a better idea.' With that, the large man disappeared into the house, mumbling under his breath something about insolence and giving him blades of grass. Michael thought himself fairly intelligent. However, if intelligence got you fifty lashes across the back of the thighs with the iron chord, then he had wished to share the intelligence of one of the dead gum branches which broke on his brother's legs. Each lash he suffered burned like a thousand knives cutting into him as the braided chord tore into the soft flesh of the boy's legs. He had screamed and screamed. His brother stood there and just watched with no means of defiance on his face. The chord whirred through the air and then cut into his legs. Time after time, until finally, he had heard the screen door clatter closed and his mother's weeping voice shrill in her distress.

'You're killing him,' she had screamed at her husband. He couldn't remember much of what had happened that time, but that was the last instance that Tony had requested the boys to source him a tool to hit them with.

As the boy ran past the Hyster's shed, he stole a quick glance and saw that the Whippet was parked crookedly on the other side of the shelter. 'Thank Christ,' the boy gasped as he pounded his way into the main facility. The sweat now fully soaked through the back of his blue chambray shirt, the material clinging to his back.

'Shit Mick, where's the fire?'

Michael's head swung around as he entered the main hanger style doors of the mill. Paul Darcy made his way towards him, his Akubra in one hand low at his side. The other mopped beads of sweat from the balding man's forehead with a handkerchief. It seemed that Michael wasn't the only one feeling the heat that day.

'J-Jack!' Michael spluttered as he came to a halt; he hadn't realised how out of breath he was. He had run a full mile flat out, however, there was still no time to waste. 'Jack, where is he?' He drove in a big breath of air. 'Now!'

Darcy looked confused. The boy had never spoken to him in that kind of tone. He looked down at the boy and the state he was in, raising one of his hands in a calming motion. 'Come now, Mick, what's wrong?'

Michael couldn't tell the man a damn thing, no matter how much he wanted a bit of comfort. Paul Darcy was apt to be the only source of comfort the boy was likely to find, apart from his mother. 'I need Jack, it's okay, really.' He sucked in another gasp of air as he hunched over and placed both of his hands on his knees. 'I just thought I would try and beat my best time from home.' The boy stood up and brought both of his hands back through his sopping wet and dusty hair. 'But I do need to talk to Jack. Could you please tell me where he is?'

Paul scoffed as he placed his Akubra on his still glistening head. He swung his grubby hand and clapped Michael on one of his sweaty shoulders. 'Bloody kids. Jack's in your father's office.' Michael winced as the man swung his arm, although he would never have thought that Paul would intentionally hurt him, the two men of his household wouldn't think twice. Blushing, Michael thanked the kind man and trotted off once more to the iron, cross backed steps which led to the mezzanine and Tony's office. As he closed the ground and heard his feet clang on the iron steps as he began to climb, he heard Paul call out to him. Michael froze, the fear of the man knowing what had happened started to claw its way up his spine once more. 'Did you beat it?' Paul looked up at the boy, his hands now on his hips. Sweat continued to run down his forehead from under the brim of his faded Akubra.

'What?' What was he talking about? Was there a joke he was missing or something? He just wanted to talk to his brother and rip the band-aid off, so to speak.

'Your time? Did you beat it?' A grin appeared on the man's face as he once more pulled his Akubra off and mopped the sweat with the noticeably wet handkerchief. Michael blushed again, his cheeks now flaming red. He had forgotten what he had told him as a lie to get rid of him.

He smiled back as he looked down at Paul from the steps, his breath still heavy on his chest. 'Destroyed it.' Then he began his climb of the iron stairs, not bothering to look back down as the man called out praise. As the boy reached the heavy, metal lined door with the fading words printed on the face, a thought crossed his mind about how different his life would have been if Darcy was his father. His hopes and dreams of marrying Susan Darcy would, of course, be eliminated. Yet, the fair-faced, auburn-haired girl would surely make better company than Jack.

More out of habit than courtesy, Michael knocked twice on the door, then clasped the door handle and began to turn it. There was no reply from inside, just the smell of a smouldering cigarette and the dusty aroma of filth and sawdust emitted from the ruined carpet. As Michael swung the door open, he saw Jack behind his father's desk. He sat relaxed on the old castor chair with both hands clasped behind his head as he stared vacantly at the ceiling. A cigarette lay burning on the rim of the ashtray, which was littered with countless other cigarettes. Jack had smoked for as long as Michael could remember, yet he never really seemed to smoke the cigarette. Once he had lit it, the cigarette had either hung from one end of his lip or was placed in the ashtray and left to burn. The smoke rose steadily, near obscuring his brother's face. Among the rest of his father's belongings, Michael could see that both massive filthy work boots were crossed on the edge of the desk. Nothing else was on the table, no invoices, no partially completed quotes. Jack was as busy as always.

The blinds were closed in the office, as usual. They hadn't been opened since the day that Tony had left. Although only a few days ago, it seemed like years to the stressed boy. Once Michael had turned and heaved the office door closed on its rusting hinges, the only light source came from the centre of the disabled ceiling fan. Smoke hung around the light in an attempt to drown it out.

'Jack.' The monster of a man still hadn't looked at his brother. His eyes were fixed on something up on the wall, but Michael hadn't turned his head to look at what it was. He needed his brother's help, so he pushed on.

'Jack, I need your help. I lost Dad's car.' He blurted it all out. The kettledrum in his throat pounded once more, and his nerves were at their end. The massive biceps of his brother twitched at that, and the big man's gaze slowly swung to look at his brother. The two meaty hands parted their grip at the back of his head, and one swung down to the smouldering cigarette that rested near his side.

'Lost?' the elder brother questioned, with a noticeable lack of concern for his brother. His eyes looked the small boy up and down as he took in his state of appearance. He raised the cigarette to his mouth and took a long drag. The smouldering end burned a fierce red, similar to the emergency brake light in the Fairlane, then dulled as Jack placed it down to rest in its usual place. 'The Fairlane's big. You'll find it if you look hard enough.' As he spoke, smoke wisped out of his mouth, it rushed and swirled, carried by Jack's breath.

'I didn't lose it. It was taken. A fat man named Kel and a filthy, skinny guy called Matt took it. I nearly hit them on the trail here. They took it, Jack!' There wasn't time for this, the sense of urgency had risen greatly in Michael's chest since he had started running down the dusty track toward the mill. As he stood there in front of his brother, the need for action rang in his ears. 'They had a blue, shitty truck. It said Trackers on it.'

Jack's eyebrow raised, and he picked the cigarette up once more to take another long drag. 'Trackers took it? You're a dead man walking boy. The old man will kill you when he hears.' He took his drag and crushed the cigarette out in the overpopulated ashtray.

'Dad isn't going to hear about it,' Michael was grasping at straws. Screaming at Jack wouldn't achieve anything, but his voice was getting shakier by the second. 'We're going to get it back. You and me.'

Jack's laughter rattled the timber curtain rods which held the rotting cloth. He rose one of his massive hands to his short cut hair and scratched at his scalp, his bicep bulged against the already torn sleeve of his work shirt. 'I ain't doing shit,' Jack proclaimed, his body still heaved with laughter as he turned his face to continue his gaze at the same place on the wall as before. A smirk left on his face from the humour of it all.

'You were the last to drive it.' Michael's voice quivered as he spoke, its pitch became shriller by the second. Jack snorted at this but wasn't interested in replying. His gaze remained on the place on the wall. 'You left the keys in the ignition. Trackers could have just come and taken it. You and I could be the heroes in this.'

Jack swung his huge feet off the table and turned to face Michael, his two meaty hands slammed palm down on the top of his father's worn desktop. He eyed Michael. The smirk vanished from his face, and his square jaw twitched as he stared. 'This is your story, you tell it how you like. But there are no heroes, boy, just you. I have no part in this. It's your problem.' He continued to stare straight into Michael's soul. Although not the quickest of mind, it was plain to see Jack had instantly cottoned onto Michael's intentions.

'There may be no heroes, but if Dad comes back and the car's not there, you and I will be goners anyway.' Michael dropped his gaze to his feet, he couldn't hold eye contact with his older brother. He glanced to the discoloured patch of carpet, where he usually rested while he read his books. 'Dad won't care if it's my fault or your fault. Mum will get it too.' He lifted his eyes slowly to look at his brother once more. His blue chambray shirt still clung to him, and the smell of the dirt, smoke and sawdust was beginning to overpower him. His nose had begun to run, and he wiped a small trickle of snot away from his upper lip as his eyes fell upon his brother. Jack's eyes no longer burned into him. The palms of his hands were still pressed to the oak desktop, his jaw muscles still flexed, yet his eyes had drifted off to the spot on the wall which seemed to command his attention so fiercely. Michael began to move his head to see what could be so interesting.

'Okay,' Michael's head snapped back. Jack's eyes were still locked on the spot to Michael's left. 'We will get it back. You and me. For her.' He lifted himself to his feet, his father's oak chair groaned and creaked as the immense weight was lifted from its base. Jack towered over Michael, and he pushed his head forward to look down at him, his eyes were filled with hate. He made his way around the desk, pushed past his smaller brother and swung open the heavy, steel-lined door.

Jack strode silently toward the Whippet. He ignored the calls of the fellow workmen and staff scattered in the mill. His footfalls made tremendous clouds of sawdust as he trudged his way through the machinery. Michael followed, likewise silent. The staff were interested in talking to Jack, not him. None ever called out to him to start a conversation or ask questions. To them, Michael was nothing.

Jack reached the Whippet and immediately went about getting the old truck running. From what Michael could tell, the Whippet used to be a luxury sedan. At some point or another, the Whippet's owners had cut the cab to pieces and had transformed it into a farm truck. Where the back seat and boot once loomed was a fairly large hardwood tray, which was now aged and scratched. The cab's metal was shaped and capped with scraps so that now the front section was open. Its only source of protection was the windscreen, which was dusty, chipped and cracked from years of traversing the fire trail. Jack sagged himself into the overhanging bench seat, flicked a switch and pumped the accelerator. As he pulled himself out, he dragged a small knob on the dash outward. He went about rummaging among the littered scrap steel and timber offcuts in the back of the tray until he dragged out a worn and rusty crank handle.

While Jack went to the front of the truck, Michael climbed into the open cab of the Whippet, happy to have a bit of a rest. His clothes still stuck to him from the sweat and as he rested his back up against the dusty and torn seat, a cool chill went up his spine. Jack was almost hidden as he bent down to insert the crank handle into the front of the bulking Whippet's front end. He cursed and muttered to himself as he braced a huge hand on the foldable bonnet of the truck and began to crank. After his fifth attempt, the Whippet coughed and spluttered, and black clouds of smoke rose from under the tray. Jack stood up, stretched his back and made his way to the cab. As he slid in behind the steering wheel, which was on the left hand side, not the customary right of Australia, he threw the crank handle into the back of the tray. With a slight grind of gears, the Whippet began to lurch, its six-cylinder engine whirred a tired wheeze of life underneath the rusting metal hood.

As the air rushed past Michael and the sound of the diff whine became more pronounced. Michael realised that Jack seemed to know where he was going. 'Do you know these people? Matt and Kel?' Michael shouted as the two brothers roared down the fire trail. As the cab of the Whippet was open, the road noise was extreme. Not only did a speaker need to contend with the rushing air or the fluttering sound of the engine, but the scream of every rusted and worn spring in the vehicle sung its protest at the slightest bump. This, combined with the scatterings of steel and timber in the back of the tray that fought among themselves for a settled position, meant that any conversation needed to be held at screaming point to be heard at all.

Jack shifted the Whippet into third gear and the transmission ground slightly as the lever slipped into position. 'The fat one is Kel

Tracker.' Jack boomed, his eyes squinted against the rushing wind and swirling dust. 'He is the frontman of their shit show. Matt is like you, useless and just drives that Bedford around for the fat one.' Jack explained that the Trackers ran a sort of wrecking yard that sat on the same fire trail as the one that led the boy home each day. Michael had never known much of this road one way or the other. He knew that once you left the front gate and went left, you arrived at the mill, when you went right, you arrived at the Darcy's lot. What lay beyond was always a mystery, and since Michael was homeschooled, he never found the opportunity to go out. His life consisted of home and mill. As Jack went on, Michael soon found out that past the Darcy's lot, there consisted of not much else but scrub and dirt road for three miles. Finally, at the end of the trail, one would find 'Tracker's Bro's Wreckers,' a shit show for rip off merchants and thieves.

Jack explained that at one point, Tony and the elder brother had driven there in the Fairlane to source a new starter motor for the Whippet. Of course, the Trackers had one, but Tony and the fat man could not agree on a price. The fat one wanted Tony's Fairlane as a trade for the questionable starter motor. Tony, not being outdone, told the fat man that he wanted a wife with tits as big as the man standing in front of him. Eventually, their father realised that the conversation would have come to blows, thanked the man for his time and left. Michael could only imagine the language that would have been coming out of his old man's cruel mouth as the father and son left, defeated. Apparently, Tony had not left it at that and approached a man by the name of Phil Webber, who was the local grader operator, Tony had questioned the man about who funds his time to keep the fire trail graded past the Darcy lot to which the answer was given that the Tracker Brothers paid for his time. Tony had suspected this, and since then, the Chinchilla Sawmill had paid

Mr Webber three times what the Trackers had paid, to always forget that anything ever existed past the Darcy lot.

The Whippet creaked and groaned as it made its way down the trail. Michael looked longingly as they passed the gate back to their home, where this mistake had all started. He wondered where his mother was and if they would see her on the road walking back from the Darcy's. Yet even though a lot had happened since the boy had risen from bed and broken his fast, it was still very early. His mother was not likely to leave the warmth of Penelope Darcy's company any time soon. Michael felt a little relieved, to be honest. The other men were bigger than him, that wasn't hard, but he had never seen anyone come close to Jack's size and strength apart from his father. There really couldn't be any question about them getting the car back unless one of them had a gun. Jack was a big man that made for a big target. 'What if they have a gun?' Michael yelled as the Whippet bounced over a pothole.

'Then we will take it.' Jack didn't seem concerned. His short-bristled hair waved frantically as he squinted and leaned forward to try to shield his eyes from the wind and dust. Michael looked out to the right once more and watched as the gate for the Darcy lot slid past. He wondered what Susan was doing. She would be in school more than likely. He could imagine her pressing the tip of a pencil into her mouth as she contemplated a math problem. How he wished he could be the tip of the pencil. A soft smile began to appear across the boy's face, and he closed his eyes so that he could dream about his love for at least a short time. Perhaps he would get a scar from this adventure. Later, when they were older, he could tell her about his great adventure with his brother and how they saved their loving mother from their father's wrath.

The dream did not last. The Whippet bounced violently, and Jack was forced to shift to a lower gear and bring the iron hulk down to lower speeds. Startled, Michael opened his eyes and grasped the side of the cab to stop himself from falling. The fire trail at this point was destroyed. It looked as though it had been ten years since it was serviced or seen the sight of Webber's grader. There were wheel ruts two feet deep in places, and channels, where runoff had completely washed the trail away. Michael watched as Jack navigated the iron hulk across the ruts and divots in the trail. He picked the high spots and, at points, even ran two of the four skinny tyres off the trail to avoid falling into ruts and washouts. The last thing either of them needed was to lose the Whippet to the Tracker's road.

The bumping and grinding continued for what seemed like an eternity. As the Whippet bounced and hitched its weight, the suspension groaned and screamed in protest. Michael's head had begun to pound away with every bump and knock, and he started to anticipate the drops and sharp rises of each blow the Whippet suffered. His eyes squinted, and his face contorted as he braced for impact. He glanced up at his brother as they went, his face had not changed, apart from his eyes, they were no longer slits against the wind. Instead, he glowered over the windscreen, his eyes darted left and right as he swung the wheel around to avoid the falls. He nodded his head toward the steering wheel in a gesture to make Michael look forward, the boy peered through the dirt and grime covered windscreen. Emerging like an overgrown relic from another time, a rusted wrought iron gate stood open before them. A worn sign above, which was near illegible, 'Track... B...s...Wre,' was all the boy could make out by the time they drove under it. As the brothers putted the Whippet through the Tracker's yard, they passed countless rusted wrecks of sedans, trucks and coupes. Many had doors missing, most of the bonnets stood open, propped ajar with scraps of steel or timber with gaping vacant engine bays looming underneath. As they rounded a destroyed wreck of a bus sitting on its rear axles, the tyres and rims long since pulled off and discarded, they saw a dilapidated two-story house. Many of its windows were boarded up from the inside. The glass that once protected the interior had long since been destroyed. From here, they could see that many of the roof tiles had been broken, now covered in mould, and pieces of corrugated iron had been thrown up there in an attempt to stop water from seeping its way inside. Unsecured, they flapped in the tremulous breeze that hummed from the east. It was obvious even to the boy that it wouldn't take much for the sheets of iron to come tumbling back to the earth.

Parked maybe twenty feet in front of the house was Tony Baker's Fairlane 500. It stood gleaming and proud among the shit and rusted hulks that surrounded it. Its nose was facing a rundown shed, which sheltered a desk and a parted-out tractor chassis. The fat man, Kel Tracker, was leaning his immense body on the jacked up chassis when the Whippet chugged around the side of the bus. He didn't make a move, just continued to lean on the rusting steel and watched as the old truck came to a halt. His eyes darted between Jack and Michael. Matt, the filthy one, was nowhere to be seen.

Jack brought the Whippet to a halt some ten feet behind the Fairlane and switched it off. The large ancient engine chuffed, causing the whole body of the truck to shudder along with it as it wheezed a final breath. To the boy, it was a mistake to switch it off since the starter motor was never fixed. No easy getaway could be made with the Whippet, or now at all, since the Fairlane was parked in by the immovable hulk they still sat in.

Jack glared over the steering wheel at the Kel, neither of them spoke. All that could be heard was the rustling leaves of trees in the distance and the clanging of the unsecured iron, which lay on the broken tiles of the Tracker's house. Jack swung his huge boots out of the cabin and rose to his feet. His eyes never left the fat man.

Kel likewise didn't speak, just continued to look from Jack to the small boy still sitting in the cab as he leaned against the chassis. Jack slowly made his way to the Fairlane and opened the driver's door. The path took him closer to Kel, and he turned his back on the man to look inside the car. Nevertheless, the fat man did not move, he just turned his head to watch the big man's progress. Jack paused as he bent to look inside the car. The iron clattered against the concrete tiles. Jack stood up, still with his back to Kel, he shook his head, and a look of anger flashed across his face. He slammed the Fairlane's door, the massive rolling iron rocked savagely at first on its suspension, then settled again slowly. Jack turned quickly and pointed a finger at Kel.

'You. Fat Man. Where are they?' He took a step closer to Kel.

Kel still hadn't moved. His eyes were on Michael while Jack looked in the car. There wasn't hate or fear in his eyes, he was just patient as if he had expected this would happen all along. When Jack slammed the car door, he calmly moved his eyes back toward the large man who now confronted him.

'Well, that attitude will get you nowhere,' his eyebrows raised as the words wheezed restricted from his fat lips. Even though it didn't look as though the man had walked any further than from the Fairlane's driver's door to where he stood, maybe fifteen feet separated Jack and Kel.

'My attitude will get me what I've come for. Yours will decide whether I go now or take a part of you for a keepsake.' Jack took another couple of steps toward the man while his jaw muscles rippled below the flesh on his cheek. His massive fists clenched, he took two more steps. Jack's back was to Michael now as he walked past another wrecked car towards Kel. His back seemed to be as wide as Michael was tall. The boy couldn't understand how the sheer sight of the man couldn't intimidate the likes of this fat Tracker.

Kel continued to calmly eye the big man, his body broadside as he leaned his weight. His arms crossed on the chassis, he remained motionless. 'I see you must be the runt's brother. Another Baker brat.' Kel wheezed as he laughed out his statement and maintained eye contact.

Jack took a few more steps, his muscles clenched and a vein pulsed from his neck as he now proceeded past the wreck to his left. 'I'll giv–' he began as a movement came from his left and below. Michael couldn't really see what was happening at first, he heard his brother cut off and begin to turn, then out from behind the wreck, the filthy skinny Tracker had risen like a flash and swung his arm up. He held a large shifter, which looked as though it fit a nut about an inch and a half across. Matt Tracker brought the shifter up across the large man's forehead. The sound was horrible as the forged steel slammed into Jack's head. His legs seemed to go out from under him as he fell to a knee, one of his big hands clasped to his head. He didn't say a word. He swayed on one knee for a moment, then fell face forward. His hands spread out in front of him, in the direction of Kel. Jack lay silent and motionless.

Michael froze. That was it. He closed his eyes and brought his hands to his face. *They've killed him, shit, now what? Jack is a monster, I'm nothing. What can I do?* He sat horrified in the passenger seat of the Whippet, stuck to the spot. He could hear both men laughing and the shuffling of dirt as they walked.

The filthy man was hooting and leaping, 'Didn't I give that big fucker what for,' he laughed and shouted. Michael managed to bring his hands away from his face and looked up at the Trackers. They had left Jack where he lay and had begun making their way towards the Whippet. The fat man swayed from side to side as he waddled towards the truck, his mouth open as he panted. Matt was still laughing as he bounced around Kel.

'Two cars now, not just one. Old Robby will be happy with us, hey ol' Kel.' He still held the shifter in his hands as he bounced around, swinging the wrench from side to side. If the boy was lucky, the fat man would wear one of the blows up his head as poor Jack did. As Kel made his way to the opening of the Whippet's cab, he laid a hand on Michael's shoulder and squeezed, his open mouth turning into a horrid grin.

'A new brother too,' he wheezed. This was the first time that Michael had been able to take this man's features in. His eyes were sunk back into his head, and massive black bags hung under each. His skin was a filmy white and coarse with rashes and pimples from the sweat. The hand on the shoulder, although flabby, was still strong. The filthy face of Matt Tracker appeared over his brother's shoulder, the rotting teeth bared as he laughed at the boy. Spit flew from his mouth as he cackled.

'I got a new truck and a new brother. Fuck these Baker's boars, I'm going to go down and get me their sow.' He ran his feet on the spot, hooting as he spat into his hand. He ran his filthy hand up over his rotting hair and smiled back down at Michael. 'Do you think your mother will like me, boy?'

Kel leaned in close over Michael and kissed his forehead with his large wet lips. A long string of saliva stretched between the boy's head and the fat man's drooping lip as he pulled away. 'Oh, I think she'll like all of us just fine, brother.' He backed away from Michael and looked at him with those sunken eyes. 'And if not, she'll come around.'

While Matt Tracker was still laughing at the boy over Kel's shoulder, a large hand was coming down over his head, open with its palm facing down. When it closed over the top of his head, the skinny one stopped laughing and stood long enough for Michael to see the joy run from his face before he was flung backward away from the Whippet. The hand holding Michael's shoulder loosened its grip as Kel swung around. Blood streamed down Jack Baker's face from the blow that Matt had dealt him. His eyes were large and burned with anger, while muscles worked in his jaw as he closed the gap between them. Although Kel had his back to Michael now, the boy could hear the fear in his voice instantly as he screamed,

'Stop! Stop!' He raised his hands to face, yet Jack's big hand swung down on him and tore him from his feet.

From behind Jack, there came an insane scream of anger as Matt Tracker clambered to his feet and re-armed himself with the oversized shifter. He raised his weapon as he ran, roaring in anger. Jack stood facing him, his hands still down by his side, unwavering, unshaken. As the filthy, howling man bore down on him, Jack caught him with both massive hands and threw him once more. This time, the man collided with the same wreck that he hid behind before felling the big man. The air came out of him as his body slammed into the rusting steel. He immediately began to clamber up again, but Jack was onto him. A giant foot caught Matt in the chest, which flung him into the side of the wreck once more. This time, he landed on his ass, his back against the steel. He was gasping for breath as his eyes bulged from their sockets. He scrambled to move as one of Jack's fists came down on him.

Matt Tracker dragged himself to the right of the crushing blow at the last second as Jack's monstrous fist drove into the steel. Steel screamed, and rust flaked from the paint as the wreck's door gave way under the power of the blow. No sooner had Matt dodged the first swing then another was coming down on him. He howled in terror as he tried to pull himself to the right again, but he was too slow. There was a bone-crunching sound as Jack's fist drove into the man's face, and his filthy head was hammered back into the side of the wreck. Blood burst from the man's nose, and three of his rotting teeth spilled from his mouth as he collapsed to the floor, dazed and barely managing to hold his conscious state.

That wasn't where Jack left it. He dropped his knee onto the Tracker's arm. Matt's body squirmed as the bone snapped under his weight, and then he began to drive his fist into Matt's face over and over again. The look of absolute hatred burned in his eyes as Jack raised his arm and brought his fist down with all of his strength. The sound each blow made was sickening, the sound that bones made as they broke, the muffled grunts of pain and with each hit, the growing sound of wetness as the blood poured from the man's face. Michael still had not moved. He watched his brother kill this man. He saw the blood running rivers down his brother's face and the bloody mess that was Matt Tracker.

Jack finally finished with the bleeding wreck of a man and clambered to his feet. He panted heavily, and the look of anger seemed all the more vicious as his eyes fell on Kel, who still lay crumpled before the Whippet. The big man grunted as he began to close the ground between himself and the Whippet. As Jack left Matt Tracker behind him, Michael could hear the gurgling of the mortally wounded man as he tried to draw life's breath. Jack, undeterred, bent over and grabbed the fat man by his tits. He pulled him to his feet and drove him into the side of the Whippet. He screamed as Jack drove his fingers into the upper left of the man's chest and closed his grip around his collarbone. The howls of pain and fear were horrific. Jack leaned his bleeding face close to Kel's, their foreheads touching. Both men were now covered in both the blood from Jack's head wound and the matted mess from Matt Tracker's face. Jack was splattered head to toe with the sticky fluid. His right hand, which was now dug half into the fat man's torso, was barely visible. The remains of his brother's face had rubbed all over Kel's filthy shirt, and the blood from Jack's wound began to run down his face. 'What did I say about keepsake?' Jack said calmly and then screamed in Kel's face.

'Where the fuck are the keys?' He tightened his grip on the man's collarbone, and the screams of pain intensified.

Kel was pointing at the house, and in between the screams of pain, a name was audible. 'Robin! Robin! Robin!'

JACK

'I hear hurricanes a-blowing
I know the end is coming soon
I fear rivers overflowing
I hear the voice of rage and ruin
Don't go 'round tonight
It's bound to take your life
There's a bad moon on the rise.'

Creedence Clearwater Revival – *Bad Moon Rising* (1969)

As the wind blew through Jack's shortly cropped hair, the corrugated iron clanged upon the roof of the Tracker's house. His breath was heavy in his chest as his meaty hand closed around the fat man's collar bone. He felt the soft skin, almost pliable, sink as he pressed his fingers into the fleshy hollow of Kel's lower throat. Behind him, somewhat forgotten, the gurgling blood filled attempts of Matt Tracker's shortening breaths still echoed. The man in front of him turned his eyes to the sound of his dying brother, a look of bewilderment spread over the cocky son of a bitch's face. From when Jack had driven the old Whippet into their shit hole of a yard, this smug silence had been replaced by shrill screams of terror and pain. At first, Kel had given up nothing, he had remained cocky with bullshit remarks in order to wind the tall man up. In that, he had succeeded, Jack was wound up.

'Robin! Robin! Robin!' Kel Tracker rasped and gasped as he

writhed in pain. He tried to struggle and break free from the giant who held him with the little strength that remained in him. The flabby wing of his arm waved frantically as he pointed hurriedly to the dilapidated house yard of wrecks surrounded. All things pointed to inside.

Satisfied, Jack loosened his grip on Kel's collarbone and felt the cool sensation as his hand slipped out of the sweaty, grimy flesh. As he swung his arm back behind him, his fist clenched, he saw the red, inflamed flesh that glistened with sweat from the spot where his hand had plunged into the man's upper chest. Jack drove his clenched fist into the man's enormous gut. He felt his hand sink once more into him as his hand was swallowed by soft flabby flesh. The blow lifted Kel up off his feet as his body crumpled around the sheer force of the impact. Jack let him go, and he took a step back as Kel collapsed at his feet. While the wheezing, sweating, sobbing heap of a man crumpled at the foot of the Whippet, Jack's gaze turned to the small boy, who still sat in the cab, frozen in his shock.

Another hit taken thanks to this boy. Another night spent with a pounding head. Another night spent wondering if it had been the pain of the blow that had been dealt to him or the build up of rage and hate that threatened to split his head open. He stood for a moment, his laboured breaths slowed and came under control. His rage boiled within him as he looked down at the boy, who sat there like a deer in the headlights. Behind him, the gurgles of Matt Tacker's bloodied breath had finally stopped. The beaten man lay wrecked, his face unrecognisable from the shit fight it had been this morning. At least it was an improvement. The big man raised one of his meaty hands and pointed at the boy, who hadn't as much as blinked an eye.

'Stay there,' Jack grunted and turned to the house. His head pounded from the impact of the wrench. Blood still ran down his sloped forehead and across his brow.

As Jack faced the house, a gust of wind blew from behind him. He watched as the corrugated iron flapped in fury, then gave up all hope of holding on to its perch and slid from the roof with a scream of rusting metal. As it crashed to the ground, Jack could feel the breeze kiss the back of his neck and the coolness of his right hand. As he made his way to the house, he thought of his brother's latest concern. When the two Baker boys were traversing the unmaintained fire trail to get to this moment, 'What if they have a gun?' the boy had asked. A gun was the last thing on Jack's mind at that stage. He looked back to when Tony and himself first graced the Trackers with their presence. There were no guns to worry about. The two men were not intimidating in the slightest to the two large Bakers. But there had been a dog.

'Ripper dog' was the Tracker's Doberman. All muscle and teeth, from what Jack could remember. The dog had taken an instant disliking to the Bakers. It had strained against its chain, holding it to the wrought iron handrail of the same broken down house that Jack now stood before. The dog had never taken its eyes off Jack and had growled low. It bared its glistening white teeth when the then younger boy had met the pits of darkness that were its eyes. But as Jack looked about the yard, there was no sign of the dog, apart from the chain that lay in a heap at the foot of the stairs. One end still looped to the wrought iron handrail, the other lay empty. As Jack passed the chain, he considered that it had been some five or six years since they had attempted to buy the starter motor for the old heap. Five or six years of hand cranking that bitch each morning, there was no wonder why he was strong. Anything could have happened to the dog in that many years, and anything probably did. As Jack turned the greening mottled brass handle and pushed the hardwood door open, he found some part of an answer.

The immediate smell of dog shit hit Jack square in the face and near put him back a few steps. He lifted a hand to his face and turned his head from the gaping darkness of the front door while he stole a breath of somewhat fresher air behind him. Saliva had begun to build up in his mouth, and he felt his stomach roll as he stepped inside. He dropped his head to miss the support beam of the door and spat as he did so. His eyes slowly adjusted to the living room's low light, the only light source being the gaping door to his back. The living space was a disaster, it was riddled with shit and rotting morsels of food. The layer of dust on the toppled dining table was enough to give the stained timber a ghostly impression. The fabric couch that had once been a pleasant cream was brown with stains and a layer of dirt and faeces. Once trim and taught, the fabric was now a threadbare shadow of its former self. It sagged where it was torn, and the browned stuffing hung out like the guts of a stuck pig. The hardwood floor, which was stained from the shit and piss, was sporadically covered by what were once expensive rugs with elaborate patterns and stitch work. Now they were worn down, brown messes, which in the low light could only be taken for rugs by the shape of the discolouration among the other scatterings of rubbish and dirt.

Jack made his way into the house and could see a stairwell in front of him. The timber handrail, the cobwebs that interlaced the supporting batons and the filthy hall runner lay crumpled at its base. It had not surprised Jack to hear that there was another Tracker. That was what he assumed the fat man referred to as he shrieked the name and flailed about. But to say that Jack had known that there were three Trackers would have been a lie. *There is always more scum on the earth than you think*, Jack thought as he made his way to the stairwell. He looked to his left as he passed an open door. The remains of a kitchen seemed to be inside. The benchtop held a partially dismantled Holden V8 engine block, its innards filling the sink. Jack saw the shape of a crankshaft looming out of the open oven as he passed. The floor was covered in a thick dark substance that had pooled under the engine and ran down the cupboard doors.

He looked up the stairs and could see nothing but darkness. Not a single light was shining in this house, not a single window allowed any form of light. The stairs creaked underneath him with each heavy footfall, and the old timber groaned under his weight. The old dry plastered walls echoed the sound as each boot fell on the hollow stairs. Halfway up the stairwell, there hung a coloured portrait of a man clad in military dress. It was difficult to see the features correctly as the photograph was so old. The low light, combined with the fact that so much dust had covered it, meant that not much more than a blur remained. Despite this, Jack could see the outline of a slouch hat, easily recognisable. He figured that this man likely served in the war along with Tony Baker, as a similar photo of Tony hung in the living/dining room of the Baker residence. Tony was a large man, which was evident even then in the photograph, with black hair and solid brick-like shoulders.

Jack stopped to brush the dust away from the image to get a proper look at the man behind it. As he ran his right hand across the image, a streak of blood was left covering some of the man's features, yet he could see a fair-haired man with a slight jaw and sloped shoulders. The man wasn't at all like the disgusting figures that lay either dead or incapacitated below. He was well put together, and there was nothing revolting about him, but if this likeness was from the same era as Tony's, then that was thirty-odd years ago.

Jack reached the top of the stairs and paused. There were three doors on the upper level, two single doors leading back over the house's lower level, and a double door directly in front of him. The anger in Jack swelled once more. He didn't want to have to look in every God damned room of this house to find this Robin. He glanced down and saw that in the darkness and the grime, a hint of some light could be seen filtering through from under the double doors in front of him. The muscles in his jaw worked as he studied the dusty door, his hands slowly formed loose fists. He knew what to expect about the situation below, but this could be anything. *Fuck it*, he thought and brought a giant work boot up and pounded the centre of the right door.

The force of the front kick broke the latch that held the doors together. The left door was pulled from its hinges, as the shock of its partner being flung from its resting place was too much for the old hinges to bear. The left door clattered noisily to the ground as the right swung open with such force its handle embedded itself in the plaster wall and propped it open. Dust and dirt swirled from the ground with the force of the entry, and a spider web that hung from a lifeless ceiling fan waved in protest. Through the settling dust, Jack saw a prestigious oak desk, which at one point in its life had been highly polished. It sat dull and dusty in the centre of the room. Before it, two plush, red fabric chairs sat facing the desk, their backs to Jack. A beam of light shone down from the roof, and below the source was a heap of cracked and broken plaster. Jack assumed that before the corrugated iron sheet had fallen from the roof, this room would have been as dark as the rest of the house.

Robin Tracker was slouched behind the desk. The slight jaw and the sloping shoulders likened him to the portrait in the hallway. However, the rest of the man had aged terribly. His hair, no longer blonde, had progressed past grey and was a dull white. It was shoulder length and looked as though it had been cut using an axe. The man's once clean-shaven face was spattered with grey stubble, and his sleek old nose had sprouts of more grey hair that loomed from the cavernous pits of his flaring nostrils. The man's face was made older with lines and wrinkles, his furrowed brow was set with grey eyebrows as slight as the man's jaw. Clad in a stained, white dress shirt, two skinny arms rested on the aging, dust-covered desk in front of him. Even in the dark and dust filled air of Robin Tracker's office, Jack could see the piercing blue eyes under the man's brow, as bright as if the man had only been born yesterday. Jack stood motionless. His brown eyes glared down at the man, while Robin's piercing blue eyes burned back at him. The only thing that made Jack take a moment's pause was the amount of hatred he saw in those eyes.

Jack was not a man for negotiation. After the men fixed their gaze upon each other, the big man gathered himself and started towards the dusty, old oak desk. He made his way between the two red fabric chairs, knocking one of them sprawling with one beefy leg. He reached the desk and placed his two hands face down. Still standing, Jack had to lean over to do this. Although he was hunched, he still towered over the old man in front of him. Jack's jaw muscle worked as he inhaled, their eyes remained locked. 'You know what I'm here for, old man. Hand the keys over.'

Robin Tracker's eyes never left Jack, and Jack saw something in them. The eyes seemed to darken for a split second over the words 'old man', yet they never faltered, they never broke. Jack could see a door behind the desk, it was shut, and only darkness could be visible under the crack. The old man pushed his oak chair back with a screech as the legs scraped against the hardwood floor. He stood in a similar position to Jack. Larger than his two siblings, Robin still had to tilt his head back as he stood hunched over to continue his eye contact with Jack.

The man's voice was riddled with sickness and infection, and his lungs sounded as though they were half full of fluid.

'The keys to your father's car are in the top drawer.' He gestured his head toward the right side of his large desk. 'But if you think I'm going to let a big bitch like you take them...' He never finished what the sentence implied, yet neither man moved. Jack's entire body swelled with the rage that lay inside of him. He lifted both hands from the desktop, straightened up and pushed out his big barrel chest. Jack continued to stare down at Robin as he slowly made his way around to the right side of the desk. The men remained silent as Jack moved, they just continued their staring contest. Once Jack had rounded the desk, he stopped. Both men now stood face to face, the oak drawer was at the younger man's right.

'This drawer right here?' Jack spoke softly, cocking his head to one side, almost teasing the older man with the question. He moved his right hand to the knob and clasped it. Jack stood easily a foot and half over this man and would have weighed twice as much. He wasn't afraid. He began to slide the drawer open. Still, Robin never moved, their locked gaze continued, and neither blinked. When the drawer stood open, the big man broke his gaze and investigated the draw. Sitting there proud as punch were the keys to the Fairlane 500. He was lowering his giant hand to grasp the keys, his eyes focused on the shining metal, when Robin Tracker lashed out.

For a skinny, old man who stood shorter than Jack, the force of the man's weight bursting into him put the larger man off balance. Robin had both hands to Jack's neck, his hands were too small to get around it, but still, both thumbs were pressed into his oesophagus. Robin pushed him backward and slammed him into the plaster wall. Their combined weight broke sections of the plaster, and white powder fell onto the men as they struggled. Before Jack could pull his hands up to grab the old man, Robin's right hand had shifted away from his throat and had begun to pummel Jack's face.

His head pounded with the blows. He was amazed at the strength this man had and at how quick he was, but what startled him were the eyes. They were no longer brilliant blue but a much darker shade, the rattled, illness-ridden breath was replaced by the powerful snorts of a man much younger. As the seventh blow came down on Jack's face, Robin grazed the section where his youngest brother Matt had laid the wrench into Jack's forehead. The bolt of pain was tremendous, and finally, Jack's rage tipped over the edge, his eyes bulged in their sockets as he roared. Both large, mauler hands came up to Robin's face and latched on. He brought his hands down and away from himself, and they dragged the old man with them. Jack slammed him onto the hardwood floor with such intense force a lamp fell off the desk. He climbed atop of him, as he had with Matt Tracker only five minutes ago and laid into him with such force and anger. Each time Jack raised his fist, he saw the dark blue eyes glare up at him, almost urging the blows to come. Jack got three good, heavy hits onto the man's face when a knee came up from under him. As his balls shot up into his stomach, the pain instantly cramped him, this old bastard fought dirty. Robin screamed as he pushed Jack off with another burst of tremendous force, which sent him sprawling. Robin clambered to his feet, his sleek nose was smashed in from one of Jack's blows, and his mouth was covered in blood. He began to bring a series of kicks into Jack's gut and face, grunting as he went.

Jack's head wound flowed with blood once more. Now, the torrent seemed further enhanced by the glancing blow that Robin had dealt him. The strike to the balls had temporarily paralysed him and had subdued his anger. Robin now stood up above him and looked down at him with those darker eyes while he kicked him. Jack caught Robin's foot in one hand and upended him, the man went down with a scream and landed heavily. Jack grabbed his face once more and dragged him closer while rising to his knees. He closed his hands around Robin's throat and raised himself to his feet. He grimaced as he took Robin's weight in his hands and lifted him from the ground. No matter how tightly Jack squeezed his hands, he still suffered a flurry of kicks and punches as he held Robin Tracker by the loose skin of his throat.

With a roar, Jack brought the old man down on his desk with all of his strength. There was an enormous snap as the legs gave way on one side and the desk slumped. The sound of splintered timber and the rush of air that exited the old man's lungs filled the room. To Jack's relief, Robin was winded by the blow, giving him a much needed respite from the fighting. Robin began to slide down the oak top, Jack grabbed his face and pulled him up the now slanted top of the desk so that his head hung over its highest lip. The fight in the old man came back all at once, and his writhing body struggled against the worn top while his feet pounded the floor in a flurry. Jack bellowed as he brought a massive fist down into Robin's face. His head snapped back as the hammer fist drove into his already smashed nose and slammed the back of his head up against the sidewall of the desk. All at once, the fight left Robin Tracker. His eyes opened and closed as his limp body slowly slid down the worn oak surface until he finally crumpled at the bottom of the ruined desk. His eyes opened once more and shone as brightly as they had before. The old man rattled and gasped as he struggled to draw breath into his failing lungs.

Jack studied the old man as he lay there crumpled. He had given Jack a pretty good hiding. If one more person tried to start something with him today, that would be it. He brought one of his hands to his face to clamp down on his bleeding wound. Breathing heavily once more, Jack limped to the front of the desk, his guts continued to throb as he went. The top drawer was still open, and the keys were still there, unmoved by the commotion. Jack picked them up and grunted as he thought about his younger brother. He began to hobble his way across the destroyed room and glanced up at the source of light as he went. He was right, it was sunlight. A large hole was torn out of the roof. Plaster had fallen away in large chunks, leaving only smaller holes to surround it. Beyond that, the roof looked as though it had been smashed from the inside out. *Smaller holes?* He thought. What *if they had a gun?* Behind him, Jack heard movement and heard the sound of a belt buckle dragged across the floor. Quickly, he pocketed the keys and whirled around to make his way back to the defeated old man. He was no longer crumpled at the bottom of the desk, he had crawled to the door to the rear of the room and was attempting to open it when one of Jack's giant boots caught him in the chest.

'Fuck ya,' Jack boomed. 'Couldn't let us leave, could you?' Jack roared at the man as the bright blue eyes screamed hate back at him. Jack studied the door which had remained closed, then he returned his attention to the old man. 'What have you got back here?' Robin lay there in silence. Jack turned the handle and pushed the door open. There was a dusty, dirty corridor, which led nowhere. Each wall was dirty and rotten, the ceiling was filthy and had black handprints scattered across its matte surface. The floor was covered in white powder similar to what was on Jack's shirt from when the old man had pushed him into the now broken wall. Everything was as Jack expected, except the furthest wall. It was new unpainted plasterboard. Jack considered the wall where he had been pushed through, then returned his attention again to Robin. The men remained silent. He made his way into the room, felt the new wall and knocked from the right edge to the left. *Tock, tock, tock, whop, whop, whop, tock, tock.*

What is this fucker hiding? The big man drove a fist into the wall and broke through it easily. He peered into the darkness, there was something looming there. He could make out a shape, but he couldn't tell exactly what it was. He drove his fist into the wall again and sent more of the plaster to the ground in a flurry of dust. His arm remained inside the wall cavity as he groped and reached. He laid his hand on the cold surface and pulled.

The plaster cracked as Jack pulled what he clutched out of the cavity. As the wall broke around the shape, the plaster fell away, and dust filled the small corridor as it erupted from the floor. Jack had never seen anything like it before. He wasn't one for watching television and couldn't pick the era that it was from, but he held a very large rifle in his hand. Unlike normal rifles, the timber stock was in two pieces, not like an old Enfield, those he knew and had even fired Paul Darcy's once or twice. The dark timber butt stock ended at a large metal hump-backed receiver. The metal was a cold, deep grey, with blemishes here and there. There was a hefty timber foregrip, but it only covered a small section of the lengthy barrel. On the left side of the receiver, there was a cocking arm and a track. It looked like an eye that stared into him. There were two protective wings in front of the trigger that surrounded a gaping hole where a magazine went. Puzzled at what he had found, Jack moved the rifle around in his hands. On top of the humpback were some words, which were made illegible by their covering of dust. He blew on the metal and squinted his eyes as he strained to read the small letters.

BROWNING AUTOMATIC RIFLE
-U.S CAL.30 MODEL 1918-

Jack looked back into the wall cavity and saw magazines lined up on one of the timber batons. There were five in total. He picked one up, the cold metal felt fantastic in his hands, but the weight of it. The gun would have to weigh twice as much, if not more, than the old .303 that Darcy owned. As he looked into the magazine, he saw that it wasn't loaded, none of them were. Everything was kept cleaned and protected inside the wall. Still, if the old man was hiding this piece of machinery, he would have ammunition stashed somewhere too.

Something about the rifle had stirred up a part of Jack. He wanted to have it, he wanted to use it. He leaned the rifle up against one of the unbroken walls and began to pull more and more of the plaster away. As he went, he found something that looked like a magazine pouch, but mice had gotten to it inside the wall, and it wasn't usable. When he removed a final section, he found a green metal tin, the words painted in black were *PROPERTY OF U.S ARMY, CAL. 30 M1 BALL.* Jack snapped the clasp on the tin and opened the lid. As he opened it, he noticed the inside was surrounded by a rubber seal, which was still intact. As he looked inside, he found it was full to the brim with ammunition. Jack considered one of the shells, the brass gleamed, and the copper bullet was dark with age, but its point remained intact. He looked at the rifle and picked it up once more and studied the section he referred to as the eye, the cocking arm and the track. The arm was toward the front of the action. With his left hand, he grasped it and started to drag it backwards. There was a lot of pressure, and it took a bit of work, when the handle was as far back as it could go, there was a soft clunk. And then everything went dark.

He didn't know what was happening. His vision was gone, he could feel the dirt under his hands, and he was in pain. There were gunshots, a lot of gunshots and people screamed. Some howled in pain, while others shouted for help. Mostly, from what he could tell, their screams were full of pain and agony as they ripped through his ears. His vision started to come back. It was the dark of night, and there were trees everywhere and fire. There were men in dark green uniforms running around everywhere, some were bleeding. Another man lay face down in one of the fires. He didn't move as his body smouldered. Parts of his flesh had turned black with charcoal, the remains of his face were unidentifiable. He watched as one of the men draped in green raised a rifle and began to fire into the tree line. 'What was he shooting at?' Now he saw more men as they tried to form a line, all of them fired into the tree line, some aimed off to his right, while others fired wildly in different directions altogether. He heard the screams, they were deafening, and he just wanted them to stop. One man pointed to the direction in front of him, and other men turned and began to fire that way. Off to their right, he saw three smaller men, also dressed in green but a different shade, come running out of the bushes. They howled a battle cry as they ran and held their rifles down to their sides with their muzzles forward. Their bayonets gleamed from the tip like the tears of a child at night. The bigger green men turned their fire onto them, one fell instantly, but the other two continued their charge. They plunged their bayonets into the bodies of the confused, larger men. More screams and blood, blood everywhere. The smaller men seemed to emerge from every direction, all of them howled their cry as they ran. Gunshots seemed to quiet, but were replaced with even more screams and blood. Screams from men as blades slid into their flesh. The sounds of rifle stocks being slammed into bodies. A smaller man stood above him now. He wore different clothes than any of the others, his face was a dark shadow, but the sword in his hands danced with the reflections of the fire, which seemed to consume everything. Blood ran down its blade, which was as thin as a razor, the shadowed man held it above his head and roared as he brought it down.

Jack snapped back into reality. Sweat drenched him. What the hell had just happened to him? He was now standing at the desk, the rifle in his hands, a magazine inserted into the well in front of the trigger. The other magazines lay in front of him, sitting in the drawer that once held the keys to his father's Fairlane 500. All of them were loaded. The ammunition tin was closed and rested next to the desk. Jack swayed on his feet. He leaned the rifle against the desk and began to walk to the door in front of him. He put his hands to his head, the throb of his migraine seemed unbearable. His wound was still bleeding. The only solace was that his guts had stopped aching from the kick to the balls. He rubbed his eyes and shook his head. What had just happened? One minute he was in that corridor, the next, he was in some fucking jungle watching people get slaughtered. He couldn't understand it. If that's what that thing did to someone, then old Robin could keep it. Jack lifted his head, his eyes wide. He had to get to Robin! Where was the old man?

Jack whirled around in time to see Robin lift the rifle butt to his shoulder and lower his head to the sights, his eyes still gleamed brightly. It was Jack's reflexes that saved his life, if nothing else. Jack grabbed the barrel with one hand and pushed it to the left as he closed the distance. There was a faint sound of metal sliding on metal, then as Jack's face moved to the right of the barrel, the weapon fired. Jack's head exploded with pain from the concussion and the power of the detonations next to his face. Yet he pushed through it, still holding the barrel of the rifle as he pushed it to the side, all other sound drowned out by the ringing in his ears as the big man brought his fist up once more to drive into Robin Trackers' already smashed nose.

The old man's grip on the rifle loosened as soon as Jack's fist slammed into him. With a grunt of pain, Robin flew back into the corridor where Jack had found the Browning and was sprawled out on the ground. Jack stood there and held the rifle in his hands while his mind spun in his world of pain, amazement and confusion. He watched as the old man propped himself up on his elbows, his eyes were as bright as ever. Jack had hit the old man as hard as he could, just as he had when he had first walked into the room. Yet before his vision, the old man had given his younger opponent the fight of his life. Why then had this punch he had just thrown had so much effect? What had happened to either make Robin so weak or Jack so strong? The big man filled the doorway as he advanced on his fallen foe.

'*Kill him.*' The voice was soft in the back of his head. '*Kill him.*'

Robin shook with illness and pain. His breath was stone on steel, and the look of disease spread over his face. He tried to sit himself up, his body was racked with a sudden cough, and he tried to bring a hand up to his mouth, but he needed both arms to stop himself from falling. Blood sprayed from the man's mouth and nose as he coughed. The sight was disgusting. '*Kill him, put him out of his misery.*' The voice was becoming more and more prominent. Robin tried to talk, but it was plainly difficult for him to do so.

'Now, son.' Jack raised the Browning in his hands, the cold steel, the warm feel of the hardwood. 'Wait.' The man was racked with another cough.

'*Life is already flowing from him. Make it quick.*' Jack's cheek pressed against the timber of the stock, the steel butt plate pressed against his meaty shoulder. '*KILL HIM!*'

Jack's vision did something it had never done before. It seemed to move back within his own head as if a cameraman had shifted the position on the lenses in his mind. The world in front of him erupted in fire and hot, spitting metal. Jack felt as though he had been thrown back into his own mind while something else stepped forward.

JACK

As the ill-lit corridor blazed an eerie yellow by the muzzle flash, the machine in Jack's hands shook with fierce power and anger. There was a soft, almost inaudible sound of metal sliding on metal as the old machine's bolt moved forward from its reward position. Then the world was consumed by the bright fires of rushing gases and the tremendous roar of the Browning. No sooner than one old, spotted brass case was ejected from its small mouth, another was being rammed in, in an attempt to feed its eternal hunger. Robin Tracker's nose had been spread across his face, and blood bubbled from his lips as he tried to talk the big man down. Then the first kiss of the hot, fire-driven lead hammered into him, and the words were lost among the hellfire of the Browning. The round entered his throat at the hollow section just above his ribs. The metal bullet punched a small neat hole in that place yet tore small ragged chunks of the man's throat and spine out of his upper back.

Jack's senses were instantly assaulted with the smell of burning gunpowder, listing smoke and particles of what remained from each charge that was thrown into the machine's mouth to be chewed up and spat out. The blood and gore of the scene was abhorrent, yet the hunger of the machine kept calling. Robin Tracker was dead with the first shot, yet there were sixteen more in quick succession. The power of the Browning as it fought and kicked in his hands, while it pounded his shoulder and urged him to go on, was exhilarating. The rifle that had felt similar to a truck axle now seemed weightless and lively in his grasp.

The man in front of him became a lesser version of himself. With each flash and thudding roar, more and more of the Robin Tracker was torn away. At around the tenth shot, the kick of the lively machine pushed Jack's aim slightly off target, and the dead man's left arm was severed at the elbow. The big man fought with the recoiling beast and brought the barrel lower and back around, never once letting up on the trigger, he found he was not able to. Robin's lower torso was torn open in a shower of blood, intestines and excrement. To have said that Jack could have relented at any moment would have been a lie; he did not feel as though he was in control of his actions. He watched as the scene unfolded in front of him through his dark eyes. He felt everything that was happening and smelt the aroma. Yet, for him, it was like looking through the brightly polished windscreen of the Fairlane, the glass so slick and clean that you could barely believe there was anything there until you reached out a bloody, filth covered hand, and your fingertips brushed the smooth surface.

Finally, the Browning's bolt slammed forward and jerked the heavy frame of the rifle along with it. It did not fire. Jack stood frozen, the butt of the rifle still braced against his meaty shoulder, his sweaty cheek still pressed down against the comb of the stock. He could smell the oils in the timber as it began to rise through its pores, sprung from its slumber by the heat generated from the furious volley of fire. The broken down corridor was now filled with the gun smoke and stank of something that could have been sulphur and shit. As the wind gusted through the hole in the roof behind him, the smoke began to dance one way and then sway another. It rolled and fought, still angry, still life left in it as it held against dissipation. Below, the remains of Robin Tracker lay lifeless, torn to pieces and no longer able to be identified as the man who rasped with illness and decay in one breath and tore Jack a new asshole in the next. Either the second or third last round had caught the man under his chin, as his head had fallen back to the hardwood floor. The bullet had taken the man's slight chin inward and had removed a large portion of his face on its way through. All that remained was a sunken mess of blood, with one lidless eye that sat among the horror. In an endless stare, as it waited and hated.

Jack let the rifle hang at his side. He raised his right hand to his head and scratched at his scalp as he studied the mess in front of him. The big man's bicep worked half as furiously as his jaw as he began to process what had just happened. Why had he let his anger take him this far? His head still pounded from the bleeding wound, which throbbed from Robin Tracker's glancing blow across the same place. His balls had continued to ache and felt as though they had embedded themselves in his lower throat. Yet it was done. He had recovered the keys to the old man's Fairlane 500, but the trouble had now cost two men their lives. It was time to leave. Not only the house, but the memory of this situation. He began to walk away from the remains of Robin Tracker. A slight flicker of thought skated across the back of his aching, pounding head of the consequences that came with the actions he had just committed. But ever so slightly, another voice that was almost sweet skated on its heels that he would kill anyone that found out and anyone who dared threaten him.

He swung a hand to slap against the blood-soaked mess of his denim jeans, further likened to black and a deep red than blue. As he felt the proud metal surfaces of the tangle of keys and the leather fob beneath the wet denim, he was satisfied in leaving. Yet he didn't move. The automatic rifle still swung at his side, its bolt was closed tight, and wisps of smoke emitted from its muzzle. Before him stood the remaining four magazines, all were loaded and stacked neatly in the gaping desk drawer. The slightly lighter metal ammunition tin waited for him on the floor. He dropped his gaze to the rifle. He couldn't possibly take it with him, the sheer size of it meant that it wasn't easily concealed. A sure-fire way to be forbidden access to the Baker's lot was for Tony to find that Jack had taken a gun home without his permission. He began to lean the heavy rifle against the smashed desk of the eldest Tracker but couldn't release his grip. The thought of Michael in the Whippet, as they made their journey to this shit hole, danced in front of him. *What if they have a gun?* The boy's words taunted him. They did have, but the outcome had been the same. They stood in Jack's way and now lay dead behind him. Jack spoke aloud to himself as he looked down at the machine, still warm, still hungry. 'Then we will take it.'

He found a large trench coat, covered in dust and the remains of the ceiling as it hung from its hook below the gaping hole in the roof. White powder covered its sleeves, and matted hair and dust clung to the fabric. Inside the sprawled coat, Jack laid the rifle. He managed to fit the remaining four magazines inside the ammunition tin, sprawled atop of the loose rounds of ammunition. He took one last look as he bundled the machine into the matted fabric of the overcoat. The bolt lay closed, the now empty magazine still secured in its well, protected by steel wings that shot forward from the trigger guard. The mouth of the beast was now closed, yet still hungry. It can stay hungry for now, Jack thought as he bundled the last of the overcoat around the Browning and secured each end with a portion of waist strap. He burdened himself with the load he needed to carry, the rifle in his left hand, its fuel in the right. The green tin weighed as much as the machine itself. As he turned to the remains of the double doors leading into Robin Tracker's office, he paused. In the time it had taken for him to secure his prize, something had moved into the section of doorway that now gaped like a partially opened mouth of a whale. The door that was ripped from its hinges sat five feet away, the corner which had penetrated the wall left it raised two inches from the ground.

Jack moved over to the figure that lay on its side, breathing heavily in the doorway. The old Doberman was half-starved. Its one visible eye was milky with cataracts. It blinked up at Jack as he neared it. A lot of its fur had fallen out and what remained was more of an ash colour speckled with grey rather than the jet black that the large man recalled. The years had not been kind to the dog. From what Jack could see, its masters hadn't been good to it either. The only kindness, if it could be called so, was to allow the dog to live the remainder of its years inside the house rather than chained to the porch handrail. Jack leaned the bundled Browning against the wall and placed the tin down in front of the dog's nose. The half-blind Doberman didn't follow the gaze of the tin, yet when the heavy metal box clunked to the ground in front of it, the whitened eye quickly darted forward. In the old dog's curiosity, it raised its eyebrows and closed its mouth with an aged expression. Its jowls concealed its rotten teeth for a moment before its curiosity waned, and it continued to pant. As its lips moved away from its teeth once more and its tongue lolled out the side of its mouth, Jack noticed that its jaws were no longer filled with the rows of gleaming white teeth. The remaining ones were yellowed or black with rot, the saliva which coated them was a white froth, like the breaking waves on jagged rock cliff faces. The cropped ears twitched back, Jack laid a blood covered hand on the scruff of the dog's neck as he crouched next to it. The white filmy eye rolled back to his face. '*Kill it,*' the words like hot iron in the back of his head. '*It would do the same for you.*'

'Do you remember me, boy?' Jack said softly in his still booming voice. He didn't pat the dog, just held it down in its position upon its side. He held no compassion for the dog. If it was his, it would have been taken out back and shot with Darcy's Enfield long before this day. Jack remembered Ripper the only time he had seen him, chained to the handrail as it strained against the iron links that held him back. The hope gleamed in its gold-rimmed eyes that just one of the iron links would give way and allow the massive Doberman a chance to sink its teeth into the Baker's boar. But the chain had not given way. The dog emitted a low growl in its throat and snarled its yellowed and blackened, rotten teeth at Jack. Still, it panted. Still, it gasped for air, as its master had. 'I thought as much,' Jack grunted as he moved his two hands to its throat and gripped.

The dwindling Doberman rolled onto its back as Jack's two massive hands clasped easily around its throat. The dog, being half-starved, had little strength left in it. A white-tipped paw clawed at Jack's arm as the white filmy eyes burned into the dark ones. The dog bared its teeth, and it tried to move its mouth around to bite at Jack's hand, but Jack tightened his grip and twisted his hands. He grimaced as he felt the loose flesh turn and the joints break under the pressure of his massive hands. The Doberman twitched its back legs, the paw that was scratching at his arm now stood out straight. It bared its teeth, and the whitened eyes bulged. Then it relaxed, the eyes rolled in their sockets, and the jowls drooped while a line of saliva started to run from the lowest points. Its legs likewise relaxed and lay in a lanky, wasted mess. No longer muscle-bound as Jack remembered, but a pile of wasted meat that was now out of its misery.

Jack lay the dog down in the doorway and released his grip, its eyes lay half-closed and vacant. At least it could be said that he did something of kindness today. This damned, bloody day.

Jack regained his feet. At least the dog's fate was not as gruesome as its masters. The wind rushed through the open ceiling, the sound of trees rustling in the distance and the clash of metal. He could hear a voice outside, but it wasn't the boys' voice. It was louder and triumphant. Beneath the wind that rushed through the trees, he heard a wheeze and heard the name, Robin. The fat one has found his strength again, it would seem. He hefted his prize into his hands once more and left the room, along with its fallen occupants, behind.

As Jack made his way down the stairs, the voice became more prominent and coherent. He heard how the fat one's older brother had turned the Baker's boar inside out, that Ripper would be eating his guts out while he was alive, and really, to Jack, it was a good story. No one should ever let the facts get in the way of such. As he lowered himself down the hardwood stairs, he took a glimpse of the military likeness of Robin Tracker, the blood stained smear still disguised parts of the man's features.

'*Not enough blood to look like him now.*' The thought raced through his head along with the image of the collapsed face with the now inverted chin. The chopped out torso and the pool of blood that slowly gathered under the corpse. '*Not enough.*'

Jack rounded the stairs and moved through the lower rooms of the house. The smell was still no better down here, the smell of dog shit and rotted food. The wasted, dusty fabric curtains hung from their rods. Hair, dust and pieces of grass clumped together almost like tumbleweeds, drifted across the ruined timber floor as the breeze worked its fingers through the gaping front door.

Through its opening, Jack saw a portion of the Fairlane's front end. The chrome gleamed in the sunlight. A highly polished bank of double beam headlights, although unilluminated, were as bright as the sun in the summer morning. Beside the car was Michael. He was on his hands and knees and spluttered while one hand clasped his throat. He heard Kel as he laughed and wheezed until he broke into a racking cough. The cough bent the man over, and that was when he came into view for Jack.

He would have been three feet to the boy's left. Kel stood up again and obscured himself from vision once more. Then a fat meaty leg swung out and the loafered foot connected with Michael's side, which sent him sprawling to the ground in a cry. Jack's jaw muscles worked as he continued to near the open front door. Each footfall was a boom in the quiet of the house. Jack found it interesting how a man who was shrieking in terror not five minutes ago was now full of courage.

'That's right, piglet. Robin has shot your boar brother for what he did to Matt.' He swung another meaty foot into the boy's gut as he lay on his side. The cry of pain from the boy made the hair on Jack's neck stand on end. 'We both lost brothers today. But that's alright.' He coughed as he laid another loafered foot into the boy. Another cry of pain. Jack's hand closed tight around his cargo. 'I'll keep the little piglet for my new brother.' The fat one began to wheeze more and more as he exerted himself in the movements to kick the boy. Another racking cough took the man, and he doubled over once more as he spluttered and spat. As the cough subsided, he looked up to Michael from his hunched over position with a victorious, evil grin. 'And I think I'll take the Baker's bitch while I'm going.'

With Jack's last footfall, it brought him to stand a few feet back from the doorway. The line of light ended inches before the tips of his boots, the rest of him still drowned in darkness. The final boom of the big man's footfall finally aroused the attention of the fat one outside. He spun his head to the open door, which remained a gaping black hole to Kel Tracker. The smile widened across his meaty, weathered face. The lines from his fat, drooping cheeks increased threefold. 'Robin, come out and meet our new brother.' The fat one gasped as he held out his hands and presented the sprawled out boy to the one inside the house. The boy rolled onto his stomach and gazed into the blackness of the Tracker's house and squinted his eyes to see through the darkness. Michael's dirty face had clean lines cut through the grime from the fresh tears that streamed down his face. His hair was matted and frayed from where Kel had rolled him across the mess of the yard. He sobbed as he peered through the door, inaudible words that didn't matter. Words never really mattered in times such as these. *'The boy.'* The sweet coolness of the thought again in the back of his head once more. *'The fat man touched the boy.'* Although this new voice had a calming effect over him, Jack's fists formed blocks of stone, and the veins on his neck stood out.

'He's not as strong as Matt, but by Christ, he doesn't stink half as bad.' Kel rattled as he continued to hold his arms out in presentation.

The fat man touched the boy, the thought echoed through his mind in his own voice and conscience. 'I told him to stay in the Whippet.'

'He touched the boy. Take your piece of him. Kill him.'

As Jack Baker walked toward the front door, the line of light moved up his body. At first, his gargantuan boots were visible, along with the dust they kicked up with each booming footfall. The pant legs of the ruined denim jeans he wore were black with grime and soaked in the blood of the men that had stood in his way. His torn work shirt and broad barrel chest were revealed simultaneously as his bulging arms, which were still heavily burdened with his prize. Finally, his short stubbled, blood smeared face, his nose red with pain from the pounding the old man had given him. His jaw set like stone as he walked, and his eyes were as dark as night. Kel's smile disappeared more and more with each step that Jack took from the darkness. The look of terror crept into his eyes at almost the same rate. His outstretched arms slowly dropped. He was helpless now. The front of his pants darkened as he took a few steps backwards.

The boy's facial expression barely changed. The look of pain and anguish was still there, but the sight of his big brother, as beaten and bloody as he was, it was plain Michael knew that it really had been a close call for him. He hung his head down in a feeling that could have either been shame or relief. Jack never asked, he never cared. His focus was on the fat one. Kel Tracker, now completely alone, looked at the bundled trench coat in the big man's hands. 'No, you couldn't have.' He edged towards the boy as he shook his head in disbelief. 'No, but Robin.'

'The old one is dead.' Jack's voice boomed as his dark eyes burned into Kel's. He now stood at the top of the stairs that led from the porch down to the dirt-packed yard. He stood three feet taller than the fat one and had to lower his head considerably to look down at the spluttering, wheezing Tracker.

'No.' Kel whimpered. As he shook his head, his jowls wobbled as if they had belonged to the dog.

'The dog is dead.' Jack's voice was still loud and firm as he spoke down to the man. It was apparent that the fat man wasn't actually looking into Jack's eyes at this stage. Kel's beady eyes sunk deep into their sockets, darted from the bundle to the tin, then back to the bundle. His eyes never met Jack's once.

'N-n-n-no.' He whimpered softer again as his small eyes darted back and forth.

'The dirty one is dead.' Jack bent as he boomed this and placed his burden on the timber porch. Still, he never broke his gaze that still had not been met.

'No. No. No.' Kel's eyes were lower as they followed the bundles that had been placed on the deck. 'You fucker!' he screamed. The boy in front of him jumped and lifted his head. Kel Tracker leaned down and latched both of his grubby hands onto the small boy's shirt. Michael screamed in terror as Kel pulled him to his feet. His arms shot out to Jack as if to grab him. Jack did not flinch, nor did he rush to Michael's aid. He just stood there, his gaze never left that of Kel.

Kel Tracker had hold of the boy, his fat arm was around the boy's skinny neck as he held him against his flabby chest. The other wrapped around his forehead as if ready to snap the boy's neck at a moment's notice. His eyes were locked on the bundled heap on the porch. Jack had begun to advance on them, slowly but surely. Each footfall of the big man's boots that came down a step was a knell to the man. The two stood their ground. The young boy now cried freely as his massive brother approached them. The fat man's arm locked around the boy's neck in fear more than anger. His beady eyes were still locked on the bundled coat. *'Kill him.'* The voice again. Calm and sweet. Encouraging.

'Now it's time for me to take what I am owed.' Jack took his final step, which brought him directly in front of the boy. Michael could not see his face, yet Kel, who stood taller, could plainly see it. His gaze slowly went from the bundled coat on the porch to Jack's face. His mouth quivered, the word, 'No,' totally inaudible but repeated. It gave him the appearance of a landed fish, dying as it struggled to breathe in the foreign environment. Their gaze finally met.

As Jack's eyes went a darker shade, the fat man's grip loosened dramatically around the boy's throat. He began to back away as he repeatedly mouthed, 'No,' the terror visible on his face. Michael, for once, didn't need to be prompted and took his leave from his stance between the two men and leapt around the other side of the Fairlane's gleaming rear quarter. Jack closed the short ground between the two men instantly. His large right hand plunged into the meaty top section of Kel Tracker's chest. His left hand clapped over the fat one's face, his palm covered the man's nose and eyes, and the gaping mouth below was still visible, 'No, no, no.' As the fish ran out of air.

As Jack's grip closed around Kel's collar bone once more, he screamed. Jack pressed his left hand against Kel's head, with his right hand now fully clenched into a fist as he began to pull. The screams were horrific. The pain in them made it sound like insanity had slipped into Kel's mind at the last second. The screams did not let up.

Jack pushed forward with his left as he used all of his force. His arm straightened in front of him; his bicep bulged with the strain. Finally, there was an enormous crack, and Jack's right arm jerked back sharply as the screams increased their intensity threefold. Kel's mouth was open too far with the agony, his voice broke as the screams became ragged and torn. His lips split and cracked and sent small rivers of blood running down his pale, milky skin. Jack's fist was still clenched around the man's detached collar bone. With one final rip, he tore it and a handful of flesh out of the man's chest.

There was a gush of blood, and thankfully the screams stopped. The blood flowed out of the man's chest and down his shirt. It ran down his gut and flowed over the milky skin that protruded past Kel's shirt. Jack removed his left hand from the man's face. The skin was pallid and filmed with sweat. His eyes were rolled back into his head, a gurgling wheeze emitted from the man's still gaping mouth. He swayed on his feet, a gurgle and wheeze, his chest ripped entirely open. Finally, he collapsed in a heap.

Jack stood over him, the man's broken collarbone clasped in his hand. Blood dripped from the mass of meat, splintered bone and flesh. He looked down, unaffected by the sight. *'Good.'* He let the meat and bone fall from his hand, it hit the dusty ground with a wet slop. Jack's hand was covered in blood, his breath was calm. He felt light, strong and powerful. Yet he didn't feel as though he had control. His jaw muscle twitched while he continued to stare down at the mess below him. This day had not begun the way he thought it would. Less than an hour ago, he was in the old man's office, as he smoked cigarettes and stared at the bloody photo on the wall. Now? 'Look at me.'

He turned his gaze to look at the boy who was peering out from behind the gleaming quarter panel of the Fairlane 500, the car that had started this whole shit fight. The boy who had started it. Michael's eyes fixed on the bloody gaping hole in the man's chest. The chunk of flesh and bone at the big man's feet. The pool of blood that spread over the dirt and gravel of the Tracker's yard. He was terrified, but alive. 'I thought I told you to stay in the fucking Whippet?'

CHRIS

'I Walk away like a movie star,
Who gets burned in a three way script,
Enter number two, a movie queen
To play the scene of bringing all the good things out in me
But for now, love, let's be real.'

Gordon Lightfoot – *If You Could Read My Mind* (1970)

The dust gathered across the single lane that cut through the scrub. Although the road was well-traversed, it had been what felt like hours since a road train or any other commercial vehicle had cut its way through the ever-increasing dust. It had seemed like an age since any rolling iron had thrown a rooster tail of red golden grit as it burned its way across the sweltering country. Even as a kite soared above the intersection, its eyes darted hungrily from tree root to spinifex cluster in search of its next meal, the dirt that attempted to conceal the blacktop from the eye began to tremble. The kite eyed the shifting sediment momentarily before it screeched in frustration and swept its wings as it trailed off to a more secluded location. In the distance, a glint of chrome and the faint rumble of an exhaust was apparent as the sleek steel crested the peak of the gently meandering slopes of the Eva Valley plains.

The man behind the wheel was of an average height and beginning to show signs of age that were becoming of some concern. The beard that cropped his hard jaw had once been speckled with red over a golden-brown. The hairs that glowed with natural oils had woven themselves into an impenetrable mask that had been seamless. Now his beard had frayed, and the edges of the greying hair jutted out like a barb on a wire, hoping to jag at the skin of the one he loved. His eyes, once a shade of hazel that replicated the mood swings, had in recent years begun to fade. Although his vision had only begun to wane in recent years, he had made no attempt to seek out medical assistance. He could still see the one he loved, and that was all that mattered. Chris Lowe was a man of fifty, his hair was slicked back with the sweat from the day, and his forearms were dark with the years they had basted in the burning sun. The hands that gripped the wheel of the HD Holden were gnarled and worn, yet there was strength left in them.

His eyes squinted as the morning sun belted in through the dirty windshield of the Holden and burned everything it touched. Darwin was always a hot place, the inhabitants were offered cool thirty-degree days of considerable heat in the winter. However, now that it was late November, the temperature had risen well north of forty. The heat didn't just seem to beat down from the sun but radiate up from the earth, which had become mostly hard and cracked under the intensity. Until the wet season came around. 'The Wet' had historically begun around November, sometimes a touch earlier. There was no mistaking the humidity as the first shower hit the deck, the ground almost hissed as the giant drops of water exploded against it. Tendrils of steam were thought to be seen from time to time as the first drops instantly evaporated against the skillet like temperature of the earth. For the most part, the showers only lasted twenty minutes, yet in that time, it had rained enough to have been trickling all day. The clouds, having dumped their load over the wetlands and the growing city, dissipated as fast as they had accumulated. They left the sun enraged by the short usurping of its claim on the sky, to burn harder than ever to remind the people that it was the King. The air became heavy, the sweat poured, and everyone instantly felt like they needed a shower. The problem was there was no point, the sweat would continue to pour no matter what was done. The moment the flow of water was cut, it may as well be turned back on for the good it did. Once the wet started, this would outline every single day, on and off. Maybe twenty minutes in between showers, maybe an hour. The sun would burn the life out of everything on the ground, the life's water sucked into the air to be stored, then the clouds would appear again like magic, and the downpour would begin once more.

Chris headed back to his property in Holtze, a nondescript suburb south-east of Darwin. With the influx of a military-based population after the war, he had decided to move further south to escape the soaring prices of city living. He had found a decent spread of land, which, as everything was when one looked at the territory, was as flat as the economy. His land was mostly surrounded by scrub, except for a dirt road that extended for two miles to link the main road to his five-acre plot. All he had to worry about was his modest home, his monstrous shed, and his wife, Angie. To say that his world revolved around his wife was an understatement. Chris doted on the woman. The first twenty or so years of his life were mainly spent alone, apart from his army days when he travelled to Africa and spent the hard days underground. Shortly after his return to Australia, he had met the love of his life, a tall, slender woman with flowing blonde hair which hung at her lower back. The more he ran his fingers through the blindingly bright locks, the more he felt he was in the middle of a good book, a real page-turner at that. Each inch rolled over his callused hands, each strand worked in a way that separated it from its neighbours. The way they twisted and twined, over and under, had him mesmerised to the point that once he had reached the very tips of its length, he wanted to start again to see what the new chapter held within.

Her eyes were oceans. Dark brown irises specked with hints of yellow and black. Every time she blinked, the lashes formed a fan of lustre in front of his desire. His heart stopped in his chest as if to pause in anticipation of being lost within the dazzling colours once more. With each blink or movement, the specks of life changed, either with the refraction of some change of light or magic unbeknownst to him. Chris could spend hours tracing their movements or noting the new spots that had sprung to existence in mere moments. The eyebrows, although a darker shade than her hair, were still light against the deep brown of her eyes, the way the short hairs seemed to bend and swoop to make that perfect line. The almost invisible freckles that shaded her cheekbone, the small peak of her chin. As Chris spent a lot of time alone, either driving from job to job or under the belly of an iron beast, his days were spent dreaming of Angie, the way her slim neck ran into her collar bones, the gentle slope of her shoulders.

Chris blinked. He shook his head in an attempt to wake himself up. His eyelids blinked rapidly as the beating sun tried to blind him in one stroke, then pushed burning red circles through the flesh of his lids with the next. The breeze that rolled in through the open window of the Holden was relaxing, and if he kept up his dreams of Angie, he would never make it back home to her. He clenched his worn fists over the steering wheel, the oil stains and scars from the day's work were visible across the backs. Post-war, Chris had earned his money servicing machinery. Whether it be the enormous diesel road trains, the old Blitz trucks of the army, or the cars and utes of the general population. He had taken to mechanics at a young age. The simplicity of engines, once they were understood, was soothing, and the hard-honest work that they entailed was humbling. While the ideas that they bred, although exhilarating, were dangerous. The HD Holden ute that threw the red dust up behind it as it ran its way up the single laned highway had been his second love in life since the day it entered. Having never owned a new car, in '65, when the HD was released, he had dreamt of owning one. After months of mentioning, envisioning and pleading, Angie had finally consented to the household purchase. In a warning tone, she pointed a slender, well-manicured finger at her husband while she smiled, that this car would be a pestilence on their lives. Chris understood what she had meant, and as she always was, she had been correct.

With every bump, corner or peak the HD surmounted, an idea was sown into the fields of Chris' mind. It had begun with the suspension. The weight of the tools that mobile-mechanics needed to carry was considerable. So, Chris changed the suspension. The original tyres were narrow and although he told Angie that he was concerned about becoming stuck, he just didn't like the look of them. So, he changed them too. The end result saw the back end sit much higher than the front, with tyres that were considerably too big for the vehicles frame. It gave it the impression of a derby bash car. Then there was the matter of the paint. The beige tone, once a nice deep, slick texture, was now a dull, faded shadow of its former gleam. Luckily in the Territory, none of this was a concern. The fact of the matter was that no one seemed to care much about anything in the Northern Territory, and that was how Chris liked it. A year ago, there had been a day when Angie had been sitting on the back porch of their dwelling, engrossed in a book while she sipped at her coffee. The HD had trundled past as her husband returned from an early morning job. The tray of the Holden had been empty, so its back end bounced and jolted as it made its way across the loose gravel. Chris had glanced at his life partner with a smile as he had passed. The look on her face was of disgust, the slightest sign of the shake of her head as she eyed her husband's second love.

Once Chris had parked the ute in his shed and had made his way back to the house with a long neck in hand. He had turned to look upon his ride once more as he left it behind. In contrast to his darling wife's opinion, he saw beauty in the tarnished utility. The camber of its front tyres, the space between the widened rear rubber and its steel tub. Knowing his wife watched his every movement, he blew the car a kiss. Her scoff was audible, and he turned back toward her laughing. She remarked that if he loved the pestilence in their life more than her, then he could sleep out with 'it' tonight. A smile spread over his face as he mounted the steps of the porch and kissed her roughly on the forehead. He looked down into her eyes, the beautiful deep brown, as his smile broadened. 'Her,' he corrected. But the name had grown on the greying man. His life needed to include some humour and in his beautiful wife's glowing eyes, he had found some.

As Pestilence spat the red dirt at an increasing height in its rooster tail, Chris waned a tired smile. He glanced at himself in the rear-view mirror and whistled at the sight of the bags under his eyes. He yawned loudly as the warm air rushed in through the open window. Hot air and dirt spilled into his open mouth. He quickly closed the gates to the onrush, yet as his bite closed, he could feel the grit inside. The road wound through Eva Valley. He now climbed the ever-slight hill toward Noonamah. The speedometer dial slowly trickled down to forty from its starting position above sixty. He allowed his work stained hand to fall down to the beard on his jaw and kneaded. A bigger engine would allow him to tow more weight while holding speed. The thought ran through his mind, all the while Angie's voice rang out in the back of his mind 'Pestilence.' Engine models flashed through his conscious regardless, as he considered the width of the engine bay, the length and clearance around the firewall and steering controls. His eyelids became heavier and heavier as he pondered and drove. At one point, he veered entirely off the red dirt filmed blacktop.

The problem with the drive from Darwin to Katherine was the road. The speed limit and the road surface were fine, it was just as boring as bat shit. If he had to make the decision between making the drive to Katherine or slamming his cock in Pestilence's door, he would have driven halfway to Katherine, then slammed his manhood into the shaped metal once he had realised his error. The road had five gentle turns at most. What the occupant of the car had to face was the same scenery for hours upon hours. Wasted sparse scrub, a single laned highway covered in red dust for the most part, as it actually turned into dirt beyond Eva Valley and the odd water buffalo and kangaroo. Every mile or so, there would be small fires. He had always wondered who had lit them. The indigenous had been his first assumption, yet someone had told him in the pub one day that the fires were actually spread by the kites in their attempt to flush rodents from their nests. In the end, it never mattered. It was all just rubbish that ran through Chris' mind as the boredom took him over, and he attempted to keep his eyes open. Finally, as his eyes drooped and his head nodded forward, the last thing he recalled seeing was the dusty road lined with scrub and wasted trees for miles.

He had awoken in a stone-lined courtyard, face down. He could feel the stone under his hands as they pressed into his cheek and the hard surface under his knees. As he turned his head to look into the ground, he saw the poor cobble work of the concrete tiles and the sloppy joinery in between. He pressed both of his hands to stone at shoulder width and hoisted himself up. On his knees, he took the time to look around. The courtyard itself looked as though, at one point, it would have been the pride of the town. It had an elongated semi-circle shape to it, the centre of which he kneeled on was paved in concrete tiles, and the outer rim was lush green grass. Separating the grass from the stonework were intermittent stone walls that extended a few feet from the ground. The walls had metal tables adjoining them. Some had been torn from the ground and were strewn across the stonework. In front of Chris were two large brick structures that extended a few stories. They followed the semi-circle from the points at each end and curled around to meet each other. Chris struggled to his feet. His body felt odd, he didn't have the standard aches and pains of his fifty-year-old body. Instead, there was numbness. He felt as though he was in a struggle to control himself. His breath became heavy with the odd sensation, and he felt as though he needed to work overtime just to stand. Once he had risen, he had a different perspective of the grounds surrounding him. In some places, the cobble work had been smashed. There looked to be shards of glass scattered in different locations. In the centre of the stone section, there was a colour pattern that had outlined the cross of Christianity. Sections of the stone walls had been destroyed in places, the tables were mostly damaged. In front of him were stone pillars. Metal gates had obviously stood between each pillar at one point. Now, they lay as twisted remnants of their former self, discarded like everything else in between Chris and the pillars. In one place, the stone pillar had been pulled down with the gate; it stretched itself out toward him, fingers of crumbled stone beckoning him.

He strained as he lifted one foot at a time and moved toward the stones. Everything beyond was blocked from sight by a smoky haze that loomed there. It swirled and billowed in an imaginary breeze, yet it never relented, never allowed a glimpse of what lay beyond. In his mind, he wanted to reach the haze. He wanted to plunge through and become lost in the abyss. Yet as he neared the broken pillar, something made him turn his head. Off to his right was a destroyed office building. Its roof lay in pieces at ground level, and part of the front wall had been blown outwards. Opposing it was a mesh gate, which remained intact and fastened shut. A woman's figure stood on the other side. She had her back turned to him. The smoky haze licked over her obscuring her from view, yet Chris felt he knew her.

As he trudged toward her, he stretched an arm out in front. The woman was tall, her long blonde hair curled and wove its way in between its own strands until it hung at her lower back. He saw the gentle slope of her shoulders and the curve of her body beneath the silky summer dress that clung to it. As Chris neared the steel gate, he tripped over a chunk of broken stone. His face hit the pavement hard as he fell, yet he didn't feel it. He looked to the palms of his hands which had scraped along the rough surface as he had fallen. The skin was grazed, and he could see trickles of blood in certain places across the heel of his palm, yet still, he felt nothing. He used all of the strength he could muster and once again climbed to his feet while his breathing became heavy and laboured. It took everything he had to make it the rest of the way to the gate, and still the woman had not moved, the tips of her long hair trembled as the smoke billowed around it. Chris held out his hands and lunged and felt his fingers grasp the smooth metal crossbars.

The air horn shook him from his sleep, and his eyes sprung open, wide yet unfocused. In his deep sleep, it felt as though he had been in that courtyard for twenty minutes. Yet, from the scenery he was slowly taking in, it looked as though he had only travelled a couple of hundred feet. The road train bored down on him, its headlights blared in the hot daylight, and its air horn bellowed. Chris swore as instinctively he swung the wheel to the left. Pestilence's front end lumbered toward the shoulder. As it did, the body leaned horribly over, and the back end felt as though it was about to lose its grip. Chris planted his foot on the accelerator, pushing it hard to the floor, and he felt the slight lapse as the power glide shifted down to its low gear. The six-cylinder plant roared in protest, a weak, hollow sound before the wide tyres hooked in and delivered him the power that he needed to push the overloaded ute off the road. The road train blurred past, with not even a sense that he had applied the brakes. The air horn still sounded as the cab disappeared from view and trailer after trailer roared over the place the Holden had been seconds before.

Chris swore louder as he swung the wheel back to the right and released his foot from the accelerator, allowing the back end to swing woefully behind the front, back to safety. His heart hammered in his throat, and his ass felt like it had sucked up the entire bench seat of the utility. His eyes darted to the driver's mirror. He saw barely anything of the truck that had almost killed him. A look of anger and shock plastered over his face. 'Fuckin' asshole,' he yelled to himself, his eyes still fixed on the mirror when Pestilence seemed to prop for a second. The crunch of metal as the Holden's panels buckled under the impact of the fleshy mass that it hit rang through his ears. His head slammed forward into the steering wheel, and his vision of the mirror was replaced by brilliant light while small circles raced from end to end of his peripheral view.

Pestilence's engine guttered under the strain and stalled. The back tyres locked under compression. The steel body veered as its backend swang around. Luckily, the rolling iron had lost the majority of its momentum in the impact, and its smashed frame came to a halt a hundred feet from the impact area. He didn't know how long it had taken for him to wake; he didn't know if he had actually lost consciousness. Yet when he was aware once more, he felt the blood run down the side of his head from the impact on the steering wheel. He felt a tremendous pain shoot from his temple, down his neck and linger in his right leg. His heart still pounded in his chest, and he felt weak, more so than ever in his life. The kangaroo had not died in the impact, but it would not survive. It lay some fifty feet in front of the battered Holden, its legs broken. It sickened Chris to watch the animal try and gain its legs. The sight as the meat and bone trembled and crumbled under the creature's weight, the panic in the animal that made it continue to try.

The driver's door clunked as it opened. Chris near fell from the cabin but for his left hand, which grasped the A-pillar. He struggled to his feet as he had in his dream, yet at least at this point, he had a reason. He took another glimpse of the broken animal that was still trying to stand on its hind legs, and he shook his head. As he lowered his head to the switch that was embedded into the side of the HD's seat, his mind clouded with the pain, and he reeled. He leaned up against the side of the tub and vomited everything he had against the Holden's side. Once it had passed, he remained there and spat the final residue of the sickness in his mouth, and breathed as deep as his lungs could bear. Finally, he flipped the switch and allowed the bench's back to fall forward.

Resting on the floor of the cabin behind his chair was a knife, yet the blade seemed too long for it to be called so. The handle was worn and small in proportion to the blade, the two halved walnut handles were pitted and grimy from age and the linseed oil which they wept in the heat. The blade was seventeen inches in length, a fuller ran the majority of the length but stopped three inches from the point of the blade. As Chris' hand clasped the small handle, a large circular ring became snagged under the Holdens chair. As he flicked his wrist, the sword bayonet was freed, and he pulled the blade into the fresh, air where it hung from his fist, dull in the bright sun.

The kangaroo watched him as he approached. Slow as he was, sometimes, death can never come quick enough. The animal didn't even try to escape him as he neared, as though it had given up, its black eyes were trained on him and followed every step of the way. When he plunged the blade down through its throat and into its chest, it tensed at the pain and its eyes closed. As he pulled the blade from its neck and the blood began to gush from the lengthy wound, its body relaxed. The solid chest of the animal sunk, and its arms fell to its side. Its mouth opened slightly, as did its eyes, and for one last second they watched him, but there was nothing in them. Finally, they rolled slowly back into its head, and it was done. Chris dragged the dead kangaroo from the road by its broken legs, the joints sounded a wet and sloppy clap with each pull of his arm.

When he dropped the animal, his attention turned back to Pestilence, and he sighed. The chrome bumper was pushed entirely back into the frame. Its grille looked as though it had never existed and was simply an afterthought. The bonnet was the worst; it had buckled and folded under the impact and didn't look as though it would be able to be repaired. As he ambled his way back the fifty feet he had travelled to put down the kangaroo that had caused this mess, tendrils of steam began to list from under the bonnet, and Chris laughed. He sat down in front of his second love and spat a bloody mess on the floor next to him. As he sat there laughing, so hysterical it was to the point of tears, the thought was stamped into the front of his brain. *Angie won't be able to say no to the new engine now.*

RANKIN

'I was born by the river in a little tent,
Oh, and just like the river I've been running ever since
It's been a long time, a long time coming
But I know a change gonna come, oh yes it will.'

Sam Cooke – *A Change is Gonna Come* (1964)

The streets of Enoggera were just how Rankin had remembered them, yet for some reason, they were different. Everything was different. The street gutters, at first glance, were as seemingly clean as they were some twelve months ago. Yet when he looked closer, he could see the waste, the layer of dirt and scum that had been glanced over by the council sweepers. A cluster of discarded cigarette butts spread out like a fan, all tossed from the same point, the door of the Barbershop, 'North Cuts.' As Rankin slowly strolled down the streets, he tried to take in everything. He had been back for only a few days, but now he had returned from hell, the more he looked at something, the more he saw.

Perspective is a curious thing. In the jungle, a person could stand and turn full three-sixty degrees as their eyes darted here and there and took in every shadow. Every shade of green, every gnarl in the timber of the surrounding, suffocating trees. Yet when that person took a single step in any direction, it would be as though they had never opened their eyes. The shadows changed with every second, making them seem alive like they were to hunt, track or watch. Rankin walked past a small shop front which was boxed in and decorated to advertise a special edition of 'Tarzan of the Apes.' A copy of the book was set on a plinth while artificial vines and leaves choked the scenery around it. Rankin's heart skipped a beat when he saw the choking jungle, and his hands shook as he stood fixed on the scene. He was only freed from his trance by a passerby who asked if he had read the book. Rankin didn't reply. He simply turned his head to look upon the stranger, and stared blankly at them, yet through them. After some time, the stranger turned and shook their head as they walked away.

As Rankin left Sydney with nothing, he had returned to Enoggera with nothing. He had no civilian clothes, and he had no car, he had no friends and no family. Just a feeling of disquiet and a thirst. He had two more days to spend in Enoggera before the Army shipped him home to Sydney, to return to his life, to forget. Rankin's hands began to tremble, they had learned this trick on the last flight Rankin had taken on the Dread. The only way he had been able to stop the damn things shaking was to down a bottle of Vat 69. The drink helped the shakes. It helped the dreams, but Christ, it had taken a toll on him. His head was forever in a cloud, his eyes bloodshot. They remained semi-focused for most of the day until about four, when the first taste of the golden fire touched his tongue and then he was on point. In the jungle, he was told what to do. Even if the task was dangerous, he did it. In the end, either everyone went home or they didn't. Everyone had a drink, and the next day they would all start again. The part that troubled Rankin about coming back to Australia, and more so Sydney, was what was he supposed to do now? When he left, he had no trade. He spent the first fourteen years of this life in an orphanage, a time which he hated. He spent the next four or five in a shelter, doing the odd job where he could, and he could generally hold a job down well enough to earn some sort of recompense. That was until the man in a plain brown suit came to the shelter to see him.

They had been given a small room to themselves. Belkin, was a small built man with a widow's peak and slicked black hair. His eyebrows seemed to be larger than the eyes they sheltered and greasy as shit. The lack of upper lip and a weak jaw made the man seem very easy to bend, yet the forceful tone of his shrill voice put Rankin at a loss. This man was sending him to war. He was telling him that he was of better service to his nation in the jungle than on the streets. Christ, the way he put it made it sound exciting, yet something about the man told Rankin that if he had decided not to go off on this grand adventure, he would live to regret it.

Rankin had two more days to walk the streets of Enoggera and pass his time before he was to be sent back to Sydney. Sent back to Sydney to… he just didn't know. The welcome parade was tomorrow, he was sure that would at least lift his spirits, which were as low as ever. The dreary mornings saw him wake in the Gallipoli Barracks, his head pounding from the previous night's drunken lustre. The returned servicemen were all being housed at the Barracks for the time being until the welcome home parade, and then they were expected to merge back into society and take up the jobs they had left behind. Embrace the women that were waiting for them (if they were still waiting) and kiss their children on their foreheads and be like the model fathers that had returned some twenty-eight years before. Perhaps he would take the path of what he imagined his father had done, to return from service to father some bastards and disappear into some backwater country town like Dalby or Bathurst. To leave behind the war's spawn, to live his own life unburdened. Yet sex and women were something that hadn't crossed Rankin's mind since Gary's death all that time ago. Every day was a war, and every evening he was welcomed back to his love with open arms and the fiery warmth of the drink's embrace.

Rankin's aimless wanderings had led him to a local park. His head was lowered, and he watched as his service boots skimmed the loose gravel path with each step. He kicked small pebbles from their lodging as he went. Clouds of dust emitted from each stroke, while the hands in his pockets began to tremble once more.

For an early afternoon, the overcast day was dreary and dark. The usually sun-kissed roads and crosswalks were thankful for the relief in the early summer days. The trees surrounding him in the park still looked lush from the spring. Well hydrated, the harsh summer days hadn't yet taken their toll. The branches were full of rosellas and cockatoos, all yammered and chirped their news to their friends. A smile crept over Rankin's face, as the thought crossed his mind that the trees must be a pub for birds. Where they all met to pick at the leaves, chat up the girls and get into fights. As the thought swam lazily through his head, he watched as two remarkably colourful rosellas sidled up against each other and pecked at each other's white beaks, the blacks of their eyes full of life. Their feathers fluffed as they groomed each other, and as the breeze blew gently around them, they took flight, and the sky became a dazzle of reds and blues. Their beautiful calls lulled Rankin into a sense of the serene.

A child ran into his sight as he chased the birds. As he ran, he flapped his arms, either trying to shoo the birds in their flight or join them in the sky. It took no longer than four seconds of this attempt for the boy to lose interest in his game, and instead, he turned and noticed Rankin sitting alone on the bench. The boy stared at him. His eyes were large and deep brown and his face was as round as his belly. The small overalls he wore were clean, the laces of his miniature boots untied. Yet when Rankin looked into the boy's face, he could only see the child he had shot down in the jungle as he screamed in his charge, presumably after he had just witnessed the fate of his mother and father. The faces of the women and men he had killed, the children. They all came back, one by one, just as they had rushed out of the jungle. Their eye's vacant, no longer in want of anything, but just as they had in life, they had wished for his death, and they still did.

The child must have seen something in the soldier's face or his eyes. Perhaps it was his trembling hands; the boy had begun to cry. In much the same manner as the boy had appeared, a gorgeous young girl came hurrying down the path, her arms likewise in motion, attempting to calm the boy from afar. When she reached the child and began to soothe him, she turned to Rankin, whose lips spread to a sort of smile. Yet the look of disgust in the girl's eyes, the scowl on her face and her curled lip drove into Rankin like the fire-driven bullets from the Black Dread's fifty calibre. She turned in a flurry of her cotton knee high dress that swirled as she turned, and as quickly as she had entered his life, she had left. She took her child, her brilliant body and her accusing look with her. Although the gorgeous young woman had obviously despised the soldier, it was the first time he had been aroused by a woman since the events of the bordello back in Saigon. His manhood had begun to press against the hard linen of his greens. The vacant feeling in his stomach had gone, yet the hands which lay clasped together as he sat on the park bench still trembled.

He rose slowly. The wound at his side, although healed fairly well, was still tight and pulled at him each time he moved. The stitches, which still held the flesh in place, rubbed at his shirt as he walked, and he knew there was only one remedy for these problems, perhaps even the problem rising in his pants. He made his way out of the park. He assumed that it was no later than three in the afternoon, yet the overcast sky and the dim streets made him feel as though he was back in Saigon, heading down a packed earth pathway to settle himself down in 'Fuck Me's.' As he continued down the street, the street lamps flickered and then shone. Their light, although useless in this mid-afternoon glumness, was a faint attempt to eradicate the sense of loss and death in the world. A faint attempt indeed, the pale light was washed out of the world by the colourful trees which swayed in the afternoon breeze and the bird's songs.

The shadows that they cast followed Rankin as he strode down the street, as if they hunted him, like the jungle in his dreams. There was minimal foot traffic, yet the street was full of cars. The windows of the cars that passed were all closed to the world as if the air outside was dark and toxic. He could feel the eyes of the drivers wash over him as they cruised past, judgemental and prejudiced. No one stopped, no one spoke. No one issued any thanks for his service or his losses. To expect any different was to be a fool. He had read upon his return that a protest in Sydney had yielded some fifty thousand supporters, all calling for the end of the war, the end of the murder. Nevertheless, the feeling still hung inside of him that everything would be different come the parade tomorrow. With 8RAR out in force, they would see the thanks of the Australian people. They would get their welcome home.

As he rounded the street corner, his eyes glimpsed the Imperial Hotel. Its dirty brick walls were covered with advertising plaques, which shone out in the gloomy afternoon as they screamed of XXXX beer and Victoria Bitter, which was a waste of a sign as no one seemed to drink that horse piss up here. A chalkboard was hung from the wall next to the old oak doors, describing the day's lunch specials and promotions. One interested him, steak and ale Tuesdays, steak, chips, and beer, all for five bucks. His empty stomach rolled and churned within him at the sight, as it howled for protein, yet his hands at his side only called for whiskey. As he pushed the heavy oak doors open and made his way into the pub, the smell of cigarette smoke hit him. At first, he was taken back to the establishment where Max and he had fought the American, yet there were no

Yanks here. The Saigon bar was clean, tiled and majestic, where this pub had rotting carpets stained with countless spilled drinks and cigarette burns where the careless patrons had simply thrown their discarded butts to the ground. The dartboard, which hung to the wall, had a photo of an Australian politician, which Rankin didn't recognise, stapled to its fascia. One well-thrown dart was protruding from the middle of his forehead. There was a pedestal fan oscillating in the corner. Each time the fan swung its face to its furthest left, the corner of the politician's photo trembled as if to escape its capture. There were only a few patrons in the Imperial at this early hour. The barman, a gruff looking man in a stained singlet with more hair on his shoulders than on his head, stood watching Rankin as he approached. He considered him over the rim of his glasses as he cleaned a pint glass with the dirty dishrag in his hands. Rankin leaned on the bar and nodded a greeting at the barman, who didn't return the gesture.

'Whiskey,' Rankin muttered to the barman, his eyes searching the other patrons to see what level of locals the Imperial attracted. Most of the patrons were male, working class, in either torn working rags, the smell of whom fought a fierce fight to be prominent over the cigarette smoke and the carpet. With each turn of the pedestal fan, it was questionable which odour was winning.

'You're in luck,' the barman barked at him while Rankin continued to cast his eyes over the rest of the pub. 'It's happy hour.'

Rankin's lip curled in a poor attempt of a smile. 'Well fuck, you better get me two then.' He leaned his lower back against the bar top. He raised a cigarette to his mouth and watched as the tip wobbled fiercely in his hand. Embarrassed, he placed the smoke in his lips and lowered both hands away, turning once more to the barman to ask if he could light him up.

The barman, who had already placed both whiskeys on the counter, rolled his eyes and said the same words that Max had spoken. 'Do you want me to smoke it for you too?' Yet he raised a large, sweat covered arm to light the cigarette hanging from the soldier's lips. The curl in Rankin's lip vanished at the barkeep's words. He drew back on the cigarette and glared at the man. He let the smoke curl from his mouth. It wisped in the air, taken by the fan's movement in the corner. With one trembling hand, he pulled the cigarette from his lips and placed it on the counter, as there was no ashtray. The burning cherry of the cigarette rested on a mottled mat, stained by years of overflowing beers and neglect, the fibres blackened and curled under the heat of the fire which rested on it. Without taking his eyes off the barman, Rankin downed both whiskeys in one gulp each and placed the glasses back on the bench in front of the man.

'Best get me two more.'

As the barman poured, he tilted his head over to a side and gestured for Rankin to look.

'There's another of your lot over there. Go keep him company.' The barman wheezed a laugh through his filthy grey beard and placed the two refreshed glasses on the bench. Rankin raised one of them, the tremble in his hand already subdued to some degree. His eyes followed the barman's gesture, and they fell upon a disgrace of a man. He looked as though he had been in the chair since the moment the Imperial had opened its doors and would be there until they threw him out. His service greens were unwashed, there were stains where he had spilled his liquor all down his front and others which looked more like vomit than liquor. From the dirt covering his sides, it looked as though he had been sleeping either in the park where Rankin sat some five minutes before or in the street directly out front of the Imperial. His hair was matted, his eyes bloodshot, his face unshaven and haggard. Of all the sights that Rankin had seen in the Vietnam conflict, he knew this would be one of the ones that hung with him. The man before him, although unafraid of getting his hands dirty, had always been clean-cut, well dressed enough for presentation and the pride in his uniform had once been evident. Rankin felt as though he wanted to be sick; he couldn't bear to watch the man he thought he knew sit there destroying himself, yet he couldn't take his eyes away. The man in the chair retched and took his hands to his face. Rankin could see the familiar tremble in them, the unwillingness to stay still.

The barman guffawed. 'If there's one good thing that comes out of you lot coming home, war seems to breed more drunks and bastards than anything else.' The barman raised the pint glass to the faint light to admire his half-assed work, 'Wish more people would wind up broken and wasted like him, might be able to afford to change the carpet once and a while.'

Rankin turned his eyes to the old barman and took in the sight of the man properly for the first time. The man was large but not from strength. Under his stained singlet, a belly stood proud over his belt. The flab on his arms quivered when he moved, laughed, or spoke. The beard, although evidentially there due to the man's laziness and lack of self-hygiene, covered a double chin, which Rankin's mind's eye saw tremble and quiver in the same manner as his arms. Once more, he downed the two glasses of golden fire which sat on the bar top. The sensation as they burned their way down his throat and sat like lead in his stomach urged the soldier's anger. The weight of the brass at his hip began to throb as if it was a part of him, almost like it wanted to drive into the man's face.

'You're a piece of shit, you know that?' Rankin's lip curled once more.

The barman laughed at that. 'Yeah, but you'll drink my whiskey the same as you would anyone else's,' and with that, he topped up the two glasses once more.

Rankin raised one of them, the curl still on his lip. 'And what if I make you eat this glass, then take all the bottles from the shelf and shove each and every one of them up your fat, pimply ass?' Rankin downed the whiskey, 'Then I"ll drink your whiskey just like anyone else's and I'll listen to the glass clink inside you as you pour.'

The barman was further amused by this, 'I'm not a small woman or a little Chinese man, soldier. You lot don't know how to fight people your own size.' He leaned his two fat arms onto the bar top as he spoke, trying to be intimidating, his large breasts hanging down as he leaned his weight forward.

The vision of the large American floated past Rankin's mind at the fat man's words. The back of his head caving in with every brass-knuckled blow, the wet sound of the blood. The woman he shot, the boy, the one in the tunnel, they all floated past one by one. The whites of their eyes visible in the darkness of his mind. The shadows closing in.

His trembling hand slipped beneath his belt as his eyes remained locked on the barman. He felt the coolness of the brass on his skin, and he felt the leather pouch release the block into his grasp. He raised his left hand, and his strong fingers closed around the barman's meaty throat. As he raised his right hand, he saw the barman's eyes pick up the glint of metal, and they changed. Then someone else was on him, hands that pulled at him and dragged him, 'Bartlett, enough!'

When Rankin released his grip on the barman, his courage returned, and he bellowed in fury at the injustice being done to him in his own establishment, 'Get out! The two of you fuckin' drunk bums, get out and stay out!'

Rankin, still unaware of who had stopped his assault, leaned forward to the bar and clasped his last remaining whiskey glass, and downed it. 'You're right, you piece of shit. Just like anyone else's.'

Then he threw the glass back onto the bar top where it shattered. He turned and looked John Rixon in the face.

He had not seen Rixon move from his seat on the other side of the bar, and he had not seen him approach. Although the way he looked was horrid, he still moved quickly enough and stable enough for the moment. Without a further word, the two men left together before any further problems arose, mainly in the working men that watched them with distaste from the table nearby.

They didn't speak a word to each other for some minutes, they just walked, side by side, down the streets of Enoggera and greater Brisbane. At some point, they had passed a bottle shop, and Rankin had gone inside to get a supply of Vat 69 while he left Rixon on the street due to his appearance. Eventually, they wound up on the park bench, where the beautiful young woman had scowled at him that afternoon. With a soft laugh, Rankin imagined the look that would be on her face if she saw the two of them now. One bottle of Vat already gone, the second about to be opened. Both of them heavy in the drink.

'What have we become?' Rixon said aloud. Rankin looked at him. It wasn't really a question, it wasn't anything, but there it was, and he couldn't find an answer that he felt was natural. He just looked at his squad leader. The man that broke as soon as he was safe. Much like himself.

'We killed children. We killed women.' Tears were welling in his eyes.

'That's bullshit, John, you know it.' Rankin's eyes burned with anger and sadness for the sight of this man in his current state. 'If we didn't, we would have all died.'

Rixon smiled softly and faced Rankin. He looked long into his eyes. Neither of his hands trembled any longer; they were solid as iron. In the saddest voice, Rixon murmured, 'I think we all died anyway.'

The two men didn't speak after that. There were no words that could change anything. It was what it was. They sat and drank until there was nothing left. Then together, they began their journey back to the barracks to sleep and ready themselves for the parade the next day.

MICHAEL

'When the night has come
And the land is dark
And the moon is the only light we'll see
No I won't be afraid, no I won't be afraid
Just as long as you stand, stand by me.'

Ben E. King – *Stand By Me* (1962)

The boy lay in his bed, unsure of what the time was, not caring to know either. This was the fifth sleepless night he had suffered since the day of the Fairlane. Physically, the boy was fine, the worst injury he sustained was a kick in the guts from the fat man Kel Tracker. Yet three people died that day, basically in front of him. Every time he closed his eyes to try to rest his weary mind the vision of Matt Tracker's face, as it changed shape and shrunk with every bone-crushing blow Jack had delivered swam before his eyes. The deep red, lucid bubble that appeared from the area his mouth once was, grew and grew. Then it burst and spread itself across the broken man's face, making way for another bubble of bloody air to follow in its path. The sound of the struggled breaths, the sound of the blood filling the man's lungs as he strained to hold onto his life. Then, finally, the gurgled breaths and blood bubbles would stop. The only thing left was to watch the pool of blood slowly gain ground inch by inch over the hard-packed dirt yard, like an army on the advance.

There was no escaping the visions. Now they had been planted

into his brain, it was as if he was strapped to the soft fabric chair that
sat in the living/dining room of the Baker's residence with wedges
jammed in his eyelids to force them open, his gaze forcibly fixed
on the screen in front of him. Yet this was no old black and white.
The pictures that flickered across the screen of the boy's mind were
vibrant with colours and definition, so clear that he could feel the
dirt in the air as the wind blew. He felt as it bit into his skin and
stung his eyes. He could smell the oil from the old wrecks and the
dwindling stink of fuel that radiated from the Whippet. He could
smell the sweat and shit from the mangled corpse of Matt Tracker.
The aroma had become so horrid that it wasn't even the sight of the
corpse that was making the boy's stomach turn but the scent.

The sheet of iron that had spilled from the roof of the old house
clattered and shivered on the ground as a gust of wind rushed across
it. Like the thought had crossed its mind that now would be as good
a time as any to hop a ride on the now bristling westerly and get the
fuck out of dodge. The boy knew he would have loved to have done
the same thing, but he couldn't. It was his own actions that had led
to this moment, his actions that had led his brother to be attacked,
and his actions that had led Jack to do what he had done. Now the
situation was so far beyond dire that he felt at any moment, his poor
little heart would just stop beating, and the good Lord would have
to take him to heaven.

The dirt bit his face as the wind blew the particles from the earth.
From inside the house, there was a long series of rattled explosions
that echoed throughout the hot and dusty day. It was followed by
an eerie silence that seemed to stretch beyond time itself. No matter
how long the boy thought about this, he couldn't determine how
long he had sat in the cab of the Whippet while he waited for his

brother to emerge from the dark cavernous door of the Tracker's house. All he could remember was the fat man getting to his feet, a new vigour in his movements. Words flowed from his mouth like the blood that had flowed from his dead brother's face. Suddenly, he was out of the Whippet and sprawled on the ground as the fat man's loafered feet laid into him. The air was knocked from his lungs, and each attempt to fill them seemed to bring in more dirt than oxygen. Michael sputtered and wheezed just as bad as the man who kicked him. Then it all stopped. He was on the ground in front of the Tracker's door. He peered into the darkness and tried to make out the shape that had emerged. Kel seemed to think it was the one he referred to as Robin. Michael couldn't say here, nor there. If anything else could go wrong this day, it was for Jack to be slain and his own life to become forfeit to these animals. But Jack had come out, and part of him wondered what life could have been if that had never happened.

The visions raced through the boy's head over and over as he rolled back and forth in his bed. The darkness of the night loomed in through the open window above his bedhead, and a cool breeze listed lazily in to kiss the sweat speckled chest of the young boy. The itchy, woollen blankets kicked to a crumple at the foot of his single bed.

It had been five nights since that day, that bloody day. They had recovered the Fairlane 500, the majestic beast had sustained not even a scratch. Once it was finished at the Tracker's Jack had scolded the boy for not remaining in the cabin of the Whippet as he instructed, then had immediately set about loading his prizes into the back of the old truck. Michael had asked what they were, but he never received an answer. Jack rested the metal tin amongst the scatterings of steel and scrap in the back of the Whippet and rested the long bundle of rags further down. While he was there, he took the crank handle once more and set about firing the old truck up. Michael's gaze was fixed on the bundle of rags. There was never an answer from his brother, but did there really need to be? The explosions from the house. The gunshots. What had his brother said on the way to this place when the scared boy had asked about guns? 'Then we will take it.'

The Whippet roared and spluttered to life, still warm from its journey it only took one vigorous swing from to get the old beast's motor into motion once more. Jack threw the crank handle into the tray from his position at the front of the truck and glowered at the boy in the cabin.

'You drive this piece of shit back to the house. Follow me there. We don't want any stone chips on the Ford.' Jack then turned and disappeared into the Fairlane. The brake lights illuminated red in the boy's eyes as the car rocked on its springs, and the engine roared. Black smoke shot from the exhaust in a triumphant cloud.

The boy shuffled over to the driver's spot and backed the old Whippet up enough to allow his brother to manoeuvre the huge Ford out of the yard. The feeling as he drove the Whippet out of the Tracker's yard was that of pure bliss. For that second at least, he had no regrets. Everything was fine. It wasn't until the first sleepless night came that he began to have issues with the horror of what had happened. The fear sunk bone-deep into him. Surely there had to be repercussions. Surely. When the two brothers had pulled into the Baker's lot, their mother was still not home. Grace Baker, thankfully, had gone into town with Penelope Darcy that day and wouldn't return until early afternoon. Jack backed the big Ford into its spot under the carport. The paint still gleamed, and the brightwork was brilliant.

The double beam headlights still reflected the sun's sheer power. Jack exited the car, the keys in his hand. He shut the door gently this time and locked it before he started toward Michael, who still sat in the rumbling Whippet.

'Keep it running,' Jack grunted at the boy as he walked toward the tray and reclaimed his prizes from the littered bed. Jack Baker disappeared into the house and was not gone for a minute when his large shape was visible through the screen once more. When he emerged, he held one of his father's long necks in his hands. Everything else that was carried in was gone, just the brown glass of the Fosters long neck was there. Already half-empty. Jack walked to the driver's seat of the Whippet and began to heave his weight into the cabin. Michael quickly got out of his way, he knew the rest of this day would be silent. No complaint would be heard from Michael. A silent day sounded fine to him after the last few hours. Really, he wanted to stay home, but he was seen leaving the mill with Jack. He should return with him. The drive to the mill was silent, apart from the metal screams of pain from the Whippet's suspension, the flutter of its motor and the sound of the dirt and gravel being crushed under the narrow tyres. The Fosters long neck barely survived past the front gate of the Baker's lot, and Jack hurled it into the scrub.

As the old car rattled its way down the trail, Michael remembered the clatter of the timber spokes on each of the four wheels. The chatter meant that soon the Whippet would need to spend a few days soaking in the creek behind the Mill. When the timber spokes rattled, it meant the timber had dried out completely, and the spokes had become loose in their joints. Tony had taught them to leave the car parked in the creek for a full day; this left the lower half of the timber rims underwater. The next day the old truck would need to be moved forward a half wheel rotation to allow the other half of the spokes to swell under the water. The difference this made was astounding. The ride was better, the steering not as faint. This process would need to take place soon before a spoke was broken, but it wouldn't be today nor the next it would have to wait until Tony returned. Neither of the Baker's boys wanted to look at the Fairlane until the old man returned.

There was a question of concern from Paul Darcy when the brothers arrived at the mill. The balding man with furrowed brow looked the bloody Jack Baker up and down, perhaps they should have cleaned Jack up before they took him to work. Jack made a passing comment about a dingo and a half-killed kangaroo in the yard and left the older man to wipe the sweat from his balding head with his handkerchief as he leaned down from the bulking Hyster's cabin door.

The two sat in their father's office for the remainder of the day. Jack smoked, his feet up on the desktop while staring off at the same place on the wall as before. Michael lay on the carpet, his head in his hands, as he tried to forget what had happened. The two hadn't even tried to look at each other. They even drove home together once the mill shift had ended, and the heavy saw blades chuffed to a stop. Complete silence.

The boy stirred in his bed once more. This was useless. Any hope of sleep had left him some hours ago. He lifted himself to a sitting position and the bedsprings complained under his weight. He might go for another midnight walk. However, the risk of running into his father was there once more. Tony Baker had returned to Chinchilla three days after the incident with the Trackers. Nothing had been said about the car, apart from the dust on it. Grace, without knowing, had defended her sons by complaining about the winds and the amount of dust that it had kicked up once it got going.

'I almost needed to wash a set of clothes twice after they had hung out there in that wind all morning,' she complained to her returned husband as he eyed the Fairlane where it lay in wait under the carport.

The risk of seeing his father was there, but it was worth it. Although the breeze that rolled through the gaping window in the boy's bedroom was pleasant, the stifling heat of the small room was not helping the situation. Perhaps he could curl up in the cabin of the Whippet. The breeze that whistled through the open face of the tool shed would mean that temperatures would be much more sleep permitting than in this oven. The boy rose and didn't bother to cover his chest as he exited the heat of his room through the open window above his bedhead. His father had returned on Friday, tomorrow is Monday, and that meant back to work as usual. As he walked through the yard to the open-faced tool shed, he looked to the sky. Not many stars at all. He had thought there would be rain tomorrow. The way the trees groaned and stirred in the scrub, the smell of the air. It had been some time since the rain had blessed Chinchilla and Christ, they needed some. Hopefully, it would be the case.

Michael smiled as he walked across the grass. He thought once more of the smell of moisture in the air and how good it felt to let his skin absorb it. He thought about Susan. Maybe if the rain came around, they could go to the creek together and swim. The broken banks always made it fun to dive into, there was far less risk of smashing his head into a rock as he dove in, at least. An image flashed across the television screen inside his mind. Susan Darcy's red hair, soaked from the water, clung to her body as her pretty pale face emerged from the depths of the creek. Her freckles outlined on her face like stars in the sky. Her mouth half-open as she let out the breath she was holding underwater. Her eyes as blue as the sky was the day the Lord created it. The boy dreamt lustily as he crept into the tool shed and lay down across the bench seat of the Whippet. The breeze was absolutely beautiful in here, yet only half as much as the thought of Susan.

Michael winced as something dug into his back all of a sudden. He rammed a hand under his back and half lifted himself. The vision of the girl with the hair as red as fire vanished from his mind's screen. There was a chunk of something dry and dusty, and he pulled it to his face and peered at it through the darkness. It looked like a piece of plaster, like from a wall. There were strands of fibres that stuck out the jagged sides like frazzled pubic hair.

What is a piece of wall doing in the cab? the boy asked himself. The two had barely spoken since. However, toward the end of that horrible day, the boy had sought his brother out. It had been around ten in the evening, and he couldn't sleep. His mother was long in bed, the meal she had prepared for herself and her two boys long devoured, the dishes long cleaned and returned to their cabinets. The house was quiet enough, except for the sound of something like a rat in a wall, gnawing away. The sound had driven Michael insane, that and the visions of the blood and gore. Michael had opened his own bedroom door and stepped into the dark corridor of the Baker's house. All lights were off, and the well-kept rug that ran the corridor's length was barely distinguishable from the dusty hardwood floor it was laid upon to protect.

Across the hallway was the door to his brother's room. Although a small house, at least each boy had their own space. A source of light emitted from under the crack, and now and then, Jack moved behind the door, and his shadow shifted back and forth. The light that his size blocked was snuffed out like a candle's glow as it died from drowning in its own wax. The boy moved to the door and knocked. The custom was embedded into him from the heavy, metal lined door of his father's office. The shuffling ceased and there was a pause. He heard more movement, then footsteps as his brother strode towards the door and reefed it open. Jack seemed shocked to see Michael standing there, his bulking shape covered most of the doorway. It was hard for Michael to see beyond him.

'What?' he said gruffly, his head partially obscured by the bandage their loving mother had wrapped around his head. She also enquired what had done the damage to her son's face, but she was as easily subdued as Paul Darcy. Jack had simply told her an ironbark limb had slipped on the trolley, and his face happened to be in its way. 'Oh, dear,' she had sympathised as she began to worry about her firstborn's cut up forehead.

'I- I just wanted to talk about...' The boy stuttered as he looked up at his brother.

'Don't start. It's not the time. Later maybe, someday.' Jack spoke softly, yet his voice still boomed as he spoke. He shut the door in his brother's face. Yet before the door closed completely, Michael had gotten a look at one of his hands. Earlier that day, these hands were covered in blood and dirt. Eventually, he had cleaned himself up to at least present something half decent to his mother. Now they were covered with white powder. The boy could remember the substance caked on his brother's hands. It was under his fingernails and filled the lines on Jack's gnarled knuckles.

What was he doing to his wall? the boy thought as he settled himself once more on the soft, worn bench seat of the Whippet. The cool breeze licked at his naked chest as the wind gusted in through the open mouth of the tool shed. The thought crossed his mind that maybe the sound of the rat in the wall was his brother, but he couldn't think of a reason for why his brother would be doing anything like this in the dark of night. As sleep eventually came over the boy, he held the chunk of plaster in his hands. He could feel the coarse, frayed strands of horsehair as it tickled his fingers. As he closed his eyes, the screen inside the boy's mind began to show him images of Susan Darcy, half-naked as he was now, in the creek out the back of the mill. Her blazing red hair dripping wet. Her bright blue eyes locked onto his. A faint smile came across the boy's face, and his grip on the plaster slipped. Finally, as sleep took the boy, the plaster slipped from his hands and out of his mind altogether. For now, at least, he was just a boy lost in his own imagination once more. The worries of the day that haunted him forgotten, and the only thing that mattered was Susan.

CHRIS

'She had a classic beauty that everyone could see,
I was the last to meet her, but she gave her life to me.
She may be rusted iron, but to me, she's solid gold,
And I just can't hold the tears back,
Cause Betsie's getting old.'

The Beach Boys – *Ballad of Ole Betsy* (1963)

The rain pelted down on the veteran and turned his jeans a shade closer to black than the pale blue they had been that morning. Mud from the road's shoulder had entirely covered his worn leather boots. The laces were now a complete clog of mess, undistinguishable from the hide they bound. The green cotton work shirt clung to his skin, and the sleeves weighed his arms so that they felt like the overburdened branches of a gum that were ready to snap and leave their weakened body forever. He kept his head low as he shielded his eyes from the torrential downpour that had accumulated from nothing and with it brought the hint of the wet. His hair ran down his forehead like dark veins that stood out from the flesh. The water that beaded from its ends occasionally blinded the man or ran to the tip of his hooked nose, where they became lost among the storm. The rain had come in so hard and fast that Chris had no chance to return to Pestilence and no chance to make it home. Visibility had been reduced to ten feet, and at that, it was a haze. He was forced to focus on the lip of the hardtop as he placed one foot in front of the other, watching as each time his mud-soaked boot slopped to the ground, it grew in size. Each time Chris felt the relief as a clump of mud lost its hold on his boots. He watched as it flew through the air and tumbled in the rain to delve back into the earth it came from. Yet, no sooner had he taken another step, the clump was replaced by another whose weight was matched only by its grip. He attempted to whistle, yet the water that coursed across his lips only permitted a drowned gurgle that was inaudible under the gallons of water pounding the earth around him.

Chris was in a dangerous situation. The poor visibility made it impossible for drivers, safe and dry in their cars, to see him. Likewise, the roar of the water pouring from the sky made it unlikely for the lonely walker to hear the vehicles as they approached. With this in mind, Chris trudged further into the shoulder. He turned his head to look behind him into the swirling rain and darkness that consumed him. He had been walking for an hour when the rain hit. In that time, three vehicles had passed, and none had stopped to assist him despite his calm waves. He reflected that forty minutes into the walk, he had actually wished for a drizzle to cool his sun-baked neck and scalp as the sweat poured down from his hairline while he felt the onset of sunburn begin to sink its fingers into his flesh. The first drop had been the size of a penny, and it hit the hard, dry earth like an artillery shell. Dirt and fine droplets of water had sprayed outwards like the shrapnel of an explosion and had left a small crater in the road's shoulder. He had craned his head backwards to look at the sky and had been amazed to see the dark clouds amassing, blotting out the sun. At that stage, he could still see about half a mile in any direction, his shoulders slumped as the wall of water came rushing in, and the darkness surrounded him.

As he took another step, the mud-caked sole of his boot slid against a rock that lay just below the surface. He struggled for purchase, yet in the end, he fell to the mud like he was just another drop of water. His face buried itself into the mud, and his nostrils filled to the brim of his sinus cavity with the same watery substance that clung to his boots. With a mouth full of mud, he swore loudly into the earth, his eyes clenched shut, and he felt the anger building in him as his profanities only allowed more water and mud to flow into his mouth. He felt the grit of the specks of dirt that he had inadvertently sucked into his mouth grind against his teeth as he spat, coughed and tried to clear his airway. Chris struggled to his knees, and turned his face to the sky and let the water rush over him, down his face and into his open mouth, cleansing while it pelted him as it washed the mud away. Each drop like a bee sting as it exploded on his face.

As he rinsed his mouth to expel the clots within, he turned his head to look behind him and saw a flicker of light in the darkness. Not just one, but two large beams cut through the downpour, bouncing as they jostled up the highway no faster than a man running. He slipped once more as he urged himself upward, yet he held his stance and managed to make his way to the blacktop in the lurching light's path. He held his hands up to the sky like a crazed stranded man waving for rescue. As the lights lumbered closer, the death rattle of a diesel engine was heard underneath the roar from the heavens. Smaller lights cut their way through to his vision. Reds and yellows glimmered off the steel surfaces they were mounted on. The driver eventually saw him and the death rattle calmed to an idle, and the truck slowed. Chris moved to the shoulder once more and headed to the passenger door. The truck was gargantuan. It had three trailers hooked up all the same round, shining steel of the tankers. He knew the truck's cab well enough, an old fifty-five Freightliner that had achieved more miles than any other truck Chris had laid his hands on. He wasn't surprised to see the face that smiled down on him in the low glow of the incandescent bubble light when the passenger door opened with a scream.

'Typical mechanic,' Rabbits Murray cackled down at him as soon as the cab door's scream had subsided. 'Spend all your time fixing other people's wrecks, and you never spend any time on your own.'

Rabbits wasn't actually his name. He was born Travis Murray of Alice Springs in the twenties. He had earned his nickname thanks to an old Greek man who had come looking for help at the Top End's Trucking Yard many years ago. Upon seeking assistance, he was told by the lady at the desk to walk through the yard and find Travis, who would be happy to help him. Whether the Greek had misunderstood his name or simply couldn't pronounce it, he had walked through the entire yard hollering 'Rabbits' over and over as if he was in a poorly outfitted rendition of a 'Street Car named Desire.' Chris had heard this story among others more times than he could remember. If Rabbits' mouth was a machine gun, it would constantly be at risk of overheating it ran that quick, the only break a man was given was when he finally remembered to take a breath. Chris had been well attuned to this, for having been his mechanic for twenty years, he had learned when to listen, nod, and offer the ever so eloquent 'Uh-huh.'

'This was nothing to do with maintenance, Rab's.' Chris struggled as he slammed the cabin door closed. The water that ran down his face cut clean trails in the mud and grime which remained. He began to work at cleaning his features on his sleeve when Rabbits handed him a grease covered towel which he had pulled from underneath the bench seat which near filled the cabin. Chris examined the rag. He didn't know whether he wanted to be relatively clean and drenched or dry and filthy. 'Christ, you haven't got anything cleaner?'

Rabbit's grin widened as he ground the old Freightliner back into gear. His eyes narrowed as he struggled to see through the old truck's windscreen. 'Beggars won't be choosers, now will they?' He shouted to be heard above the rain and the diesel, which now powered up to move the immense weight forward once more. As the truck began to crawl, the cab bounced as the transmission whined and howled in protest against its labours. Chris dragged a hand over his face once more and pushed the hair away from his eyes so that he could see his friend all the clearer. Rabs was an aging man, his hair which had once been jet black all those years ago, was now snow white yet as full as the day they met. The man needed glasses yet refused to admit it and struggled along as always, his eyes gave the tell-tale squint as the crow's feet spiralled out from the corners of his usually bright and round eyes. His face was heavily wrinkled and sun damaged from the years of driving his old truck up through the centre delivering his fuel loads. The cabin of the Freightliner was mainly glass. The enormous windscreen offered a fantastic view of the road, yet it offered little to no protection against the heat of the sun that pelted through it.

Chris noticed that his friend was about as drenched as himself, and a hint of a smile came over his face. Chris had laboured in pushing Pestilence from the road before he set off on his journey back home. The car was in a bad state, yet the last thing he wanted was for the old girl to wind up under the axles of a beast like the one he now sat in. 'I trust you didn't run my girl over on your way through?'

Rabbit's face exploded into a mess of wrinkles as he laughed. 'I got myself soaked trying to find you in this,' he gestured through the windscreen at the road outside. The Freightliner's powerful headlamps were only enough to give a forty ft headway through the storm. The rains swirled through the light and beat down on the glass to conceal not only the road but the small limp wipers as they flapped almost uselessly at their top speed, overwhelmed by the amount of water that rushed over them. 'I'd say your old girl is about finished, though.'

The smile vanished from Chris' face. He rested his head against the plate glass of the passenger window. He let the oily rag fall to the floor and made no attempt to retrieve it. Rabs continued to yammer on about his day, his life and everything else Chris didn't care about. His mind went to Pestilence, his second love. Angie was safe at home, yet Pestilence was out in the rain, her front end wrecked, her cooling system destroyed, a shadow of her former self.

By the time the road train had dropped its passenger at the looped entry to his property, the rain had been replaced by the angry sun, accompanied by the humidity. The sheer heat sucked the water from Chris' clothes, yet they never felt dry for the rest of the day, and his smile never seemed to return. He had kissed Angie on the cheek briefly as he walked through the door and headed straight for the phone. The Lowe's lived in a relatively old house, yet it was large for its age, and Angie was constantly on top of maintenance and cleaning, hence it presented superbly. As Chris dialled the trucking yards, he turned to look at his wife, whose happy expression at seeing her husband had turned to wrath at the filthy footprints he had trekked into the house and the ever-increasing puddle underneath him, which seemed to grow by the second. He had begun to mouth 'Sorry' to his wife when the dial tone was replaced by a click and the trucking yards receptionist whose voice he recognised as Lucy McDowell's, a heavily obese woman with the voice of a lusty debutant who ran men's minds wild.

Chris introduced himself and kept the conversation quick and to the point. 'The car is a beat-up Holden HD, the front end all smashed in.' Angie's eyebrows furrowed at this. He had forgotten to actually tell her what had happened. 'Please get the driver to be careful with her… I mean it,' he corrected himself as he withered under his wife's look of disapproval and hung up the receiver.

Angie didn't say a word. She simply looked into his eyes, a look of concern on her face. Chris gazed at his wife. Her beautiful flowing hair was tied up in a bun, and she wore one of his old stained work shirts.

The sleeves were rolled up to expose the silky skin of her arms, which were speckled with dirt. Her hands were clean as always, protected by her gardening gloves which lay neatly on the mantle by the door. She frowned her perfect lips, and the hint of a line ran across her brow. 'How much is this going to cost?'

The smile finally returned to Chris' weathered face as he ran one of his hands through his beard, and he felt the dampness that still lay deep in the dust filled curls. The Holden was his passion, he felt alive when he drove it. He dreamt of its potential, but next to the woman who stood in front of him, the utility was nothing. 'We will see what the damage is first. I'm pretty sure the engine is gone.' He had to try it on for size.

'Is it actually gone, or do you just want it to be gone?' His wife had always known him, known his comments for what they actually were and known his intentions before he had. Chris' reply was only a wink as he left his love to clean the mess that he had brought into the house while he readied his workshop for the task ahead.

The workshop had been left open from that morning. The rain had not entered as far as he thought, but the humidity had penetrated the full extent. His setup was tremendous. It was placed on a two-thousand square ft of concrete. The three walls that consisted of its main structure were built of cinderblock, while the front was a conglomerate of steel bracing and sheet that created a bay door that swung open on the twenty ft high block walls at either end. As Angie kept the house in neat order, he had kept his workshop in a similar state. Although the concrete was stained by oils and fluids from the numerous vehicles he had pulled to pieces over the years, the benches were clean, and his tools were always returned to the correct spot. Chris believed that said a lot about a man, and the last thing he wanted to do was to go looking for a 5/8 spanner that he was sure he had just placed 'there' a moment ago.

He pulled his shirt over his head and flung it over a steel brace on his bench. He let a sigh escape his mouth as his eyes fell upon the phone which hung from the workshop wall. A different line to the house as this was for his business, and he didn't take business calls when he was with his wife. He picked up the phone and dialled the number he knew in his head, the number he had been thinking of dialling for some months now but had refrained. The voice of his love in the back of his head 'how much is this going to cost us?' It didn't matter how much, what mattered was making her the best she could be. When the gruff voice on the other end answered, 'Top End Motors,' Chris smiled as he ordered the 327 Chevrolet long motor and bell housing to suit the Power Glide transmission.

Two hours later, the wrecker came ambling up the long drive to the Lowe's house and workshop. The hulking shape of the HDs rear end hung behind it, the twisted bumper dragged along the loose gravel drive as it went, as if to further degrade itself in front of him. When Pestilence had been reversed into the bay of his workshop, the wrecker lowered it. Sweat lined the driver's face as he glanced dismissively at the rolling iron as he did. Before he left, he took another look at the Holden's twisted front end and tutted as he handed a clipboard to Chris with a pen. Chris looked down at the sheet, 'This waiver is to signify that the consumer has received the property in the same condition that they have left it and that the Top End Trucking Company is not liable for any damage sustained,' Chris frowned as he signed across the dotted line. As he handed back the clipboard, the wrecker's driver lugged himself back behind the wheel. 'Oh, and by the way, I think the motor in that's gone, it left a line of oil from where you left it all the way here.' Chris smiled and closed the door of the wrecker's cab for him.

The work was slow, tedious, and continued well into the night. He wrenched the smashed grille out from behind the bumper and began the junk pile. To the pile, he added the radiator, destroyed upon impact, and the chrome bumper dented and partly ground away during the tow. The Holdens lazy engine, the hole punched through the sump, was little indication that the engine was destroyed, but if it helped his story, he was happy enough to see the end of it. While he waited for the Chevrolet engine to be delivered, he began to trim the crumpled body sections in the places that weren't necessary. He opened the hole in the front of the frame to allow more air to flow through, and he removed anything he felt was unnecessary to the engine bay and the vision he had in his mind. Bolt by bolt, the car became lighter, and the scrap pile grew and grew.

The final task he set himself for the night was to construct a bar to replace the crumpled chrome bumper that still glittered from the bottom of the scrap heap. He spent half an hour sitting cross-legged on the floor of the workshop, staring into the gaping hole of its front frame, imagining what he could make. He let his mind run wild with any possibility, every option. Finally, he clambered to his feet with a smile from ear to ear and like any true mechanic, he began to speak to himself.

'All well and good to give it more power, but hit another one of them big red bastards, and you'll be in the same place.' He selected the main bar and dragged it out from under his workbench. The railway track had been hardened perfectly, making cutting it to length a nightmare but it was nothing an oxy couldn't fix. When it came to mounting the bar, he was left with no option but to reinforce the front end, *you change twenty things, for the sake of one idea*. He mounted the heavy iron rail on an angle to encourage anything he hit to get sucked under the wheels rather than go over.

When he had finally finished mounting it, he lowered the vehicle to sit on its own wheels once more, the already low front end hit the ground. Chris scratched his chin as he marvelled at the weight of the bar. 'I know it's heavy, but Christ. It hasn't even got an engine in it' He raised the car into the air once more and continued to swear at himself for not thinking things through while he agreed with the ever so eloquent name Angie had dubbed the Holden. As the rear suspension had been upgraded, the front now came under Chris gaze and it too was beefed up.

By the time the door was closed on the workshop, the front bar had been installed along with the upgraded front suspension. The vehicle's stance seemed very high at the front, even with the front bar, which would have added another three-hundred-and-fifty pounds of weight, yet Chris was satisfied as he knew the weight of the new engine would be immense. He had showered in the workshop and had left his filthy work clothes on the stained concrete floor before he walked across the gravel drive completely naked. His head craned back so that he could gaze at the stars above him in the pitch black of the night. The air outside was fresh compared to that inside the workshop, and he felt his skin ripple in gooseflesh as the heat still held within the gravel, stung against his bare feet.

The house was dark as he entered; Angie had long since retired. He could see the slight mess of the couch in the living room to his right, where she had spent most of the evening by herself. The book, *Of Mice and Men* lay on the coffee table, an envelope was visible in the darkness marking her last page. As he passed the lounge, he stopped briefly at the hall cabinet, which sat to the right of the hall leading to their bedroom and bordered the entry to their dated kitchen. The photographs were positioned neatly in their frames, not a speck of dust to be seen or felt. The moon reflected from the glass of one of the photos as it begged for his attention. It was of their wedding day, so many years ago now. Angie looked as beautiful as ever. Even in the darkness, he could see the beautiful gold speckled brown, the natural vibrance which echoed into his soul. He smiled as he thought back to that day, she had glowed with an aura as her smile spread across her face while the priests words had washed over them. Just that memory of her had been enough to drown out any hardship he had ever suffered. Any thoughts of the war, the German's and those horrible days of the North Africa campaign, were but shadows that flickered in his mind, afraid of the light that she cast. Still to this day, all of the worries of the world seemed to tumble from his mind with just a glance from her eyes. All the pain from his aging joints were no match for the magic of her touch. Better yet, no matter what had angered him or set a scowl across his face, she could always make him laugh.

He crept up the hallway, his now clean hands lightly brushed the plasterboard and picture rails as he went, being careful not to make a sound. As he reached the door, the barrier to her, he placed his ear to the hardwood timber. He heard the soft, steady rhythm of her breathing, the slight whistle in her nose. He pushed the door open slowly so the hinges didn't creak. The curtains were drawn to let the moonlight flow through the window and wash across the floor, like the way her golden hair flowed through his fingers. The room was fairly large, but the furniture which skirted the edges were left in the darkness, unwanted now, of no concern to anyone. His feet plunged into the soft rug that bordered her side, and Chris smiled as he gently placed a hand on her cheek.

She had been lost in a shallow sleep when he had entered, and when his rough hand kissed the softness of her cheek, her brow furrowed. His smiled widened at this as he witnessed her fight a losing battle to hold onto the dregs of her dreams and finally, she opened her eyes. At first, the two just met each other's gaze and for Chris, that was more than enough.

'Hey honey,' he said as his smiled softened and he brushed a rogue strand of hair from her face.

'Bugger off,' she muttered as she turned away from him, batting his hand away.

Chris laughed as she moved away from the bedside and he slid in behind her. 'I'm sorry I've been busy.'

'With *her*,' she added sardonically. He sighed as he wrapped his arms around her and kissed behind her ear.

'It's just a car,' he admitted as he took the bait, noticing she hadn't pulled away from him. 'But, it's our livelihood.'

With this comment, she turned and looked at him. He noticed that the shallow sleep had completely left her, and that she had not pushed him away again.

'I know, but there's more to life than money.'

'You're right,' he agreed. His hand moved to her breast as if to suggest something that was indeed more important than money, or the car, or anything that wasn't in this room with them right now. He leant forward and kissed her and she kissed him back. The sheets whispered against their bodies as she turned to face him fully.

The taste of her was exhilarating, the way she urged him to go on, pushed into him with her chin, her breasts and her hips all in sequence. She guided him into her, and he felt her warmth as he entered. His manhood throbbed as she worked underneath him, her hips rolled, and her legs closed around his back. His hands pressed into the soft linen at either side, and he lifted himself slightly so that he may look into her eyes once more. She opened her mouth slightly as he pulled away, as if she was beckoning him to come back for more. The beautiful mess of her golden hair had tangled itself in a lustful mess spread against the pillows. Her eyes were closed slightly, the specks of gold irradiated by the silky light of the moon, still shone from beneath their lids. Her eyes burned into him, yet she couldn't seem to hold her focus on just his eyes, her gaze trailing over his body. She ran her fingers up his arms which were solid to hold him

Matthew Cirson

above her. Then she clawed at his chest, which was firm like steel and bristled with coarse, jet-black hair. She pushed a hand onto his side and rolled him over.

As she straddled him, her breasts swayed gently in front of his face. Her nipples, as hard as iron, as he closed his thumbs and forefingers around each one and tugged as she moaned and gripped his hands close to her breasts. She rocked her hips in a circular motion, faster, then faster again, until finally, they both climaxed together, and she collapsed on top of him. She breathed heavily, her body rising and falling with his own. He kissed her on the forehead as she rolled off him and back to her pillow, his loins wet from their love. With the heat of the moment still heavy on her breath, Angie leant over and kissed him again softly. Then as she had when she had been dragged from the depths of her dreams, she looked at him.

Chris smiled once more as he felt the weariness of the day come over him, all he wanted now was to sleep. Her eyes moved from his to the pillow that he rested his head on, and with a swift movement she swept it out from under his head. A small groan escaped his mouth as his head fell back and he questioned 'Why'd you do that for?'

'That's my pillow. You can go back out to *her* now. You're on my side of the bed.'

Chris laughed as he took her by the hand, then promptly fell asleep, no doubt in a snoring mess, on her side of the bed.

186

RANKIN

'Have you seen the old man outside the seaman's mission?
Memory fading with the medal ribbons that he wears
And in the winter city, the rain cries a little pity
For one more forgotten hero and a world that doesn't care.'

Ralph McTell – *Streets of London* (1969)

The rain pattered down on the littered streets of Kings Cross. As the wind buffeted the street's occupants, the rain swirled along with the discarded movie tickets, candy wrappers, and newspapers to create a wave of garbage and water, forcing everyone to lower their heads as they made their way down the dark, bustling streets. As Rankin made his way through the crowds, his eyes were not blinded by the flurry of mess and water but by the accusing street lamps which burned down on him like the spotlight of a police cruiser. His head kept low, and his eyes squinted, he was pushed off balance more than once by a passer-by, who never turned their head or offered him a second look. He had attempted to light a cigarette as he walked and had discarded match after match as he struggled to light the wet sulphur on the abrasive section of the soggy cardboard. The cigarette paper, still unlit, was already weakened and torn by the flurries of water and waste. The cars moved slowly, all completely unrecognisable to Rankin as they held their steady crawl. Their headlights gleamed off the chromed bumpers of the cars in front. The red eyes of their tail lamps watched like the fiery eyes of a large cat that waited for its prey to lower its guard. Their hulking bodies all seemed black in the night. Their panels gleamed as the water trickled down and shimmered over the skewed perspective of the sidewalk that reflected on their paint. People who were four inches tall, that never looked at each other, never spoke. Their collars turned up to the wind and rain. Above them, the eyes of the God which put them there burned like the sun as it waited to flare and take them all.

If Enoggera had been too quiet for Rankin, Sydney was by far too busy. To add salt to the wound, the local shops had changed their names to appeal to the American soldiers who were flown in and out of Sydney for their two-day recreation passes. Places that had once been aptly named 'The Royal' or 'The Stockade' had now been brandished with red, white and blue banners. Makeshift signage now labelled them the more attractive 'The Eagles Rest' or 'The Alamo.' Posters of women dressed up in skimpy britches and top hats to resemble the beloved Uncle Sam while they posed in provocative ways. Men dressed in smart grey three-piece suits, with American flag bowties fastened around their necks, were the only ones that spoke on the streets. They yelled their sales pitches to passing troops, 'Do your duty to your allies and help the ladies they have left behind,' or 'the only thing better than the American dollars against your hip is what's between the thighs of the girls we have inside.'

What seemed to disgust him more than the prostitution was the level they went to make their shops appealing to the foreigners. It was one thing to welcome an ally with open arms; it was another to do everything in one's power to fleece them of their coin. Yet the Americans were always so willing to hand over their greens in any event, if a restaurant wanted to go to the extent of changing its menu to label chips as 'French Fries' or soft drinks as 'Soda Pops,' just to have the marketing edge, then good luck to them. As like with almost everything in the world today, if it doesn't breed money, cost money or look as though it does, then no one gives a shit about it.

The return to Sydney had not improved his mental state, yet he was relieved to leave Enoggera. All of his hopes of his life picking up after the parade were ill-fated. Even the sight of all the Americans was preferable to the faces that lined the street that day. The wind gave an especially strong rush, and he was blinded by the rushing water in which it carried. With his eyes closed tight, he continued to press on until he was nearly bumped off his feet. Rankin blinked his eyes in an attempt to clear them while his hands went out to steady himself. A businessman with a long moleskin coat glared at him from under the visor of his fedora. 'Walk with your eyes open, dickhead,' the man barked as he continued down the street, his head still turned to fix his filthy stare on Rankin.

The cotton of his shirt clung to his body and accentuated his muscled shoulders, the slightly hunched back and his solid stomach. His jeans were tight against his legs, wet further from the torrents of water that breached the walls of the gutter each time a car trundled past. His sandy blonde hair, already speckled with the odd grey, pressed to his forehead. He ran a trembling hand up and over his head and felt the cool water gush down the back of his neck. The time had come to quench his thirst once more.

As he pushed through the doors of the 'The Pint of Liberty,' he was astounded to see the number of Americans there actually were. He had spent a lot of time in drinking holes in Saigon, God knew he had, but it seemed there were more Americans in Sydney than in South Vietnam. Most of the tables were full, and the bar was completely blocked by a wall of men and women. It was easy to tell the Americans apart from the Australians, the accent aside. The American men always seemed to have women around them, no matter how they were dressed. One man might dress himself up to appeal to the ladies, the second man would wear his military dress, while the third would wear his military fatigues. The ones who wore their military clothes were easily identifiable to be American and never seemed to be without a girl hanging from their arms or their cocks. The ones who dressed plainly seemed to be less successful until they started spending the American money and talking in their stupidly slow southern accents.

A few of the other patrons shot him dirty looks as Rankin pushed his way to the bar. Nevertheless, the laughter, the singing and the shouts of joy continued around them, and they soon forgot about the rude man at the bar. It took what felt like an hour to get served, the women with low cut tops and water running down the curves of their breasts seemed to be better patrons to the overrun bar keeps, yet finally, the liquid fire was placed in front of him. As he raised the glass to his lips, he looked around at the faces of the people that surrounded him. Their smiles, the joy in their eyes, the way their bodies moved—this was by far a better reception than what he had received in Enoggera. As he moved his eyes along, there were no Australian flags, no 'Welcome home boys.' Just American flags, American lingo, and Australian women clinging to American men. He lit a cigarette and dragged deep as the whiskey worked at the stone in his stomach. As he exhaled slowly, the smoke amassed in front of his face and momentarily obscured the rest of the pub from his view. His mind darted back to the streets of Enoggera. His lip twitched into a snarl, and he turned to the bar once more and ordered a double as he leaned over the highly polished top and smoked while he reminisced.

The streets had been cleaned, the glass windows of the shop fronts had been polished, and even the benches that lined the streets had been given a once over to remove any sign of dirt or stain. Everything had to be immaculate. To see the street in comparison to how it had been the days before, although not an enormous transformation, an effort had obviously been made. The assumption could be made that people were happy to have the parade, yet as 8RAR began to fill the streets, sectioned into their platoons, all dressed up and clean, the assumption had turned to doubt.

Rixon cleaned up better than Rankin predicted. The bags under his eyes, although still visible, had receded mostly. The scraggly beard cut away to reveal the gleaming soft skin that lay underneath. His hair had been washed and then cut back, his fatigues had been burned, and he now donned his full military dress, displaying his rank and last name. He looked as though he was twenty years older than the man that had sent him into the tunnel a few long weeks ago, yet still a lot better than the man who stood before him the previous night. Rankin likewise had cleaned himself to a similar extent. Although he had started in a better state, he couldn't help but feel that he didn't polish up to the same level. Perhaps he was made of a different metal. He felt uncomfortable in the pressed linen; the tie seemed to choke the life out of him and his feet already felt as though they were gaining blisters in the highly polished boots.

Rixon's section was the fourth from the front of the parade, which was led by the top brass, then by the band, 'A' company's first section, and then finally came them. Rixon marched in front, his back straight as if his head were locked on invisible struts. His arms swung in time with others that surrounded him and the beat that was laid out by the band in front. Although no soldier was allowed to turn their head and look at the people lining the streets, sights were stolen through the sides of their eyes and on corners where the parade wove its way through the streets of greater Brisbane. If a man took a count of the signs that read 'welcome home' or 'good to have you back,' he would not have needed the digits on his second hand. There were no flags bar the ones that were carried like banners by the bearers that surrounded the top brass at the front of the procession. But even they hung loose and barely stirred in the pace that was held.

The number of people that lined the streets was promising at first, yet street after street, their numbers waned, and with their numbers, their passion fell sharply. As the procession neared the end of the main street and turned for the barracks once more, Rankin's view let him stare straight into the faces of a group of people who leaned on the rails of the corner. Their eyes, which scanned the soldiers as they marched past, were dull, and their mouths were solemn. Their hands either held onto the rails loosely or clasped together in front of them. None of them clapped. None of them seemed to be in the mood for shouts of joy or thanks. As Rankin neared them, one of the men who had been smoking held his cigarette butt in his hand and flicked it into the crowd of soldiers as they marched. Rankin followed the butt, the small embers that danced and swirled as the charred paper flipped over and over again. Tendrils of smoke trailed behind it in the air as it went until he watched it disappear into the first section. His eyes darted back to the man who had flicked it. He hadn't moved, he had simply turned his head to look another way. The soldiers in front did not stir at the act; their heads remained straight, and their arms continued to swing in motion. The few people that had surrounded the smoker had not subdued the man, they had not done a thing. They likewise watched the cigarette tumble through the air with Rankin and who knows how many other soldiers and continued to watch the procession in their own silence and thoughts.

Rankin believed he had seen the woman and child from the park, the same woman whose tight body hidden beneath her light summer dress had driven the arousal from deep within him. She held the small boy in her arms, his bottom rested on her hip as they both stood in silence. Her hair flowed in the subtle breeze once more, as dark as the depths of the jungle, yet beautiful in its own right. The flowing locks tickled her son's cheek, making it itch. As he scratched his cheek, his face remained blank while he vacantly watched the soldiers march by. He didn't ask his mother anything, he only scratched at the spot on his cheek, which was irritated by the kiss of his mother's flowing hair. There was a moment where Rankin's eyes locked with the woman. He could see the deep brown of her gorgeous round eyes, slightly hidden beneath the long lashes that protected them. In the deep brown, there was a sign of recognition as they met the grey-blue of the veteran in the masses. Then her lip curled in a scowl, and she turned her face away.

Toward the end of the march, Rankin's spirits had been destroyed. His feet throbbed in the unworn, polished boots. His thighs chafed against the pressed fabric between his legs. The parade was closer to a march of the condemned than to a welcome home. The citizens lined the streets to watch the murderers, home wreckers and bastards that they had bred and sent away, only to have them come back worse than ever and unleashed in the streets. In the final legs, the march led them across the front of the Imperial, and the barman was out on the curb. His white singlet blotted with fresh stains, the hairs on his shoulder standing on end like the barbs of a cactus. He scowled through his filthy grey/white beard as they passed. One of his patrons hiccupped beside him as he leaned against one of the many light poles which lined the streets.

The man seemed to be heavy with drink. As he raised his head, he looked straight into Rankin's face. Rankin's timing wavered for a split second as the man's face came into view. At first, he had believed it was Gary. His first friend to die, drunk in Saigon, the only thought on his mind was his cock and how he was going to plunge it into a girl like a sword through a dragon's heart. But the features of the man's face were nothing like Gary's. His widow's peak was in stark contrast to the high forehead of his friend, blue eyes against brown, and a wasted stubbled chin against a smooth rounded one. The man swayed on his feet as he took in the soldiers before him, a wry smirk on his face. As Rankin's section moved up onto his perch, he retched as he reeled his head back and spat into the parade a snot-filled glob of saliva. The mess fell pathetically short of the men it was intended for, but the notion was taken well enough. None of the men reacted; as if they had never seen it take place.

When the parade was broken up at the end of its course, the top brass congratulated the men on their safe return, thanked the town of Enoggera for its hospitality and the men were sent back to where they called home. Sydney had never been home to Rankin, yet it was the only place he really knew. He had left an unfortunate orphan with nothing and had returned a broken soldier with some money and the apparent debt of his nation. The money had been enough to secure himself an apartment in Redfern. He had furnished it with the bare necessities and had bought himself a small selection of clothes. To his surprise, he had managed to find a job close by in a mechanic's workshop, assisting in various ways. Although he was not a qualified mechanic, he preferred to work with his hands and had learned a lot through the man who had taken him on. Allan Ross, a gruff old Scotsman who had accumulated a lifetime of junk and waste to horde in his workshop. In the four weeks he had been back in Sydney, and the three weeks he had been on the job, he had arrived to work late seven times. The rest of the time, he was hung over. He didn't expect to hold the job for much longer, but as long as there was another job around which could pay him enough to drink himself to sleep each night, it didn't really matter.

He tipped the glass back and drained its contents, his hand as steady as a doctor, the stone in his gut eroded by the fire. The bar had filled to where there was no room to sit. To reach the bar, a patron had to breach a wall of two people deep. He felt someone push up against him, and the glass almost slipped from his grasp. Angered and fuelled by the drink, Rankin spun around to confront the pusher. The woman was small of frame, and her hair was a fiery red, cut at her shoulders, its ends curled back in to kiss the sides of her neck with its perfect tips. Her face, as pale as it was, was broken up by the large, perfectly rounded blue eyes and small lips which were as red as her hair. She wore a smart white blouse over blue jeans and red heels. She looked up into his eyes, and to Rankin's surprise, she didn't scowl or look away. She smiled at him.

'I'm sorry, there are too many people here. I just wanted to reach the bar.' Her long lashes fluttered at him, and her voice was soft and soothing, yet audible over the crowd. Rankin's lip curled in a one-sided smile. He moved to the side and made room for the lady to move in beside him. In true barman style, as soon as the beautiful woman rested her pale white arms on the bar, he appeared.

She ordered a gin and tonic, and Rankin spoke beside her, 'And one more of mine.' When he spoke, she looked at him, confused, as if something he had done had not been what she had expected.

'You're Australian?' she said, as her eyes darted back to watch the barman go about her order. As she turned her head, he decided to take the rest of her in. Her nails were neat and freshly painted to match her lips and hair. She only stood about shoulder height to the veteran, so the sight down the front of her blouse was tremendous.

'Born in Sydney.' Rankin kept it short as the whiskey was apt to make him say words he would regret. He saw the corner of a smile on her lips as her head still followed the barman on his journey. Rankin looked behind the bar and noticed that it was backed with a mirror.

Her brilliant blue eyes were staring into his through the reflection across the bench. Her smile remained. Embarrassed, Rankin diverted his gaze. She had more than likely watched as he looked her all over. He tried to move beyond the embarrassment, and he asked, 'Did you think I was an American?'

She turned to look at him full in the face, and those brilliant blue eyes caught him once more. 'I did, but I was pleasantly surprised to find that you weren't.' She extended a delicate hand, still holding his gaze, 'I'm Mary.'

Rankin took her hand, 'Rankin.' The smile came naturally as he said his name. He knew it was unusual. Her eyebrows raised as she shook his hand and mouthed his name as if trying to pronounce it. He laughed aloud and clapped her softly on the shoulder, 'Ran-kin,' he enunciated, 'I know it's a bit different, but it's better than more of the same old apostles.'

She laughed, 'Yes, you're right. I do know too many Johns and Lukes.'

The night with Mary had been the best night he had spent in Australia, even before the war. He paid for her drink, then another and another. She looked him in the face as he spoke to her and didn't turn away. She laughed as he told her stories that were fit for her ears of his life. Mainly about the Black Dread and the beautiful views that were there to see from the open side at a thousand feet above the ground. She listened intently and didn't cringe when she heard he had returned from Vietnam. She matched him drink for drink, and her eyes stayed bright, her lips a burning red that beckoned him closer and closer. Until finally he gathered up enough courage, as she was mid-way through an actually interesting story of how she had arrived in Sydney from Melbourne, he leaned in, a little too quick and kissed her. Her lips were soft, and at first, she stiffened against his touch, then he felt her body relax, her neck loosen and her mouth open to accept him. Her tongue moved longingly against his, and her breath was warm. When she moved away, her blue eyes burned with lust, the tip of her bottom lip in between her teeth, and her hand was on his wet shirt as it clung to his skin, 'Do you have somewhere to go?'

Rankin was breathing heavily. Although he had bedded girls before, he had never had someone he thought of as a woman, and none he hadn't bought. 'Only with you,' he said softly, their faces still close. She took him by the hand and led him to the door.

The journey back to Redfern was a blur, yet at least it had stopped raining. They spoke more as they walked. She finished her story about how she had moved to Sydney from Melbourne, as she followed the love of her life. Only for him to suffer from the disease of a wandering eye, among other things. Once she had discovered his deceit, Mary had been left with the dilemma of leaving to return home with no money, or staying and continuing to build her career in sales advertising. Like Rankin, she had little to no friends besides her work colleagues, who were mainly men and had no interest in partying with so many Americans around. Mary disliked the American soldiers as much as them but wasn't for letting it spoil a good night out. The more she spoke, the more Rankin fell for her, the kindness in her voice was something he was unaccustomed to, her touch, her hair; the list went on.

When they arrived at Rankin's apartment, he led her into his sparse living room, which consisted of a single chair and a small table positioned to look out of the window. The floor lacked any form of covering, but it was clean and presentable for what it was.

He gestured to the near-empty room, 'Welcome to my humble abode. No need to take your shoes off.'

She laughed and threw her head back in her joy. Her hair bounced and swayed with her movement, and Rankin was powerless but to watch her. When she stopped laughing, she moved close to him and ran her fingernails down the back of his neck, across his shoulders and down his chest. She once more nibbled the tip of her bottom lip as she looked up into his eyes, the brilliant blue locked onto the pale eyes of the man she clung to. Rankin hesitated. He said, 'I'm sorry, there's not much else here. I haven't had…'

She stopped his words with her mouth, and the kiss was passionate and more forceful. He ran his hands up and down her back, feeling the silky fabric move over the soft skin that lay underneath. He could feel her breasts pushing into his chest as their lips worked together, their tongues in a dance of lust and passion. As they continued to kiss, they moved towards the only other room, the bedroom. She unbuttoned his still-damp shirt to reveal his chest, and the small bristly hairs clung to his skin as his sandy blonde hair clung to his face. As she opened the fabric, she sat on the side of the bed and saw the scar on his side. She paused slightly and turned her brilliant eyes to his. Her lips pursed in a worried look.

'Does it hurt?' Rankin was hunched to look down at her, and his hands had fallen to his side. He was powerless to say or do anything, so he shook his head slowly. Mary's eyes went back to his side. She ran her fingernails around the scar and kissed it softly. 'My poor soldier,' she said. She kissed lower and lower until she came to his jeans and his belt.

With trained hands, she unbuckled him and allowed his trousers to fall in a heap to the floor. His manhood stood proud as it swayed in front of her. She stole a quick look at his eyes once more, smiling as she took him in her mouth. Rankin looked to the ceiling. The sensation that ran through his body was like none he had ever experienced. His legs locked, and his back arched as she pleasured him. The moment seemed to continue for hours, the sounds of every movement, the feel of every touch. He moved away from her and stood her up. Gently, he unbuttoned her blouse, and his manhood still throbbed from the thrill. He threw her blouse aside and squatted as he undid her jeans and dragged them down her long legs. What was hidden beneath the clothes was better than his poor imagination could allow. Her thighs left a small gap just below the slight bulge of her lower lips. She had a flat stomach and slim hips leading up to large breasts, which were still saddled in their brassiere. Rankin ran his hands up her sides, his fingers grazing the skin so that she erupted in goose flesh where they contacted. He removed her brassiere and leaned in close to reach around her. He threw it aside with the rest of their clothes and pushed her onto the bed. Her breasts bounced with the movement of her body as she fell back onto the soft mattress. He stood and looked at her for a moment as she lay with her arms open, inviting, on the white sheets of his bed. Her pale skin seemed almost to blend entirely with the coverings in the low light, but her red hair and lips stood out with her blue eyes like fire and ice. Her breasts trembled with each breath she took, he lowered his eyes to her slit, and his hands began to shake.

He was taken back to the last time he had been in this situation; he saw the girl with the hair lip as his fist slammed into her face. Her screams and cries loud enough that the MPs rushed in to drag him off her. He saw Gary, dismembered as he lay on the bed, his face pale, the white satin pillow pushed to his crotch, turning a velvet red with each passing moment. He saw the strangled mess on the bed, Gary still inside of her, although two feet away, the blood and gore that seemed to flow out from between her legs. He felt the stiffness fall out of his cock, the peak wavering as it fell to point at the floor. In about ten seconds, he was completely limp. He raised his shaking hands to his head, still fixated on her vagina, his eyes wide.

'Get the fuck out.' He spoke in panic, ashamed of himself, horrified by the memory.

Mary's look of shock was not to be unexpected. Shuffling herself up the pillows, she closed her legs at the look Rankin was giving her. She brought a pillow to cover her breasts, her eyebrows furrowed.

'What is wrong with you?'

Rankin panted and his heart raced in his chest, his hands shook worse than ever. On his bedside table, a bottle of whiskey stood. Only a couple of ounces remained, but anything was better than nothing. He rushed for his saviour. As he moved, Mary, who was startled by his sudden lunge, screamed and flung the pillow toward him, but her aim was poor, and the pillow went wayward. Before Rankin could reach the bedside table, the pillow had crashed into the bottle and had sent it tumbling to the floor, where the glass shattered, spilling its contents everywhere.

'No!' Rankin screamed as he ran his hands over the broken glass frantically. The shattered glass tore his hands to ribbons as he clutched jagged pieces. The whiskey, which coated the pieces, burned inside his wounds like they were laced with napalm. In absolute agony, in a dire panic and rage, Rankin stood up. His eyes were dark.

'You're a fuckin' freak!' Mary screamed, in absolute hysterics. She was trying to clothe herself as she stared at him, her blue eyes no longer brilliant and large, full of love and happiness. They were narrow and accusing, full of fear and prejudice. She was trying to put her arm through her blouse when Rankin hit her full in the face, and she crashed to the ground without a word. The right side of her face was dark and angry. The red lipstick had smeared up the side of her cheek from the blow, and a small trickle of blood ran down from the tip of her bottom lip, where Rankin's fist had driven into her teeth. She cried as she attempted to crawl away. Her feet propelled her backward while she lay on her back. Rankin approached her quickly, still naked, his limp member swayed angrily with each step. She began to scream in horror and pain as Rankin began to hit her repeatedly.

'I'll make sure no one ever wants to fuck you again, you fucking bitch!' He roared in her face as he hit her again and again. She hadn't stopped screaming when the door was broken down. This time it wasn't the MPs that pulled Rankin off the girl as he swore and spat; it was his neighbour. Mary sobbed and cried as the hands pulled him away from her. There were other voices as well, someone shouting for the police to be called.

The man that pulled him away from Mary gasped as he strained to drag the crazed veteran away from the poor girl.

Rankin heard, 'Crazy son of a bitch,' behind his back just before he was hit over the back of the head by something that was cold and hard. The fight went out of him, and he lay motionless, semiconscious on the floor, his eyes in and out of focus. Behind him, he heard Mary cry, and someone swore. He could see the broken whiskey bottle, the shattered glass was everywhere, mixed with the blood from his hands. A small dribble of whiskey trickled across the floor towards him.

Just a little closer, he thought as the blurred trickle of golden life edged across the floor of his apartment. *Just a little closer.* He opened his mouth and tried to stretch his tongue as if he was kissing Mary, but the whiskey was a more reliable lover. He should have known that. The trickle edged ever so closer to his outstretched, straining tongue, he had the chance to think, *Just a little closer,* one more time before the darkness overcame him, and he fell into the depths of unconsciousness.

MICHAEL

'You may say
I'm a dreamer, but I'm not the only one
I hope someday you'll join us
And the world will live as one.'

John Lennon – *Imagine* (1971)

The boy had awoken from his slumber on the frayed seat of the Whippet. Still half-naked, he had risen and re-entered the house through the rear screen door. The smell of frying eggs and greasy bacon had lifted him from slumber easily enough, yet the fatigue didn't leave the boy for most of the day. He had broken his fast on his portion of eggs and bacon, noticing to his own dissatisfaction that all of the yolks had broken and run while in the pan. The remainder of the gold liquid was cooked through, and not a portion remained in its liquid state to soften the hard bread that accompanied his meal. While he supped, his mother had informed him that his brother would not be going to the mill today due to his head injuries. It was best that Jack rested up. Michael could only think of the day that awaited him now. His father, Tony Baker, had never approved of either son skipping a day at the mill. Not that Michael had ever done any labour there. It was their father's belief that a man should always start the day with routine, a throwback to his days in the military. As far as the boy knew, his father believed he should end the day in routine also, half-drunk, livid with anger, striking out at his own family.

Michael was happy enough to have his father home. He felt a sense of detachment from the day's past. With his father home, perhaps he could settle back into a routine. Although the day hinted of rain, the morning still held the heat of the previous days. Black clouds swirled above, unchecked as they roamed the bright blue skies like sheep in a paddock. Hopefully, they would amass above Chinchilla later that night and spill their hold down on the sun-kissed land below. God knows they needed it. The Fairlane was long gone. It was a wonder that the sound of the engine firing didn't wake the boy as he nestled into the frayed fabric of the Whippets bench seat. The old man and the majestic beast were gone, and it seemed the old truck would also get a respite for the day.

'Mum, do I have to go to the mill today?' the boy asked as she went about scraping the remainder of his meal into the compost bucket. Jack was getting out of it; why couldn't he?

'Don't you want to spend time with your father today? You know he's been away,' Grace enquired. She didn't raise her eyes from the sink as she moved her hands underneath the soapy water. Steam rose from the hot water in ribbons to mingle with her long dark hair that swirled among the woman's shoulders with every small twitch and movement of her head.

To be honest, the last thing the boy wanted to do with his day was to spend it on the dirt-encrusted carpet of his father's office. It was a nice day, still warm, but the lack of sleep the last few nights had taken its toll on the boy. He felt as though the bags under his eyes were large enough to touch the table he sat at. His back ached from the lack of support the Whippet's worn and sagging seat had offered, and the beginning of a headache lurked somewhere just under the surface. In all honesty, the boy just wanted to go back to bed.

'I'm spent, Mum,' the boy said in his sookiest, *please mother me* voice. His eyebrows raised slightly above his enlarged, watery brown eyes, both of which were red from exhaustion. 'I haven't been sleeping. I don't know what's wrong, but I just want to go back to bed.' The boy slumped his shoulders and hunched over the table in an attempt to look as pathetic as possible. Anything to get out of a day at the mill.

The boy's mother stilled her hands beneath the hot water and turned to eye her son. Her hair flourished as she did so, it seemed to take minutes for the straight brown strands to settle once they had started. Although a typical mother to dote on her two children, she always seemed to be one not to step into bullshit. Yet either Michael's act had been worthy of an award, or the boy had actually looked as pathetic as what he was aiming for, as his mother began to wear a worrying look over her face, as her eyes whisked over the boy at the table. She took in his posture, his bloodshot eyes and the fact that he hadn't even managed to don a shirt before sitting himself at the table for breakfast—all of it seemed to weigh in the boy's favour.

'You don't seem yourself today.' Her lips pursed as she frowned at her son. 'First Jack, now you. What is happening to this family?' She turned back to the dishes and continued to work away at a particularly stubborn morsel of burned bacon, which for the past three minutes had resisted any attempt by Grace to remove its blackened flesh from the now sudsy and slippery pan. 'Once you're done, you can go back to bed and sleep, nothing else. If your father comes home and finds you anywhere but in bed, you know what he'll say.'

A sigh of relief rushed out of the boy's mouth as he settled his back against the oak dining room chair. The kiss of the cold timber against his still warm torso made him spasm slightly, but now as he settled, the currently cool timber was such a nice feeling, one to start a nice day. His act had worked. 'Thanks, Mum. I'll apologise to Dad when he gets home.' The boy pushed back the chair, and a yawn escaped his gaping jaw as he rose to his feet. His eyes had begun to water. Maybe his success in fooling his mother should not be put down to his acting skills after all. Now that his belly was full from the warm eggs and hard bread, Michael felt dead tired. He raised his arms above his head again and yawned with a tremendous noise as he stretched both of his skinny arms. Grace had turned to watch her son once more as he stood there. With a laugh, she flicked her wet hand in his general direction. Drops of warm soapy water flew from the tips of her fingers as she swung her hand.

'Come on now, enough of that.' The woman laughed, 'Go to bed before you make me start.'

Michael mumbled his apologies as he wiped his belly with one hand while rubbing his red, weeping eyes with another. He made his way back to his bedroom and looked forward to climbing back into his sagging mattress and perhaps pulling one of the woollen, itching blankets over him for a while for some comfort. As the boy opened the door to his bedroom, a cool gust greeted him. The window above his bedhead still remained open, and thankfully, the slight breeze had positioned itself just so that it gently worked its way into the room. Behind him, still at the sink working furiously at the chunk of charcoaled bacon, his mother yawned loudly and then yelled after him, 'See what you've done now?!' Michael laughed as he closed his bedroom door and lay on his bed.

He pulled a blanket over his naked chest and laid his head down gently on the duck down pillow. Clumped and knotted, the pillow was in a good need of an airing and a shakedown, yet anything was better than lying on the bench seat of the Whippet. Now that the room was cooler, he was sure to get some sleep. As he lay his hand down in front of his face, he noticed a white mark on one of his hands. He squinted his bloodshot, watery eyes and strained to see what it was. He dabbed at the spot with a finger, powder of some sort, like plaster. The boy remembered the plaster chunk in the Whippet, what was it? He thought of Jack across the hall, what was he doing? But the thoughts, as with last night, never took hold, as the blanket he had thrown over himself had already begun to drive him crazy with itch.

Michael threw it off, rolled onto his back and thought randomly, *I haven't read my book for a while, that will put me to sleep.* He yawned again and lifted himself to a sitting position while his red eyes scanned the room for 'The Lord of the Rings.' Eager from the snap of an idea to delve into the book, at least that way, he could report to his father that he had achieved something in his day at home, apart from just sleep. However, try as he might, he couldn't find the damned book. He had searched in all the usual places, his backpack, his cupboard, under the bed. His room wasn't that big, but if his mother was to be believed, you could hide a herd of bull elephants amongst his few possessions. As it were, he could definitely hide a book.

Each new idea, under that shirt or under those piles of socks, had been rendered useless, and it seemed that the boy was left with his imagination for the rest of the day. Defeated, he lay on the bed once more, and he yawned again, his arms and legs stretched as he did so. It took him less time to forget about that book than what he had spent searching his room for it. 'It will turn up,' a quick dismissive thought threw it out of his mind altogether. Within another five minutes, the boy had fallen asleep, a stone-hard, dreamless sleep, the kind where your body repairs.

A clap of thunder reached into the boy's state of sleep, grabbed him by the navel and dragged him back into the world. Bewildered, the boy looked around his now dark room. His face was wet from the rain which had shot in through his open window, and as he peered outside, he could barely see a thing. The world had gone dark with the storm that had brewed in the skies above. Rain cut horizontally through the air on the back of tremendous winds that shook the window in its frame and howled like a pack of dogs in the night. The boy had absolutely no idea how long he had slept, and he couldn't tell whether the darkness was from the storm or if he had slept through the whole day. His head pounded with a headache from dehydration, and his muscles still felt weak from sleep. His arms strained as he pulled on the window and dragged it downwards in its tracks. The moment it closed, the world seemed to quiet. The howling wind was still audible, though, as was the rain as it slammed into the corrugated iron tool shed outside. It was quieter in his room, yet he couldn't hear anything else in the house. Still disorientated, the boy climbed from his bed. As he wiped the water from his face, he picked up one of his still dirty work shirts from the previous week. The temperature seemed to drop with the storm, and the boy felt a chill through his spine as he slid the smelly work shirt over his head, not bothering to undo the buttons that sealed it.

As he opened his bedroom door, he could see that Jack's was still fastened to the outside world. No light emitted from under the crack. Grace was in the kitchen, right where Michael had left her. She worked in the sink, probably still on the same chunk of charcoaled bacon, yet her hair had changed. In the morning, he noticed that the steam from the hot water had listed through her long brown hair as it hung down by her shoulders. Now it was knotted into a bun fastened by elastics at the back of her head. As the boy ambled into the dining room and sat back at the same chair he had before he went to bed, his mother turned to him and smiled. Always loving, this woman. 'Good evening, sleepy head.' She said gently as she smiled at her youngest.

'What?' the boy said, still half asleep in his state. Had she said evening? 'What time is it?' He felt as though he had only just gone to bed, surely, she was teasing him.

'It's near six o'clock. Your father will be home soon.' She turned back to the sink. From his position, the boy could see that she was plucking a duck in the sink, getting ready for dinner. Thunder cracked outside the Baker's house, and the structure seemed to tremble on its foundations. 'It's really coming down now, powers out and all. It's a good thing you stayed home today, I think.' His mother spoke softly, barely audible over the rain. Barely visible in the darkness of the kitchen. The only source of light came from the kitchen window, but even then, only darkness seemed to be glooming out there. Now and then, a flash of lightning would strike down at the earth in the distance, and the dining room would be lit up like daylight. Enormous shadows cast onto the walls, forming Grace's silhouette. Her hands worked with the skill of a butcher as she shed the duck of its plain brown and green feathers, her eyes searched through the rain dark window in front of her.

'Where's Jack?' Michael asked, his eyes now drawn to the window above the sink. This was some storm, his mother was right. Thank God he stayed home in bed, imagine walking home in this. The house smelt of rain, which was beautiful, but storms like this always left damage in their wake. When it subsided, the Bakers would find either the tool shed mostly destroyed or countless trees obstructing the fire trail. The Whippet would need to be salvaged from under the collapsed shed and would spend the entirety of the day carting the men around the fire trail, bouncing and sliding across the waterlogged dirt road from one deadfall to the next.

'Still in his room. Haven't seen him all day,' his mother sighed. The poor thing was probably excited at the prospect of spending time with her two sons for one blessed day, only to find loneliness. 'Hope he's feeling better, the poor sod.'

Michael was sure that Jack was fine. He had the suspicion that the big man probably used near the same act his younger brother had to get out of a day at the mill, although he would never voice it to his mother. The thought of big Jack Baker, all muscle and bone, sooking up to his mother pretending to be sick made Michael want to laugh out loud. It was something he wished he could have seen.

A gleam of light shone through the kitchen window, and Grace turned her head to investigate. The light danced across the kitchen and dining room as the twin beams of the Fairlane 500 bounced and swayed while the big hulking iron made its way through the gate from the fire trail.

'Your father's home,' Grace proclaimed, with no emotion in her voice at all. She was probably thankful that tight ass Tony had not spent the money to buy her the electric oven that she had asked for, as nights like this would have been a problem for her. She would be able to provide a meal for her family using the old wood fire oven and stove system, which they still had. Fire did not require electricity to work, at least not in the Baker's residence. As the Fairlane moved down the drive, the light shone directly into the kitchen window, his mother turned her head and squinted her eyes as she did so. The shadow cast by the twin beams of the old car was like that of a dragon in the way it spread itself across the plaster. The boy was mesmerised by the shifting and changing darkness and never replied to his mother.

As the car came nearer, the lights dipped and jumped with each rise and fall of the uneven surface of their drive. The shadow changed from a dragon to a warrior, then finally back to a woman as the bright light disappeared when the big car moved down to the side of the house, to the safety of its carport. He came back into the world from his slight daydream and rubbed his eyes again while he sat silently at the table. There was nothing really for him to do but greet his father when he walked through the back door and sit silently while his red-faced old man lectured him on having a routine, so on and so forth.

Perhaps the boy would even cop a hit upside the head. Everything depended on the day that Tony Baker had, the rain tended to make people happy, but happy people tended to make his old man mad. Only time would tell.

Outside, the sound of the Ford's engine died, and the remnants of the light that still emitted from the twin beam headlamps was extinguished soon after. The wind continued to howl with such anger and ferocity, and the rain continued to pound into the corrugated iron of the tool shed. The sound of the car door closing never came. Eventually, the hulking shape of the old man was visible at the rear screen door. The big man burst through the door with such force and speed anyone would have thought he had the devil on his ass, and his eyes were fixed on the boy. The man's face was red with anger. His hair, though cropped, was wet and clung to his head as water dripped from its tips and ran down the red face of Tony Baker. The man wore his blue chambray work shirt, with no embroidery, darkened by the amount of water that lay within the weaves of the fabric. His hands were also wet, water traced the thick, coarse hairs on his arms and dripped from his fingers as he stormed toward the boy. In his right hand, he held a book. The cover dripped with water and mud, which caked near the entire front cover. He held the keys to the Fairlane in his left hand, which he lobbed onto the kitchen table as he stormed past it to the boy. His mother, startled by the look in her husband's eyes, had not said a word, she just stood helpless as she held the half-plucked duck in her hand at the sink.

As his ferocious father rounded the table, he began to move his right hand up with speed. He roared the words, 'I hope you enjoyed your day!' as he brought the sopping wet and mud-caked, hardcover book into the boy's face. The force of the blow knocked Michael backwards off his chair, and his flailing legs came up to kick the underside of the kitchen table. There was a crash as the table settings, and the keys flew into the air and crashed back down again onto the oak top. His nose squashed into his face as the cover of the book slammed into it. He felt the wetness of the cover and mud splatter into his hair as he went tumbling backwards to the hardwood floor. He could taste blood as the world spun around him. The oak chair he was sitting on crashed and broke beneath him, splintering timber and back braces snapped under the boy's weight and the force of the fall. His head reeled from the frontal impact, then blackened for an instant as the floor rushed up to hammer into its rear. 'Are you missing something?' his father roared at the boy sprawled on the floor. The sound of his mother's scream was barely audible. Michael had no sense of what was happening. His father towered over him, his figure illuminated by another flash of lightning in the distance, the expression on his face was pure anger. The big man threw the book into Michael's gut, which made him rise into a semi-crunch. In his pain and bewilderment, Michael had time to lift the cover of the book to his face. He tried to make out the title on the mud-caked cover before his father's hands pulled him to his feet and dragged him towards the screen door.

'I want you to see what you have done!' The father screamed as he dragged the boy. The book was still in his hand as they neared the door. His mother screamed something to her husband as she chased them. She still held the duck in one hand while the other was to her face, spreading feathers throughout her hair and over her clothes. The big man slammed the boy's head into the screen door, just as he had done so many years ago and continued to drag him around the house. Behind him, he heard the screen door slam closed on its hinges, then open and slam once more as the shrieking Grace Baker followed them into the rain. The rain stung his face and his arms as it hit. The wind was so strong that the boy felt as though it would blow him away if not for his father's iron-clad grip. Tony threw his son down in front of the Fairlane's front end. The heat from the enormous V8 engine could be felt from even here.

'Look at it! Look what you've done!' The big man screamed into his face as he pointed at the chrome grille of the big car. Once straight and seamless, the chrome grille and bumper of Tony Baker's prized Fairlane 500 was crumpled and pushed inwards from a point. 'A tree fell in front of me.' His father was still barely an inch away from him. 'I try and slow down to turn around, but the brake pedal was jammed by your fucking book!' He roared those last words. The boy could smell the tobacco on his breath; he felt as though spittle had also landed on his face, but it was impossible to tell with the rain. The Fairlane's carport was a roof with four legs. The rain rode the back of the rushing winds and came straight under it. No shelter could be found under a roof with no walls.

Grace stood behind them, duck still in hand but with both hands to her face, struck silent by the sight of the crumpled chrome fender. Tony raised his hand and struck the boy open-palmed across the face. The blow drove Michael to the ground, and his face fell into the soft, wet grass. Water got into his eyes, and the taste of blood became mixed with mud and grass. Tony pushed his son's face into the ground with one of his hands. 'Do you have anything to say?'

Michael couldn't talk even if he wanted to. The hand on the back of his pounding head pushed his face into the grass every time he opened his mouth, either to scream in terror or cry out, more grass and mud seemed to rush in.

'Tony, please stop this!' Grace pleaded with her husband; tears visibly streamed down her face along with the heavy rain and duck feathers.

'Shut the fuck up!' Tony roared at her, yet relenting his grip on the back of the boy's head enough so that he could lift his head to draw in a wet breath of air. Just past the tool shed, a bolt of lightning struck a gum tree; the sheer light was blinding, but the crack of thunder that hit them was almost instant. The tree exploded in a mess of splintered timber and burning leaves. The impact shook the ground beneath them and drowned out the furious argument between husband and wife. Splinters of timber rained down on the three as they shouted and screamed at each other in the rain. The flash of light had started to drown out, but the ringing in the boy's ears seemed eternal. Tony's grip on Michael was gone, his attention was now on his wife as they argued. His father pointed at the crumpled chrome of the Fairlane, while Grace pointed at the crumpled mess of a boy lying in front of it. Michael's resolve broke, he needed to get inside out of the rain, away from his father. He needed to get to Jack; he had helped him before, and maybe he'd help again. As he got to his feet as fast as he could the rain pelted down on him like miniature bullets crashing into his skin; they burned as they hit. He shot past his parents, seemingly unnoticed, and burst through the screen door. His feet pounded the hardwood floor. The house was still submerged in darkness, not a sound apart from the boy that ran for his life. The table was askew from where his legs had slammed into its underside. He was almost past the table and into the hallway that led to his own room and his brother's when two hands clamped down on his shoulders, and he felt their weight drag him down to the floor.

'JACK!' The boy screamed as his father took him to the ground and began driving his fists into the boy's face and body, 'JACK, HELP ME!' He screamed as he cried. The tears filled his eyes as his father's fists slammed into his body. Michael realised he still held the book and tried to shield himself with it, but the book barely softened the blows. The sound of the man's fists pulverising him was sickening, as if someone had a bag of meat and was hitting it with a bat. One blow took the boy in the brow, and the world reeled once more.

In his semi-conscious state, the boy saw his mother hit Tony across the face with the only thing she could think of, the half-plucked duck. This made Tony pause for a split second. A clump of wet feather clung to his cheek, along with a sinewy slime from the meat. The big man left the boy and turned on his wife as she continued to hit him with the duck. When a fist took her in the chin, she went to the ground, and the big man went with her. Dazed as he was, he could hear what he thought were the thundering blows of his father's hands hitting his mother, but they were out of time. Instead of sounding like a bat hitting a bag of meat, it sounded like a hammer on a wall; it echoed through the house. The boy lay and watched as his father lay another fist and another into Grace's body. She had stopped screaming, her hands weren't even up in front of her, and she didn't even try to defend herself. As one final massive blow fell onto his mother's face, her body flinched, and her leg kicked from underneath her husband. Then she laid still.

Tony Baker rose from his wife, his hands red with blood and turned on Michael. The boy was still dazed from the blow on his brow, yet he pumped his legs and his arms to try and take himself backwards. Tony bore down on him, his hands still in fists, his face was red with fury, and the feather still clung to his face. He leaned down to grab at the boy until a voice stopped him.

'Enough!' Jack's booming voice shook through the kitchen and made Michael jump. Tony began to advance on his eldest son but stopped dead in his tracks. Michael lifted himself to a sitting position to look at his brother, who had finally come out of his bedroom, but he feared that Jack was too late. Another bolt of lightning struck the earth in the distance, and the kitchen was illuminated for another second. Jack's head was no longer bandaged. A great scab was on his forehead, but no blood ran down his face. His torso was bare, and his massive hairy chest seemed to be wider than the hallway he stood in. He wore clean blue jeans and his work boots, everything cleaned by his mother, everything presentable. In his hands, he held a rifle that seemed as though it was from another century. The barrel seemed tremendously long, and its receiver was bulky and dark, the metal was knurled and discoloured with age, the timber as dark as his brother's eyes. The hole at the muzzle of the gun seemed to stretch forever, and his brother's arms bulged from the weight of it.

'You'd bring a gun into this house? What would your mother think?' Tony spoke quieter now but firm as ever as he tried to stand over his son. There was still a threat in his stance, but he did not advance any further on his eldest son. Likewise, Jack stood motionless, his dark eyes fixed on his father, the muzzle of the rifle trained on his old man, his jaw muscle working.

'What would my mother think?' Jack boomed. 'Why don't you ask her?' The men continued to stare each other down. Neither of them moved or glanced toward Grace, only Michael did. His mother still hadn't moved. In the darkness, he couldn't make out her face, but she had taken some pretty big hits. The boy hoped she was okay.

'You going to shoot your old man?' Tony tried a different line as he went to move past his wife and edged towards Michael. With the slightest movement of his boot, Jack raised the rifle in his hands, the hulking shape loomed in the darkness, the size of it. Jack never answered his father. The two men stood silent for some time until Michael, overwhelmed with the whole thing, sobbed. Tony turned his gaze from Jack to look at the boy still on the ground, tears rolling down his cheeks. 'We all pick our weapons in life, son,' Tony spoke softly now. 'Your brother here uses his tears like a woman.' The old man turned his gaze back to his eldest son, the muzzle of the gun still trained on him. 'You pick yours now.' Tony lunged at Michael, his fists raised. The boy lay there unmoving, shocked at what was happening. His father turned on his feet to face him, he lowered his head and raised his fist, ready to lay into him again. His brother turned smoothly and calmly, turned the rifle's muzzle in his hands.

The kitchen was filled with light once more, but there was no lightning this time. It was filled with a tremendous sound of earth-shattering thunder, but the sound didn't come from the heavens. Fire spat from the muzzle of the big rifle, over and over and over again. It kept coming, the flashes of light, the sound of the devil's breath never ended. Everything kept coming, except his father. Blood sprayed the walls and peppered Michael's face. At first when the warmth hit him, he didn't even realise it, he just blinked. As if something as simple as blinking could wipe it all away. As each shot rang out, his father became a lesser version of himself. Torn apart inch by inch, until finally he fell, dismembered and disembowelled. His life stolen from him, carried away by the thunder of the machine in his son's hands. His father's disfigured body lay on the ground and still the fire didn't relent. More blood flowed, and more fire cut through the air, nearly exploding Michael's ear drums with its tremendous roar.

Finally, it stopped. Jack didn't move at first, only his jaw muscle continued to work. Michael was frozen. He didn't know whether to cry, run, or curl up and wait for Jack to do the same to him. His father lay at his feet, an unrecognisable mess. The sheer power of the old thing in his brother's hands shocked him. How could a man so strong, so fierce as Tony Baker, be turned into this puddle of mess that was seeping into the hardwood floor just like that?

His brother walked towards him, the rifle still in his hands. Each footfall seemed to boom in the boy's ears like the rifle had done just a moment before. Michael couldn't move. He was covered in the life of his father; the whole room seemed to be covered in it. The dark figure of his brother stood over him, his mother motionless at his back. Jack's face was covered in darkness, his chest rose and fell slowly with each breath he took. He shifted the weight of the long, dark rifle in his massive hands and removed a solid, long magazine from the ancient grey bulk. He placed it on the kitchen bench, and from the pocket of his freshly cleaned jeans, he pulled another and jammed it in place. *Why does he need another?* the boy asked himself as his brother racked a handle on the left side of the bulking grey frame. Michael couldn't talk, he could barely breathe, his chest felt as though a tonne of bricks lay on it.

'This was all you,' Jack boomed as he raised the rifle and settled the stock into his shoulder. The gaping muzzle was not even a foot away from his face. Smoke still listed from the enormity of its hole. It hung there as it swayed with the big man's breath. The boy struggled a breath in, his mouth was dry. *This is my last.* The thought swam in his head.

Light poured into the kitchen window, as before, but it lingered, unlike lightning. Jack's face was illuminated, as was most of his upper body. The grey metal looked somehow even darker in the light than before. The black eyes of his brother disappeared as he squinted against the intensity of the light on him, he began to turn his head towards it. As he did so, the light began to sway and move just as the brilliance of the twin beams from the Fairlane had earlier. Just as suddenly as they appeared, they were gone, and the faint glow of red replaced it. Outside, the sound of an engine that roared at the red line could be heard as it faded. Someone was running away.

Jack turned his head to the boy once more and lowered the rifle slightly. 'Your life belongs to me now, understand?' His voice was softer, yet it still boomed in the now deadly silent dining room of the Baker's residence. He turned, stepped over his motionless mother and walked toward the rear door. He stopped only to pick something up from the oak table Michael had broken his fast on this morning. He left and took the rifle with him. Michael lay there while shock still soaked into him. Outside, he heard the faint whirring of the

Fairlane's starter motor, then a roar as the engine sprang to life. As the roar intensified, the hulking iron could be heard stalking through the fierce rain, off in chase.

It took Michael what seemed like hours to move after Jack had left. His father still hadn't moved, yet a horrible smell had begun to rise from his destroyed body. Fluid of what seemed like every colour flowed from his flesh. It was the fluid, as it progressed toward him, that made the boy move. The feeling of being covered in the remnants of his father's body was more than enough for him; he didn't want to bathe in it. He struggled to his feet; his legs trembled horribly underneath him. He took two steps and vomited, his whole body wretched while he strained, as bile more than food flowed from his mouth. His eyes burned from the number of tears that had poured forth from them today. However, he knew this wouldn't be the last of them for a while.

He was still holding the mud-caked hardcover book. He lifted it to his face with one trembling hand, and with the other, he wiped at the cover. The mud and grime had worked its way into the coarse lining, and it took some effort for the boy to work his way through the filth to the gold lettering which lay beneath. As each cursive letter became visible, the effort in the boy's strokes and wipes became weaker. Once the words 'Rings,' 'Fellowship,' and 'Tolkien' were clearly legible, he let the book fall from his hands altogether. The mud-caked cover landed flat in a pool of his father's blood and bile and splashed it onto his bare legs.

Once his body had relaxed enough for him to move again, he struggled over to his mother. The half-plucked duck was still in her hand. However, the grip on its neck was loose, rather than being clasped like before. Her eyes were open slightly, her mouth as well. Her face had taken a horrible shape from the blows her husband had given her. The skin around her eyes was dark, and blood ran from her nose. Michael placed a shaking hand on her cheek; she was warm to the touch.

'Mum.' He pressed her cheek for a bit, but she didn't respond. He placed both trembling hands now on her face and shook her slightly. 'Mum?' His voice broke, and the tears were coming again. The boy placed both hands on her shoulders and shook her as hard as he could. 'MUM!' He screamed at her, his eyes closed with the tears, and his voice was gone in sorrow. Grace Bakers's head lolled as her son shook her. When he stopped shaking her, her head rolled slowly to her right, her mouth still open, and only the whites of her eyes were visible. A small trickle of blood began to run from her mouth. With nothing left to do and nowhere to run, Michael curled up next to his mother and wept.

PENELOPE

'I hope you got your things together
I hope you are quite prepared to die
Looks like we're in for nasty weather
One eye is taken for an eye
Oh, don't go 'round tonight
It's bound to take your life
There's a bad moon on the rise
There's a bad moon on the rise.'

Creedence Clearwater Revival – *Bad Moon Rising* (1969)

The storm had not affected the Darcy lot as it had the Bakers. Penelope stood over the sink of their fairly modern kitchen when an enormous gust of wind vibrated through the house. The children were always afraid of storms like this, but deep down in her heart, Penelope loved them. She loved the way the wind threw her shoulder length, auburn hair behind her as it hit her full in the face. She loved the rain, the smell of it in the air. The feel of it on her skin, as it ran down her freckled arms. Most of all, she loved the way it took her back to when she was a child.

Penelope reminisced with a soft smile on her face while she stood at the sink and peeled potatoes. She had grown up on a wheat plot from nearby Jandowea and had often worked on the family's fields. Although, she was not at all unhappy with the life that her and her husband had made for themselves, she missed those early days.

She missed the feeling of a hard day's work, even if it was on the back of her father's old header. She missed the sun beating down on her and most of all, the rain when it came. She loved the way the wheat shook in protest as the wind and the water pushed it about like a small child in a playground. She loved the smell that came out of the ground when the water hit after so, so long without.

Admittedly, it wasn't far from Chinchilla to Jandowea, but when she had followed Paul to play house, she had never returned to the wheat fields. There had been no need, she was more use to her family standing where she was, in front of the sink making their supper rather than walking through the fields.

She sighed as a crack of thunder rumbled outside the window and glanced through the window before her. More often than not, her husband Paul would visit the Baker's lot before journeying the rest of the way down the fire trail. This was one of those nights. She could picture her Paul in the quaint living room of the Baker's small house while his handkerchief mopped the rain from his forehead as Tony and himself witnessed the carnage of the storm through the kitchen window. Probably a beer each, cigarette smoke thick in the small room, as there is no place outside the Baker's residence to enjoy the taste of a cigarette without being drenched in this torrential, awe-inspiring rain.

She tutted to herself as a bitter feeling crept over her. *All good for Paul to go out and earn the money, drink and smoke cigarettes each and every afternoon.* What did she get to do? Playing house had sounded like a game, but playing it had meant she'd given up so much more than the wheat fields. Paul was such a generous man, he wouldn't allow her to do the chores he saw fit for a man to do. Cutting timber for the fires in winter, fixing fences when old gums came down and trashed them, to name a few. Both of which were chores that she had completed as a child. Although chores in nature, she had enjoyed them.

Now she was tasked with sewing miniature overalls for her youngest so that he could look like Paul.

A long streak of lightning cracked its way across the sky to explode six-hundred feet from her window. She frowned as the brilliant light cast shadows across her face. More fences would need fixing tomorrow. But that wasn't her problem now, was it? She sighed as she placed the freshly peeled potato into the pot along with the others. She didn't hate Paul. In all honesty, she loved him with all of her heart. Sometimes, she just felt like one of the geese they used to keep, wings clipped so they couldn't stray.

As another ferocious streak of lightning hammered down to land somewhere on the other side of the mills firetrail. She wished her husband would just come home and be safe. The thought of him driving the wet and muddy fire trail on a night like this in their old Holden ute made her nervous. The old cars were not as stable as the newer ones on the road, and they couldn't afford a new car. Paul had been saving to buy himself one of the newer HQ series but had spent the money on the new kitchen for his Penny. To be honest, Penny probably would have preferred the car.

Penny. Her husband was always shortening people's names, whether they liked it or not. She turned the handle on her electric oven to begin preheating. She screwed up her face as she looked at it. She appreciated the convenience of the new oven and cooktop, no more smelling of an old bushfire, no more singed hairs from flares, no more kindling and ash. After long days, it was a hell of a lot easier to just turn a switch than to build a fire.

Grace Baker had eyed the oven lovingly, the first time she had visited. The clear glass, the plastic knobs, the coiled stove elements, she had run her hand over the cool elements and sighed under her breath. Penelope felt for her. The poor thing never seemed to be spoilt the way Paul had tried to spoil her. Then there were times when she envied Grace as well. Penelope couldn't see Tony Baker complaining if Grace did as she pleased, as long as dinner was on the table when he got home.

'Mum.'

A voice behind her. Penelope screamed, the pot of potatoes next to her toppled over into the sink. She swore beneath her breath and then held a hand to her mouth as she realised her daughter had probably heard her.

'Susan Darcy, don't you ever sneak up on your mother ever again, do you hear me?' Penelope's left hand was to her chest as her heart thudded within. Her cheeks were bright red with her embarrassment of swearing in front of her child. She knew they were in country but she didn't want her girl to grow up with a mouth like that.

Susan was a sweet girl who had her mother's deep red, fiery hair and her father's blue sky eyes. Her faintly freckled cheeks were dimpled from the smile on her face, and she swayed slightly with amusement, both of her hands clasped together behind her back. She was donned in a summer dress, the floral pattern similar yet different altogether to her mother's, the way the roses interwove the lilacs. The edelweiss like stars in the night sky ready to greet the morning as the old song suggests.

Penelope pulled a face at her daughter, who returned the gesture by sticking her tongue out and crossing her eyes. She laughed as outside, the storm raged on, lightning flashed, but the well-illuminated kitchen and dining room of the Darcy's residence was barely affected.

'It is a warm night,' her daughter replied. 'It's bad when it storms on a warm night.'

'Hmmm,' Penelope thought about the statement as she continued to smile down at her daughter. It was always bloody warm in central Queensland, but she supposed when it stormed, it never did it half-assed.

'Mum, is Dad going to be okay in the storm?' Her smile faded at this enquiry, her hands still clasped together behind her back. As she looked up at her mother, her eyes seemed to grow. Penelope smiled at her daughter. So many kids these days were only out for themselves and what people would give them, not her Susan. The darling child would always help and always thought of others before herself. A trait that would no doubt see her grow into a wonderful woman.

'Your father will be fine. Now, where is Billy?' The youngest of the Darcy family was Billy. If Susan's face held the promise of her mother's beauty, Billy's was a carbon copy of his father. His fair hair and round face, shone his innocence through his worriless smile.

'He's sleeping,' Susan said. Lightning cracked again nearby. This time, the lights flickered slightly. Penelope frowned as she raised her eyes to look at the globe in its batten. The light emitting from the glass bulb was bright once more, but the last thing she needed was for the power to go out. Despite Grace's fondness of the electric stove and cook top, it would be the Darcy's going hungry tonight if they lost power. Not the Bakers.

Amid the roar and clap of the thunder, a faint whirring noise could be heard. Penelope peered out of the kitchen window. Two beams of light cut through the darkness. 'See Suzie, your father's home now.' As the woman reassured her daughter, a smile did not spread across her face but another frown. The headlights jolted in the darkness. The beams came toward the house too quickly for the old Holden's standard crawl down the drive. She strained her eyes to see the Holden clearer through the rain speckled glass. A gust of wind howled deeply through the crevasses of the house, and the pane of glass rattled slightly in its frame. As the old Holden hitched and bounced down the drive, the beams of light went with it. Penelope saw the back end of the old ute slide out to the left dramatically as the driver took a gentle turn. Penelope's concern deepened as the

Holden ute roared toward them.

Wet stones and gravel sprayed the porch as the old ute slid to a crooked halt, partially off the drive. The brightness of the headlights vanished off into the fields as the sound of its tired engine was cut. Her husband spilled from the car. He didn't even close the driver's door as he ran flat out to the kitchen door. As Paul climbed the steps, his feet went out from under him, and he sprawled on the deck with a loud thud. The impact would have hurt. His Akubra fell to the ground, as the fabric was darkened by the rain that pounded it. Paul left it where it lay, and sprung to his feet to burst through the door.

'Paul, what's wrong?' Penelope quizzed as her brow furrowed. His face was pale and his hair was wet and clung to his scalp. The bright blue of his eyes seemed somewhat greyer tonight. He tried to grab his wife. Something had scared the man to death. 'Paul, what's happened?' His eyes didn't settle on anything for more than a second before they darted off once more to another corner of the room or the window. She felt like slapping him so to bring him to his senses.

'Oh, Christ, Penny,' the man said as he ran to the door and flipped the switch for the lights in the kitchen. The room was thrown into darkness. Her husband ran to the kitchen window and leaned into it. His grey-blue eyes squinted to see out into the storm. 'Oh Christ, honey.'

'Paul, you're scaring me,' the confidence in her voice waned at his. She had never seen him this way, although she saw herself as a strong woman, she didn't marry a sook of a man. Something terrible must have happened for him to act like this. An emptiness filled her stomach, and her arms were covered in gooseflesh.

'Mum. What's wrong?' Susan was still in the room. In the commotion, Penelope had forgotten about her daughter. Her hands were no longer behind her back but down by the sides of her summer dress. In the darkness, the hints of edelweiss could still be seen across the light fabric. The woman rushed to her daughter in the darkness and held her face to her stomach.

'It's okay, honey. Your father's just worried.' She watched as Paul ran out of the room and into the cellar. He muttered, 'Oh Christ,' as he went. Susan had begun to sob; the mother, although not much of a crier was tremendously upset to see Paul this way and was not far behind her. He had scared the shit out of them. The thunder roared above them, and the wind howled again. The house shook as the built up air rushed around its foundations. The rain continued to hammer into the side of the house, and the kitchen window was a blur of rain and shadows.

Paul emerged again, his old Enfield rifle in one hand, a tumble of ammunition in the other. 'Paul, what is going on? You're scaring us,' she said, the tone of her voice shakier than she would have liked with the terror that had crept up inside her. Her husband looked at her and paused, the bolt of the Enfield open, two rounds in the magazine, another in his hand which trembled so much the point of the bullet was a blur in the darkness.

'Tony's boy went mad,' he stumbled across the words. 'He's killed all of them.'

'Michael?' Susan cried, her tears now soaked into the floral pattern of her mother's dress. A dark spot had begun to form where her face was pushed into her mother's belly.

'I-I- I went around to see Tony.' The man's voice shook even worse now; his eyes were back on the breech of his rifle as he tried to put another round of old military ammunition into the magazine. His hand quivered so badly he dropped the bullet, it bounced and skittered across the highly polished hardwood floor. 'Oh Christ,' the man moaned again as he went to his knees to retrieve the metal casing. The scratching sound of the brass case, as it rolled around in circles on its rim, was cut short as the man grabbed it. His voice became heavy with panic and grief. 'I had my lights off in the truck so as not to blind them as I came in. I was at the back door when it all happened.' He trembled so badly now that in the dark, he had tried to put the round of ammunition into the rifle backwards. He fumbled and struggled to push the metal case downwards into the magazine while he became increasingly frustrated with each failed attempt. 'He shot them all, hon.'

'Who shot who?' Penelope, in her fear, had not taken in all that her husband had said. She didn't understand why the rifle was in his hands, why they were in darkness. The heat from the oven warmed the kitchen; otherwise, the atmosphere had become icy, unliveable. A cold chill ran up her spine.

'You better call old Jerry, I–I–I…' the man trailed off. Now he was asking her to call the police? Jerry Thompson was an aging man, but he was the only source of law around town since the police station at Chinchilla had closed due to a lack of resources six years ago. Jerry operated out of his own home, but that was still an hour's drive, maybe two hours in this god-awful weather. 'I panicked when I got into the car. I turned the headlights on…' his voice was low now, and she could hear the tears that he was fighting back with every sentence.

The girl at her stomach cried uncontrollably now; the whole situation had become too much for the sweet girl. Penelope rubbed her back with one hand and kept her head pressed into her belly with the other. Her eyes fixated on her husband. 'What are you saying, Paul?' Still bewildered by the scene, she couldn't grasp what he meant.

'He fucking saw me, Penny,' he looked up at her from his kneeling position, the rifle still in his hands, the last round of ammunition that he held now finally placed into the cross stacked magazine. 'I saw his eyes; he had some big old cannon in his hands. He shot them all and saw me. Oh Christ, oh Christ.'

He rose to his feet and his legs shook under his own weight. He leaned on the kitchen table as he struggled. One hand delved into the pockets of his denim jeans to drag out his handkerchief, which he ran across his forehead and jammed back into his pocket. His hands trembled, and his whole body quivered as if he was cold. 'Honey, you need to call Jerry…' he began as a light so tremendous and powerful shot through the kitchen window. Their shadows were cast onto the opposing wall, bulking great shapes. Both adults raised a hand to their eyes to shield them from the brightness. Through her fingers, Penelope could see four bright circles, a car with twin beam headlamps. The girl at her stomach still cried, while her husband to her right still muttered 'Oh Christ.' She felt hollow. 'Paul, who is that?' Her voice was quiet, almost inaudible over the wind, and their eyes were fixed on the four bright circles. Deer in a spotlight, they were all pinned to the spot, unmoving.

'Honey, call Jerry. Get the kids upstairs.' His eyes never met hers. The light shone brightly on his face and accentuated every line, every deep crevasse on his worried, stressed face. The receding hairline glowed with sweat and rainwater in the twin beams. He walked to the kitchen door, which rattled in its frame as the wind outside shot another terrible blast into the house. Everything seemed to shake; it wasn't until the wind gust settled for a moment that Penelope realised it was just her and the child she clung to.

Penelope shrank to her knees and held her daughter at arm's length. Her eyes were visibly red in the darkness of the kitchen. The twin beam lamps shone through her hair and made it look like fire, the way it wrapped around her face, the way it stuck to her wet cheek. Penelope ran her thumb under the girl's eyes to dry her cheeks and tried to reassure her that everything would be okay. A clap of thunder hammered in the skies above, and both of them jumped slightly, thinking it was the old Enfield that Paul held.

'Honey, I need you to go upstairs. Get your brother and go in Mummy's closet, okay?' Her tone was calm, but there was an underlying hint of panic. The girl began to shake her head; she still bawled. She brought the girl to her chest and hugged her tightly. 'Oh, come now, it'll be okay,' she rubbed her hand up and down the child's back. 'Come now, upstairs, go get Billy. I'll be there soon, and so will Dad. You be brave now.' She held the child away from her again. The tears had begun to subside. Her eyes still as red as her hair, her bottom lip pushed out. 'Okay?' Penelope asked slowly and quietly. Her husband was at the kitchen door now. She needed to get onto the phone. The girl nodded, then turned and ran out of the room. Small sobs could be heard as she disappeared from sight.

The kitchen door flew out of her husband's hands, caught by a gust of wind and slammed up against the frame of the house. Paul raised one of his hands to shield his eyes from the wind, rain and dazzling lights of the unknown car in their drive. Penelope rose to her feet and rushed to the pantry where the phone hung from a wall. As Paul walked out into the wind and rain, she raised the receiver and placed it to her ear. The only sound was the wind and rain; nothing came from the receiver at all. Dumbstruck, Penelope looked at the wall unit of the phone, she hammered the dial switch ferociously, staring blankly at the unit as it hung. Nothing.

Outside, she could hear Paul shouting, 'Jack, we don't want none of this.' Although Paul had a loud voice, over the storm, he sounded like a mouse; his voice still had a faint quiver in it.

Penelope stood and watched her husband move toward the twin beam lamps in front of him. His left hand, still raised to the wind, the rifle low in his right. The receiver was still pressed to her ear, so hard that it hurt. She wanted to be able to hear any faint sign of a dial tone or the operator at Chinchilla.

Still nothing.

Paul had come to a stop outside, his left hand now lower to support the rifle. The four circles were still about twenty feet in front of him, nothing else of the vehicle was visible in the darkness, just the damn headlights. Her husband shouted again; the words were lost to her in the wind. He raised the rifle in his hands and fired a round at the car. Like her husband's voice, the gunshot was barely audible. Penelope's hand went to her mouth, *My god,* she thought, *he shot at them.* This was bad. What was going on? The volley of thoughts ran through her mind. The shot from the old Enfield seemed to have done nothing, the lights still shone, and neither Darcy could see a thing past them. Her husband still stood there, rifle raised, silent. The wind howled around him; the rain partially obscured Penelope's sight of her husband.

To the left of the beams, not far, a fainter light strobed in the darkness, yet unlike the white and yellow of the halogen headlamps, this was red. As red as her daughter's hair, fire in the darkness. As it flashed, something happened to Paul. He staggered in the rain; the wind must have pushed him off balance, it looked as though a bit of shrub had hit him in the back. Where his denim vest was blue, his back was now a strange red. The red strobe flashed a few times more as one of the fire-driven bullets passed through her husband and smashed through the window of the kitchen. Penelope began to scream.

Paul fell to his knees, the rifle still in his hands. The strobe was gone; the fires burned out. Some of his blood had splattered on the glass around where the bullet had driven through, embedding itself into one of the white boarded cupboards that filled the kitchen. Penelope still screamed, tears streaming down her face, as she watched as her husband tried to lift his rifle, but the old Enfield seemed too weighty for the injured man. A shape loomed before him, the twin beams still shone. The kitchen door clanged against the frame of the house once more as the wind churned through the air. An enormous man emerged from the darkness; his bare torso rippled in the light as the rain pelted into his flesh. As his massive chest blocked the brilliant light from one bank of burning lamps, the light inside the kitchen dwindled. He stood in front of her husband, an old grey machine in his hands, as he towered above Paul. Her husband raised a hand to the man. It stretched out to him, almost as if he pleaded with him. The hulking shadowy shape of the big man didn't move. There was another flash of fire red, she watched as half of her husband's head disappeared in an instant, and his poor body, crumpled to the ground, the old Enfield fell with him.

Penelope let the receiver fall from her ear. To her, the world had gone quiet. She moved her mouth, she screamed, pleaded with the heavens for what she had just witnessed to be a hellish nightmare. It had to be wrong. The hulking shape outside moved, but not to the car; it came to her voice. The light shone in her eyes again as the hulking shape moved out of its line. The phone receiver swung on its chord and butted softly up against the wall with each pendulum. Penelope ran, her auburn hair trailed out behind her, just as her daughters had done. The light floral dress pressed to the front of her body as if to strangle her as she ran toward the stairs. Behind her, the sound of the storm still raged. Softly, under it all, there were heavy footfalls in the gravel. The woman shrieked, her voice was lost to her. She didn't know what she was saying; she didn't care.

She flew up the stairs, and tears rolled freely down her face. Her hand slid up the well-polished handrail. Her tennis shoes pounded lightly on the hall runner, which worked its way up each polished step. In the kitchen, the first booming footfall echoed. Penelope raced into her bedroom and slammed the door behind her. In the closet, she heard two sobbing voices, her two children. She opened the door too quickly, and both children screamed in terror. She sat down with them, the children all screams and sobs now. The woman was lost; her husband was lost and still the booming footsteps could be heard on the stairs. She pulled the closet door closed with one hand while she pulled her children to her side with the other. Susan's hair got into her eyes, and the tears fastened the child's hair to her cheek like glue. Billy's hand reached for her face and almost clawed at her; he was so needy.

'It's okay,' the woman said to her children, 'I'm here. Mummy's here.' She shushed her children; the tears still rolled down her own cheeks. Her mouth was loose, no longer taught with terror. The shock had settled into her. The booming footsteps echoed along the upstairs corridor, the soft rug that lined the floor doing very little to soften the blows of the big man's feet. Then they stopped.

Outside, the wind continued to howl its protest. The kitchen door could be heard below, still swinging on its hinges as it slammed into the frame of the house. Nearby, an old gum gave up its fight against the pounding stresses of the wind and rain. The sound as its trunk snapped and the smaller branches cracked while the large gum uprooted itself from the loose earth shot through the woman, and the cold chill ran up her spine once more. Then the bedroom door slammed open with such force all three of the Darcy's in the closet jumped. Her children began to cry again, all that Penelope could do was shush them gently as she rubbed their backs. Their hands pawed at her, the red hair stuck to her cheek. Her vacant eyes fixated on a small blemish on the rear of the closet door, her back pressed up against the wall. 'It will be okay; Mummy's here.'

The soft loop pile carpet of Paul and Penelope's bedroom did a sight deal better than the hall runner at softening the booming footsteps of the big man in the room. She watched in horror as the closet door opened slowly, almost gently, and the sobs of the children stayed low. Before the Darcy's stood an enormous man of height and size. The long, grey machine was in his hands, and the children did an excellent job of remaining calm. Penelope hushed them once more, 'It will be okay,' the big man in front of them raised the machine in his hands. Outside, a flash of lightning streaked across the sky, and the big man's face was illuminated. Penelope saw the darkness of his eyes, the muscle working in his jaw and the scabbed gash on his forehead. Before the fire took them, she rubbed her hands on her children's backs and thought to herself how she could ever find joy in the storms that created so much damage and carnage. Like the one that had cut their family off from any chance of help. The one that had brought this thing to their door.

'Mummy's here.'

RANKIN

As the steel bar door of his small cell was slammed home, he watched silently as the reverberations shook the dirt on the floor and made the small specks jump and quiver with fear. He hadn't said a word since the night he was laid out on the floor of his own apartment. No words came to mind of the reasons why he had committed the crime. No words of defence nor defiance, as the courthouse judge and jury had peered down at him over the rims of their glasses and the timber partition's tall walls, which separated them from the criminals and lower people. The looks on their faces as photographs of Mary's beaten face, the swollen right eye closed by Rankin's right hand. Her bottom lip was torn open by her teeth, which were now smashed, and her perfectly pointed nose had been disfigured and twisted under his wrath. Yet one blue eye, with the hint of brilliance, burned into him through the slit of the eye he had failed to close. For the grace of God, Mary had not entered the courtroom during his trial. He did not want to see her face; the photograph was enough to torment him. The bailiff had taken the photograph around to show every single person in the courtroom before Rankin was allowed to lay his eyes on it. The murmurs of anger, the hateful looks from the women in the room, the vacant expressions from the other men. There was no need to say anything in his defence. Nothing he said would achieve a damn thing. So, when they asked him to explain himself, he brought his eyes slowly from the photograph of the once beautiful Mary to the eyes of the Judge and then the jury. He paused on each set of eyes, one by one. He noticed the colours change, brown to blue, then grey and green. Furrowed eyebrows, concerned expressions, eyes welling with tears. Then once he had made contact with every set of eyes in the room that were about to judge him, he let his vision fall back to the photograph.

A man who is trained by the Australian military is classified as a weapon of war. He stood accused of using his body to inflict grievous bodily harm upon the absent plaintiff Mary Bywater. In the lack of defence presented by the defendant, Rankin Bartlett was sentenced to seven years in prison. That is what the small sixth page article listed at least under the title 'Vietnam Vet Brutalises Woman.'

Rankin never paid attention to the name of the hole that they threw him into. He doubted that prisoners of war read the word of the arches they were led under, whether it ever made a difference to them. Somewhere, he had read that the words written on the entrance to Auschwitz were, 'work sets you free' and wondered whether it was all just some twisted game. To allow prisoners to hold onto their hope, let them have that brief breath of air before their heads were plunged back into the water. Nevertheless, the prison that held him was built in the days when stone was favourable to any other material. Its high sandstone walls squeezed in on him as he stood in the grounds and looked up to their peaks. Barbed wire coils traced every edge that a man with a child's imagination could dream that an inmate within could scale. The reality was that the sandstone walls, although weathered and filled with ridges, were too smooth a surface for any man that Rankin knew to grasp a foothold. Meals were uninteresting, as were the other prisoners. Hard men that, for whatever reason, had been crammed into this shit hole to rot away their lives until a tap on the shoulder meant the time had passed and the doors were now open. From what he could gather, it would be some years before any of the thirty-eight prisoners would be given any such tap.

Although the prison held a large number of inmates, only a fraction were held within the maximum-security section. There was still a sense of dominance within that fraction. Fresh meat was ridiculed, harassed and bullied as if they were back in a schoolyard. Upon Rankin's arrival, he could tell the current victim was a small man by the name of Richard Dweyer. A squat, balding man who had the stature that brought the saying with it that it was easier to jump over him than to walk around. He had a long, hooked nose, which hung out like an overlook of his meaty lips. His eyes were small and beady and gave a man the impression that he was being gazed upon by a rodent rather than a man of the age of forty. During the first meal service he attended, Rankin was led into a room about the size of a small community hall. There were worn timber benches spread in an orderly fashion throughout. The floor was polished concrete and was lit by six large hanging halogen lamps, which burned down on the inmates like six hot suns only eight feet away.

Sounds were all amplified within the hall of concrete and sandstone: guard's heavy boots slapping against the concrete, the metal meal trays that clanged onto the timber benchtops. The raucous laughter of the imprisoned as they jeered at each other and threw insults at the guards as they walked past. The inmates were spread out more sporadically, each group of comrades bunched up together with the outsiders speckled in between, hunched over their meal trays each man was handed through a small window at the end of the hall. There were only three guards present, and they stalked the outside perimeter, their eyes darted back and forth while they hovered for what seemed years over the groups who Rankin could only guess were the ones to offer up the most trouble. Their batons in hand, like the beat cops from the old English novels.

A man with the biceps of small boulders and a chest that resembled an oak barrel, stood over Dweyer and picked the choice pieces of grey meat drowned in gravy for himself. He jammed each sopping piece into his mouth and chewed loudly, open-mouthed as spittle and pieces of his supper were ejected as he spoke.

'You're only a small man, Rat. You don't need all this food, do you?' Across the hall, a group of other men watched and laughed while the guards who continued their circle work around the edges continued their pace and their course. The small man was hunched over his tray, visibly terrified, and didn't answer.

As Rankin took his tray, his eyes searched the room for a secluded area to sit, where he didn't have to talk to anyone or look at them. He had no intentions of making friends in this shit hole. He noticed that while the big man harassed the rodent, no one's eyes had fallen upon him. He walked past the group a second time and took a seat that, although segregated him from most groups, left him seated in the middle of the room. One man's eyes fell upon him and lit up as they realised he was a new addition. The weedy looking man slapped his neighbour on the shoulder and gestured at Rankin as he sat there eating, his eyes fixated on his plate. The neighbour considered Rankin for some time, took in his hunched back, his sloped shoulders and the way he ate, then turned over to the big man who now sopped the remains of the gravy up with the rodent's last hunk of bread.

'Brian,' the man called, loud enough for the entire mess hall to hear. The man turned his meaty neck so that he could gaze on his caller as he jammed the dripping wet bread into his mouth. 'You still hungry?' The speaker gestured as the other man had at Rankin, and the giant oaf smiled as his eyes fell on the newcomer.

Brian strode over to Rankin, proud as could be, he continued to chew loudly, a grin visible across his large, stupid, tattooed face.

He stood across the bench from the newcomer and proclaimed, 'You know what? I think I am.' A heavily tattooed hand plunged into Rankin's mash potatoes. Rankin raised his eyes to look at the oaf as he slapped the mash into his mouth and spread it half across his face. That the man was a pig, there was no doubt. 'There's a rule in here, new meat. All your food is mine until I say you can eat. And since I don't remember saying it, your food is mine.' His voice was a droll rumble whose echoes bounced from wall to wall in the burning halogen light.

Rankin eyed the man, a sneer spread across his lips. He raised his fork, and grey meat hung loosely from the end. Mushed peas and specks of mash clung to its surface. Rankin delicately placed the morsel into his mouth and began to chew, an expression of bliss of the taste spread across his face as he smacked his lips and hummed his delight. The entire hall had fallen silent. Everyone's eyes, including the guards, were on the two. Even in the small window at the end of the hall where the meal trays were handed out, the cook's face could be seen, eyes large with anticipation.

Brian growled and reached over the table once more. As he leaned, he was forced to stretch, a lot of his weight placed forward over the table. As his hand was inches away from the tray, Rankin seized it and pulled. Brian's surprise was audible as he spilled forward over the bench. His face smashed into the tray and sent a shower of peas and gravy everywhere as the giant roared in disbelief. Rankin grabbed his shoulders and pulled him further over the bench, so his head overhung. He strained as he rolled the man over. All the while, he had not stood up from his chair. Rankin drove his hand deep into the mess of his own tray, and he clenched a glob of mash, gruelled meat and peas and drove it into the big man's face. Brian coughed and spluttered as he struggled to breathe under the mess of potato and gravy. Chunks of meat clung to his brow. His nostrils were completely blocked. Rankin pushed more into his mouth as he opened and tried to breathe. The whole room was quiet around him.

'Still fuckin' hungry?' he questioned. His voice echoed around the room. 'Nah, fuckin' eat up mate, a growing boy needs his strength, right?' A hand came up to wipe at his face and to clear his eyes. As it withdrew, Rankin held his fork above the man's right eye. It wavered there with his trembling hand. Nevertheless, it never swayed an inch away from the oaf's eye.

Brian spluttered as he tried to lift his immense weight from the benchtop, his teeth clenched until he saw the fork, then he froze, his neck strained to hold his block of a head up. The eyes didn't focus on Rankin, only the fork, the tremble in their tines as it wavered above his retina.

Rankin leaned close and whispered into the man's ear, 'Touch my fucking food again, and I'll eat your fuckin' eyes, then your tongue, then your ears. I won't kill you, I'll just let you walk around blind, dumb and deaf for the rest of your useless fucking life.'

The guards descended on Rankin and took him to the ground, pounding him with their batons.

For that stunt, he had spent the rest of the week in solitary confinement, which in reality was no punishment but rather a reward. Rankin had no wish to spend any amount of time with the other inmates. He didn't care why they were there. He didn't care who they were, he just wanted to be left alone.

The incident in the mess hall granted him three weeks of solace, the other inmates hadn't enough courage to attack him again for that time. Then, in the showers one day, four of them had fallen upon him. Five naked men slipped on the wet tiles as fists and feet flew through the air, it was a shit fight. Rankin came out bleeding, his nose spread across his face, but the others had taken it just as badly, one man had lost his footing in the first seconds of the fight and had slammed the back of his head against the tiles. To Rankin's knowledge, he had never seen that man before or ever since. That was the last time they had tried anything on him. They seemed to dislike the way that Rankin liked the conflict, the sneer on his face as he glared at them, the blue-grey seeming to burn straight through them. The look on his face made the other men lose their taste for blood. Their safety in numbers didn't count when their friends were uneasy and were worried at what they had bitten off.

As the weeks went by, Rankin became fond of prison life. He was awoken at the same time every day for breakfast, he had yard access at the same time, and then supper at the same time. Every day was similar in most ways, and he found it refreshing. The only time he wished he had more of was alone time in his cell. The want for whiskey had peaked at about two weeks in, his entire body had broken into shakes, and the sweat poured profusely from every pore. He had remained in his cell for three days straight, refusing any food, water or exercise, before finally, the guards had taken him to the hospital ward. The time he had spent in that ward was a blur. Semi-conscious, he had slight memories of tubes coming out of his arms. Panic-stricken, he remembered clawing at them and tearing while men draped in white and light blue gowns rushed into the room as he collapsed back into his subconscious.

The dreams were the worst part. He was visited by each of his friends, Gary, Will and Max. Each was disfigured in their own way. Gary's face was white and shrunken, and his eyes were deep within their sockets. The pale grey eyes were unblinking as he opened his mouth to talk to him. Dirt and chunks of silk began to flow, but the words were clear and echoed in the back of his mind. 'You should have killed that bitch for what she did like I killed mine.' His teeth were rotten, and even as he spoke, his incisor worked loose and was taken away with the trails of dark earth and red satin.

Will was next, the flesh on his face torn from rot. His hair clung to the half-eaten skin, patchy as massive clumps had either fallen out or were ripped from their place. His eyes were gone altogether, the sockets empty and gaping. Inside, worms and beetles slithered and crawled; they ran down his cheek and disappeared into the gaunt hole where his nose used to be. When he spoke, his voice was rattled with infection, and he began with a cough that shook the bones deep within him.

'They shit on the spikes before they dug them into the ground, Rank.' His lips curled as he spoke, the worn tendons pulled and tore as the flesh fell from his face. 'They laughed as they wiped their asses. Your blood is poisoned like mine, Rank, but you didn't die. You didn't, but I did.'

Max was the last of his friends to visit him throughout his dream state. His throat was torn open, and blood ran down in a continuous gush. He looked as though he had been dragged behind a truck for miles. One of his ears was gone, and the bright white of his skull shone through a tear in his forehead. As he spoke, the blood flow from his throat lessened, but instead, it began to pulse through every other orifice on the man's face. It spurted through his mashed nose and trickled down the side of his head from the small hole which marked the place where his ear used to jut out. The flow out of his mouth was the worse, it sprayed as he spoke, and even in his dreams, he could feel the droplets burst across his face. 'No matter how big they are, a brass kiss to the head, and they all go down the same.' He laughed at the end as the vision of his friend disappeared into nothingness. The blood rained down like a torrential shower in the jungles and painted everything.

He was called on by two others before he woke, and these two visions burned in him like fire. The first was Mary, her right eye shut forever by his fist. A trickle of blood ran down from her lower lip and pooled on the ball of her chin. As she spoke, her hair flowed around her face and sometimes hid her wounds, while at other times, it showed them in all their gore. Her voice was harsh and hateful, unlike the soft, beckoning tones from that night.

'You no dick loser, woman killer and basher. You should have died underground. That Powers boy died, yet you got out. You losers only save yourselves.' Her one visible eye burned an icy blue jet into him. He felt his gut burn when the gaze set on him like she had sunk her perfect nails into him and clawed at his intestines. As if she wanted to watch the life flow from him as she dragged out his guts for what he had done.

Finally, it was Rixon who called on him. His body swayed as his eyes pinned him. His head was at an off position to his neck as the rope that was tied around his throat trailed up into the air. The rope seemed to go up forever, to vanish into the darkness. The strands of the rough spun chord groaned as his commander swayed one way and then the other. There were large bags under his eyes, his mouth was ajar, and a thin trail of vomit ran down from the corner of his lips to leave a large stain on the front of his service greens. Yet, out of all of them, he looked the best. 'We all died over there, Bartlett. You just haven't realised it yet.' He offered no other words, he just continued to stare. His eyes followed Rankin as he swayed.

When he awoke in his cell, he had no idea what day it was, nor how long he had spent in that torture chamber of his mind. Yet the shakes his body had been racked with were gone, the pains in his gut were replaced by a fierce hunger that burned within him. His whole body howled for food, not for whiskey. As he lay on his bunk, he watched his hands trembling, the thirst that had been in him was ferocious, but the water he was served at meals did not quench it.

He was able to secure cigarettes, and he smoked them when he had them. But the one thing he wanted, the life's milk of whiskey, was always out of his reach in this cold, damp hell. Now it seemed that part of his life was almost over. His hands still shook, but it had been two months at least since his last drink, since he had tasted its glorious warmth or felt the sensation run through his body. As he lay there and watched his hands, he knew that the part of him that loved whiskey would always be there, would always be waiting for him to feel weak, fall into drunkenness, and be free.

As his hands trembled, the thought ran through his mind of what they labelled him, 'A weapon of war.' If he were a rifle, he would be handed into the armourer for servicing. The clapped-out frame and shaky grips would be undesirable to the boys that left for their patrol that day. If he were a vehicle, he would have been dumped a long time ago in favour of another more reliable choice. Even a man's own two feet would be a trade up to the poor state he was in. Even as a knife, edge once pristine and razor-sharp, with years of neglect and abuse, even the hardest steel would become pitted and rusted. The once razor edge now dull and rolled, in need of a rework. The set of knuckle dusters, once gleaming brass, highly polished and perfect. Now green with decay, the edges blurred and softer than before.

All the negativity, the harsh words, they raced over him. There were so many clouding thoughts that boxed him in. He felt as though he was underground once more, with death right in front of him, but he was just too stupid to see it, too naïve to realise that the whole world wanted him dead. Yet here he was, imprisoned but alive. He spent a lot of time thinking, as there was nothing else to do. He would lie flat on his back and study the blocks of sandstone as they trailed across the ceiling. The lines that traced the joins, the small cracks in the mortar. He thought about how many small cracks he had in his own foundations, all the flaws that could have brought him down to his death, but here he was.

He stood up, his back ached from the lack of movement and the stale position on his thin foam mattress. His eyes were tired and strained to see anything in the ill-lit cell, which was now his home. His muscles felt as though they had all gone to waste, they ached and complained with any movement. He lowered himself to his knees, his back to the cell door, and placed two hands shoulder width apart on the cold floor. As he eased himself down, he felt the cold radiate outwards and try to overcome him. It tried to suck him into itself, yet he loved it. His will would be strong enough to overcome this shit hole. He stretched his legs straight out, his bare feet clasped at the concrete for grip. With his arms bent, he raised his head to look straight ahead and saw the mortar lines trailing up the wall. At the base of a single line, it was gone altogether. Chipped away by years of hopeful inmates trying to find a way out, yet the mortar clung the whole way up even though its base was gone.

His arms bulged and he lifted the weight of his upper body skyward. He held himself there for a couple of seconds and thought, probably the only positive thoughts he had conceived since his conscription. A rifle could be serviced, its parts reworked and honed to bring the weapon into a usable condition. A vehicle could be rebuilt, its engine stripped and cleaned, being reassembled with new parts to renew its lease on life. The blade of a knife could be honed, the dull, rolled edges filed down to reveal the gleaming razor edge which was hidden just below the surface. Brass, if anything he compared himself to, seemed fitting. Funnily enough, they were the easiest to repair. A simple polish and shine and the metal block would gleam in all of its of former brilliance. He sneered and began to complete push up after push up. His muscles strained, yet the feeling in his gut was wholesome and pure.

'I'm strong enough to beat this shit.'

JERRY

'A handle hid out in the dark
A hand set the spark
Two eyes took the aim
Behind a man's brain
But he can't be blamed
He's only a pawn in their game.'

Bob Dylan – *Only a Pawn in Their Game* (1964)

'I've told myself time and time again. Jerry, you are getting too old for this shit,' the aging policeman muttered to himself as the state-owned Ford Falcon bumped and hitched over the rutted fire trail. The lines that were eroded into the gravel and stone of the road were only matched by the deep crevasses which lined the man's face. The bags under his eyes had appeared shortly before his thirtieth birthday, but now, as he neared his sixtieth, they were more apt to be called satchels. His wife had grown tired of pleading with him over and over to put the office aside and spend more time on her and himself. Yet year after year, the lines etched their way deeper into his face, the ache in his back worsened, and with each passing winter, more people left his life.

It had started with the closure of the Chinchilla Police station. With that, he had watched his whole family outside of home vanish before his eyes. He remembered watching as Harry Lewin packed his Toyota station wagon, piling each child in as if they were a piece of furniture. Then he drove past without even a look or a final wave goodbye.

His wife had taken a similar approach to leaving town, although instead of being packed neatly into the backseat restraint of an old Corona, she had been perched high up in the cab of a B-double. The old was replaced by the new. It seemed to happen with every turn of the clock. The old Holden Special was replaced by the Ford Falcon. Rusted, pitted metal, worn with the dullness of the years in the sun, replaced by gleaming white and sparkling chrome. The old lined face was replaced by one near half the age. Not even a hint of crow's feet erupted from the corner of the bastard's eyes. And yet here he remained, alone yet dedicated to his job, the office, his only place in this world.

He felt his stomach roll over and pulled the Falcon sharply to the shoulder. The wheels churned through the stones and dirt, howling in protest as the car came to a halt. The door had barely swung its entire path before his breakfast had come up. His body shook and waned as he wretched over and over again, each shiver calling up the sight of another bloated body, another blackened face. Finally, his frame began to settle, and he clasped the front guard of the Falcon as sweat lined his palm and traced his wrinkled brow. He was racked by another fierce tremble, which started in his legs and worked slowly up his spine until his entire body was jittering like when Norma O'Hara had suffered an epileptic fit in the town's greengrocer. As the shock settled into him, he strained for breath. His old lungs sucked in the hot afternoon air. Hot, yet thankfully fresh in comparison to the Darcy's bedroom.

Jerry had been phoned two days ago by the owner of the Chinchilla Saw Mill, Terry Macress. Mr Macress had expressed his concerns for Paul Darcy after two weeks had passed since the Manager, Tony Baker, had phoned to explain that the Darcys had skipped town.

Darcy had always been a solid worker for the plant, and in Macress' eyes, he was in line to replace the short-tempered Baker as manager. However, despite the phone calls to either the Darcy house, the Bakers lot, or even the mill, no one would answer either the calls of Macress or of Jerry himself. Finally, the situation smelled bad enough for the aging lawman to warrant further inspection.

The afternoon sun punished the land as fiercely as if it were ablaze. The moisture that had cut fissures into the tracks had been sucked back into the sky, leaving nothing but cracked earth and weakened trees in its wake. The first sign of a problem was found in the Darcy's drive. An enormous gum had cracked beneath the power of a lightning strike and had fallen across the neatly graded drive. As Jerry pulled the Falcon up to assess his route, he saw the ground had been churned and destroyed around the tips of its branches. The mud had moulded under the weight of a vehicle as its occupant lit up the wheels to pass through into the night. The ground would have been near sopping clay to have moulded and collapsed the way it had. Now, it was as hard as iron. The tips of the ruts were crumbling as the last dregs of moisture left them in their cast. Through the trees that lined the residence, he saw shades of white paint and the outline of an old ute, so he left the Falcon and walked the few hundred feet of drive that remained.

The sweat had already begun to soak into his shirt, pooling at his lower back where the cotton was pressed to his skin by the Falcon's lumber support. When he saw the door of the old ute ajar, the keys still in the ignition and a pool of water in the footwell, his mouth became dry. Although the town was relatively small, he had never visited any of the occupants on this stretch of fire trail apart from the Trackers up the end. Robin and Kel's halfwit brother had often gotten himself into trouble. He had often wondered who had lived down these long and windy drives as he had passed but had never had the need to find out.

The house was in beautiful order, the fact that the utility out the front would be left in such a state made him furrow his brow. The car was empty to the main extent. Papers and letters littered the cab. Nothing stood out to him as he slowly approached the open cabin door. The knob for the headlights was engaged, alas, nothing shone from the old faded lenses. Jerry turned the key, twisting it to start, but not even a click could be heard in the bowels of the engine.

He knocked only once. As his worn gnarled knuckles rapped on the oak door, it swung inward on its hinges. The house was dark, but even in the low light that clawed its way in, desperate to see what had become of the Darcy's before the lawman, he could see the footprints. Caked mud pressed into the linoleum of the kitchen, more than one set. However, only one continued into the house. Large ones, larger than the set that was spread throughout the kitchen. Unlike the smaller smeared and distorted prints that had shown the panic of their owner, these larger ones were perfect. As if the man that had created them had taken his time as he walked into this house. The mud that had once been soft had now dried, and the peaks of each scattered print crunched under Jerry's weight as he entered the kitchen.

'Hello,' he called into the house. 'Police.' Nothing could be heard, no movement from upstairs. As he took another step into the kitchen, he felt the sole of his boot connect with something, and a thin metallic sound was heard as something small and hard rolled in a circle under the dining table. Jerry kneeled, his eyes still not adjusted completely to the low light of the kitchen, his hand padded a few times before the cool kiss of metal was felt under his palm. As he squinted and held the cartridge case away from his old eyes, he noticed it was a loaded .303 casing, the faint specks of light glittered through the corrosion on its case and bullet. Jerry put it in his pocket and clambered back to his feet. No people, house empty, car open, a random bullet left on the floor.

'Chinchilla Police, anyone here?' Jerry called once more as he loosened his service revolver in its holster. The larger footprints led up the stairs, yet as he went, it looked as though they crossed back on each other. Fainter prints over the well-defined, distorting them to the eye, then fainter ones again, going back up the stairs, all the same size. At one point, he placed his foot over one whose outline was clear as day. Being a size ten himself, the print would have easily been from a size three to five times higher than his own. He whistled under his breath and continued to climb the stairs. The smell hit him before he had reached the top, thick and sour. Jerry's mouth went dry as his boots padded softly on the hall runner.

Nothing could have prepared him for what he saw. Some of the bodies were bloated, the man's especially, as his was left intact. It looked as though he had been thrown into the room. Half of his head was gone. Nothing made sense, nor would it ever again. There looked to be two small children and a woman as well, four bodies in the closet, a mess of limbs, blackened faces with distorted features. The woman's chest had sunken, and her right leg was dismembered at her thigh, which lay only inches away. Jerry coughed and brought his handkerchief from his pocket and placed it over his mouth. He looked at the way the jaw hung on the woman, cockeyed and dislodged, her nose smashed inwards.

The child to her left had lost most of their arm as it was wrapped around the woman's waist. Black cylinders that could only be fingers, were scattered like leaves to the wind. The other child's head was tilted back, her mouth ajar, and a line of faded hair ran down from (what could only have been) her head and rested among her lips. Her face had shrunken in drying, the lips receded from the gums, and her eyes had fallen back into her skull. Among the blackened rug and the blood that still covered the boards were bullet casings; most heavily stained by the blood that had eaten into the soft brass. He didn't count. He didn't want to stay in the room, yet there were over a dozen to choose from, he picked up one that had escaped the blood and left.

He stood outside for what felt like an hour, not knowing what to do. He had wanted to try to call town, but who would he call? The next police station was over at Dalby, and there was no point in asking for help just yet. His first thought was of the Trackers; thieves and cretins that they were, but killers? No, he didn't think so. In any case, no Tracker had the size foot of the gargantuan ones inside. Yet, they were his best option. The walk back to the car had been the thing he had needed. The jolting of the Falcon over the destroyed trail, on the other hand, near brought up his breakfast more than once. The hot air listed lazily through the open window and mixed with the cool air pumping through the air conditioner's vents to make a sick feeling that only worsened his state. None of this was helped by what he found in the Trackers yard.

The sun, the rain, birds and, from the looks of it, a fox, had all taken their toll on the two bodies that had been left in the yard. Parts of a man's jaw were jutting from the mess of brown shit, the white gleaming brightly against the rotting hair, fabric and flesh. One had been laid face down, presumably, Kel for the size of the remains, birds and animals had stripped the flesh from his back, something had tried to make off with part of his gut but had given up, leaving a trail of stinking brown lines trekking over the packed earth of the yard. The ground had turned dark with corruption, and the smell, although not confined, still lingered lower than the oil that seeped from the wrecks that surrounded him.

One hand kneaded at his temple while the other clasped the handkerchief over his mouth. There were more bones than flesh left of these bodies. Although they had been left out in the open for animals to get at them, he didn't believe there had been a tremendous amount of time between the killings.

He didn't bother knocking on the door this time; it was already open. The smell from within was worse than the other house, but different. Shit and rotting food, dust and wet dirt cut through the fabric of his handkerchief. Still, he held his stomach. The hole in the roof of the office had likewise allowed animals access to the house, that and the open front door. Of the dog, mostly bones remained. He found it dragged partly down the stairs, part of it left at the top of the flight, the rest could be seen in a pathetic pile at the bottom. The dog was a big breed from his memory, so he didn't think foxes could have dragged the carcass, so perhaps wild dogs had gotten in. He had heard reports of packs of the bastards in the hills to the east, hiding in the forest.

Frowning beneath the fabric, he continued around the office. The office doors had been destroyed. One had basically been torn from its hinges and thrown across the room, chairs were overturned. In the centre of the room was an ancient oak desk which at one point would have been a beautiful piece to own. Now the legs were smashed, and the desk sat lopsided, with a considerable lean. Once more, he found casings strewn across the floor, mainly in the corridor behind the desk that held another body. As he walked around the desk, he could see the damage, a hole in the wall as if someone had pulled something out from behind it, the way the plaster had burst outward. The hardwood floor was stained heavily around the body, but no moisture remained, only a shrivelled corpse, destroyed in a similar fashion to the little girl and her family.

'Seven dead.' The sound of his voice was almost a whisper as his body still shook. He had driven back out from the Trackers and had passed the drive into the Darcy's lot when the sickness had taken him. Slowly, he straightened his back and looked back down the road toward the Trackers. It seemed darker than before, almost menacing. The trees knew the secret they held; they knew who had committed these horrors, yet they always kept their secrets to themselves. The groans of their limbs, the rustling of the leaves high above, their only way of grumbling their disapproval. He plunged his hand into his pocket and pulled the three metal casings, and examined them in his trembling hand. One .303, unfired. Two longer fired cases, black scorches ran down their necks and speckled the shoulders. The brass was dull yet uncorroded. He flipped the cases and squinted his old eyes as he read the headstamp. 'W.C.C' the two fired cases read and numbers below them. 'Two out of at least thirty.' There was no doubt in his mind that all these cases were fired from the same gun, nor was there any doubt that the man who had pulled the trigger was the same in both instances.

As he turned to look down the other direction of the fire trail, the brass casings still in his hand, the world looked lighter and more promising. Some hundred feet beyond where he stood was another drive, unmarked yet visible from the road as it led off to his left, the same side of the road as the Darcy's. He spat the last remnants of his breakfast to the ground and returned the three casings to his pocket. The Falcon clunked into gear and purred down the dirt track once more.

The house he found was simple; he was relieved to have found no bodies littering the front yard. The lawns were kept neat, there were no cars to be seen, and only the thin treads of an old truck crossed the dirt in all directions. The screen door was closed and latched, the door beyond was hardwood and aged. Jerry rapped his knuckles on the metal, listening for any movement as the metal door rattled on its hinges with each blow. Nothing. Jerry waited some time, then tried the handle. It turned, and the screen door screamed as he pulled it.

He loved the country; he loved the quiet, the people and the nature, yet the feeling he had now of being alone in the quiet unsettled him. He would give the world to hear a bird sing, a dog bark, but where he was, there was nothing. Not even the tickle of the breeze on the back of his sun reddened neck. The hardwood door was likewise unlocked, it swung inward silently.

The kitchen was dark, yet clean. Rows of old cupboards lined the wall to his right, leading to a woodfire oven and a sink. An old Kelvinator fridge sat ticking softly in the corner. To his left was a dining table, likewise clean. Only a book was placed neatly on it, its edges lining perfectly up to the lines of the table. Jerry entered the house, allowing the screen door to hiss and howl as it closed on its strut behind him. He was relieved not to smell anything odd; everything looked okay. He squinted his eyes as he walked through the kitchen, searching for anything, he came to the woodfire stove and paused. He could see that there were short legs holding the weight of the immense cast iron block, the room was dark, but there may be something underneath. He lowered himself to the floor, allowing his chest to press against the hardwood boards. Down here, he thought he could smell something, something that had soaked into the timber, but he couldn't quite grasp it.

A glint of metal caught his eye as he turned his head to peer under the oven. He could see the small opening of a case mouth, mostly hidden in darkness. He slid his hand outward and felt the cool kiss of the brass on his fingers. He knew already, without even looking properly it was the same as the others. He could see the W.C.C in his head as he pulled the case outward. With a sense of dread yet excitement that he had found another clue, Jerry stood up. Squinting in the light to examine the case head, he suddenly froze. As he raised his head, a figure was standing in the hallway across from the table. Jerry gasped at the sight of the figure and dropped the casing. It clattered as it bounced, then slowly it rolled, the sound ground into his mind as it bored over and over until finally stopping at the figure's feet.

'Son,' Jerry said softly as he held his hands out. 'I'm with Chinchilla Police.'

There was no reply. The boy stood in the hallway his head lowered to look at the casing that had come to rest at his feet. The boy was roughly chest height to Jerry, and he wore shorts but no shoes and no shirt. His small bloated belly made it look as though he hadn't eaten in days, his arms were thin, and the shorts were clasped with an old belt that had holes punched into it. Slowly, the boy raised his head. His dark hair was long enough to cover his eyes when his head was lowered, yet as he straightened, Jerry could see two small brown eyes beneath his fringe. His shoulders were small, and his ribs could be seen through the flesh.

'Are you alright, son?' Jerry tried again. The child's mouth quivered, and his eyes were sad. The child still didn't reply, but he moved to the table and sat down behind the book. 'Is this book yours?' Jerry asked in an attempt to get something, anything, out of him. The boy pushed the book across the table. Both of their eyes followed its path. The writing faced the boy, but he hadn't noticed before, the cover was mostly destroyed. The hardcover was caked with what looked to be mud, then something else. The words 'Lord,' 'Fellowship,' and 'Ring' were visible, and that was all. Jerry slid the book closer to himself and kept his eyes on the boy as he did so. His facial expression was still sad and somewhat vacant. He opened the book, expecting to see white pages, maybe stained with whatever had damaged the cover. Page after page was red with dried blood, soaked the whole way through. Some letters were visible as the font pressed through the gore. Jerry looked at the boy. His face broke up, the bottom lip quivered more and more with each passing moment, his eyes were screwed up, and tears had begun to flow, streaming down his cheeks.

'Where are your parents?' But the boy wouldn't talk. Outside, he heard gravel crunch as a vehicle approached. Jerry turned his head, his eyes wide with anticipation, and his heart pounded in his chest. He returned to the screen door in time to see the tail end of a makeshift truck cut behind his Falcon to swing around the side of the house where the sheds were lined. 'Who is that?' The lawman asked the child, but still, there was no answer. Straightening, he pushed the screen open and stepped back out into the light. Feeling the gravel and dirt crunch under his boots as he took each step.

As he neared the shed, his eyes adjusted. He saw the front end of an old car or truck of some description, jutting out into the light. The cabin was set far enough back that it sat in the shade. The old man's eyes struggled to cut through the shadows and see through the glare of the late afternoon sun. Yet he heard the springs of the truck sigh as some weight was lifted, and he saw the slight movement of the cabin rise. The man that emerged from the shed was the largest he had ever seen. He stood an easy seven foot and seemed to be as wide as he was tall. Dark brown eyes hit him with their accusing stare, and his jaw flexed as if he was chewing something. He had a faint scar on his forehead, which ran diagonally across from the middle of his brow and then up over his right eye. His neck was a solid mass, and his shoulders were like cinderblocks. Two heavily muscled arms hung at his side, one clasped a bag that clinked from the glass inside, and the other held an open long neck. The man was only young, that much was evident by his face, but his eyes and his demeanour looked a lot older.

'Sir, I'm with Chin—'

'I don't give a fuck,' he cut him off. His voice was grinding stone, deep and booming. He took a few steps toward Jerry as he downed the last of the long neck in his right hand. As he lifted his arm, more muscles bulged from his sides and out from his back.

Jerry backed up with each step the giant took, yet he was still gaining. 'Who is that inside?' Jerry asked hurriedly; his hands were in front of him in a calming gesture. The giant stopped at that, the glass shattered in his right hand and blood started to run through his fingers. A look of hate came across his face as he scowled at the aging lawman. The bag at his side crashed to the ground, and the sound of glass breaking and the smell of beer filled the air.

He spoke low but firm, his voice booming still as it ground into his ears. 'Never,' he started to shake his head, his voice raised with his anger, 'speak of him.' Ending in a roar, the giant advanced on him, his eyes darkened in his rage. Everything happened so quickly, it wouldn't be until later that he remembered what he saw, but the hands shot out towards him, and he reacted.

Instinct and luck was all he could put down to what allowed him to leave that place. His service revolver came out, the hammer cocked, yet the tremble still shook in him. Having the revolver in his hands did nothing to deter the fiend, and there was just enough time for Jerry to fire a wild shot off target. The report echoed in the silence, pounding off the walls of the house and shed. The giant stopped; his eyes were closed as if the concussion had given him a migraine. Then the air rushed as he exhaled, and when he opened his eyes once more, Jerry could see his brown eyes focused on the barrel of the thirty-eight that was trained on him.

'It's time you left, old man.' The voice was low once more, the anger gone in his voice and his eyes. 'You'll leave with your life,' the big man was as calm as a cool breeze. His eyes were unblinking and never left those of the lawman. 'But never come back to this place.' With that, he turned and entered the house. The screen door erupted in a scream of rust and iron, and the slam jolted Jerry as he realised he still had the revolver in his hands. Trembling, he fumbled to place it back in his holster, and he breathed deep. That maniac was too much for him to take by himself. Now was the time to call Dalby.

He never felt as though he was one to run from danger, but the advice the lunatic gave him seemed to be the best thing for everyone. A man that big, he doubted the thirty-eight-calibre revolver would have stopped him before he tore his head off. If Jerry died there, then no one would know about the child in that house. He needed to get help as soon as possible; he thought quickly about the brass casings and the amount of them. He said to himself as he sagged into the driver's seat of the Falcon, 'Stay safe, boy. I'll be back.'

JERRY

'I fought the law,
And the law won.
I fought the law,
And the law won.'

The Bobby Fuller Four - *I Fought the Law* (1965)

Smoke rose from the tip of his trembling cigarette. The tendrils were disrupted by the continuous spasms of his gnarled hands. Still, they rolled and washed their way through the air to pool in the ceiling of the Falcon like a shallow puddle. His old straining eyes watched the tip of the butt as it jittered back and forth. The Falcon pulled down a small breach in the dense wall of the scrub. He tried to remember when it was that his hands had started up their funny little routine of twist and shout. Had it been in the Darcy's, or had it been the sight of the dog, all chewed up and pulled to pieces?

Jerry had always favoured the company of dogs over humans; they never seemed to hold grudges like their masters. Always happy to see a man when he came home from work, the only thing they wanted was to spend their time with the human they loved. Humans, on the other hand, the wanting, the lusting, the hating, it was just one thing after another. The ambition, motives, and angles that each twisted son of a bitch worked up in their minds to either play the long con or the short. Whether it was their goal to commit a mass murder down the row of a fire trail or screw the mechanic who had been working on their car down an extra couple of bucks because, as everyone knew, times were tough. They chewed up everything in their wake and spat it out like it was nothing. When the remains of what they had devoured lay on the ground in front of them and looked up for some sort of reprieve, they turned their heads and walked away, never to look back or offer a second thought.

People and memories enter and leave one's life in the same simple manner as flicking a switch and turning a light on. How they leave doesn't just depend on the switch, the power could cut, the bulb could blow.

'Some fucking truck driver half your age could take it away.' His voice was a low crackle, his throat dried from the copious amounts of cigarettes he had lit, taken only one or two drags on and otherwise just watched the ash track its way down the stem of the paper. The ashen section became heavier and heavier, unbalanced and weak. Finally, with one tremble of his fingers, the stem would snap, and the ash would tumble down. Twirling and spiralling specks of burned tobacco and paper as it went, to finally crash to the carpet of the Falcon or explode against the fabric of his pants.

He had felt sorry for the dog. An animal which is always loyal to the end, left to decay and become a feast for another of its kind, but the image the old lawman couldn't shake was that of the small and malnourished boy in that house. He had never seen a living thing look so broken and defeated as that child had been. His mind darted from the dog to the boy and finally to the giant who had almost taken his life. As the last chunk of ash fell from the depleted butt of his cigarette, he whispered to himself in an almost rhetorical tone. 'What is it?'

But what was 'it?' There were so many questions he could ask himself right now. Why did this happen? Why was he here on the side of the road, waiting for the stars to come out, waiting for the stroke of a new day? What is it with the boy?

That was the question. It all came back to the child in the kitchen. Why had all those people died, presumably at the hands of that seven foot monstrosity, yet that boy survived? He thought about the flash of anger on the young man's face at the mere mention of the child, the way his eyes darkened in their sockets. It was as if his pupils had enlarged to swallow the iris' and the pools of white, but they hadn't. He didn't know the words to explain it even in his own mind; just the vision remained of the eyes as they turned dark, like a spoon full of coffee had been added to water. Then as the gunshot rang through the quiet afternoon air, the darkness had vanished. What is it about the boy?

Jerry had fled from the small lot of land with his life. Badly shaken, he had torn grass from roots and trailed a long rooster tail of dirt and silt through the air as he powered the Falcon from the yard. He had near been in town when he had finally caught his breath and had allowed the car to slow to a crawl and finally stop. He had tried to bring his breakfast up again, but nothing remained, but bile and gut-wrenching agony as his stomach twisted and wrung itself, trying to purge any form of substance from its depths. Rather than just the tips of his fingers twitching and shuddering through his dismay, his entire body was racked with shakes to the point of shock. He sat there for what felt like hours, at the town's border, the old rusted sign 'Welcome to Chinchilla. The town of sawdust and coffee.' 'Sometimes you can't tell which is which,' had been carved into the metal below the brilliant white letters of the latter. He had tried to have a cigarette to settle his nerves, but the taste of the stale tobacco over his empty, churning stomach made him want to wretch all over again. Instead, he ventured into the town and fled to the safety of his office.

He had placed the iron kettle on the stovetop and sat at his kitchen table, his face buried into his old hands as the tips of his fingers kneaded into his lined forehead and temples.

'Too old. Too old,' he muttered into his palms over and over again. The boy had needed him, that much was certain. He never spoke, but his eyes had cried out for help all the same. The sense of duty and the feeling of heroic prowess was low in his stomach at that stage; a coppery taste had formed in his mouth. Then the sight as those gargantuan hands came down on him, the large face twisted with anger, and his bowels had essentially let go. The big bastard had allowed him to live and leave but never to return, and Jerry, like a good little boy, had hopped into his car and burned rubber the whole way back into town in fear for his own life. He had left the child, weak and malnourished, who probably watched through the kitchen window as his only hope drove out of the gate.

He slammed his fist down on the table and swore at the top of his voice. His shame was red on his face and the sickness in his guts added to the fatigue. 'Since when does a man of the law get offered terms instead of him stating the way it is?' He roared to himself and no one. 'Useless old man, since when?' The iron kettle began to whistle behind him, and he felt the anger begin to calm in him. As the whistle reverberated in his ears, a voice was carried up his spine. It spoke softly and calmly, as if right into his ear.

Since the only lawman is an old, used up piece of shit like you, that's when. Jerry swallowed his insecurities. He had made his third coffee for the day and had taken the mug into his office to begin the phone calls.

The first phone call was like the first drag of a cigarette in the morning after a big night, you needed it but Christ, you could've done without it. Terry Macress was a man of business, and to some degree, Jerry was as well. He wasn't able to disclose who had been killed, how or when, but when Macress had failed to answer some of his questions, using the whole, "I'm a very busy man," Jerry let slip that bodies had been found. The line had gone quiet for some time until, finally, Terry's tongue began to loosen. He offered complete descriptions of Paul Darcy and Tony Baker, even to the point of explaining that Tony was one of those big, ball-breaking bastards, and that was the only reason he had been placed in the position of manager. Macress believed a firm hand was good for children but even better for staff. Intrigued by his statement, he pushed further into this Tony Baker. He asked for the colour of his hair, the actual size of the man, how did he speak and with each answer, the feeling of success and fear sunk deeper into his stomach. Tony Baker was the name of this big son of a bitch. Before he let the conversation end, he asked two more questions. The first: 'Is there anyone else of that size at the sawmill?'

The line went quiet for a time again, and he thought that Macress had become impatient with this whole thing, but then he clacked his lips in a sense of realisation and continued. 'It's been a long time since I have seen him. The boy was only about fourteen the last I had seen him, but by then, he was near damn taller than I am. I'm not sure what he looks like now. Tony never spoke of his family all too much...'

'Tony Baker has a family?' the lawman enquired. He slapped his face with his free hand, angry with himself over being caught up in the man's size rather than his life.

'Yes, sir, you wouldn't know it from talking to him, but he has a lovely wife, whom I've dined with a few times, and ahhh, is it two... Yes, I believe two sons. Maybe a son and daughter, or is that Darcy? I never do pay attention to these things...'

Two sons. Or maybe one of each kind. Jerry cleared his throat and asked his second question. 'Mr Macress, where could I find Mr Baker? I mean, where does he live?'

'Well, if he's not at the sawmill, he lives on a small fire trail that shoots off nearby. I should know that as I own both of the houses there. He lives on one, and the Darcy's live right next door.'

Jerry let the receiver fall onto the cradle. His disappointment and stupidity burned in his ears like the whistle of the kettle. He took another sip of the coffee dregs that he had brewed and grimaced at the taste of it. The boy and the book that was soaked in what could have been mud or blood, or even both. The man that could either have been Tony Baker or his son, as Macress never did mention how long it had been since he had seen the fourteen-year-old. The age of that big bastard in the yard was hard to pick. His face was free of wrinkles, but his eyes were sullen and deep. The scar across his forehead and the way his jaw worked like a man chewing on the old leaf was another thing. There was nothing for it, he would call for assistance from Dalby.

That phone call, at least, was as pleasant as it could be. He spent twenty minutes getting through the exchange, Chinchilla three through to Jandowae four onto Dalby one. Once at Dalby one, he was put through to the Police Department and was put through to the front desk. Being the fifth person he had now spoken to on his quest to talk to his own boss, Captain McLennan, he had become sick of repeating himself.

'Constable Jerry Thompson, the last man in Chinchilla, I need to speak to McLennan,' he said with a soft sigh.

The lady on the other line smacked her lips as she audibly chewed on gum. 'I'll transfer you now.'

The line was filled once more with clicks and clacks, and then another woman spoke up.

'Dalby Police Department, Captains office.'

Jerry rolled his eyes and repeated himself with more disdain in his voice, 'Constable Jerry Thompson, the last man in Chinchilla. I need to speak to McLennan.'

'Captain McLennan is very busy at the moment. Can I take a message?'

Jerry slammed his fist on the table and pressed the receiver firm into the side of his face. 'Listen, lady, we have seven dead bodies here and are almost drowning in shell casings from the gun that cut these people down. You put him on the phone and do it now or I'll drive up there and dump these corpses on your desk and let you show him each one.'

The line clicked and clunked once more, and finally, the rusty tin voice of Captain McLennan came on the line. Jerry explained the entire situation, explained his suspicion of the use of a machine gun, the deaths of seven people, and a suspect that was too large for Jerry to handle himself. McLennan remained silent throughout the entire debrief. It took him only a second to reply once Jerry had finally gotten around to asking for help.

'How many do you require?'

'Four, well-armed, should be plenty.'

Once more, McLennan didn't hesitate. He didn't seem exasperated by the conversation; a job was a job. People die every day in the city, and seven people dying in the country didn't help McLennan. It was just another problem to add to his growing list.

'Three. I can spare only three. They will be in town late tomorrow morning. I'll inform them now. They'll meet at your office.' The line clicked and faded. Jerry returned the receiver to the cradle once more. Three was better than none, and four was better than one. Still, he didn't like it. His mind returned to the boy in the kitchen and the brute in the yard. They were part of the Baker family. Things had started to fall into place but were not as perfect as he would have liked.

As the sun waned behind the hills and the sky became a red rash, Jerry cleaned his service revolver. The single shot he had taken in fear and dire need had left small remnants of unburned powder, and the smell of the burn was all over the pistol. The ordeal did not take long, but it was something that should be done before and after an operation. He felt the tingle of anticipation quiver through his spine. The taste of copper flooded his mouth. He pushed each shell into the cylinder one by one, lining the words 'Winchester' and '38 SPL' so that each were in line and angled all the same. He knew this didn't matter, but it was sort of a ritual for him. Make sure everything with the tool is right, and the tool will look after you. He clicked the cylinder home in its frame softly and felt the gate engage. He gave the frame a final wipe down with his cotton cleaning rag and holstered the revolver. Then he clambered into the Falcon and headed out of town.

Jerry discarded the cigarette butt out the window as he leaned his head out for fresh air. The cigarettes had not diminished the taste of copper in his mouth. All they had done was to remind him that he had not eaten and the state his stomach had been in only hours earlier. The sun had removed itself from the sky hours ago, and the clock on the dash of the Falcon now read a quarter to twelve, midnight. He fired the Ford up and let it idle down the road. He refrained from using the headlights in an attempt to keep his presence hidden and hence travelled slow. Even still, the cool night air flowed in through the open window and tussled with the stale, smoke ridden air that he had been stifling in for the past four hours. The fresh mixed with the old to make him feel light-headed slightly, and he tickled the accelerator to increase the flow.

The Chinchilla sawmill stood dark in the night. There were no gates to mark the border of its lines, just a mess of dilapidated fences, half-collapsed. A large gloomy shed with old hangar style doors, which were now chained shut, the day's labour complete. Across one side of the fence was a line of smaller sheds and one old carport which housed the manager's car, which he knew from the rotting plaque nailed to the iron. There were no cars to litter the yard, only a large logging truck, its cabin closed to the night air, its windows rolled up, and the largest forklift he had ever seen. The words 'Hyster' were stuck to its side. Years of beatings and hard work had left its cabin dented and worn, and so the sticker was peeled in places and scratched to near oblivion, yet it was still legible.

The dirt crunched under his boots as he slowly paced across the yard. He had left the Falcon in the manager's spot, the window up and keys still in the ignition, should he need to make a quick getaway. The moonlit night painted a beautiful contrast to what would have been seen during the day. Light washed over the metal walls of the shed, rather than burning and beating everything down like the sun. Shadows were cast in a soft, blurry manner, that made them look as though they were the soul of whatever had wilted in the blazing sun and poured out over the ground. The chains that held the hangar doors closed were loosely wrapped. Even so, the doors had that much flex and play in them it was obvious it was only designed to stop honest people from breaking in.

'Lawmen are honest,' he whispered to himself. A ghost of a smile shimmered across his face as he lowered his head and slipped under the chain and through the corrugated doors. 'Honest enough.'

Inside, the mill was dark. Despite the gloom, the roof looked as though it was a starry sky as the moonlight seeped through each burred hole. Years of wear, tear and holes being drilled into the roof had left an eerie effect. The old, well-maintained hulks of the boilers loomed in the darkness. Heat still radiated off them from the day's hard labour. The Canadian trolleys sat squat unloaded, brooding on the beating they had taken. Looming out of the darkness in front was a squat mezzanine with an office at its landing. Jerry set off steadily.

His feet tested each step before he committed, unsure of obstacles or trenches cut into the hard dirt for the boilers, pipes, or the belts that drove the sawblades.

Finally, the first sound of rubber hitting cross-hatched steel steps clanged through the darkness. Jerry let his hand run up the rail and felt the pits of the metal as he passed. The door was shut but unlocked and the hinges groaned as the heavy metal lined door pushed open to reveal a dank office. Jerry moved even slower into the office, not wanting to disturb anything or break it, which would be a sure way to let the big bastard know he was still being watched. He ran his hand up and down the plaster of the walls beside the door he had just entered. He found a small switch and flicked it. The light from the ceiling fan flickered once, twice, and then finally illuminated.

The carpet was mostly rotten and dark with dirt and grime, except for one small patch in front of the desk, which was relatively clean. Atop the desk sat an ashtray, which was overflowing with butts. Many had spilled from the brim and scattered over the paperwork, which likewise had been thrown carelessly onto the desk. Jerry took a small look at the invoices, at times brushing crushed cigarette butts to the side to better read the small print. 'Overdue' were stamped on some, 'Last Notice' on others. Jerry sifted through the drawers, which revealed nothing more than cigarettes and boxes of matches. He turned to look at the rest of the room, disappointed to find nothing on the desk. Directly behind the desk was a window, completely covered by a large, dusty curtain that looked as though it was decomposing on its eyelets. He found the centre of the two folds with some searching and pulled a side back to look through the dirty glass. Down below, the boiler and Canadian trolleys still sat gloomily. The hangar doors were still shut, and a line of moonlight could be seen cutting its way down the centre.

Jerry turned his attention back to the office. As he stood behind the desk, it became apparent that there was only one photograph on the wall, high up and to the right of the only door. Squinting to make out the figures behind the plate glass, Jerry walked across the carpet; his footsteps sounded as hollow as a knuckles rap on an empty tank. Behind the dust were two boys. One noticeably larger than the other, he had a solid square jaw for a boy of a young age, solid shoulders and cropped black hair. The only clothing he wore was his noticeably dirty jeans, his upper body oddly solid from what could be seen, as in his arms wrapped in the shirt that he once wore was a squalling baby. The child's eyes were closed, and even through the dirty glass, he could see the hint of a tear on the boy's cheek. Below the photo was a brass plaque, pinned into the timber frame and etched into the metal, was the script 'Jack and Michael Baker (1960).' Jerry looked at the face of the eldest of the two children, the already solid jaw, shoulders and height. There was no doubt the two in the photo were the ones in that yard, the Bakers lot. As Jerry continued to stare at the photo, he noticed a soft smile on the one that he thought to be Jack, and he thought how odd the smile looked on the face he had only seen in anger. The soft lines, his forehead unmarked; they were brothers. Was that the reason why the giant had gone to anger so quickly because they were brothers?

In the quiet office, Jerry tried to understand this man and his motives, when a soft rumble and clatter was heard from outside the hangar doors. His eyes turned to the curtained window, the somewhat dim light from the ceiling fan lit it up like a signpost on a highway. Jerry quickly made his way to the door and flicked the switch as he exited the office, the soft smile on Jack's face still on his mind. He gently swung the office door closed behind him and felt the latch click as he heard a vehicle halt directly out front of the hangar doors.

'Shit,' he said to himself. It hadn't been smart to leave the Falcon in plain sight, keys in the ignition and all. The vehicle that had stopped at the hangar doors remained idling for some time. Through the crack in the centre join, Jerry could see a line of a bulky cab, and he heard the rattle of the old engine as it idled. Quiet as a mouse, he made his way down the steel cross backed stairs and crouched behind a giant twelve foot saw blade. The engine of the vehicle cut, and he heard the rattle of the body shake as the engine died under it. He strained his ears to hear what happened outside; he heard the suspension of the vehicle squawk as its weight shifted, then crunching footsteps.

The panic in Jerry rose; he needed to get out of this place before he was found and questioned. If it was the big man from the Bakers lot, then he would be killed, revolver or not. Jerry spun around; each crunching footstep burned into his head as if it was a timer for a detonator. He moved down the corrugated steel wall of the structure and pressed at the bottoms as he went. He heard the car door of the Falcon slam shut and the clinking of broken glass as the driver's window gave in. Footsteps again now, faster, heavier. He needed to get out. Just before the chains on the hangar doors began to clink, Jerry pressed on a section of wall, and his hand pushed the steel sheet outward with ease. Sweat ran down his face, as Jerry pushed his body through the gap. The chains that held the hangar doors were being pulled through their holes.

The moonlight washed over him as he scrambled into the night air. As far as he could tell, he was at the back of the compound, trees and bushes stretched out into the night. From where he stood, he could only see about thirty feet in front of him, and so he ran. He pushed through the spinifex and the gidgee bushes that bordered the uncleared section of the mill's yard. His shoulder bounced hard off a large gum and nearly sent him rolling down a descent that he didn't see coming. He stumbled most of the way down the descent, his boots slid along the loose dirt and slipped on the dewy grass patches that lined the hill. Finally, his feet were bound up in a tree root, and he slid the rest of the way down on his chest, his hands pressed out in front to lift his face from the ground. Behind him, the mill was quiet. He couldn't hear the hangar doors, or footsteps or even the corrugated iron sheet he escaped through being disturbed. Nonetheless, he pushed onward slower now, careful not to make too much noise. His boots ground the soft dirt beneath him, and with every third or so step that he took, a twig snapped under his weight. Eventually, he crossed a beaten down track that had been cut into the bush and graded a long time ago. It was obvious that the track had seldom seen use, as the spinifex had worked its way back through, and at one point, a small sapling had begun to sprout.

Jerry thought it best to continue up the track. The further he got from the mill and his pursuer, the better. The loose soil ground under his feet, and in the distance, he heard dogs barking, an entire pack of them from the sound. His mind went to the dog at the Trackers yard, all dismembered and torn limb from limb. He had always liked dogs, but the fact of the matter was that they were a beast all the same. The same beast that would curl up at your feet or lap your hand, would tear strips of flesh from your face if it was starving.

The moonlight cut through the tree canopy fairly well, even as the scrub thickened. The track wound around an enormous grey gum, and as he turned with the beaten road, a glint of red was visible in the darkness. Jerry paused and partly back stepped to conceal himself behind the grey gum. The glint of red did not move, as Jerry moved his head around to try and see what it might be, he imagined that it could only be a tail light. Cautiously, he advanced down the track, his head lowered, the revolver in hand. The further he went, the shape was revealed by the moonlight. One red glint turned into two, and a chrome bumper shone through a gidgee bush that had been crushed by the vehicle's weight. A Fairlane 500 in near mint condition was parked hidden in the scrub. Jerry stood in awe, looking over the car from twenty feet, confusion rolled through his mind. He circled around the front of the vehicle; everything looked as new as the day it had rolled off the factory line. Chrome upon chrome, the fenders gleamed in the low light, except for a few imperfections. A small hole had been punched through the windscreen, and a spider web of cracks had coursed out from its centre. That and it looked as though someone had love tapped a tree with the front end, nothing too serious. Jerry neared the car, his eyes focused on the spiralling web of cracks in the windscreen, but as he neared, his stomach began to roll.

An odour of rotting flesh surrounded the car. So potent that it near made him vomit the moment its teeth had sunk into him. The air was thick and seemingly hotter the closer he got. He pulled a handkerchief from his pocket and slapped it to his face to try and staunch the smell, but the attempt was too little, too late. He brought up the remains of the coffee, which wasn't much. Each time he tried to suck in another life-giving breath, he brought in more of the odour, which made his stomach wretch over again. This time green bile had come up with the remains, and the pain in his stomach was threefold what it had been that morning. With all of his will, he pushed himself up with his revolver hand while the other pressed the vomit and bile-soaked handkerchief to his face. He summoned the last ounce of willpower he had left and continued to the sedan.

He tore open the driver's door and peered into the coupe. Nothing but the smell. The interior was beautiful, so well-kept, and just under the smell of rotting flesh and decay, he smelt the leather and shampoo in the carpets. Jerry looked about the cabin, refusing to get into the sedan, and he found the boot release. The solenoid clacked as he pushed the button, and the heavy steel panel rose on its struts. When he pulled his head out of the cabin, it seemed that the smell had increased tenfold just by popping the boot. He closed his eyes, which had begun to water, the coppery taste washed in his mouth along with sediment of bile and vomit. He breathed in deeply a few times, his eyes still closed. The pain in his stomach clenched and near doubled him over as he tried to bring up the courage just to walk to the back of the car. He opened his eyes, straightened up and said to himself, 'The child needs you. You're doing it for him.' His voice was a gurgle of pain and saliva, yet he moved forward.

The only part of the two bodies that distinguished them as male and female were the clothes. One wore a torn work shirt that was black with rot. Blue jeans that were only distinguishable due to the unstained cuff on one ankle and old work boots. The other wore a summer dress and seemed to clutch the carcass of a bird. The flesh had turned black on both bodies, the heat of being left in a metal box in the summer heat had sped up the decay. Although fairly water tight, the Fairlane's boot had not stopped the insects from getting in, and both bodies crawled with maggots and worms. Their clothes looked to be covered in dirt, grime and muck. He had seen all he cared to, Jerry had held his breath the whole time he had stood there, and he desperately needed fresh air. As he spun around, his vision blurred with the water that had welled up inside of them. Four steps were all he managed to take before his old body had finally run out of puff, and he was forced to stop and breathe. He heaved air deep into his lungs, spluttering and panting, making so much noise that he only heard the boots crunch on the earth when they were right on top of him.

Jerry started to raise the revolver, but a large hand closed over his own. The big man squeezed and twisted the revolver hand, breaking bones in his palm while the other grabbed his throat. As the revolver fell to the ground, his right hand crushed, he was lifted by his throat some two foot off the ground. He was near suffocated by his own weight. There was no soft smile on Jack Bakers' face this time. The square jaw worked in anger, and the brow was furrowed, the scar lit up by the moonlight. His eyes were black holes, deep in their sockets, under his heavy brow.

'Why...?' Jerry croaked as he strained to talk, 'He's your brother.' The hand that clasped his throat tightened. Jerry's good hand still clasped his handkerchief as the other clapped uselessly against Jack's meaty forearm.

Jack's voice was so deep it resonated through Jerry's body as he spoke. 'This is all because of him, all of it.' The hand around Jerry's throat squeezed tighter and tighter. 'I'll kill each and every one of you bastards that try to get close to him.'

His airway had closed and Jerry couldn't speak. His hands hammered at Jack's arms, face and shoulders; each flurry became weaker and weaker as the strength left the old lawman. Just before he lost consciousness, he heard Jack speak once more. They had begun to move, Jerry's body still suspended in the air.

'Come, I want you to meet my parents.'

RABBITS

'Sittin' in the morning sun
I'll be sittin' till the evenin' comes
Watchin' the ships roll in
And I'll watch them leave again.'

Ottis Redding – *Sitting by the Dock of the Bay* (1967)

The morning heat rolled over Travis and even as the ocean swelled below, him he didn't dare to tempt fate and steal it's cool kiss. The days of long hauls had begun to take their toll on the old man, the bags under his eyes resembled the satellite dishes of the Larrakeyah barracks. The once plush seat of the old Freightliner, which had become his life, had been pressed into submission by the weight of the aging man who perched himself atop it. The feeling of comfort was replaced by the slow cancerous ache in his back and his restless legs that kicked at night. His eyes nearly fell from their sockets as the old truck dragged its chain of fuel tankers, the eighteen-hour slog down the Stuart Highway and back again. Decades before, he was able to make the complete trip three times a week, a feat that had been unprecedented for a single driver of a truck. They spoke of him fulfilling an early grave, and as with most things in life, he laughed it off; a man with more backbone than brains. Yet as the years etched the lines into his face and as the ache worked its way into the depths of his spine, he dropped his service to two complete runs a week. Then he found that three runs over a fortnight suited him better.

Finally, the man's body had aged worse than the iron hulk it rode in. Weak and near breaking point, he had allowed himself a single run in seven days, with a three-day gap between returns.

The tip of the pole in his hand gave the slightest of tweaks, and his old eyes strained to focus in the streaking sunrise.

'Take the bait, you mongrel,' he muttered under his breath. the sweat had already begun to form under the pits of his arms. Only quarter past six in the morning and the mercury had already risen past the thirties, humidity over eighty. He frequently spent nights in Darwin, either camped in the Top End Trucking Companies' lodgings, which they allowed overnighters to use or, as he much preferred, out in the bush somewhere safe and away from the lizards. He had seen only one man taken by those damn things, which was enough to make him never want to see one again. The way they watched a man and learned from him, only their eyes visible from the surface of the murky waters. Analysing and calculating, each flick of the lure was a gamble for a man such as himself, and if one ever thought he was safe in the flood plains, he was a bigger fool than he knew. As far as he knew, they had been a mile away from the closest river when he had seen the crocodile strike. They had been chasing pigs, caught up in the blood, and the moment. The sound of the old Enfield's they carried as the thirty-year-old ammunition either fizzled in the breach or detonated in a cloud of cordite and recoil. He remembered the sounds of the boars retching, their sows and litter squealing as they fled the fire and pain that came with man. The croc had been fourteen feet in length. It had laid that still off to the right of the track among scattered logs and leavings, its mouth open in such a way that it resembled the fork of a fallen bough. The low coverings of the canopy that protected the dry ground below from the intense heat ran a speckle of shadows over its ridged spine. Each peaked spike melted into the shadows of the scrub and the drying timber that surrounded it. It happened without warning; the jaws had clamped around his hunting partners' mid-section. The clap as the prehistoric monsters' jaws slammed into the soft meat was only conquered by the rush of air escaping its prey's lungs. Any fight the captured hunter gave was insignificant to the strength of the dinosaur, that's what seemed to stick with Travis. It knew it had him. The eyes and the curl of its rough hide at the edge of its terrifying jaw all seemed to be laughing at him. Travis fired his Enfield countless times into the beast, and he knew that the wounds would kill it, but too little too late. The monster backed away from the remaining hunter, its prize still clamped tightly in its jaw. As it disappeared through the coverings and spinifex, the eyes of his partner locked with his. Fear, that's all there was. He had no breath to speak with, nothing to end his life with, no phrase or request, just the look of fear as he was dragged away from salvation to be the dinosaur's last meal.

The horrific memory of that rotten day sent an eery shiver coursing down his spine. The shame rolled over him, for try as he might, he couldn't remember his hunting partner's name. His eyes quickly darted from the tip of the rod in his hands to the water that surrounded him and paused on any stick or log or tremble of the water's surface. Really, he was asking for death sitting where he was. The crocodiles did not just inhabit the inlets and small rivers that cut their way inland from the vast blue beyond, they owned it. Any boat trip along the coast would show their dark silhouette every seventy feet or so. Small figures and then the occasional freak of nature, the monster from the depths that sunned itself on the beautiful sands which were unable to be used for anything but what it so desired. In a way, the people of Darwin reminded him of Adam and Eve. They were stranded in such a hot, desolate land, with the most beautiful ocean one could ever imagine just within reach. The cool waters promised to soothe their sun-kissed hides, begged them for their company in its world so alone. Yet just below the depths lay its true intentions: come, embrace what I am. Let me show you my true self.

From the time he had left the Narrows and the comfort of his bunk at the trucking yard, it had taken just shy of an hour and a half of leisurely strolling to bring him to his favourite place to drown a prawn at East Point. From his position, he could see the city of Darwin itself starting to wake. The people's minds were on the rain and more so the wind, if they would get any at all today. The wet had started early but had begun to fizzle out. As the new year came and went just like another day as it was, the dry spells between downpours became longer, hotter and more unbearable. The rains that came to break up the monotony left the town and the people wanting, with only the specks of moisture to cool their cheeks from the glass of water that was just poured out on the floor in front of them. Their mouths and their throats still dry, their stomachs yearned for the taste. It didn't seem as though their prayers would be answered. The skies were mostly clear. Just the wisp of the white elegance and their hopes being pushed away by the wind currents above.

As Travis watched the fleeting clouds, a speck of movement in the sky caught his eye. Its form was visible for a split second, then vanished behind the faintest speck of white. The sound of the jet's engine slowly rolled across the water as if it was the tide coming in. As the elongated jet became visible once more, the sound of the rolling jet stream became louder. Another wash had joined its voice to the first, then a third. The planes flew in a line, wing to wing. Travis sat there with his head craned back. As the planes neared the coastline, their line took them straight over Darwin itself. He could not bring himself to look away. The planes were odd-looking. He had never known any airship to look the way these had, skinny and long, too long almost. Then, as they neared the coast, Travis could see black holes appear in the underbelly of each. His mouth was ajar, as if he knew what he was seeing, but he couldn't believe it. Small specks of iron fell from each. They glinted in the sun as they plummeted to the earth, the jets' engines howled as their pitch increased, and they banked from their course. As he followed the three specks of metal, which tumbled as they rolled through the air, the sun caught their metal casings momentarily. Rabbits was left with a thought that seemed childish: Are the falling people going to use their parachutes?

As each speck of metal hit the ground, they exploded in walls of fire that curled their lips at the buildings they consumed and begged for more. He watched in horror as one of the larger office buildings reacted as though it had been kicked from behind. Its middle blew outward, and its roof canted downward as the brick and mortar tore apart. From a distance, it was like watching a toy set fall over, but the sound of the fires, the crumbling of foundations, chilled him, yet he still wasn't able to move. As the fires consumed yet another tower and the destruction flowed outward, a tear ran down his face as he wondered how many people had died in the blast. Stones and chunks of steel were thrown into the air, trailed by the fires of the grief that had devoured those which had stood. Their fingers clutched at the debris as if to try and pull it back into its ever-hungry mouth. Finally, the debris lost its momentum and came crashing down on the city below, crushing cars and the roofs of houses that it impacted.

Cannons fired from his right as Travis whirled his head around to see the shadowy hulls of four long grey naval ships that sat low in the water. Once again, they seemed weirdly different to the elegant grey hulls of the ships he had seen grace the presence of Darwin's coast. Yet since the war in Vietnam, he had seen fewer ships and fewer planes, year by year, as they were committed or moved to other bases around the continent. The canons fired intermittently, smoke billowed from the bow of each ship as they advanced on the coast.

The third ship's cannon fired a volley directly into the side of a building that had survived the bombing unscathed. As the shells impacted the solid concrete wall, fire swirled from the chunks of rubble that tumbled from the heights, then the other ships zeroed in on the target and shell after shell impacted the concrete. With each hit, the face of the structure was torn away. Through the dust, fire and smoke, Travis saw inside the buildings, the gaping insides of the animal whose outer skin was ripped and torn by the evil of the men who had set on it.

The rod in his hand bucked and weaved, its tip bent double. Travis jumped at the sensation of the rod fighting in his grip. His eyes were wide, and his whole body trembled. As he scrambled to his feet and ran, the butt of the rod was slowly sucked underwater. It bobbed again once more as if to take one last breath and then it was gone forever. Like a man's last breath before the monster who caught him devoured its last meal. As his bare feet pounded the earth, his heart hammered in his throat. People's screams became audible, and the fires of the city rose and curled above the peaks of the highest buildings that remained. It lapped at the stone and concrete walls and the tiled roofs as it devoured everything below hungrily and greedily, never satisfied with what it was given. Behind him, the sound of jets came once more, the rolling roar whose intensity rose as it neared. Below the roar of the exhaust, the whistle of the turbine held a steady note as it sucked the life out of the air it cut through. They passed overhead, so low he felt that if he had jumped the moment before, he would have been cut in two by their wings or impaled upon the spikes on their nose caps. The jets were a dark brown with an odd camouflage pattern. They fired rockets on targets that Travis couldn't see, then banked and soared up into the air, giving Travis the sight of the red star on their wings.

The realisation set into him, yet the question of what country had committed these murders didn't matter as much as it had happened, and he needed to get out. The jet's engines roared as they soared upward into the air. Their wings cut through the thick, hot air like a blade through flesh. He never slowed his pace, and his old lungs screamed as they sucked air in and expelled the hot waste. Faster and faster, his legs pumped as his chest roared with pain. The sound of the jets hadn't even rolled in the air when they were replaced by the shrill pitch of more turbines screaming up behind him. Once more, he felt his body get pushed to the earth as the pair of brown eagles swooped over him. A horrible churning noise came from their hulls as they spat leaden fire into the earth and churned the ground only a few hundred feet in front of him. He didn't see what they had targeted, but as they banked and followed the flight path of their partners before, the sounds of dying screams and moans were heard below the afterburners.

The jets soared upward as they twirled with the joy their pilots must have felt for the massacre that ensued. As he continued to run, a quick glance to his right showed him the advance of the four long destroyers in the water, the one closest to him seemed that near he could almost reach out and touch it. He could see small men aboard the decks, just walking and pointing as the ship's front cannons continued to pound the mainland. The ship's side that faced him was lined with machine guns, yet the men who operated them didn't seem to be in a rush to use them. All but one watched the journey of the death from above, as wave after wave of the brown eagles swooped upon the land, churned up the earth and crumbled what the locals had made.

As Travis ran, others joined him. People who were fishing like him, going about their days, getting ready for work or journeying to their destinations. A man appeared in front. His legs waned as he clutched his chest. He was dressed in blue overalls, and he clung to the broom he must have used only moments before. He heard the sobs of a woman as she thundered to keep up, the babe at her chest screamed for the noise to stop. As if in a triumphant roar, three of the ship's side machine guns opened up, and the air was filled with hot fiery wasps that buzzed past their heads. The cleaner in front fell first, his right leg torn in two at the knee. As he fell, it was as though he never felt the impact, his remaining leg still pumped as he continued to clutch his chest with his free hand, then he was behind, and Travis never looked back.

As he neared the outskirts of the city, he could see a mass of people climb through the wreckage, they waved their hands and called for help as they attempted to save those that were trapped inside. As he ran past, he didn't see any official men, no army, police or firefighters, just everyday people trying to help.

'Run!' he screamed at the top of his voice. The voice was like that of another man, harsh and coarse like a crocs hide as it worked through his throat. As he continued to pant and hold his pace, he saw a glint of sunlight cut through the smoke and dust as another hunk of metal fell from the sky, well on the other side of the crumbled building. This time, the fire worked as though it had a mind of its own. It laced the building and covered the men and women that scattered its wreckage. As it curled and worked its tendrils through every crevasse, the heat burned into his face and body as if a burning man twice the size of Travis had walked right through him. The smoke that emitted from the building was as black as the devil's heart. The fire was as red as his eyes and lifelike. From the black cloud before him, people emerged, their bodies blackened and the fire clinging to them. They had not the breath in them to scream or cry, they just ambled. He saw another man, who had escaped the fires, try and help one whose skin was dark and cracked. The clothes he wore were burned into his flesh, his hair melted across his face. As the helper's hands grasped the others, the flesh pulled away from the bones like mud from a stick. The black surface moved like a cake of hard earth over a soft watery base to reveal the sheer white gleaming bone, which stood out in such contrast to everything so dark.

The ships were still visible in the bay as they swung broadside, their guns turned to the land to douse any survivors they could find. A single jet came from west of the coastline, its engine powered as it hugged the land. As it entered the space above the water, a missile ignited under one of its wings and propelled itself forward while it spat fire and twisted through the air like a snake writhing on the ground. It impacted the ship closest to him, and the ship's front cannon exploded in a fireball, the barrel visibly twisted under the force of the impact, yet the ship remained afloat. The friendly jet attempted to soar into the air, but the brown eagles descended on it out of nowhere. Its wings were shot from its frame, and it hung in the air like a bird, saddened by the knowledge that its flight of life was finally over. Travis darted his head back to watch the course of the falling jet. He was trying to get off the street when his foot clapped into the side of something soft and heavy, and he tumbled down to the earth while the shrill pitch of the jets turbine still gasped for air. As he hit the ground and slammed his forehead into the blacktop, the jet crashed through a building to his left. He peered through the curtain of blood that ran over his eyes. The pilot in the cockpit struggled and fought to get free. He pounded his gloved hands on the hard glass that had imprisoned him. Fire could be seen through the glass that became cloudier and black with soot until only the sight of his hands that still pounded the glass and the rising red embers were visible. The turbine whined and rose in pitch and Travis clapped his hands over his ears as it finally exploded.

The force pushed him along the blacktop, his bare feet and arms torn to ribbons as they scraped along the rough bitumen. The world went dark, yet it wasn't his eyes that had given out. The combined smoke and dust from the explosions and napalm clouded the sky, but underneath, he could still see the bay. One of the four destroyers had craft leaving it, some had even birthed large rafts that carried what looked like tanks and troop carriers. The small vessels inched toward the shore like the lizards he hated. The time to watch and survey was finished, and the time to kill had come. Travis pulled himself upward, his injured feet and legs screamed and his heart still pounded to the point it felt as though it was about to burst from his chest.

He needed to get to his truck. Not that the truck would outrun planes or tanks, he just needed to get home. He took up his journey to the Narrows and his Freightliner once more, his pace considerably slowed. His breathing had become raspy, and he felt nothing but searing pain from both of his bare feet. He limped and lurched as fast as he could into the alley between two untouched buildings. The sounds of jets had dispersed. All that remained was the crackle of fire and the moans of the life that escaped the mouths of those that had been hit. He stopped inside the alley and felt some sense of cover and safety. He took a well-needed breath and rested himself against some bins. The woman that had followed him from the East Point lay on the road, her skin blackened by the dust and debris from the jets fire. She howled in pain and distress, her face upturned to the sky as she cried for Jesus Christ in words that were so inconsolable that the Lord's name was all that Travis wanted to hear. Her child was still clutched to her chest, lifeless and limp. Its body surprisingly clean in its surroundings. Like anything pure and innocent, cleanliness and purity does not save one's life.

'Come on,' he urged himself. His worn hands rubbed his face as blood filled the cracks that appeared and moved with each facial movement. 'Run like the rabbit you are.' His breath echoed in his ears, his heart rate finally slowed to something below a trill. His right hand worked its way across the brickwork as he moved along the alleyway. A feeling of safety seeping through him as his fingers felt the firmness and the warmth of the brick. At the end of the alleyway, he could see the road leading out of Darwin. It was clogged with cars that had attempted to escape. Wrecks were overturned, and vehicles were on fire. He could see the large holes punched through the thin metal of the vehicles strewn across the lanes, the ground beneath them torn from the guns of the jets. People scattered the road in an absolute mess. The cannons that had punched easily through the metal lining of their cars had torn limbs from people, decapitated some and had left nothing but waste and remains of the corpses. Their life's blood left to pool where their bodies lay, as if it were nothing more than an old forgotten coffee, tossed out on the earth.

The air was shaken once more by the sounds of aircraft, and three enormous planes became visible through the alleyway as they headed inland. They were hundreds of feet in the air, and they travelled like bullocks wading through a swamp. Behind them, they left a trail of parachutes as hundreds of men listed slowly to the ground. The time to breathe had gone, and now he needed to run. The softer beat of the propellers echoed in his ears as, once more, his bleeding feet pounded the pavement. He had covered most of the distance to the Narrows by now, yet the urgency was still high in his throat. The paratroopers behind him had already landed, bringing more death with them. As he felt his feet trample the remains of the people under him, the sounds of automatic rifle fire rang out in the streets of the city behind him. The mother with the child had continued to howl to the heavens as he made his way through the destroyed Holdens and Fords. He tried to keep to the outgoing lanes to give himself cover. Those who tried to mount the median and make it to the freed-up incoming lanes had been lodged. Their cars still ran as they sat empty, their owners abandoned them in their chance to flee.

A burst of fire behind him silenced the mother, and he knew he had very little time to reach his home.

Above him, the men which listed down came so close that he could see the features of their faces. The slanted eyes, the young stubble on their chin, and the look of duty and honour on their faces. He swore as he continued, knowing that soon he would be forced off the road. The paratroopers had seen him on their descent, and he knew they would come for him. He found his opportunity some forty feet further on, and he plunged through an already shattered glass door of a half-collapsed building, not even noticing the shattered glass tear his feet to ribbons. Outside, the roar of the enormous plane engines had dissipated, replaced by rifle fire and the continual pounding of the ship's cannons. He made his way through the building, over desks that had been overthrown in whatever explosion had rocked the structure's foundations. He climbed through an office window and slumped behind a desk. His heart pounded so fiercely that he needed to rest. His lungs heaved air into his body and repeatedly, he swore to himself in a heightened sense of panic. Suddenly, a slight movement in the office made his heart stop, and he turned to face what it was.

Two children lay hidden partially under the crook of an office desk that had been thrown against a wall. Clean lines had been cut down their dirty cheeks as the tears streamed. Their sobs became more pronounced as they both peered out at the man who had fallen upon their hideout. Travis held a finger to his lips and shushed them as gently as he could, yet he could see how badly his finger trembled through his peripherals. Outside, he heard the thud of a man's boots hit the concrete hard and the flap of canvas as the parachute crumpled around him. The soldier that had landed did not speak, yet movement could be heard and eventually, to Travis' horror, he heard the crumbling of shattered glass under the soles of heavy military boots.

With the sounds of the man's footsteps echoing through the office, the children flinched and sobbed harder the closer he came. Travis tried to quiet them as they clutched at each other and their mouths opened to wail. Travis stood up in a panic and pushed his back to the wall, his shoulder only just concealed from view from the window he entered by. As the soldier slowly penetrated deeper into the offices, he began to move slowly around and out through the office door, he left the children to sob and cry behind him. For a man with bleeding feet and torn arms, he moved silently through the offices, not even concerned with the blood he left behind in the darkness.

The children's sobs followed him as he went, as did the haunting thoughts that he should go back to them. How could he be such a coward? Yet he needed to get to his home, his Freightliner, his only means for escape. He continued to move, his head low until finally, he caught a glimpse of light through the darkness. His breath hitched as relief ran through his body. As he moved toward the light and went to exit the building, he heard a sharp cry of fear and pain, followed by the automatic rifle fire which echoed through the rooms. It lasted forever. Travis sat there in the light of the morning, his back to the building, the hole torn in the brickwork to his side. He stared at the bloody footprints that he had left behind since he had crossed the broken glass. He listened and hoped for one more sob but there was nothing.

CHRIS

'But Listen! I hear a man moaning. 'Lord'
I know I hear a man moaning. 'Lord'
You didn't hear a man moan at all
You didn't hear a man moan at all.'

Bonnie Dobson — *Take Me for a Walk* (1962)

The ground trembled beneath Chris as he crouched behind an abandoned Kingswood on the littered highway. Heat from the ticking engine bay still radiated out and soaked into his back as he pressed against the gleaming guard. The sky above him, heavy with the lingering afterburners of the jets that had raped the tranquillity, was a dark red, as if from the pain of it all. The jets turbines churned the smoke that loitered, and their wings sliced through the blue vacancy like it was their life's single purpose. Among the cannon fire, jet wash and the sounds of some monstrous engines, the streets were filled with the sobs and moans of the city workers. A woman some streets away had howled an incoherent stream of sorrow, anger and fear until a rattle of automatic rifle fire had silenced her. Others simply wept, struggled or moaned as they looked down at what had become of them, as they surely knew what was coming next.

Streams of blood coursed from the banks of the gash on his right arm as he peered over the glistening white bonnet of the Kingswood. He could see that the telecom offices had been levelled. A building once proud and majestic to stand some thirty stories tall in its rendered concrete shell was reduced to nothing but rubble, fire and soot. Its remains spread out in front of it like the guts of a sow in slaughter. The chunks of concrete and wire traced steel reinforcement, all twisted together like the fingers of a broken hand. There was a Ford LTD, which must have been making its way up the levels of the adjacent carpark, which had likewise been brought down in the barrage. Only its rear end was left visible among the rubble. The once straight and perfectly angled roof was now crumpled and creased against its front doors. The rear end, which looked as though it had come straight from the showroom floor, hung suspended. Both tyres were frozen in their position, the gleaming chrome exhaust still protruded, yet there was no wisps of smoke to hint of its power. Only its left indicator remained as a sign of life as it continued its monotonous flash of purpose while the fires from the surrounding rubble caressed the sides of its shell.

To say that Chris had regretted coming to town today was to put it lightly. He had seen the glimmer of hope of bringing Pestilence to life this day. He had fitted the new engine and bell housing, the rail iron bar, and had braced the front chassis. He had even managed to find a second hand bonnet in excellent condition for the right price. All he needed was some simple insulated copper wire to complete the build, and that was it. Before dawn, he had hitched a ride into town before the heat, and the humidity had begun to bleed into his aging flesh. He had taken no more than five steps from the door of Flood Plains Auto Parts when the two large, overly long planes had traced their slow crawl across the great blue above. They worked their way through the cloud cover to conceal themselves completely at times and if it wasn't for the roll of the jet wash, he probably would never have noticed them. It wasn't until he followed the progress of three glinting objects as they fell from the clouds that he had begun to run, as he clutched the roll of wire in his hand.

The blast had thrown him forward so viciously that he had felt nothing but weightlessness and hot air rush past his ears and body. He finally came crashing down on the tarmac, where his face slid painfully across the rough surface. His ears had given up all their efforts of being some sort of help and instead rung angrily in their protest. When he had come to a halt, he had wasted no time in picking himself up and continuing his pace. The sun already burned down on his back as he did all he could to keep pace with his shadow stretching out in front of him. Yet as he ran, his shadow became lost in a wall of debris that had been thrown into the air, along with the smoke and dust cloud that the sun had failed to penetrate. As the soles of his work boots pounded the concrete path, pain throbbed a rhythm in the forefront of his skull, and the debris had finally begun to fall around him.

As Chris looked wildly around to find some hope of shelter, he noticed that he wasn't alone on the streets. People were all around him. Some ran alongside, others just stood there, stunned, as they watched the cloud of smoke and fire rise behind those who fled. He watched a woman get run down as the driver of a Toyota four-wheel-drive made a hasty U-Turn in the street in an attempt to escape the chaos. He watched as the grill bit into her side, and her arms shot out in front as if to cling to anything that gave some hope of life. Then the meaty front left tyre of the Toyota ran up her back and folded her underneath as she began to roll and catch under the axles and chassis. The driver pressed down harder, and soon after the wagon had disappeared, Chris paced past the woman's mangled body.

Another poor, deserving motorist had attempted to cut their way up the street in a small Datsun and had clipped other terrified runners in its path. As the 1600 came level with Chris, there was a horrible crunch of crumpled metal along with the screech and howl of the torn frame as it scraped along the tarmac. The rubber bulged and burst under the added weight as a large chunk of concrete came crashing down on it. The chaos continued as two more bombs were dropped. The dust and smoke consumed the streets, which made it impossible to navigate the obstacles which had presented themselves in the mess. Shortly after the second round of explosions, Chris had fallen on the sidewalk. As he hit the ground, his breath came out of him, and he lay there in shock for just a second. As he attempted to pick himself up, a shrieking woman crashed into him from behind. She spilled over him and drove Chris back down again. Others stepped on his back, one heavy clad boot pressed his face into the concrete, and although his eyes were open, he could not see for the life of him how many people had trampled him. All he could hear were the slaps of their shoes on the pavement and the roar of engines as more cars and trucks flew past. Debris continued to rain down around him, and as he crawled his way up the side of a building, the horrible sound of a plane's machine cannons sounded. Chris lost all the breath that was left to him as he heard the grind of the soulless metal within. The planes' tracers cut through the haze and churned the ground up not a hundred feet in front of Chris. The sound of the ripping machine gun cut everything else, bar the angry ring, from his ears. Before the first burst had finished, another had opened up to spray hot tracer down the street this time. He felt the ground shake under him, and something agonizingly hot flew up from the road next to him to tear up his arm.

Chris threw himself down once more, although by the time his body impacted with the pavement, the jets had already passed. The smell of fuel, soot and dust was in his nose as the haze shook under their power, then lifted and swirled in their slipstream. He hoisted himself up once again while his arm cried in pain. He noticed only now the thud of the cannons from the other side of the buildings to his left. Above him, a shell ripped through the glass wall of the office building he leaned on and tore into the concrete side of the shopping mall across from him. The section of the mall collapsed with the impact, and more dust and smoke arose. Then fires reached through the debris like the arms of a prisoner that stretched out its cell and howled to be released. Chris had seen enough, he turned and continued running.

The haze cleared as he put more and more paces between himself and the crumbling CBD. The highway had been torn up by the jets' machine guns, along with the cars and people that littered it. The fierce power was abhorrent. The bodies of cars were torn from their chassis, and even the blacktop was pockmarked from the reign of hellfire. He had made it only a part of the way down the highway when the Australian Jet was brought down. The explosion and the whirr of its turbine rising in pitch before it let go was only matched in horror by the napalm that was dropped on the crumbling telecom office. Chris had recognised the rolling wildfire from the news on the war in Vietnam. The way it clung to whatever it had hit, the blackness of the smoke that came from it, the way it rolled and curled its way through the air. A group of five or six people had helped each other traverse the torn highway. They were caught on the very edge of the fiery chaos, and as Chris continued to run, he was helpless but to watch the figures. Their black bodies ambled and rolled over the likewise burning bonnets of the cars they cowered behind. No features able to be identified from each person as they died slowly. Just black puppets on fire.

The men with parachutes had landed shortly after, before Chris even neared the burned bodies. He watched as one soldier who was helpless in his direction was sucked into the still burning napalm. He screamed as the licks of napalm sampled his boots, then his legs and finally took the plunge in a bite. The soldier struggled along the rubble. He tripped and tumbled in his panic while the crumpled parachute, which was also alight, snagged on everything. It took what seemed an hour for the man to stop fighting. Like the others, he became a black figure, indistinguishable from the rest.

Chris knew he needed to get off the highway. the majority of parachutes had come down between himself and his home. Angie's face appeared in his mind, her smile, touch, and love. He needed to get to her. They would bring Pestilence to life together the same way a mother and father brought their firstborn screaming and kicking into the world, and together, they would flee. For now, he knew that the cars would have to do as cover so he could work his way through the highway, then disappear into the swamps up by the Narrows and risk the crocs rather than men with assault rifles. He took his time and calculated each step, trying to stay as low as possible. At one point, he saw two of the men that had come down in chutes as they were talking in their strange tongue. They were both small men in stature, their eyes slanted, and their chins were faint. They had red stars on their uniforms and carried the AK-47s that he had once again seen on the news with the war in Vietnam, but these men couldn't be Vietnamese. The two men talked as they sat on the rubble, as if waiting for something. A man in a suit crawled from the rubble of an adjacent building to that of the telecom. They didn't speak or gesture. One of the two just raised his rifle and fired.

Once the parachutes had come down, the cannons stopped and the jet's streaks seemed less of a threat. Rather than look to the skies for falling debris or listen for the tearing sound of the machine guns, Chris's eyes scoured the skirts of the highway. He saw men who calmly lay in wait on the rubble, and then he saw those in the grass only feet from their parachutes. Some formed groups, others just waited. That was what frightened him the most. What were they waiting for? Surely the worst had come. While the sun made a feeble attempt to cut through the smoke and dust, Chris first noticed the faint tremble of the grains of dirt at his feet. In the distance, the sound of large diesel engines, far larger than any he had worked on, roared into life. He had flashbacks from Africa and remembered the iron hulks of the German Panzers, which made the sand quiver in fear as they approached, and his mouth went dry. That was nearly thirty years ago, and he didn't want to relive it. He took one last look at the failing indicator of the LTD and turned his thoughts on his path back to Angie.

He hadn't progressed more than twenty feet when the first tank became visible. It trekked its way over the cars and the people that littered the streets. None of them moved, just the littered remains of their first wave. The tanks were larger than what he had seen in Africa. They were rounded, green, and their cannons stretched out in front, angled to the sky to avoid being hung up on the destroyed car bodies they rode over. The upper half a man's body was visible above the open cupola, as he sat above the rolling iron and looked out at the devastation. The deep rumble of the diesel and the clatter of the tank's tracks over the blacktop drove into Chris' mind and body, it almost made his heart change its rhythm in fear and anticipation. Metal screamed in a shrill protest as the Datsun that had succumbed to the chunk of concrete, crumbled beneath the weight of the monster. The commander didn't even steady himself as the tank crushed the shattered frame of the Japanese sports car. To the left of the commander, a heavy machine gun wobbled and swayed on its mount, just in reach. Chris watched the tanks progress, almost frozen in fear as it clattered and rumbled up the street. Small men emerged and fell in behind the armour. Sometimes one, then two, until a small column had formed, and Chris understood why they had waited. Far behind, another tank had slowly trundled its way into the open as it took the same course as the first. Way off to his right, behind buildings and rubble, Chris heard the tell-tale boom of another tank's main gun and shivered as a building collapsed beneath its power. He looked behind him, only five or so cars of cover remained to him and then a two-hundred-yard dash to the tree line.

He made his way to the final point of cover, to his surprise, he noticed the car was running. As he leaned on the frame, the body of the Corona rolled forward slightly, Chris steadied it. The small motor purred gently beneath its frame. He peered into the cab and saw the remains of a woman in the driver's seat. A hole punched through the windscreen in front of her was replicated through her back as her head slumped over the dashboard. Chris worked his way around the Corona; his eyes scanned the tree line for any signs of men in hiding. As he pulled the door handle, it clunked, and the door swung open silently. He could hear the crunch and grind of the tanks behind him as they made their progress. He let the woman fall to the ground, and she left a mess of blood and matter behind her. The road listed to the right in front of him; only a hundred feet of cars and corpses littered the highway behind him where the first tank pushed forward. If he could take off and clear the distance to the bend before they got him, he would be in the clear. To get the trees in between the small Toyota and the menacing tank would mean his safety, for the moment.

He threw the coil of copper wire to the passenger well, depressed the clutch and pushed the gear lever into first. The car shuddered and stalled as he let up the clutch.

'Fuck.' Only now did he see the handlebar of the motorbike protruding from under the front end. He glanced in the rear-view mirror, but the rear windscreen was obscured by blood and gore. He pushed in the clutch and turned the key. The Toyota came to life on the third turn of the starter; he slammed the shifter into reverse and popped the clutch. The small Toyota rocketed back into the

Landcruiser behind them. The Honda under the front dragged only for a second before it was flung out and off to the side. Chris thanked anybody above watching over him as he pushed the shifter into first once more. As he popped the clutch and the Corona shot forward, the rear windscreen exploded in a shower of glass and shrapnel. He felt a shard dig into his neck as he urged the car onwards and pushed it into second. This time, a glance in the rear-view allowed him a picture of the green tank with a red star as it bore down on him. The soldier who protruded through the hatch fired the heavy machine gun in a wild fashion as the tank's body climbed and fell over the wrecks in its path.

Chris aimed the car at the tightest line for the trees. The Toyota bounced and bucked as it jolted over the median and onto the opposite lane. Bullets snickered and rung off the car's body. In front, he could see a soldier firing directly at him. The destroyed windscreen was scattered once more with bullet holes, and large chunks of already shattered glass fell in wasted clumps to the littered floor. Chris lowered his head behind the dash and aimed the car to where he thought the soldier stood. He punched the throttle, and the small engine whistled as its revs climbed. The automatic fire got louder and louder in the seconds after Chris had lowered his head, then the car lurched and bounced as the metal frame rammed into flesh. The sound it made as the body was sucked under the wheels was sickening, yet the feeling as the car cleared the obstacle and the revs continued to climb felt glorious. The frame was racked by another burst of the heavy machine gun fire, and steam began to emit from under the bonnet. 'Come on, girl, it isn't far,' he urged the Toyota as he shifted into fourth, and finally, the trees were between him and the tank.

The tank had continued to fire through the trees, he heard the thumps and the cracks as ancient old trunks split under the withering fire, but none came close to him. Chris continued to look through the rear-view as he urged the dying car onwards and waited to see the muzzle of the main gun emerge from the bend. He knew it wouldn't be long. He turned his eyes back to the road and nearly shit himself. The faded blue cab of the old fifties Freightliner hurtled down the road at a speed well above the usual cascade. The tyres shuddered as Chris pulled the Toyota off the road and onto the shoulder. He worried the wheel as he went and hoped that the small tyres wouldn't bog into the grass at the speed he was doing. The Freightliner thundered past in a roar of diesel and dust. He caught a glimpse of what could have been his friend behind the wheel, but the figure there was gaunt and pale, his face contorted in what looked like inconsolable anguish. The road train seemed to go forever, the cab, then the A trailer, and finally the B and C. All the tankers were full from the deep bellow of the diesel as it laboured. Chris gently ushered the car back onto the tarmac and continued to put the hammer down. He drove blindly while watching the tanker's back grow smaller in the mirror.

Just before impact, the Freightliner sounded its air horn. For an instant, that deep roar filled the earth until its cab jolted upward so that Chris could see it above the trailers. The world behind him was engulfed in a fireball as near eight thousand gallons of fuel went up. Everything became brighter and even at the distance he was, he felt the heat. He allowed the car to slow slightly. He glanced back through the completely destroyed windscreen to make sure he wouldn't impact anything else. Satisfied, he allowed the car to slow to a crawl and then finally stop, so he could watch for a moment longer and think of his friend.

As he watched the flames fight among themselves like unruly children, a shiver ran along his spine and his eyes widened. The muzzle of the main gun emerged through the flames, it raised itself into the air as the remains of the tankers were crushed beneath its hull, and then it fell back down to the earth and continued to crawl. As it emerged from the fire, it became its own, like a fireball of blackened steel, set on revenge for the car that had escaped it. Chris watched in horror as he saw men climb from the belly of the beast while they burned alive. They screamed and rolled out of the hatches. He watched as one of the men fell down the front of the still rolling hull, only to be pulled under the tracks, the life crushed out of him while the fire turned his face into a melted ruin. Chris did not want to see how far the tank would roll unmanned. Instead, he turned his head away, mentally thanked Travis once more, and continued down the highway back to his house and his wife.

He had been sure that he was going to run into more of the soldiers on his way. He had seen discarded parachutes and the corpses of men and women. The trucking yard where Rabbits and his Freightliner had emerged from to take their final charge was now ablaze. From what Chris could see, the Narrows was more or less a large fire now. The military base that lay beyond looked as though it had been the second place of attack for the planes; they had concentrated on terrorism first. As he drove, he watched the menacing jets lay down the gut-wrenching machine gun fire. It was followed shortly by a burst of napalm, which ran across the ground in a wall of fire that bulged and curled up at the end. The military had done nothing for the people in the city, not that they could have, and likewise, Chris could do nothing for them.

In another ten minutes, he bounced the Corona into his drive and pushed it down the stretch of dirt. As the steam became more and more prominent, the engine began to labour and shudder. In the end, it let him down some five hundred feet from his gate. Chris ran in the beginning. As he passed four parachutes that hung up in the trees, he began to sprint. His breath burned in his lungs, his feet pounded the graded earth and kicked dust as his sweat-soaked him in the early morning heat. As he entered the gate, everything seemed fine; nothing was out of the ordinary, nothing had changed. The workshop doors were still open, and Pestilence lay in wait; her new headlights watched him like the predatory eyes of a panther. He went straight to the car and reefed the door open, then he plunged his hand behind the seat and retrieved his bayonet. His hand clenched the small handle as he faced the house he had lived in for over twenty years with his wife, his love. Gravel ground beneath his feet as he stepped cautiously across the drive, his eyes fixed on the open front door.

He placed one boot on the porch steps, then another. More of the house was revealed with each step he climbed. The living room was ransacked, pictures of himself and his beautiful wife on the ground. Their frames cracked, splinters of glass scattered over the rugs and the polished floors. The couch had been overturned, and the lamp which sat on the small table next to it was in pieces. Its once-white lampshade had the distinct mud and grime of a footprint on its crushed side. He entered the house and went straight to the hall table that held his favourite pictures, all of which were scattered now like the leaves from a tree in autumn. The glass crunched under his boots, and the frames of the photographs he had held so dear fractured under his weight. The bayonet hung loosely from his grip at his side; its weight was a comfort to the man as he neared his closed bedroom door. He stepped softly from the hall runner to the bare patch of hardwood boards that lay just before his door. He placed his hand that clutched the bayonet on the door next to his face and rested his forehead against the cool kiss of the painted timber. For a split second, the eyes of Pestilence raced through his mind as it sat and watched his progress from the workshop. She was more obedient than any dog, yet machines would give their loyalty to anyone who could control them. Chris furrowed his brow, took a deep breath and turned the gleaming brass doorknob.

CHRIS

'I threw a pebble in a brook,
And watched the ripples run away,
And they never made a sound.
And the leaves that were green
Turn to brown.'

Simon and Garfunkel – *The Leaves That Are Green* (1966)

As he lay face down and his cheek pressed into the cobblestones below him, he opened his eyes and stared blankly across the courtyard. His hands were down by his side, his body limp. He had been this way for what seemed like an eternity. Stagnant, he was satisfied enough to lie there as long as his mind would allow him. In the time he had lain there, there had not been a single sound. Not the rustle of a leaf, not the song of a bird. Not even a whistle of a gust of wind as it rustled through his hair; he couldn't even remember if he had taken a breath.

Overthinking, as if he had just emerged from the depths of a pool, he gasped. His eyes opened wide to reveal the vast white oceans around their hazel islands. He spluttered as he continued to suck in long, deep breaths and tried to hold them to slow down his sudden panic. But no sooner had he begun to inhale than his chest had heaved the air out of him, like a greedy dog that eyed his brothers' plate before he had finished his own. Chris slowly brought his panicked, heavy breaths under control. He rolled onto his side and propped himself up with both hands. With each glance at his surroundings, his mind settled. Yet, his hands trembled and quivered as he ran them over his face and kneaded into his eyes. Finally, he gained his feet and once more, he stood in the middle of the cobblestone courtyard of his mind.

As he let his hands fall to his side once more, he noticed one of the brick buildings which skirted the courtyard. His eyes squinted at the spectacle, but his body urged him to get nearer. He raised a hand to shield his eyes as he moved. The building, although brick and stone in construction, burned as if it was the black head of a match that was struck along the cobblestones to begin its beautiful existence. The flames guttered as they tried to hold their purchase on the smooth brick and mortar of the building's walls. Yet as each tendril and lick died in its curl, there seemed to be more and more come up from nothing, determined to at least blacken the shell of the stone beast if not to destroy it at all. He stood there, transfixed. The flames ran up the brickwork like there was a fuel source, but there was nothing. No lines of fluid etching its way down the brick, and no blackened compound was pushed into the pores of the stonework. The brick was just on fire, yet the mortar shone a bright white. As if to shun the fire, the bricks remained their earthy brown, red and black.

Without getting close enough to tempt the fire from trying the oil-stained mechanics rags he wore loosely on his body, Chris peered to see through one of the windows on the ground floor. There didn't seem to be any movement inside the house. Only a single portrait of a man and woman on their wedding day was visible as it hung from a nail bent into the wall. Chris studied the photo as best as he could from a distance and through the fire, but even so, the curls and length of that blonde hair that he knew and loved would never be mistaken. He wanted to get closer; he wanted to see the details of her face. As he urged closer, he tempted the flames and their heat; he could see the nail in the wall begin to fail in its perch. He only needed a few more steps, and he would be able to see her once more. As the sole of his work boot touched the grass and the first hungry lick of the fire touched his outstretched hand, the nail lost its grasp in the plastered wall, and as if suspended in time, the portrait slowly fell from sight. As they went, flames erupted inside the house in such a powerful fury that the window was blown outwards. Glass clinked as shards and shattered chunks clattered to the courtyard. The heat intensified tenfold, and Chris was forced to take steps backward. The sound of the fire was surreal; it didn't roar as he expected. The crackle of the heat as it broke down its fuel did not exist. He stood there for a moment. What would happen if he were to enter the flames? If he walked open-armed into the abyss and let it take him? Felt those silent embers running up his legs, soaking the oil-stained jeans? To let them taste and test before they finally sunk their teeth into him and delivered a life-crushing blow.

He turned to the steel fence which marked the outside perimeter of his courtyard. The stone pillars which held the border were still crushed on the ground. Smoke wisped through the air and billowed at an invisible barrier as if it didn't dare to reach out over the cobblestone. He took his time as he ventured closer to the steel mesh and strained his eyes to cut through the smoke. There was movement within, but he could not quite see what it was. As he reached the fence, he crouched low to try and look below and found that he could see a curb and street which wound its way past the courtyard and hooked on a dogleg out into the smoke. He could see the feet of people as they shuffled down the road. Women's high heels and men in business pants and shiny black shoes. At one point, he made out the torsos of two small children as they walked hand in hand. They looked dirty and dishevelled as they comforted each other, their heads bowed so that they could watch their feet and not stumble on debris. No one spoke or looked at each other; they just continued their pace onward into the smoke.

To his right, he remembered there was a gate that would allow him to escape from the courtyard. He could see that it was still closed to him, yet on the other side, there were two men with their backs to the steel. They overlooked as the droves of people walked only feet away from them, barely visible. One man was tall and broad-shouldered, he was dressed in Australian Military dress, with a slouch hat and parade issue Enfield slung at his shoulder. The brass gleamed from the swivels of his sling and the polished chrome nose cap cut through the haze, too proud to go unseen. The man to his side was of a smaller frame and dressed in brown military dress, with high boots and a dagger shining at his side. The rifle that rested on its stock by his side was the AK-47 of the invaders. Neither of them turned to look at him as he neared. He called out to them, yet they still didn't turn, didn't even speak. As he stood behind them, he tried to scream, but not even a whisper escaped his lips.

He felt the anger mount in his belly once more. He clenched his fists and pounded on the gate. Yet as soon as his flesh touched the cool metal surface, there was a soft 'whump,' and he watched in horror as flames spread from nowhere up his arms. The flesh underneath turned into a blackened mess as the skin melted and bubbled in front of his eyes. As he fell, the flame consumed him. He felt it crawl up his neck, catch his hair and finally suffocate him.

The last thing he saw, was that *finally* the Australian Soldier at the gate had turned to consider the screaming, burning man behind him. Under the slouch hat, there was only rotting flesh that half clung to the pale white bone. The man's left cheek hung down in a filthy brown flap that still had grass and dirt embedded in its moist, rotting flesh. His right eye was gone, but his left floated in its socket, deflated and yellowed by age. Its brown pupil had leaked and formed a horrible patch at the lower right section of its whites. Where his nose once was, remained a gaping hole where only darkness could be seen. His lips had receded to expose what remained of his gums and his yellowed teeth. As the single floating eye looked down on him, the soldier laughed in a rattled, heaving splutter, which sent a shiver up Chris's spine. Then he lost his vision, the world fell silent, and there was only darkness.

The motor whirred. Nothing. It whirred again and caught. It spluttered to life and desperately tried to hold on, yet failed. A pause. The motor whirred, and just as it could be thought a hopeless cause, it caught and erupted in an earth-shattering roar of power, hunger and desire which could be heard for miles in the otherwise desolate area of Holtze. The ground seemed to tremble beneath the tyres of the beast that had now drawn its first breath of life in its final and imperfect state. For it, for its maker, the hunt had now begun.

In the darkness, the headlights of the monster illuminated the cinderblock rear wall of the Lowe's workshop. It was fairly bare now, just one man, unconscious, slumped against it. His head hung low, but his arms spread like Christ on the cross. Chains ran from his wrists outward to secure him to either the hoist or the oversized workbench. To either side of him was a car ramp, spaced maybe a foot back from the wall. It didn't matter; it was only a guess. The engine pounded the air in its sloppy dissonant rhythm. It didn't want to idle; it wanted to sing. The shifter clunked into low, and the first kiss of the power was given to the back wheels, which spun in enthusiasm as if excited by what it could see in its wake. Yet they spun only for a moment. A shrill pitch echoed in the shop and cut through the rumble of the exhaust for a short time, only to be consumed like everything else by its low, deep mutter. The iron frame rolled forward, and it lurched with the dissonant rhythm of its idle. The front tyres reached the ramps and the front of the Holden began to climb. As it did, the railway track caught the chained man gently by his forehead, and as it rose, so did his face, until finally, they were both at the height they needed to be. Slowly the car edged closer and closer, as did the distance between the wall and the hardened iron rail, less than a foot now, and it stopped.

There was a soft 'clack, clack, clack' as the iron beast's handbrake was engaged, and the driver allowed his foot to come off the brake. The engine tested the strength of its stopping power, teasing as if it wanted to go those extra few inches. Chris walked around to the front of the car and peered into the open engine bay as he passed. He watched as the Chevrolet plant rocked on its mounts while it surged with raw power. Finally, he reached the man caught in the jaws of the cat. His eyes were still closed, still in the blankness of his subconscious.

When Chris had awoken, he had lain on the gravel of his drive. It took him some time to work out where he was. The house in front of him was on fire, his hands and arms were burned. As he saw the house he had lived in with his beautiful wife for so many years burn and crumble under the roar of the fire which burned so fiercely, he had lost part of his mind. He had tried to run into the chaos as he screamed Angie's name, yet the pain in his hands and arms was too great, and he retreated to the safety of the drive. As tears streamed down his face, he saw another figure lay motionless on the gravel, twenty feet beyond where he had lain himself. With a raised sense of hope in his stomach, he had rushed over to who he had hoped was his wife. Yet, instead of long, flowing blonde hair, he found short-cropped black bristles. Instead of longing brown eyes, he found closed narrow slits of an Asian man. Instead of a summer dress, he had found a military uniform. Beside him, lay his 1907 bayonet. Dirt and gravel had stuck to parts of the blade that were covered in thick, red blood. If this unconscious soldier had escaped the fire, then so had she. The thought pounded through his head, over and over. The man before him was the key to finding her. She was too beautiful. They had taken her, and he would find her again. As he secured the loops of heavy chain around the soldiers' wrists, he paused as he thought to himself, 'how am I going to speak to this man?' Then something inside him, deep within, assured him, Angie's whisper across the back of his mind, *'he will lead you to me.'* As his house, his home, crackled and collapsed in a flurry of embers and memories, he had chained each wrist to his bench and his hoist and had set about putting the finishing touches on Pestilence. If he needed to find her, what better to ride, than his pale horse.

The temperature of the Chevrolet's iron block climbed quickly. As Chris stood silently, there was a small click as the clutch of the viscous fan engaged, and the heavy iron blades of the cooling fan swung into motion. The rush of air being sucked past the man's face made his eyes flicker, and finally, they opened wide with surprise and horror at his position. His eyes darted around and then fixed on Chris's. His arms strained against the chains, and underneath the snarling mouth of Pestilence, he could hear the rubber of his boots slapping against concrete and steel. Chris let him panic. He knew the fan would turn off in a little while. Rather than scream to be heard over it, he let his captive bask in its fury.

His head not quite pinned between railroad iron and concrete, it bobbled around in panic as the man sobbed and pleaded in pig English, 'Family. Please.'

There was another small click as the viscous fan's clutch disengaged, and the blades slowly came to a halt. Chris leaned in close to the man, their eyes fixed, the quick panicked breaths of the chained man audible over the steady yet dissonant rhythm of the V8.

'Where is she?' It was more of a whisper than anything, the words quiet yet clear, the understanding coming into the man's eyes. He knew what had been asked, that much was clear, but the flurry of words and panicked shrieks of 'No' and 'Family' from the man were frustrating. He leaned his body into the open engine bay of the Holden and tweaked the throttle lever on the enormous 600 Holley. The motor blipped in a short roar, and the body surged against the brake that held it pinned. The car rocked as all of its forces worked against one another. The brake held, but not completely after the body had settled; both men knew at least an inch of space had been lost.

'Shhhhhhh…' Chris calmed the man who had shrieked violently at the car's progression and had begun his flurries of please and families once the iron frame had settled again. He placed a burned finger to his lips and repeated, 'Where is she?'

This time, the man considered, his eyes darted everywhere. Perhaps he looked for an escape; perhaps he just looked for something to say. 'Sh-sh-sh- she?'

'Yes, she. Her,' he pointed to the house desperately. 'Where is she?' His face was so close to the soldiers that he could smell his horrible breath.

'Sh-sh-she, family?' The man spoke as he attempted to remain calm. 'Family.' His arms strained against the chains.

'Yes,' Chris growled, his eyebrows furrowed. The anger in the pit of his stomach rolled and churned. 'Family.'

The man nodded and smiled. A strained, forced attempt. His eyes were frightened. 'Family,' he chuckled a soft, reassuring laugh. 'Very,' he considered words to use, 'Beautiful.'

The engine blipped once more, and the body rocked and urged against its brakes as it tried to reach out. The man screamed once more. The iron of the makeshift bull bar had now pressed the side of his face against the cinder block; he didn't have much time left. Only one or maybe two more blips of the throttle would crush his skull. His face was pushed inwards slightly, but there was no pain for him yet. Chris smiled at him; the man's breaths had become even quicker.

'You don't have long, my friend. You need to tell me where she is.'

'Sh-sh-sh,' he began again, the sound now odd as his lips and mouth strained to move under the pressure of the iron.

'She, the woman, long hair, beautiful, yes. Where?'

He shook his head.

The Engine blipped, and the viscous fan came into motion once more. Beneath the roar and the mutter of the exhaust, small cracks could be heard as the man's jaw was dislocated under the pressure of the iron. Under the smell of the fuel, exhaust, smoke and charcoal, Chris could smell the piss of the soldier as he cowered in front of him. Once more, he waited. He had the rest of the soldier's life to wait, and the soft clinks of the Holden's handbrake as it strained under the power of its new V8 plant told him he didn't have long to wait. Finally, the fan slowed to a stop once more. The heat that radiated from the engine bay was immense, and he saw the sweat of fear and heat course down the soldier's half-crushed face.

He needed to ask the question in a different way. Chris leaned in close, the pain still streaked from his blistered hands and arms. 'Is my family with your people?'

The man nodded ever so slightly, his face pinned against iron and cinderblock, but it was a nod.

'Okay,' he sighed. He had only time for one more question, and then he would need to start his chase, but before then, Pestilence would take her tax.

He straightened and his eyes darted around his once neat workshop. He racked his brain as he thought about a straightforward question to bridge the language barrier he was stuck on. Finally, his eyes fell upon an old worn poster with the map of Australia, but with slang names for cities. A glimmer of hope shone in his eyes; Chris nearly skipped as he made his way across the polished concrete to retrieve the map. When he returned, his prisoners' eyes once more darted every which way, and he strained against his restraints. Chris wagged a finger in front of his face as if he talked to a child and tutted with each finger movement.

'You haven't answered all of your questions yet. You couldn't possibly think about bailing out now?'

The soldier had no idea what he had said, but nodded profusely and continued about his family. The word 'beautiful' made a few more mentions. Chris had begun to wonder if he meant Angie or his own family.

He shook his head as he dismissed the matter, and he kneeled down once more. He held the map out to the soldier at a distance so that with his left hand, he could point at the map. The prisoner had pulled so hard on his restraints that he had stripped part of the skin on his wrist. A trickle of blood ran down his now relaxed hand and pooled at the tips of his fingers.

'Where? You point. Show me where.' Chris spoke loud and slowly as the body of the Holden quivered with a small surge from the idling engine. Extending one finger, the soldier pressed his bloody skin against the page, nodding and feigning a smile. Once more, he spoke of a beautiful family in his pig English.

Chris stood up; the man's eyes followed him, wide with question and concern. Chris thought about his courtyard in his mind, the rubble of the pillars and the smoke. A question of a smile hinted on his dirty face, 'Will I see you there? In the smoke? Will I see you in the burning house or at the gate? Was it you that wouldn't let me pass?' He didn't know why he wanted to ask those questions, but now that he had, they seemed to be the most important thing to him.

'Why won't you let me pass?'

The Asian man tried a forced chuckle and a smile; their eyes never broke contact. He struggled with words once more. 'Family... Beautiful...' until the fan churned into motion once more and the stillness was destroyed by its hunger. The soldier thrashed against his restraints. Chris pulled the throttle lever hard and everything was lost in the perfect roar of power. The rubber howled and spun freely on the polished concrete. Their eyes never broke contact as his head was crushed by the beast that pinned him. Chris watched the soldier's jaw separate from his face, his flat nose protruding longer than it ever had, the sequence of progression as the skull gave way and the iron bar surged onward.

There was no life left in the soldier, only in the beast.

The roar subsided and resumed its shaky mutter. Chris stood there for a long moment, his face blank. The anger in his gut was gone for now.

He looked to Pestilence. Her front raised still on the ramps, her body trembled as if from excitement. He ran a blistered hand down her flank and felt the vibration of the rough idling V8 surge through her as he moved down her side. He stepped away to admire her from afar, her stance, her power. Her headlights bored into the cinderblock wall only inches away, while the iron bar pushed hard up against it. Chris smiled softly as the main beam of the house he had lived in cracked and collapsed behind him, and the flames surged up in the night air. The hunt had begun, and the pale horse would ride that night. Before he set about his plans, he took a final look at the map of Australia that he had presented to his prisoner. A round blotch of blood stood out in stark contrast to yellows and blues. The stain mostly covered the slang name, but the bracketed italics of the correct name was still visible: *Brisbane.*

RANKIN

'No reason to get excited,
The thief kindly spoke,
There are many here among us,
Who feel that life is but a joke.'

Jimi Hendrix – *All Along the Watchtower* (1968)

Each day ran into one; there was no difference. Eat, shit, exercise, eat, sleep, and sometimes in reverse order. Exercise was everything now, his body the one item of solace in this whole mess. He couldn't polish his brass knuckles, and he couldn't maintain his service rifle, so he concentrated on his muscles. His biceps bulged from the weights in the yard, and his chest hardened and became more defined from the presses and the push-ups. The line of his shoulders connected higher to his neck than they had ever before and his core, although scarred by the line which etched its way across his side, was harder and stronger than ever. Everything was an exercise. To get out of bed, he attempted to make his way across the room without touching the floor. He wrapped his hands around the bars of his small window and braced himself against the wall with the soles of his bare feet. There was nowhere else in the room to grab a foothold apart from the barred door which held him enclosed. Leaning back, he looked over his shoulder at the bars behind him. He shuffled his feet and bent his toes in to secure their grip on the weathered sandstone walls. The sandstone grit between his toes, bit into his skin and threatened to rip and tear at the slightest friction.

'One, two,' he began to bounce in time with his count as he felt each muscle tense and then relax in preparation for the mighty leap, 'three!' He pushed up and outwards with his legs and twisted his body in the air while he stretched his arms out in front of him. The propulsion his legs gave him was more than enough, almost too much. The hair on his head, which had grown to an untidy mess in his time spent doing his acrobatics, brushed harmlessly against the mottled concrete ceiling. He felt the cool kiss of steel in his palms as his hands wrapped around the bars of the door. His feet likewise came forward, like a duck's legs spread out for its high-speed landing.

'Perfect.' The smirk spread across his face. He bounced his weight backward and brought his legs up behind him, leaving only his grasp on the steel bars to support his weight. 'Come on, come on, as many as you can.' Up and down his body went, fast at first, too fast, almost uncontrollable. His mind was the key to his weapon, and it wasn't long before it kicked into gear and lowered the speed of his muscles. He finally began to ache as he went on, but that was what he wanted; he almost craved it. There was nothing else in his life now but his body and the pain of his muscles when he had overworked them. With each passing day, he found that needed it more and more.

Sometimes he thought back to when he started his sentence, his body racked by the shakes of his withdrawals. Although they still held their strength due to his youth, his muscles waned early on. His first hundred attempts of the leap across the room had failed. The gritty sandstone had torn the flesh from his feet more than once, and the soft sandy brown was now stained in places from his blood. Other times, he had simply fallen short or flat on his face. The other prisoners in the block laughed and shouted insults at him, even though the majority couldn't see him. But he only sneered and continued. He worked harder and harder to push the pain beyond its limits until sometimes he either threw up or collapsed in a heaving heap on the floor or on his bed while his heart pounded in his chest.

The most miraculous of changes was in his head. The dreams of his brothers in arms and the dreams of Mary had thinned in their occurrence. He knew they would always haunt him, deep down at least, but the negativity, the cloudiness of his mind, had vanished. He no longer woke up drowsy, and he couldn't remember the last time he had a headache. His vision seemed clearer. He still smoked far too much, but that was more out of boredom than anything else. *Everyone needs at least one vice*, he thought.

For a while, he found that the bigger and fitter he got, the more the attacks came. But time after time, he beat them back. Whether it be in the yard, the shower, or in the mess. No matter how many came, no matter what they said, he took all they had to give and dealt it back tenfold. The more they gave, the more they hurt. The big dumbass that had started it all had tried a couple of more times. As he knew, the bigger they were, the slower they moved, but Brian the brawn was the slowest man he had ever seen—he couldn't understand why he was so revered. Each punch he threw seemed to take a year to reach its target. The only way Rankin figured he could hit someone was that he had been lucky enough to pick fights with people even dumber than he was. Stupid enough to stand there and let the slow hammer drop. Even as he thought about it, he couldn't remember if Brian had ever landed a punch on him. Rankin had ducked and weaved time after time; he had driven his fists into the big man's body to work the ribs and kidneys. He never heard about it, but he was certain the stupid prick would have been pissing blood for two weeks.

The attacks always ended as abruptly as it began. A bunch of guards intervening, who at first had just watched the show, happy for some excitement. Once, they had seen one guy get hit with either a ripping hook or a tremendous uppercut, and the fear that a prisoner could die on them while they watched and laughed got the better of them. Then they would all rush forward as if they had only just seen the commotion. Batons whirled through the air, and the 'thwomp, thwomp' of the slender black shafts was heard as they were laid into flesh. Then the cries of the prisoners who actually had the nerve to act surprised when they were hit. Of all the times he was hit, all of the fists, all of the kicks, the batons hurt Rankin the most. One blow had bruised his ribs for three weeks. The patch had swelled up black, brown, then yellow and ached to the point where he even considered that some of his ribs had been broken. But he never complained. He never fought the guards, although he saw it in their eyes that they wanted him to. Nothing would have pleased them more to have had an excuse to lay open his skull, or break bones, or even visit him in the night as they had with Summers.

Jeremy Summers was an inmate that Rankin knew of in passing. As Rankin never spoke to anyone, satisfied with his own company, he had never known what Summers was about. He was an average height man with no real muscle mass to him; his chest was covered in poorly done tattoos of skulls, flowers, and women with a little flame thrown in for effect. The biggest part of Summers had been his mouth, he remarked with what he thought as hilarity at everything to do with anyone. Guards, prisoners, the big and the small, it never mattered. He never knew what Summers had said to have earned him his midnight visit by four of the bigger guards, and he imagined that it didn't really matter. Summers used to occupy the cell below Rankin's. He remembered the footfalls on the grated steel walkway in the night, too many to have just been a normal patrol. He remembered the grind as the old steel bars had slid open. The screams which would have woken the entire block at first, had become muffled. He remembered the sound of the batons whiz through the air, the unmistakable sound as they bit into flesh and the grunts of the men that worked him over.

Although the screams of protest from Summers had undoubtedly alerted the other prisoners to what had happened, the cell block was otherwise silent. The grunts had stopped, as had the beating. The cell door had slammed back shut, and the heavy footfalls echoed through the stone hall until they disappeared into the night. Rankin thought he had heard the struggle for life that had continued through the night below him. He thought he had heard attempts for breath, even scratches on the concrete floor as the broken man had tried to crawl to his bunk. Rankin lay there awake as he stared into the darkness; he didn't feel much of anything. Neither fear nor pity for the loudmouth, not even an ache in his muscles from his day of labour and his intensified solitary training sessions. Eventually, he fell asleep and had enjoyed one of the better nights of sleep he had encountered during his stay.

The next morning, a ruckus occurred when the morning shift of guards had opened all the cell doors and waited impatiently for the prisoners to move into the mess room. Obviously, they counted one short, and Rankin saw the guards with furrowed brows as they made a second and third count of heads in the mess room. They acted as if they were teachers that marked the roll call for the morning classes and realised that someone was missing. It wasn't until weeks later that he had heard prisoners from another block discuss that Summers had committed suicide by hanging himself in his cell. Apparently, he had torn his bedsheets into strips and had carefully tied them end to end. He then weaved a portion through the bars of the small window that sat high in each cell and had created a hangman's noose for himself.

One of the prisoners in the conversation didn't seem as ignorant as the others and had said, 'That's not high enough to hang yourself.'

The other didn't want a small thing like facts getting in the way of a good story, reasoned that just explained how desperate he was for an out. He tied the rope around his neck and placed all of his weight against the makeshift noose he had made. Finally, he had passed out, and in his unconsciousness, had succumbed to the effects of his own weight against the strips of bed linen.

Rankin reflected that too many people believed what they were told. In the end, he didn't really care much one way or the other. Summers didn't matter to him and neither did any of the guards, nor the prisoners. Nothing that came out of anyone's mouth mattered; it was all lies anyway. Trust, love, hate or fear, none of it was true. There was only one thing that each person needed to worry about, and that was themselves.

His brothers in arms had been there for him at the beginning; that much was true. But as they died, parts of him died with them. Sometimes, he thought that perhaps it was better that he never had another friend or lover. Other times, he lay in his bunk, his manhood as hard as hot iron below his sheet and all he could do was stare at it like it was a rash, as if he wondered what he was supposed to do with it when it got like that. He rarely thought about women anymore. Each time a set of tits came into his mind, the curves of a woman's hips or the flow of her hair over her shoulders, he would think of the hair lipped whore. He would think of Gary, then finally, he would think of Mary, her face smashed up, her teeth broken. Love was not an option for him, unless it was for himself. But how could he love what he was?

The cycle was vicious and neverending: pride in who he was swelled up inside of him like the bruise on his ribs, then came the fall of hatred. There was no self-pity, he didn't have room for that, just the disappointment in how he had failed in everything he had achieved in life. There was one moment in one of his 'darker' turns where he had ridiculed himself, put himself down so low, how it was no wonder that he had never had a woman that he hadn't paid for. What self-respecting woman would touch a man like him? He tried to defend himself, but a soft retort of: *What about Mary?* would echo deep from the caverns of his mind. As soon as it did, he felt himself stoop lower and he tried to sink further into the mattress that he lay on. He put his hands to his face and waited for the thought that he knew would follow. He anticipated it so much that he spoke it aloud himself.

'We all know what happened to her.'

The only way out of it was pain. Each time he sank low, he punished himself with exercise. He would do push-ups until he collapsed. He would press his toes into the odd ruts of the sandstone and do sit-ups until his guts screamed in agony. Still, he pressed on. The pain was the fire that burned the dark thoughts from him, and the sweat was the water to cool the heat of hate. And so, he continued to punish his body throughout the night and at every point he could during the day. By the time six months had passed, he was in the best shape he had ever been in. Better than the day he had left for Vietnam and tenfold the man that had marched the streets of Enoggera.

He had his one and only visitor seven months into his sentence. He lay on his bunk once more, tracing the lines of the cracks in the concrete and the crumbled mortar between the sandstone blocks, when he had heard the footsteps on the steel grate. Too many to be a patrol. He didn't take much notice until they stopped outside of his cell. He sat up as the barred door swung open, his hands on his knees in loose fists, ready to defend himself if need be. When the guard, a big burly man with arms like tree trunks, told him he had a visitor.

Rankin just continued to stare at him like it was a poor attempt at a joke.

Rankin stood, centred himself in the room and slightly bent his legs.

'So, this is the part where you give me the old Summers treatment?' His mouth turned to a sneer as he spoke the words, his shoulders hunched.

The guard gave him a funny look and screwed his face up. As the guard eyed his stance, Rankin realised that the baton was hung low on the guard's hip and wasn't even loosened in its strap. He didn't know what to do, so the two men just stood there and stared at each other for some time while the other guards who stood outside shuffled impatiently.

'I know I'm a handsome man, Bartlett, but I do have other shit to do today, so if you're finished staring at me, would you get the fuck out?'

The expression on Rankin's face vanished as his eyebrows furrowed. It turned out the burly guard wasn't full of shit. As the possibilities of who it could be and why ran through his mind, Rankin lowered his head and continued to eye the guard. 'Well, what are we waiting for? I can see flattery will get me nowhere with you.'

He felt all the eyes of the inmates on him as he strode with his escort through the cell block. No one spoke; he barely even heard a breath, just the four sets of footfalls. His head jerked every now and then as he peered through the bars at the inmates within. Rankin didn't bother; he just watched the man walk and amused himself at the way he pushed his chest out and strutted in a way that made it look like too much of an effort. He loved the way people tried to make themselves look big, as if it was intimidating. Big men didn't scare Rankin, especially not ones that tried to make themselves look even bigger. They walked for what seemed twenty minutes through doors that required them to be buzzed in by a fat man who watched them through a thick, milky pane of glass. Other doors required a key to be unlocked; Rankin watched patiently as guard after guard rumbled through a mess of keys at the end of a bit of tied wire or another that hung off a ring the size of a man's fist.

They led him to a door that had tarnished brass lettering pinned across the metal sheet lining. 'Interrogation room,' Rankin read. His brow furrowed. What could he be getting interrogated about? The only thought that sprung to mind was Summers, and he glanced at the burly guard who led him in and told him to sit.

The room was smaller and colder than his cell. There were only three pieces of furniture, two small metal chairs and a polished table in between them. As Rankin sat, he felt the cool kiss on his lower back and the undersides of his forearms. A plastic ashtray sat in the middle of the table. He tried to slide his chair closer to the table so he could get himself more comfortable, but the chair refused to budge. The guards left him without another word, and the door slammed closed. He looked under the table and saw that each leg of the table and two chairs were bolted to the floor.

He pulled his cigarettes from his pocket and fiddled with the packet. Cigarettes cost a fortune in this place, almost a dollar a packet. Seeing as though he earned fifty cents a day either digging holes or patching stonework in the yard, he looked at cigarettes like they were worth something for once in his life. He still smoked them too quickly to make the packet last the two days, but he preferred to smoke them if he had them; one never knew when something would happen. Like now…

As he struck a match and lit his cigarette, the door opened once more, and Rankin's shoulders slumped. A man in a drab brown suit entered the room; he carried a plain battered suitcase and wore the type of glasses one bought from a cheap store. His hair was messy, and his faded tie hung loosely around his neck. The man looked as though he had been to hell and back. A light film of sweat covered his forehead; it started at the point of his widow's peak and resonated out the shit, greasy slicked back hair that he still remembered.

'Running late?' Rankin commented as he tapped his ash into the container and pretended to look at a watch on his bare wrist.

The man ignored him. He placed his suitcase on the table and unclipped the latches. As he sat down to rummage through the innards of his now opened suitcase, Rankin's eyes burned into him. The man still had not met his gaze and Rankin continued to smoke and glare in his direction as the flustered man went through file after file until finally, he spoke.

'Bartlett, Rankin, of Sydney.' The man held up the file, as if in triumph that he had found anything in the jumble of shit he hid between the leather folds of his case.

Rankin didn't answer him, he just continued to stare until his gaze was finally met. He didn't know if there was any recognition in the other man's eyes; there didn't seem to be. He placed the file on the cool tabletop and continued to speak.

'My name is Belkin. I'm a—'

'I know who you are,' Rankin cut him off. He spoke as he exhaled a breath of cigarette smoke into the man's face. His upper lip twitched as the cigarette smoke rolled around his face, and Rankin could tell he wasn't a smoker. His smile widened at this. 'I recall it was you that took me off the streets some years ago. I know I was younger then, but I'm surprised you don't remember me.'

Belkin had begun to gather his composure and he exhaled, blowing some of the lingering smoke away from his face. He held Rankin's gaze as he said, 'I meet a lot of people in my job.'

'Oh, I'm sure you do. All the downtrodden mongrels, no doubt.'

'And the fact that the first time we met was in a shelter,' Belkin broke the gaze to look over the file that was spread out in front of him, 'and now only the second time we have met, and correct me if I'm wrong Mr Bartlett, but this doesn't look like Kirribilli house?'

Rankin laughed at the comment but held his stare. He didn't reply. The son of a bitch had got him with that one. Instead, he took another drag on his cigarette and exhaled it in Belkin's face once more, his smirk from ear to ear.

'You have been in prison for a little over six months.' Belkin stated, 'A lot has happened to your country in that time, Mr Bartlett, and a situation has occurred where your country requires your service once more.'

Rankin laughed again; that was probably the only thing he could have done. The laugh was long and hearty, and he craned his neck back and closed his eyes as he pounded his cigarette-free hand down on the table. When he finished, his face was expressionless. The anger had swelled in his stomach. He now understood why the tables and chairs were bolted down in this room, as the next thing he would have done was to break Belkin's head with the one he sat on.

Instead, he crushed out his cigarette while Belkin sat patiently and watched him. He leaned over the table and lowered his voice to a growl.

'A lot has happened to me too, and not just over the past seven months, mate. I can fucking tell you that much.'

Belkin's expression remained unchanged. He sat silently while Rankin had his rant.

'I went over to that shit hole once, nearly died more than once, sure as shit, all my friends died. Then when I come home, it's "Thanks, mate. There's the door, fuck off."' His voice had risen to a shout as the anger swelled inside of him. 'No wonder I wound up in this fucking place. Now, you're coming here to ask me to go back? Well, get fucked, sunshine. How does that sound?'

Rankin slammed his hands down on the table as the door to the outside hall opened. The burly guard poked his head in with a serious, "intimidating" look.

'What's the carry-on?'

'It's alright, thank you,' Belkin said with a reassuring shooing gesture. He turned to consider Rankin once more, leaving the guard to scowl at them both behind Belkin's back before he shut the door once more.

'You're correct with part of your statement,' Belkin said flatly. 'Your country does indeed require your services as a soldier. However, the plane trip will not take quite as long as the one to Saigon.'

Rankin spat into the corner as he continued to scowl at the man. He tore another cigarette from his packet on the table and struck another match.

'Exactly five days ago, the mainland of Australia was invaded by the Chinese.'

Rankin shot him a look of disbelief. His cigarette sat between his lips, unlit, as Belkin continued.

'Although only a small force landed at first in Darwin, our estimates are that over fifty thousand enemy combatants are now on our soil. Our bases and those that the American's held in Darwin were caught unawares, and we have no choice but to expect that every man is a loss.'

'Wait, wait.' Rankin held up his hand in front of his face. 'Bullshit, this is got to be bullshit.'

Once more, Belkin continued, his expression unchanged. 'Mr Bartlett, I'm afraid not. The situation is quite dire. A small section of Chinese are working their way down through the Northern Territory and have begun to cut east, while a larger main section has butchered its way through any defences we held at Cairns and has begun a southern march.'

All the wind had been taken out of Rankin's sails. He sat there and stared at Belkin with his mouth slightly ajar, speechless. Eventually, the smouldering tip of the match burned down far enough to singe his fingers and he blinked as he tossed the stem into the ashtray.

'Okay...' he started. He didn't know what to say. 'What's the story then?' He was surprised in himself that he was actually going to hear Belkin out, but as with the first encounter with the bastard in the brown suit, what choice did he have?

'The story is that the Federal government has issued a decree stating that any ex-servicemen currently in the corrective systems are being offered full pardons for their service against the Chinese threat.' His shrill voice was still flat toned and unempathetic. 'So, either you can continue to rot away in here, Mr Bartlett, or you can reclaim your freedom and fight for that of your countrymen.'

Rankin let himself fall back into the support of his chair. His shoulders slumped as a feeling of numbness came over him. Once more, this bastard had him by the balls and now squeezed them to see if there was anything left inside.

'My apartment?' Rankin piped up. He had been screwed enough by this bastard; it was the time to screw back for once.

'All of your assets will be returned to you upon signing this contract.' A piece of paper was slid across the table toward him. The Australian Coat of Arms was printed boldly on the top and centre of the page. Rankin picked up the pieces of paper; there was so much bullshit in these things. He placed the pages down and looked Belkin in the eyes once more.

'Well, what choice do I have?'

CHRIS

'And if you read between the lines
You'll know that I'm just trying to understand
The feeling that you left.'

Gordon Lightfoot – *If You Could Read My Mind* (1970)

By the time Chris had come to his senses and had begun to prepare himself and Pestilence for their journey south, the sun had started to set. The body of the soldier that lay half-crushed was covered in a black blanket of flies. He had stopped his preparations at one point just to look at what had become of the soldier. His face, now disfigured and collapsed, seemed to move inward and out as if he drew breath. The one eye that hadn't burst, bulged out from its socket. Yet the movement of the flies gave the impression that it winked an unknowing secret. Almost as though the man had kept one last piece of information from him. Chris frowned as he brushed the hair from his face. The fly's legs left the smallest trails of blood, trekked across the man's brow and across his eye. They rubbed their forelegs together in front of their many eyes to express their greed for the platter at their feet. Really, when it came down to it, the human being may be able to stand tall, talk and bask in their own creations, gods in their own right. Yet once they perish, they are taken by everything they walked over to reach their pedestal.

Only fools thought they were superior.

This grim thought was reinforced only minutes after he had set off from his homestead to find the woman who was his true home.

Air rushed through Pestilence's open driver's window. As the freshly revived Holden devoured the dirt track from his property, its occupant sat expressionlessly. His eyes were unblinking as mosquitos the size of small sparrows were flattened against the curved glass windscreen. The humidity in the air made it uncomfortable no matter what he did. His armpits felt wet and heavy, and his balls felt as though they were having a spa party with his ass crack. The headlights cut through the darkness to reveal the entrance to the single laned Stuart Highway as it emerged from the scrub. Although the penetration that the Holden's halogens provided was usually tremendous, this night, the air was thick with smoke while the sky, rather than its usual pitch of darkness, was scarred an eerie red. The air that rushed past him and blew his hair into his eyes carried a smell of ash and burned rubber on it. Nothing was as it should be; there were no flashing lights of emergency vehicles in the distance. No sirens wailed into the night. It was as if he was the last man alive north of the invader's vanguard. As far as he knew, he may very well be.

As the Holden hitched itself onto the tarmac from the dirt track, the highway south had led him past an undulating river system. Crocs had become a larger threat to everyone as the years had gone past. The once king of the river mouth, bashed into submission by a lizard even larger, was forced to move further downriver to claim his territory. They seemed to get bigger every year, and more seemed to appear. It wouldn't be surprising to find some fifty to a hundred miles south of the ocean as they basked their great bodies in the sun. As he had crawled the pale utility through the strewn wrecks of crushed cars and an overturned school bus, he glimpsed something move in the water. He pulled the Holden over and watched as the heavy idle of the V8 rocked the steel on its frame.

The crocodile was enormous, scarred from years of territorial scraps, its eyes were ancient and hateful, and they burned through him as they considered each other. The way it lay in the water, its mouth was mostly hidden, buried in the mud and reeds, yet its body lined the water bank like a stone wall to reinforce its rills. It shifted and something emerged out of the water, but it vanished too quickly for Chris to identify. To say there was something in the crocs eyes was wrong; there was nothing. They were as empty as a veterans who had survived the German onslaught in Africa, seen the horror yet lived through it.

As if it wanted to show off its catch, the croc moved its stumpy legs and began to climb the bank toward him. In its mouth was one of the Asian invaders. Its mouth hung open, his face disfigured, the skin a milky colour from the time it had spent underwater. His rifle was still slung around his chest, yet partially crushed under the power of the prehistoric jaws that held it. The croc turned its head as if to give Chris a better look, then after a short while, it turned and trudged back into the water. One of the soldier's hands dragged against the ground as they went. As the dinosaur disappeared below the depths, the hand floated. Eventually, that was the last thing visible in the reeds and murky salt: a waving hand, a finger, then ripples.

Just like with any sign of life, the ripples eventually dissipated, as would the fires behind him. The soldiers had burned everything they could as they marched through. Darwin was left in rubble, and the Army base razed to the ground. The people they found were shot on the spot and then they rolled the tanks over them and continued on their way. Chris had heard the convoy pass as he had worked on his car, his second love. It seemed to go forever; the metallic grind of the tank's treads audible over the crackle of the fires. The diesel roars of trucks, jeeps and personnel carriers, that noise seemed unending.

Chris had seen the first survivor in Humpty Doo. It seemed that the wiry, silver-haired old man had had a similar idea. Chris had taken a short detour from the Stuart to seek supplies in a small town only a short distance from the intersection. Once more, he had seen torn down homes and people lying dead in the street. One man who had attempted to flee, by the looks of it, had been shot in the back and had been left sprawled in the middle of the road. A tank had then driven over his legs; the immense weight of the vehicle left nothing usable of the meat and had left them squashed and spread out over the ground. The bones had been splintered and couldn't be distinguished from the sinew and muscle matter. Thankfully, the petrol station had been left untouched; that's where he found the old man.

As the Holden had rumbled into the street in the late afternoon sun, the man had spun, his eyes wide in terror as he backed himself to the bowser. The exhaust sighed as Chris killed the thirsty V8. He sat in the car for a moment to consider the man whose lips quivered as he kicked the jerry can at his feet and spilled petrol all over the concrete. Chris shook his head as he watched gulp after gulp of amber fluid pour out over the ground.

'That shit has just become gold, and you're pouring it down the drain!' he yelled at the man through the open window as he pointed down at the can behind him.

The old man didn't seem to have realised that he knocked over his can, and when he turned his head to see it, he made a mess of righting it. Chris threw the cab door open and lifted himself out of the car. His arms still pained him from the burns they had received. He had spread some cream over them before he left and had wrapped them in rags soaked in cool water. But the water had soon turned hot and had disappeared. Now he didn't want to look under the rags at all.

'Did you see them come past?' Chris asked the wiry man as he assumed control of the bowser and began to top up the can that had been spilled.

The old man seemed to look at him out of the side of his head like he had a bad eye, but both eyes were wide and clear, and his mouth was lined with gleaming white teeth that looked too clean and straight to be real.

'Yeah.' The sound was short, twangy and inflicted to say it was obvious. 'They drained the diesel tanks.' His hands and lips trembled once more as he pointed over to the diesel pumps. They sat fifty yards to the right of the old run down service station and allowed enough room for old road trains like the pale blue Freightliner to swing around and fuel up. The diesel hoses were left lying on the ground. The bowser itself had been half ripped from the earth as the truck that had harvested its fuel backed over it.

'What about inside?' Chris gestured into the shop itself. He needed jerry cans, as many as they had. If the invaders planned to stop at every fuel station and harvest anything they could, he was lucky to find this one not ablaze, let alone with petrol left.

The old man shook his head as Chris put the cap on the can for him and handed it over. The man snatched it and headed straight for the open driver's door of Pestilence.

'Whoa, hold on there, mate, that's mine,' Chris said firmly as he clasped a burned hand over his shoulder. The old man turned around as quick as anything and their noses almost touched; the wide eyes were directly in front of his own. He felt something hard and cold push into his stomach and a metallic click.

'It's mine now,' he cackled a low and snivelled at the end. Chris heard the dentures slap against his gums as he moved his mouth.

Chris laughed; the only survivor apart from himself and of course, it's a thieving old man. Chris raised his hands and backed up a step.

'Okay, okay. Just—'

'No "just."' The old man snorted. 'It's mine, and that's that.'

'I just want one thing out from behind the seat. It's worth nothing; it just means something to me.'

The old man stared, then shifted aside to allow Chris access to the cabin; he held the revolver low with the barrel tilted up. It seemed the further the man backed off, the further he cocked his head, which gave the impression of an old rooster gone mad. As Chris rounded the door, his hands still raised, the older man jerked the revolver higher and cocked his head further as if to say he was watching. Chris had paused and raised his hands higher still, his eyebrows raised with them. Slowly, he turned his back to the old man and reached in behind the seat of the Holden. It took no time to find it, and the coolness of the steel tang, his hand closed around the old oiled grips.

As he spun back around, he brought the blade of the bayonet around with him and swung to the place in his mind where he had last seen the revolver. The old man's eyes widened as he realised what was happening and began to raise his arm. The steel crashed down on his wrist with a sickening thud. The silver-haired man screamed in pain as the revolver clattered to the ground and spun on the concrete as it went. The 1907 bayonet was never made as a slashing weapon, and the edge on the seventeen-inch blade was dull, but the weight of its spin and the force in which Chris had swung it had half dismembered his hand. It hung off at an odd angle, and it looked as though his wrist had been broken. The old man's eyes closed as he clutched his mangled wrist to his chest. Then he turned, ran and left behind the fuel, the revolver and Chris to his journey.

He had watched the man run screaming into the smoke and wondered if he would see him again in his dreams. Would he, too, walk down that long road among the others and hold his limp hand to his chest as he went? A chill shiver ran up his spine as he bent down and collected the revolver, which had come to rest only a few feet away. He pushed the latch on the side of the frame and let the cylinder swing out; six brass circles gleamed inside. All of them had their primer intact. As he slammed the cylinder closed, his eyes raised to the Arnhem road to follow where the wiry bastard had disappeared. 'Bastard was going to hijack me,' he said dismissively to himself. He then pushed the revolver down the back of his belt and went to search the service station.

The station had been ransacked in a similar fashion to what he remembered of his own house. Goods were spread over the ground, packets of chips had burst under the hurrying foot of a soldier or civilian, and the innards spread out everywhere. He had managed to find four more jerry cans and stacked them by the front of the door. He took some paper bags, filled them with dried foods, canned beef, and tuna, and added them to the pile. He took everything he could manage. Once he had filled Pestilence's tank with leaded, he filled the cans. Only enough petrol remained to half fill the last, yet he still walked away with twenty gallons in reserve and a full tank. Without knowing how far a tank would last with this new engine, a knot formed in the pit of his stomach. He began to regret his choice of the power and noise of the 327 over the slow, reliable put of the 186.

With the goods he had taken from the service station stowed safely in the tray of the Holden, alongside the satchel of tools and spare parts he had taken from his workshop, he went back into the station one last time in search of water. Before he found it, he had come across the shop owner. He was half folded back over his chair, a bullet hole in his forehead. His eyes were as wide as the man's who had tried to hijack him. Chris hated how his eyes stared vacantly at the ceiling; it reminded him of the soldier's crushed head, the waste. He ran his fingers down over the shop owner's face, and when he removed them, the eyes were closed. He ventured into the back and hissed in pain as he slowly removed the dry rags from his arm. They had become stuck to his skin in the heat, and puss and blood ran out of the cracks in his flesh as he tore the fabric away. He ran a tap and held his arms under its running flow, his eyes shut, and his head leaned forward to touch the cool metal of the spout. He stayed that way as the cool water caressed his unrecognisable forearms for twenty minutes or so until the pain had slightly subsided. Then he lathered what was left of the cream he had taken from his workshop and had taken a soft white bandage from the shop area to wrap over his arms.

That seemed an age ago now, although only hours had passed. He was now mostly all the way to Katherine as he followed the trail of carnage, death and waste the invaders had left behind. As the red tear in the sky shook with anger and the smoke became heavier, he knew he was close. He backed off on the throttle, and the engine surged as it used its own force to slow the car. The smoke became so thick that he could barely see ten feet beyond the iron bar even as the headlights blared. With the window open, the smoke filled the cabin and made it hard to breathe, but it was too late to stop it; Chris just coughed as he limped the HD around the final bend to reveal the burning main street. He paused for a second before crossing the threshold, then he killed the halogens and proceeded into the town.

If the invaders had failed to burn brick and stone in Darwin, they worked out a way to get it to catch in their short reprise. Brick workshops blazed fiercely from the fuel they had stacked around them and what lay inside, while others they had simply run down with tanks. An Indigenous family lay scattered on the median; and Chris frowned at the sight of them. 'They weren't a threat to anybody.'

The service station that stood at the entrance of the town had been set alight, and the knot in Chris' stomach tightened. In the three hours he had driven, he had nearly used half a tank. The fires that burned down the main street were too fierce to even attempt a course, so he took the first left into the town and ventured into the small industrial sector. Sadly, it had seen the same treatment. Bodies burned black even in the night, faces wrought with fear and pain. He saw a man who had died holding his Kelpie in his arms. The dog's body was torn from a volley of bullets to its gut. Everything he saw churned the anger deep within him but, at the same time, broke his heart and his mind. If they had taken Angie through this shit, how was she supposed to stay alive?

Just as he thought a search of the town would be a waste, he saw a flash of lights ahead and stopped the ute. The roar of the fires around him were powerful enough to drown the sound of a jet, let alone a V8, so he left the engine idle. Out of the smoke came a small jeep. Two men sat in the open cabin; they bounced as the jeep jolted over bodies and up the curb. It was as though the driver had attempted to run a tyre over every corpse he could. Angie's voice echoed in his mind, *'We are just like the animals we walk over.'* As his hand clasped around the steering wheel, the jeep turned down an adjacent street and vanished. Chris gave them a brief head start and then let the Holden slink down the road. He nosed the front end into the street and peered through the smoke. The jeep had come to a stop in a driveway some way down the road; as the smoke was still fairly thick, it couldn't have been far. The men carried fuel cans into another building, presumably to set it alight. As they walked into the house, he straightened the car up on the road and waited.

Shortly after, the soldiers exited and had begun to remove even more cans from the back of the jeep when Chris lit up the high beams of the Holden. As he did, he slammed his foot down on the throttle, and the V8 roared. In the heat of the fires and the night's humidity, the rubber was soft and the tarmac sticky, so the back tyres didn't even spin in the slightest. Chris was thrown back into the seat as the front end lifted with the propulsion. As the howling beast came down on them, the soldiers' first instinct was to shield their eyes from the blinding light. By the time they had started to reach for their weapons, Pestilence had cut the distance between them by three quarters. As she mounted the curb to cut between the jeep and the houses, Chris saw through the windscreen that one man had raised a rifle while the other had turned to run when the railway track bit into them.

The soldier that had turned was hit in the lower back. He was sucked under the car, and Chris felt and heard his body break under the steel. The one that had stood his ground was caught full in the gut. His body and face came forward to slap the bonnet and spray blood all over the glass. Chris jammed the brakes after the body underneath had cleared and watched as the soldier was flung from the bar to roll heavily to a stop on the road.

The Holden came to a stop and Chris killed the engine to save the fuel. He held the silver-haired man's revolver in his hand as he exited, in case any remained alive, but the soldiers did not move. The one that had gone under the car was a complete write-off; there was not a bone in his body that looked as though it would have survived. Under the green uniforms, the flesh was red and torn and his limbs all lay at odd angles. Instead, Chris went to the Jeep, and opened one of the caps on the jerry cans they had left. Chris smiled as he smelt what could only be petrol. He added another eight jerry cans to his collection between what was inside the house they had intended to burn and what was in the back of the jeep. He had decided to take a look around when the soldier that was thrown onto the road rolled over.

Chris turned his head and considered the crumpled man for some time until he heard a muffled cough. He drew the revolver once more and advanced. As he neared the broken soldier, he looked over the sights of the short revolver. The wounded soldier lay on his stomach, his assault rifle underneath him. Chris stepped on the butt of the assault rifle with one foot and kicked the soldier over with the other. The sound as bones ground against broken joints rattled through the air, and the man spat blood and groaned in pain as he settled on his back. From the looks of his body, most of his ribs were broken, if not his spine. Chris held the revolver to his throat.

'Brisbane?' he asked softly.

The man beneath him struggled to breathe. His body convulsed in what could have been a nod as he was wracked with a cough, and bubbles of blood formed in his gape to splatter Chris' face and clothes. Chris blinked and a smile spread across his face. With his right hand, he pulled his wallet from the back of his jeans and opened it; inside was a clear plastic section where he had a single photograph stored. There, safely behind her shield of plastic, was a photograph of a beautiful woman with long flowing blonde hair. He held the photo to the dying soldier's face, 'Do you have her?'

Whether the soldier actually managed to look at the image before he coughed again and spread blood over Angie's photograph was questionable. Once more, he convulsed and made the same nodding motion as he gasped for breath. His eyes rolled into the back of his head, and with his last breath, he uttered a single phrase before he collapsed under the weight of his broken body and died before him.

'All white devils… die in Brisbane…'

RANKIN

'So, when this day was ended
I was still not satisfied.
For I knew everything I touched
Would wither and would die.'

Johnny Cash – *Flesh and Blood* (1970)

The sandstone walls loomed, darkening the world and his demeanour. He had thought that when he signed the contract that was placed before him, he would at least feel better. Instead, his head became a bustle of traffic that had come to a screaming halt. His ears began to ring as thoughts traced over one another and a slight feeling of regret seeped into his soul. The ink had not even had a chance to dry on the page as it was snatched back by Belkin, tossed into his briefcase, and the outer slammed shut. If the chairs weren't bolted to the floor, he imagined Belkin's would have tipped at the speed in which he stood.

Arrangements were to be made for him to be released that very day. He would have a day to organise his affairs, and then he would be taken to Richmond, where he would be armed, given a uniform and sent to help the effort in the North. Belkin pushed out of the room, and the shadowed mass of the guard filled the door shortly after. Rankin was taken back to his cell with the feeling that he had just been sentenced to death. He imagined the guards calling out to the other prisoners that they had a dead man walking, but no one spoke. No one congratulated him on his freedom; no one cared.

Although Rankin never cared about anyone in that place, he felt afraid to leave it. Inside his cell, he was king of all and master of none; he had overcome his addiction to alcohol. He had gotten into the best shape he had ever been in his life, and he had become accustomed to being alone.

As the cell door slammed closed behind him for the final time, he didn't know what to do. Should he try and gather his belongings? No, he had none. Should he to try and get some sleep? He knew full well that there was no hope of this. Instead, he walked over to the small window placed too high in the stone wall to offer any view and grasped the bars. As he strained his arms, he lifted himself upward and held himself for as long as he could so he could look down on the world below. He saw a guard lean on a metal railing as he looked down on some prisoners in the yard below. He stood high on one of the corners of the bordering wall and frowned while he smoked a cigarette. The steel guardhouse behind him resembled a pillbox like those that lined the military bases in South Vietnam. He watched as a fat white and brown pigeon fluttered to sit on the peak of the pillbox's roof. It fluffed itself while it drove its beak into points on its wings and chest. Finally, it took to the air. Its wings whistled as the fat bird worked them furiously. As it left, it dropped a line of white shit as if it were a plane dropping a bomb. It fell and fell and vanished from Rankin's sight.

He felt hollow, excited and nervous at the same time. He constantly felt as though he needed to have a piss, but every time he whipped it out and pointed it at the stainless-steel bowl in his cell, only a trickle or two, if at all, would come. Eventually, another guard came, alone. The door slid open, and the guard asked if he was ready. Rankin stared at him; he had walked in and out of this place more than a hundred times, yet to step over the threshold seemed to take all he had in him. As his foot touched the steel grates, his ears began their chorus of tinnitus, and his head felt as though it was apt to detonate and bring the walls of his sanity crashing down, like the C4 in the tunnel. He was taken to a room where a man stood behind a cafeteria-style window.

After signing more papers he was given a plastic bag which had the clothes he was arrested in, or what remained of them. His keys, his wallet and more importantly, his dog tags. His thumb traced the pressed metal and he felt their coolness; the letters dug into his thumb as each bump and swirl coursed its way around. Then he was taken to a small room where he was told to change into his own clothes and left in peace. Perhaps he thought at some point, it would've been nice to wear civilian clothes again rather than his inmate rags, but Rankin found no joy in this. The jeans were the same pair he had worn the night he had met Mary. The same shirt, stained by the water or the whiskey. The shirt barely fit; the loops around the buttons strained against the thread as he fastened them over his chest. The jeans fit tightly as well, but he never knew whether it was the feel of washed denim, shrunken and taught or whether it was his body renewed in its form. Once he dressed, he exited the room and handed the guard the plastic bag with his prison clothes in it. He sighed when he did this and looked at the older man. 'What's next?'

The guard smiled. 'Now you leave, son.' He clapped him on the shoulder and continued down the hall. Rankin expected a grand exit for the great steel gates to boom through the silence as they slammed behind him. Instead, he was taken to a small steel door that stood alone on the immensity of the sandstone that it was fixed to. The guard asked him if he had everything and laughed like it was the joke to end all, then he swung the door open. Behind it was a street, cars were parked in the gutters, their tyres sunken in the piles of hardened leaves that had cast and fallen. Ass Rankin stepped through, a couple walked hand in hand, busy in chatter. He felt the pavement beneath his feet, and he felt the wind rush along the wall to cut through him easily as his skin erupted in gooseflesh. Not sure what to do or where to go, he turned to talk to the guard, but the door behind him was already closed. He was out.

Rankin placed a hand on the steel door and felt the cold bite of the metal on his skin. He took a deep breath and began to walk down the street while his fingers slid first over the smooth steel and then hit the course sandstone. He walked the length of the wall and looked at each silent hull of the cars he passed. The rustle of the leaves was stirred by the autumn breeze that filled his head. He walked and walked. Without knowing where he was, he only knew that he needed to get to his apartment. He pulled his wallet and flipped the leather open. Twenty bucks, he was as wealthy as they came fresh out of prison. He walked until he was satisfied that he was lost, but still, he enjoyed himself. He thought back to his walk down the streets of Enoggera. How everything seemed hostile to him back then, but now the streets of Sydney seemed warm and inviting even while the breezes threatening claws sunk deep into his bones. He managed to find a train station with one of those native names that he could barely pronounce, but he didn't want the hassle of a train. In the end, he found an HR Holden with a slender, long haired youth behind the wheel. He got into the cab and told the driver his address.

The news that Belkin had given him about the invasion seemed wrong; people in Sydney walked and talked like nothing could touch them, and maybe it couldn't. It didn't look like people had the concern or the anticipation that he had about the invading force that pushed South. He laughed softly to himself as he thought that they only had that luxury because of people like him. He had one day to sort his affairs, and then he would be back in the fire, the blood and the steel. The driver tried for small talk, but Rankin ignored him, too encapsulated in the world outside of the Holden's window. One thing that settled him was that the more the cab traversed the streets, the more he realised he had seen nothing to do with Americans. Their ally, the one that led them blindly into the jungles, was not here to help them. The sky was free of the black hulls and the whirling blades. The people's ears weren't pounded to death by the rattle and clatter of the M2s on their sides that demanded that when they spoke, all were to stop and listen. The trucks that they passed on the roads carried food and products, not men and guns. *Not yet anyway*, he thought.

Eventually, the Holden pulled up, and Rankin peered out at the large, brick structure that held his apartment. His home for such a short time and one of the worst memories he cared to remember.

'Three bucks, mate.' The driver sighed as he threw the Holden into park, its six cylinders revs climbed in its idle.

'Three bucks?' Rankin exclaimed as his voice raised in surprise. 'Christ, you drove me downtown; you didn't give me your virginity.' Nonetheless, he shifted in his seat and pulled his wallet out from under his ass.

The taxi driver rolled his eyes as he took the twenty and exchanged it. Rankin took the change and got out of the car, and mumbled something about highway robbery. The Holden's exhaust chuffed at him as it pulled away as if it turned it's nose up at the man who questioned the price of its ride. Rankin watched it merge into traffic and then take a left at the next street; it failed to indicate the entire time.

'At least I know nothing's changed,' he grumbled to himself as he turned to walk the narrow path in the grass to enter his apartment block. If he thought stepping over the threshold of his cell was hard, the climb of the stairs to his apartment was worse. Each step took more and more of his will to bring him to that place. He slapped at the keys in his pocket and, for good measure, the bulge in his ass that held his wallet. He sighed as he exited the stairwell and walked the dark corridor to his door. Once more, his mind was flooded with nightmares, his ears whined in their pitch, and his gut felt like lead. 'The things I would have given for a drink,' he muttered as he pulled his keys from his pocket.

The lock turned, as did the knob, and the door swung open silently. Nothing had changed; no one had cleaned his mess for him. Glass still glittered in the sun that drifted through the dusty windows. The smell of the whiskey that had spilled was gone; all that remained was its container and the dried specks of blood on the floor. He closed the door behind him and looked over his small dwelling. His bed sheets were still on and still left in the mess that Mary had put them in. The pillow that had started it all was still up on the bedside table. He opened his fridge, unsure what to expect, and shut it again in disgust. When they had taken him and the power was cut, no one thought it would be a good idea to take his milk out. He spat in the sink; if he survived this invasion, he would worry about it when he came home. 'I'm not hungry anyway.'

He walked out of his kitchen/dining/living room and sat on the edge of his bed. The smell of dust was in the sheets. He could take them and wash them at the laundromat, but what was the point? He had one night in this place. One night to sort his affairs, of which he had none. The only thing he really came here for was in the drawer to his right, but he didn't want to look at them just yet. He didn't think he could bear to. He had taken Max's dusters from his body and had brought them from Vietnam to Enoggera and now to Sydney. He figured that if the idiots had left the milk in the fridge, they had left everything else. He hoped as much anyway. His eyes turned to the drawer while the fight inside of him began. The fear to see against the curiosity to know that they were there. He wrestled with himself for what felt like hours; in the end, time didn't matter; he had nowhere to be. He grasped the drawer's knob and slid it open.

The brass had dulled, greener than gold. When he had closed the drawer the final time before being taken away unconscious and delirious, it had shined to the point of being almost white. He had ground away the rough edges and fixed almost every imperfection that Max had instilled in it by using dirty .303 cases. The shirt he wore had begun to itch at him. He tore it off, happy to have his skin free in the cold staleness of his apartment. The dusters clinked against the porcelain of his bathroom sink as he tossed them carelessly from the door. The old rusted can of 'Brasso' that he retrieved from beneath the kitchen sink, sloshed with age as he began to shake it and eventually it began to thin. Then he poured the contents on his shirt and over the brass.

As he worked away to polish the brass in his sink, he thought back to the basin in the bathroom at the establishment in South Vietnam. He remembered the way the blood ran from his fingers as the water trickled over them. The way it pooled in between the loops of the brass block. The red was browner than it should be, like mud from a stagnant bog, as it danced against the backdrop of the green and gold. Then it ran down the drain, like everything else in his life, and vanished somewhere below. The green ebbed away to expose the brilliant gold beneath. He continued to rub and knead, his mind completely absorbed by the process. When he washed away the residue, the metal shone proudly in the sunlight that still managed to penetrate the room. Less than an hour of light remained.

He went then to his wardrobe. As bare as it was, it still held what he wanted. He took the belt from the hanger, the same one he wore in Vietnam, its leather pouch still stitched tightly to its side. The brass clip was as mottled and green as the dusters were a moment ago, but they still held the flap fast in its rivets. The smell of old leather, sweat and blood filled his nose. He popped each fastener and heard the strength that remained in them. He placed the dusters in their pouch and hung the belt once more, ready for his trip tomorrow morning.

The rest of his clothes were in a similar state to the bedsheets. Everything smelt old and untouched, the fabric was hard and somewhat gritty, but it would do. As he suspected, his jeans had begun to stretch against his thighs, and his old boots were as good as they always were. He had no military drab left, apart from his dress uniform. He wasn't proud enough to wear that, so he laid out the only other shirt he thought clean enough to wear, an old plaid work shirt.

The rest of the night was filled with his attempts to keep his mind from wandering back to Mary and his friends. For a moment, while he lay half-naked on his bed, he thought he could still smell her, and he became obsessed for a short while. He picked up pillows and smelt them as he tried to remember the smell of her hair and the taste of her lips. The more he thought about it, the more he became aroused. His manhood stiffened beneath his jeans, ready for action even though it had been shelved for the same amount of time as the dirty old dusters. He unbuttoned his jeans and let his manhood stand up freely. He stroked himself while he thought of her. Her face, her tits, her hair, the feeling of when she had him inside of her mouth. He closed his eyes and became lost in the thought of her.

He imagined that he never hit her, that he didn't freak out. That she had allowed him to enter her and push his way inside. He imagined her breasts as they bounced with each hip movement. He imagined her closing her eyes in pleasure. Her fingernails dragged along his back and left red lines of lust etched into his flesh. His arm worked furiously, his eyes closed to the world, his mind lost in Mary. He dreamt that she bit his neck, tenderly and playful, her face buried into him. He rolled her over and entered her again. Her white skin was like silk, her lips as red as her hair. He closed a softly clenched fist around her hair and lightly pushed her face into the pillows as he continued to push himself deeper and deeper. His eyes were shut, his arm still worked, when in his head, he pushed down with his hand harder and harder to press her face further into the pillows. Her arms began to fight him, and he pushed her head down and pushed deeper into her with each stroke.

He opened his eyes, and his arm stopped moving. His manhood was still hard and throbbed, inches away from its desire, yet already signs of softness in its foundations waned its strength. As his member softened completely and lay flat against the rough fabric of his jeans, Rankin lit a cigarette and took a long drag. Love never seemed to work out well for him. Not that he had ever known it. He was all too familiar with lust, drive and energy. He supposed women kissed you and stroked the hairs on your chest afterwards, the same whether you've paid them to do it or not. Touching can't change; the feeling cannot be any different.

'So why do I feel as though I'm missing something?' he complained as he blew the smoke to the ceiling. It rolled over itself and clung like it was a source of life.

His body had become the machine it was supposed to be. He was stronger, faster and more dangerous than he had ever been. But his mind kept clinging and holding on to the past; he felt weaker with every thought of her, every thought of Max, Gary or Will. It sapped him like a leech. The more it ebbed away at him, the worst it became. The grief, the regret, all surmised this embodiment of himself.

Suddently, he stood up and swore through the cigarette clamped between his lips. He swore only at himself, the weaker version of him that could only be remorse. Without bothering with socks, he jammed his feet into his boots and hurriedly tied the laces as smoke burned at his eyes. Bare chested, Rankin reefed open the front door and locked it behind him before he stormed down the corridor, cigarette still in hand.

His feet rattled like machine guns as he flew down the stairs. On his decent, he passed another man who offered him an odd expression, and he moved to the side to allow the shirtless man to pass.

'Slow down, you idiot,' the man called after him, 'and there's no smoking in here.'

Rankin never slowed, and he still puffed on the cigarette. He lifted one hand and flipped the bird back to the whinger on the stairs as he went.

He burst through the front door of the complex at a run and tossed the butt as he left the path for the pavement. The moment he left the doorway, the cold air beat down on him. The wind still rushed through the streets and chilled everything in its path. He hit the streets and let it all out. The soles of his boots pounded the bitumen, and his arms pumped through the freezing winds. Faster and faster, he pushed himself as he tried to leave the thoughts of her behind. He had never been much of a runner, and the smoking didn't help as already his lungs had started the regret cycle of the last cigarette. The feeling he had now as he rushed down the street, faster than he had ever run before, was exhilarating. In prison, he hadn't the room to jog, let alone run. The overcrowded yard was more suited to weights and games like basketball than to set up a track and jog the exterior. He found it annoying when people moved here and there to block one's path, so he never even bothered. Now he wished he had. His hair was caught by the wind and thrown in every direction. Then when the gust settled, it laid back on his scalp once more, pushed down by his speed.

With each step, he focused more on himself and his body rather than the people he had left behind. Max left his thoughts, Gary and Will. When only Mary remained, he pushed himself even harder;

his lungs howled for air, his legs cramped from the pace. The pain started in his gut, which was now empty as it roared for food. He saw her face, beautiful at first, then broken and then she was gone along with the rest.

He slowed his pace, his chest still pounded. All he had achieved was to run to the end of the street, but the street climbed a gentle incline, and it wasn't as short as others. Nonetheless, he'd had enough; his mind was clear. He walked most of the way back, his legs ached, and his chest was on fire. That was until he cooled down, and the wind caught him once more as he jogged back to his apartment. That night he put his head on the dusty pillow that had been thrown at him some time ago. No sooner did his head touch the fabric did his eyes close, and he enjoyed a long, peaceful, dreamless sleep.

The next day he woke and showered in cold water as his hot water system had been turned off. He dressed himself in the clothes he had laid out. He took one last longing look at his apartment, now that he had the chance and left. The cab ride to Richmond Air Base was long and expensive. He had thanked himself for taking more money from the tin in his wardrobe as the ride cost him eighteen dollars. He laughed to himself when he handed over the twenty and left the cab without taking his change. Yesterday he had complained at a three-dollar cab ride, today's fare was six times the price and he paid it willingly. Funny what a good night's sleep can do.

When he reached the airbase, he saw that others had arrived at the same time. Some men were dropped off by their families, dressed in military greens, while others were in casual clothes like himself. He sneered when he saw a young man being dropped off by his mother, who had prepared his military dress for him. He doubted they'd need that get up any time soon. To see veterans dressed in casual clothes mixed in with those in military dress made him feel the furthest from being a soldier in his life. He felt more like a mercenary, a hired killer brought in when volunteers came up short. The problem with conscription is that there's no negotiation of the price; he remembered Belkin's words to him.

'Either you can continue to rot away in here, Mr Bartlett, or you can reclaim your freedom and fight for that of your countrymen.'

It was twice now the bastard had gotten him. Conscription meant that he didn't have a choice, and the first time, he didn't, but Belkin worded it in a way and led him to the point that made him think it was his own choice. Same as this time, sit and rot or go and fight. Six years wasn't that long; he could've sat and waited it out. But that's not the way he was geared.

The prodigal soldiers were led to a marshalling area. Rankin watched the families embrace, the women cry, and the men act bravely, then he turned his back on them and left them there at the gates. He marked his name off, was given a haircut and was made to shave. They took his clothes, boots, and shirt, and they threw them all on a pile and made him and all the other mercenaries dress in the open. One man objected and tried to take his boots back; Rankin could tell why; they were nice boots, and the man was a fool to bring them. The Commander stepped up to the complaining soldier, so their faces were less than an inch apart.

'You are not going to Brisbane to go out on the town; you are going to kill Chinese men. They won't mind if you're not wearing nice boots, and neither will we.'

When all the men were dressed, shaved, and armed with unloaded rifles, they were organised into makeshift platoons and stood in a manner that made it look like they were a genuine Australian military company. Rankin was amused to see they even positioned the idiots that had come in full military dress toward the front to make it look like they were officers. They were told to stand at attention while the air base commander addressed them. Then they brought out a podium draped in the arms of Australia and a microphone. Military personnel then escorted men with cameras and their own microphones so they could see the military might before them.

The cameras flashed, and shutters clicked as they tried to capture the glory in the faces of the mostly battle-hardened men in front of them. The soldiers from Vietnam who came home with no thanks, only to step up and fight for their country once more. Then a white-haired man, in full military dress and with a very stern face, stepped up to the podium and cleared his throat. Rankin prepared himself for the biggest load of bullshit he was ever apt to hear.

'Returned Servicemen.' The Colonel began. 'You have honoured your country in Vietnam, some of you even through Korea and the Second World War.' His tone was soft, almost regretful.

Rankin sneered at the opening line. The way he spoke, they were just being rounded up to be thanked. 'More like blowing smoke up our asses because now they have a use for us.' He grumbled under his breath. The man next to him shot him a disapproving look, then straightened his back to look like the proud veteran he was.

'Your country has now called on you once more not to travel to some far away land to fight someone else's war. But to defend our own against a foreign threat.' Shutters clattered away while a man with a large, heavy camera edged closer to the Colonel.

'The Chinese have used tactics and methods that can be compared to those used by Nazi Germany in the thirties and forties. They have struck hard and fast and have continued to do so ever since their feet have been on our soil.'

His tone became aggressive and he almost spat every word.

'But when they meet us in Brisbane, that will come to an end. They have had a fine time dealing with unprepared bases and our women and children. But let us test their metal. Let us test their strength against ours.'

People in the press group clapped.

'Let them see what it's like to stand against the Australian military. The blood of the rats of Tobruk run through our veins, the spirit of the light horsemen of Gallipoli. The men that traversed the Kokoda Trail.'

The shutters clattered even faster; the flashes became more intense, and the clapping became louder and more furious.

'The Australian forces have united to stand together, and with you men of hardened steel to stiffen their backs, we will turn the tide and push them out!' He slammed his fist down on the podium as he said this, and everyone cheered. Everyone except Rankin, who just stared at the Colonel, while the men around him clapped and cheered as their rifles hung from their slings.

The cheers still rang in his ears as their rifles were taken from then and then they were crowded onto the planes. As Rankin was herded past the supply dump to his plane, he saw some of the crates that waited to be loaded. Along with crates marked 7.62 and L1A1, the military designation for the SLR. There were even more crates marked .303; he saw a man pile old Enfield's and Bren guns messily into the crate and then hastily fastened it shut once he saw others looking.

'Hardened steel,' Rankin muttered. The thought flashed through his mind. He didn't dare say it as he didn't want the men beside him to know, but if the military was dragging out the returned servicemen and the rifles of those that had returned thirty years ago, he doubted how their metal would test when it was thrown into the forge of Brisbane.

RANKIN

The high spirits that the Colonel had instilled in the soldiers' hearts continued on the flight. The cabin was alive with chatter, and the men carried on as if they were drunk. At one stage, twenty or so men had taken up a chorus of 'Lookin' Out My Back Door' by Creedence, while a group further down the plane was already halfway through the Beatles 'Come Together.' The racket of the scene drove Rankin insane. What made it worst was the commercial air liner the military had chartered was non-smoking. Rankin sat in a middle seat of a row between an overweight middle-aged man who had told every person he could that he had served in Korea and a boy who looked as though he had maybe seen a week of 'Nam. Rankin estimated that he alone was on his fifth retelling of the Korean story and placed his face in his palms. He kneaded at his temples as the beginnings of a migraine bled its way into his brain. He felt as though the veins in the side of his neck were about to pop when the fat bastard next to him nudged him to see if he was still paying attention to his story.

'Look, mate, do us all a favour and just shut the fuck up,' Rankin said as he snapped his head around to reveal his bloodshot eyes. The overweight man leaned back, offended and muttered to himself while he looked around to capture the eye contact of another poor veteran.

They had been in the air for over an hour and the smell of sweat and men's odour had filled the plane. The singing and the loud-mouthed chatter continued. A hand reached over his seat and he felt something slosh against his chest. 'Take a swig and pass it down the line, soldier,' the veteran spoke. The bottle dropped from the man's grasp and fell into Rankin's lap. He looked down at the golden liquid in its glass cage. The way it rolled and broke its waves against the banks. A message in a bottle would eventually find someone to read its message, in the same way that Rankin would always wind up with a bottle of Vat in his hands.

His mouth felt dry, and his stomach felt like lead. A drink would cure him; it always did before. He took the cap off, the smell of it washed over him like the ocean spray. The voice in the back of his mind told him he had come so far but, at the same time, said that one sip wouldn't hurt. Rankin extended his hand to the boy next to him. The boy jumped as his arm made contact with his shoulder. He glanced quickly to Rankin, then down at the bottle and back again. The look in his eyes was as though he was about to apologise for getting touched. He looked frightened, and Rankin questioned whether the supposed returned serviceman next to him was even old enough to drink.

'Easy mate, do you want any?' Rankin asked in a calming tone as he raised the bottle to continue his gesture.

The boy looked at the bottle once more as if seeing it for the first time, then lowered his eyes to his lap and shook his head as he continued to look out the window. Rankin refitted the cap and leaned forward to pass the bottle forward.

'Oi, you weren't even going to offer me any, were you?' the overweight loudmouth bellowed.

'Ah, Jesus, mate here.' Rankin tossed the bottle into his lap. 'At least while you're drinking, you can't talk.'

Their time in the air continued to drag along. Rankin's migraine had peaked by this stage, and he was forced to rest his head back with his eyes closed and refused to speak to anyone. Each time the fat loud mouth bumped his arm or his leg in his over-enthusiastic motions, the vein in Rankin's neck pulsed. He regretted not taking a drink; at least he might have slept.

Thankfully, it wasn't long after that they announced the descent into the Amberly Royal Australian Air Force Base. Rankin lifted himself in his chair and tried to look out the window, but the boy's head completely blocked it. He was forced to endure the rest of the flight by listening to the low whine of the turbine engines as the liner soared lower to the earth: that and the mindless white noise from the rest of the plane.

Like teenagers on a weekend away, the entire cabin erupted in cheers when the tyres made contact with the earth.

Across the plane, men called out war cries like, 'Let's show these fuckers what were made of,' and 'Time to kill some Chinese boys!' Each of these were met with a volley of cheers and hoots, yet Rankin sat silently. His eyes on the back of the chair in front. They began to shuffle off the plane, and the war cries continued as they went. As the plane emptied, it became quieter, the air seemed fresher, and his migraine dissipated. Rankin stood as the loudmouth began to shuffle down the aisle in a sort of sidestep. Before he exited the row, he looked at the boy to his left.

Panic was in his eyes, he wrung his hands as he softly shook his head. Rankin sat back down.

'Hey man, it's alright,' he said to the younger soldier and placed a hand softly on his arm.

The boy tried to pull away, as the tears streamed with a never-ending flow. 'No... No, it's not,' he choked out.

'It's okay to be scare—' Rankin started trying to soothe him.

'I can't!' He screamed, the plane became instantly silent. His face wrinkled up and became a shade of pink. Saliva had started to run from his lips as he blubbered. 'I can't do it again.'

Rankin put an arm around him and pulled him close. He let the boy's head fall on his chest and felt the heaving of his tears as he poured it out. 'It's okay, mate, let it out.'

Rankin eyed the soldiers that passed; all of them looked as they went by, some with concern, others with humour. One man muttered 'pussy' as they shuffled past, and a few others chuckled. Rankin eyed him, a broad man with dark short-cropped hair, a square jaw and a barrelled chest. His face was ravaged by pox marks, which had left him one of the ugliest dials Rankin had seen, that would make him easy to remember. They made eye contact as the ugly bastard stepped off the plane and Rankin sneered.

Most of the plane had vacated by the time the boy had begun to calm. Rankin lifted him away from his chest and sat to look straight into his eyes. 'What's your name?'

'Half... Halfpenny, Sir.'

'Don't call me that. What's your first name?'

He still blubbered and shuddered as he took in his breaths. 'S-Sam.'

'Good, Sam, good. You've served? You look young.' He kept his voice low and soothing. His hands squeezed the boy's shoulders.

'I served in Vietnam, but only for three months.' Tears began to swell in his eyes again. 'My brother died while I was there. He was a pilot.' The tears started to flow, but Rankin knew he needed to let it out. 'My dad... My dad killed himself when he found out... they took me home to care for my mum.'

Rankin was forced to pull him close to his chest again, as the tears had once more become uncontrollable. The plane was empty now and an officer came aboard to see what the hold-up was. His eyes rung red with anger when he saw the two, who still sat in their seats.

'Not paying you lot by the hour, you know!' he shouted.

Rankin held his hand out and shook his head at the officer, while he pointed down at the young man in his arms. The officer walked up to them, his chest puffed out.

'What about your mum now?' Rankin asked, regretting the question more as each word came out of his mouth.

'They said I had to go and protect everyone's mum. Not just my own,' he spluttered, the words muffled by the fabric of Rankin's shirt. 'I've seen enough people die, I don't want to go there. I don't.'

'None of us do,' Rankin muttered as the officer took the last few steps to their row. 'None of us do.'

The officer proceeded to tear ten shades of shit out of them for holding up the procession. Rankin tried to explain the problem but he was having none of it. He helped Sam out of the row and left his hand on his shoulder as they walked toward the exit.

'Stick with me, Sam, you'll be fine.'

Sam looked back at him, a thankful look in his eyes, which were still red from the tears. 'Thanks... I... I, never.'

'Rankin Bartlett.' He smiled at him. The two men shook hands as they climbed down the stairs that had been rolled up to the side of the plane.

The attitude was somewhat sombre in the base than that of the plane. Men had straight backs as they stood to attention while they waited to be split into their details. The large green cargo plane that was full of the crates of ammunition, rifles, a Centurion tank, and an M113 personnel carrier was likewise being unloaded. They all watched as the Centurion clattered and rumbled its way off the plane, the barrel of its main gun raised against the drop of the ramp.

Everyone who had served in land forces knew the Centurion. The sight of Australian armour always made a soldier feel at ease. The picture of the lone Centurion from Richmond, as it made its way to join the other eighteen that were lined up along one end of the compound, was tremendous. The 1st Armoured Regiment was the only unit left in Australia that had tanks, and the entire Regiment was in Brisbane now, their tanks and their crews spread across the bases.

As they were all organised into the same sloppy formation they took up in Richmond, they were told where they would be deployed. The chatter continued like they were a line of frontline forwards gearing up for a scrum until four straight-backed, tight-lipped Sergeants called for attention at the top of their voices from the front of the ragged company. The small talk soon died out, and Rankin took a glance at Halfpenny to his side. His cheeks were still wet from the tears, but his grasp retightened on his resolve.

'Men,' a voice called from the front; Rankin could not see the speaker through the sea of closely cropped haircuts but prepared himself for another speech, 'welcome to Amberley Air Base of the Royal Australian Air Force. Hope you enjoy the sights because you won't be here for long.'

As he spoke, a line of international trucks entered the compound and divided. Half of the trucks went to the right of the company, the other to the left. They pulled up in a line formation, and soldiers began loading crates into the canvas-covered backs.

'The trucks you see behind me will be your ride to the front. The enemy is upon us.' If there was any small talk still alive at this point, it ended. 'Our forces have been spread between the Enoggera military base North West of Brisbane, and an outpost which has been created at Deception Bay to defend the eastern road. Your strength will be added to the ADF personnel already stationed there and your lines will be added to strengthen their gaps.'

Rankin didn't know which would be worst; Deception Bay and having the flank open to the sea, or Enoggera and seeing that shit hole again.

'If you were a rifleman when you served your name will be called along with a base. Those going to Enoggera, will go by the trucks to your left. Those going to Deception Bay, will go by using the trucks on your right.' There was a pause and the silence rang through the air. 'Good luck, men, and don't let these bastards get to the river.'

The name-calling began as soon as the last word had died on the speaker's lips. A new voice, one of the sergeants, 'Aagard, Ryan: Deception.'

Then another voice 'Allendorf, Martin: Enoggera.' The roll call continued as men started to move off either to the left or the right. 'Allwood, Brian: Deception.'

'Anders, Simon: Enoggera.'

Rankin kept his head bent forward, his hands clenched in fists at his side until finally. 'Bartlett, Rankin: Enoggera.' His shoulders slumped. It looked like he would be back to where it all began. He lifted his head and began to move out of formation when a hand wrapped around his wrist. Rankin turned his head; his back was already up, and he saw Sam's face through a cloud in his head, the look of abandonment in his eyes.

'Sorry.' Rankin said, as he moved to his position, 'I'll wait for you, okay?'

'What are we going to do if I get called to Deception Bay?' Sam asked in a quivery voice.

What could he do if that happened? Everyone was running around like chickens missing their heads. Maybe that was the way around it, just go to the wrong truck? Mistakes can happen when people rush.

'We will deal with it when it comes,' he said as he clapped

Halfpenny on the back. Rankin smiled to himself, the only thing that was good about this situation was Sam's last name wasn't anything like Zachary.

It took only another three minutes of name barking before they heard the name they waited for. 'Halfpenny, Samson: Enoggera.'

'Thank Christ,' Sam exhaled as the two of them made their way through the already heavily diminished lines of the company. They continued to their left, while Sam beamed at Rankin as they walked.

Rankin raised his eyebrows as he looked away from Sam's gleeful face and to the line of International's that already teemed with men. Whether he liked it or not, he had a friend. No matter which way he thought about it, Sam seemed more like a responsibility.

Before the line of trucks stood a clerical officer who held a clipboard. His face was partially hidden by his glasses and he never seemed to look up from the pages in front of him.

'Names?' he asked as they arrived, making it seem more like a field trip than a war effort by the minute.

'Bartlett and Halfpenny,' Rankin said and watched as the clerk ran his pen down the list and checked their names. The man gestured to the trucks and barked at the people who stood behind them for their names.

They climbed into the back of the first truck, the inside of its tray already full with crates of rifles and ammunition, canned food and water. Rankin rubbed at his mouth; at least they would eat like Kings off bully beef. Everyone had hated it in Vietnam, but as he had never had a taste for finer things, he never complained. The men lined the bed of the truck, their backs to the canvas, their eyes peered over the crates that were tied down between them. It didn't take long for the engines to fire up. He heard the rattle and the boom of the tanks, heavy diesels across the compound fire almost simultaneously. They left Amberley, their feet on the ground for less than an hour.

The convoy of trucks travelled at a lower speed than he had thought they would. They were hindered by the speed of the Tanks and M113 personnel carriers that made up their vanguard and rear. The tanks had been broken up into three groups; of the nineteen, nine would go to Deception Bay, being the lightest defended currently. Enoggera would receive two, and the remainder would stay back at Amberly as part of a reserve unit made up of mechanics, clerical officers and older veterans.

Sam tried small talk, but Rankin was never much for that. He just continued to look at the black printing on the sides of the crates. Curious about what lay inside. He found more with .303 and some lengthy blank crates that he imagined held the rifles. He wondered what he would be handed when he got off the truck, what hand he would be dealt.

Sam now spoke like the loudmouth on the plane, but the words went in and out of Rankin's head and failed to grasp any sort of hold on his mind until he thought of something that he had found amusing.

'Samson?' Rankin said, a queer smile on his face as he glanced at his new friend. 'Who is called Samson?'

Sam looked abashed by the name and dropped his head, 'I hate it when people call me that,' he mumbled as he spoke to his feet.

'It's alright, like I can talk. Rankin,' he said, emphasising his own name. 'Just never heard it before.'

Sam seemed lightened by his sleight on his name and lifted his head to continue to beam. 'Dad used to say I was going to grow up as strong as Samson and that's why he named me after him.'

Rankin laughed, 'No doubt. So what was your brother called then? Hercules or something?'

Sam gave him an odd look. 'No, his name was Adam. Why?'

'Oh, no reason, no reason.' He gave back as he shook his head and turned his gaze to look out the back of the truck, the only place that offered a view of the outside world. Scrub had turned to highway. A stream of cars loaded with suitcases, belongings and families, extended back in the other direction. He raised his eyebrows again at the sight and shook his head, this wasn't even the main road out of Brisbane, he could only imagine how the highway South looked. Eventually, highway skirts went from littered trees to houses. He saw glimpses of houses with doors ajar, belongings left or forgotten in front yards. A dog on the sidewalk watched in silence as the dark green International followed the clattering of the Centurions tracks.

By the time they reached Enoggera, the sun was at its peak, and he fondly remembered the southerly breeze of Sydney as he ran half-naked and half-mad down the street. It was stifling under the canvas, and the men that had been cramped together on the plane and now on a truck were beyond ripe. The fresh air hit him as he clambered off the truck, his service greens stuck to his back, and the heavy fabric of his trousers was damp. His hand fell to the pouch on his belt, and he felt the coolness of the metal below the leather. He felt safe with the dusters at his hip, like Max was with him. At the sight of the base, he was all too familiar with, his migraine began to encroach once more. The barracks, the command centre, nothing had changed, but nothing felt the same. It felt odd to see soldiers run and yell as they barked orders. The beginning of his day had been filled with the laughter and cheer of the men he was surrounded by. None of them were laughing now.

An aid station had been erected alongside the mess; there were men on stretchers under portable shade, and bandages were hurriedly wrapped around arms, legs, torsos and heads. Stains of red reached past the white as if looking for the heat of the sun. A civilian ambulance had just pulled up, and a stretcher was being dragged out of the back. A small girl lay still, one arm hung off the edge while the other was wrapped around a doll at her chest. The bearers placed the stretcher down on a table and were immediately met by the triage nurse. The nurse took one look, placed her fingers on the girl's throat, shook her head and moved on.

'Get those crates off the back of those trucks; you're not here for a fuckin holiday!' a sergeant roared at the idle men. Everyone sprang to work; crates of ammunition were pulled and stockpiled in the open, lined up along with the food and water. Rifles were left to the side. It took twenty minutes for everything to be counted for stocktake; clerks scribbled notes and wrote numbers one through six on the crates.

The same Sergeant that shook the men back into action tore open the crates with rifles. To Rankin's surprise, the first crate that was opened contained SLRs. His eyes widened when the first rile was pulled and handed straight to a nearby soldier as his carry weapon. He pushed people out of his way as he raced to the front and dragged Sam behind him.

'Don't worry; there are other crates. We will get one,' he complained.

Rankin shot him a look. 'You haven't seen what's in the other crates yet,' his voice was harsh. One after another, The SLRs were being handed out as the crate became lighter by the second.

The sergeant reached in, pulled out one, and handed it to Rankin. 'Protect our sons and daughters with it, son,' he said in a solemn tone then kicked the crate to the side. 'Open another.' The next crate was dragged over and as soon as the first edge was cracked, Rankin's shoulders slumped. The heavy metal receivers of the SLR's weren't visible, nor the pistol grip or the charging handle. Old heavily oiled timber sweated in the sun and brass butts dented and beaten from use, struggled to offer a simple gleam in the brightness of the day. The sergeant pulled out an Enfield and handed it to Sam; others were being handed out around them. While some were being given the heavy Bren and pouches designed for the large banana-shaped magazines. Soldiers cried out in disbelief, those that held SLR's soon saw what was happening and took off out of sight. Their hands wrapped around the timber grips of their rifles so tightly that Rankin didn't doubt the timber would be dented from the pressure.

The muzzle of the old rifle came up to the centre of Sam's sternum while its butt rested on the ground. Rankin looked at him, looked at his SLR, then snatched the Enfield from his new friends' hands.

'Here, take it.' He pushed his weapon into Sam's chest and gave it a longing look as he did so. The SLRs were a modern combat rifle, capable of semi-automatic fire. One trigger pull, one shot. The Enfield he now held was the same model rifle the ANZAC's carried in Gallipoli, half the magazine capacity of the SLR and bolt action instead of gas power.

Most of the other soldiers had realised what was left for them, and cries of outrage filled the air. 'The Chinese have AKs, and you're giving us souvenirs?' a man said, his face red from the injustice.

'Be thankful you're getting any fucking thing!' The sergeant roared to quell the protestors. 'You want SLRs? You take them from the boys that fall in front of you. In the meantime, these rifles have seen us through two world wars. They won't fail you and you won't fail us!'

Rankin took Sam away from the crowd. 'If I'm not wrong, shit's going to get pretty ugly here in a minute. You hold onto that rifle like it were money.' No sooner had the last word left his lips than someone shoved him hard in the back. Rankin stumbled forward and just managed to keep his feet.

'Pussy gets an auto and I get this? Like fuck!'

Rankin spun around, his gut heavy with anger. The same pox scarred bastard from the plane had one hand around the barrel of SLR in Sam's hands, who fought to keep hold. Rankin rushed forward, his hand went to his belt by instinct and he flipped the tab.

He felt the coolness of the brass and in one fluid movement he had slipped the dusters on his fingers and driven his fist into the gut of the attacker. He felt the air go out of him. Spittle speckled Sam's face from the rush and he crumpled. Rankin sunk his boot into him for good measure, then kneeled over him. He pushed his face so close that his lips were pressed to his ear; he could feel the sweat of the man below him as it ran from his thick hair. 'You come near him again, crater face, and I'll put a fresh one in your fucking forehead.' He punched him in the lower back and the man twisted below him. 'Every time you piss blood now, I want you to think of me and what I said.' He pushed the soldier down into the ground and stood. Around him, the scene had gone from bad to worse. Fights had broken out in places, unloaded rifles were being used as clubs. There were roars of men all around them, then a gun shot rang out.

Everyone went quiet.

Rankin was surprised to hear the shot. As far as he knew, no one had been handed ammunition. Then he saw the sergeant, who now stood atop the crates, his Hi-Power in his hand as it pointed to the sky. Around them, active soldiers closed in on them, men who were wounded, clerks and mechanics. All of them with looks of anger and disappointment on their faces.

'We are not the enemy!' the sergeant roared. 'Take it out on them!' His face was beyond red and had begun to take on shades of purple. He pointed his finger North as he screamed the last, 'Anyone of you fuckers that wants to start any more shit,' he spat these words, accompanied by saliva and accusatory pointing, 'I'll fucking do you in myself. Fuck the Chinese.'

The Veterans stood there, their heads down like abashed children. The rest of the rifles were handed out in silence. A few of the soldiers that had approached to offer the sergeant support remained to keep an eye on the newcomers, but no further quarrel sparked. Once everything was divided up, he called the men that were handed Brens and the very few that were handed M60s. He then announced to all of them that he would assign men to trucks. He pointed to each International and counted aloud one through six, then he pointed at each Bren gunner and did the same. As there were only three men holding 60s, he sent each of them to the trucks that held the least men so far.

Once this lottery draw had been announced, the sergeant turned to the rest of them. 'You'll see numbers on these crates one through six. Each of you knows which truck you rode in on. Machine gunners, go to the ammunition crates, and the clerks will fit you out. There are twenty of these gunners; I need twenty support people who will stick with them and carry their ammunition. I'll ask for volunteers and I fucking expect them. The rest of you pick up a crate that's numbered the same as your truck, take it there, load it and then proceed to ammunition collection. Whatever remains will be loaded onto the trucks as per the numbers.'

The whole exercise took another twenty minutes. More than twenty men stepped forward to volunteer as ammunition carriers, Rankin thought many did it out of shame. As this happened, there was small chatter once more, but nothing more than short to the point exchanges. They watched the Bren gunners stuff magazines into their pouches, each of them struggled with the weight of the cumbersome dinosaurs. The crates of food and water were carried to the trucks and stowed. The time came for ammunition fit-out.

Each of the men with Enfields were given old bandoliers stuffed with five round stripper clips. Men with SLRs were given webbing to suit and multiple magazines already loaded. Each of them was provided a helmet and a small pack with a canteen full of water, a few days' rations and a small first-aid kit. Then the sergeant's voice rang out once more to call all of them to their trucks, to their positions, to war.

MICHAEL

'The wild and windy night
That the rain washed away
Has left a pool of tears
Crying for the day
Why leave me standing here
Let me know the way.'

The Beatles - *Long and Winding Road* (1970)

Nothing made sense and nothing ever would. The outside world had become far too hostile and far too tragic, so for what seemed like months; he had retreated deep within himself. He had barred the doors of his mind, great iron monstrosities that were welded and bolted together with bits and pieces of junk and parted out cars. The heavy steel chassis of the mill's lumber truck stretched to the heavens, braced by the Whippet's panels. While part of the Fairlane's brilliant chrome, made up the handle. Even in the darkness of his mind, the chrome glinted and twinkled at him. It laughed as it sparkled amongst the inch thick stacks of corrugated iron that were riveted together to form a patchwork of rusted sheets. Pipework from the mill's enormous boiler framed the doors to give them strength, while a quartered twelve foot saw blade was bolted over the top.

He had pushed those giant doors closed the day it all happened, while he lay on the floor next to his mother. The book he had loved only inches away from him, thrown to the ground in the confusion.

He had watched as the blood that flowed from his father's body advanced on the novel, as the slowly rolling waves broke against the hardcover and began to swirl around its flanks. The pages held strong against the fluid at first, already damaged by the water and mud, then the pages began to soften as the remnants of Tony Baker became a part of that book forever.

He had barred the gates before Jack had returned; the storm that still raged around him seemed to quiet the instant the two halves became one. His own projection of himself wasn't sore, wasn't beaten. It was as if he had gone back in time to before this had all started, the boy ready to walk the long and winding fire trail to head to the mill. No scratches, no cuts, as long as the doors remained closed, he would be alright. As he stood back and admired his protection, he sighed, he had forgotten a lock. He squeezed his eyes shut and focused with everything he had. In front of him, he heard corrugated iron shift against the cold steel. When he opened his eyes once more, a long steel shaft appeared across the door frame. Eight foot long, it hung loosely in its guide. Michael grasped the pole's handle, he slid it across as rust flaked from the steel. Finally locked against the horrors of the outside world, he turned away from the gates to create his ultimate paradise.

A path of brilliant white pebbles etched its way through the lush grasses before him. The path cut its way through a forest that was more alive than anything he had ever seen. The scrub of Queensland was thick in many places but it never looked as vibrant as what he saw before him now. Vines etched their way up the trunks of trees which were as gold as his mother's wedding band. Although sparsely spaced on the forest ground, the canopy was thick and covered the entire sky, yet somehow, he had no trouble seeing. He thought this is what Tom Bombadil's forest must look like. Michael half expected to see elves jump out from behind the tree closest to him, but nothing happened.

Shortly, he came into a clearing where brilliant sunlight broke through the foliage, now allowed to touch the earth, dazzling his eyes. The trees and their canopy had subsided as he moved closer, white pebbles turned to flat slates of stone. The path widened and his heart leapt at what he saw. Vaster than the creek down the back of the Baker's lot, was a lake. Calmer than anything he had ever seen, with water so clear he could see each pebble that littered its banks, along with the sandstone that formed its edges. He gasped as his fingers touched water and he watched as the ripples seemed to run from one end to the other, almost fifty feet away.

The sound of song birds that nattered of lovers and moonlit nights to their partners filled his head. He let himself drown in the beauty of the scene that surrounded him, and felt the tension in his mental spine melt away. He had removed his work boots and let his toes tempt the water, the cool kiss ran shivers of delight up his spine. Just as he thought he could spend an eternity there, soaking up the pleasures of a beauty he had never known, the iron gates began to shake on their hinges. The sound drove him from his dream within a dream, he clambered to his feet and ran the rest of the way to the gates.

They had come alive. The cross bolt rapped madly against the iron below it, as the steel pole trembled in its sheath. Michael didn't know what was happening, whether someone or something was trying to get in. He needed to see what was on the other side. He closed his eyes once more and focused all of his effort on the door. Beneath the rattling iron, he heard metal shift and rivets pop their seals. Iron bent, then welded itself anew. Once he opened his eyes, he took a step back, amazed. Before the gate stood a rusted iron scene of the Baker's living room. The boxy television stretched out of the gate and flickered with snowy static. Spaced ten feet back was his father's chair, but instead of the worn through fabric, rusted corrugate acted as arm rests. Instead of needle work and staples, rivets and bolts held it together. As he neared the iron chair, the static shifted on the screen and began to form an image. Bewildered at what he saw before him, he sat down and gave the screen his full attention.

He saw the kitchen table where he had sat for every meal, with vision far better than the old screen in their living room. On the table was his book. Slowly a hand came into the picture and slowly slid it out of frame.

'Hey,' Michael pounded on the steel armrests of the chair, 'That's mine!' The image did not turn, he swore at the television. 'Turn you bastard! Who took it?' As if by his own command, the vision panned softly. The book was open on the table now. Even through the screen he could see the blood-soaked pages, the words replaced by large clots of mess. He could see the trousers and waist of a man who stood behind the table. The image panned upwards, and as it did, he finally saw the man's face. It was heavily lined, and a look of genuine concern was behind his old eyes. His mouth moved as if he spoke words that Michael couldn't understand; only one word stood out by the shape of his mouth, 'Okay.'

Michael wished he could talk to him; he even looked over at the cross bolt that now rested gently on the door. He thought he should move towards it and throw the gates open, but when he looked back at the vision, the man was gone.

Just then, a sound cut through everything and his makeshift world exploded in a roar of fire. It echoed and bounced off the gates, which harmonised the steel and iron as they rattled ferociously once more. Michael jumped on the iron chair, and almost lost his balance. The gunshot seemed to come from the trees, rather than the speakers of the television, the sound clearer than anything he had heard come from the old machine in their living room.

Confusion racked the boy as he turned his head to the screen once more, then he screamed as he lost his balance and fell from the chair. The breath rushed out of him as his back slapped against the white pebbles. In front of him, the gates had stopped their commotion, but the vision of Jack in the doorway still burned into his mind.

Shaken by the image, he had returned to the lake to drown his worries but something urged him on. Rather than sit by the lake side, he ventured further to see what lay behind. He was met with a green hedge wall that stretched to the sky and vanished in a swirl of smoke and wispy fog. In its centre stood a carved arch, spaced up the sides were the faces of people he mostly knew. He saw Paul Darcy, his father, Susan was there as well as the two horrible Trackers that had stolen the Fairlane. Above them was an older man with longer hair he didn't know. He marvelled at the way that the features of the faces in the hedge were done; it was so easy to tell who they were even in a wall of leaves. As the marble tiles went under the arch, they were met with another hedge wall only mere feet away, which was likewise straight as a die. Michael walked into the pathway and turned his head to the right, the path seemed to stretch on for a few hundred feet and then it vanished off to the left. When he turned his head to the left, he saw a mirror image.

'It's a maze,' he said. A real hedge maze in his head. He had always wanted to see one, but the Baker family had never travelled. He was sure that the Darcy's would have seen one; they seemed to go everywhere. Michael took a few steps down the left path and began to turn the corner when he heard the iron gates erupt again. He swore, turned on his heels, and rushed back toward the opening of the maze. As he went through, he noticed there was another face carved into the archway; with the introduction of this face, every other one shuffled around to allow it more space to fit. He recognised the man with the lined face instantly. There was no concern in his eyes, only peace. The lines on his face were etched into the hedge wall with such realism that Michael thought he could see a bead of sweat run down his forehead.

As he reached the gates, they still quaked on their hinges. Rust sifted down through the air with each movement and settled on the screen of the television. He took a moment to stand there and watch the gates as they rattled. In one place, a bolt had worked loose and tumbled to the earth; it skittered across the pebbles as it landed. Could the gates collapse? He still didn't know what caused them to shake, but he supposed there was only one way to find out.

When he once more settled on the iron chair and gave the screen his full attention, it looked as though he was in the Whippet. He could see the cracked windscreen; and the battered frame of the passenger's side of the cabin. Again, the vision began to pan and it didn't take long for the screen to reveal Jack behind the wheel. His head was low to keep his eyes below the line of the windscreen. His face was sullen; he didn't offer the boy a glance as they traversed the road together, seemingly at a high rate of knots by the trees he could see whizzing passed his brother's head.

Where were they going? It wasn't often that any of them had gotten the Whippet up to a speed like that as the roads didn't really call for it. The old truck was happy enough sitting at twenty down the fire trail; it didn't need to go much faster. Michael tried to lean closer to the screen to see the speedometer, but Jack's giant hand hid it from sight. As he sighed and gave up on the idea the vision panned back to the windscreen. The gates had fallen silent once more and Michael sat there to watch the road through the television screen. Only one thing held his sight, a mountain in the distance, as it slowly became larger.

He didn't know whether he had dozed off, whether it was even possible for himself to doze inside his own head. Still, when the gates erupted in an explosion of clanks and rattles, Michael had been snapped to attention and had fallen from his perch once more. This time he felt pain down his side, a throbbing in his head and an ache up his back. Michael couldn't understand how he could possibly hurt himself in his own mind. He stretched and winced as he sat down again on the chair. This time the TV screen was a little garbled and projected a lopsided image. He took a little while to work it out, but it was as though his body lay on its side as it watched what happened. They were in a forest, similar to the one he walked to reach the gate. Even through the screen, he could see how the scrub differed from the dry landscape around Chinchilla. The road Jack had taken was chopped out and steep. In some places, the dirt had eroded to such an extent that rocks had been exposed. They jutted out and waited for any unsuspecting vehicle. Jack leaned next to the Whippet, the front end was down on the ground, and splintered timber was spread out around him.

'Jack looks pissed,' he said. He was about to ask himself what had happened, when he saw his brother hold the splintered and cracked timber rim of the Whippet up to inspect it. They had forgotten to soak the spokes. Michael made a noise of shock, he held his hand to his face as his first impression was someone was going to get into trouble for that. But the memory of the fact that there was no one to get in trouble from anymore came back and he was left depressed once more.

As Michael looked on, Jack disappeared and returned a while later, burdened by a large stone. Panic began to rise deep within Michael's stomach as his first thought was that his brother was about to crush his head in with the small boulder. When Jack placed the rock down by the side of the Whippet, he relaxed. Jack squatted at the front of the hulking frame as if he was going to start it and Michael watched in awe. As his face went purple with strain, Jack began to lift the old machine. Metal groaned as the frame was lifted into the air, then placed softly on the boulder. It's right hub raised so Jack could work on it.

Shocked once more by his brother's strength, Michael left the screen and the iron gates behind him. He returned once more to the lake to retrieve his work boots and welcomed the sight of the carved hedge faces as he entered the maze. No new faces had joined the pack; their features were still peaceful and calm. This time he chose the right path. His engineer boots padded softly on the marble tiles as he wound his way through. The sound of the song birds was behind him now; the only sound came from his boots and the rustle of the hedge as an imaginary breeze wisped through the maze. Left, then right and left once more, he wound his way through the maze in his mind, unsure what was at the centre, and he didn't care either. Just left, then right and left a few more times. He never found a dead end, not once, just more hedge and more gleaming marble tiles.

Eventually, he came to another archway. The faces were carved into it again, all the same faces, all in the same positions, but the look of peace in their eyes was replaced by that of fear on some and anger on others. A look of warning from the kind man with the lined face, a look of hatred from his father. The old man with the long hair had eyes that were just orbs and nothing else; his mouth hung open, gaunt and lopsided. Michael passed them, his brow furrowed as his gut was left unsettled. The ground below him turned to mud, and the tiles ended in a broken section, with shards that protruded at odd angles, partially sunken into the brown waste. Before him stood another open lake, over a hundred feet from bank to bank. At its centre stood a statue, forty feet tall. The edges of the lake were not sleek sandstone as with the other, but jagged shards of dog's teeth and bone that shot up like prison bars, designed to hold the statue in. The carving was perfect. Jack's face was solid and stern, the scar ran a jagged line up his forehead, and his jaw looked even more square set from where Michael stood. His chest was bare, hair that looked as though it was barbed wire ran a tangled mess across its broadest point, and a thin trail ran down to his navel.

Michael took a step and felt his foot sink deep into the mud. He sprawled forward; one leg was trapped while the other scraped uselessly against the sloppy surface. He let out a cry in his surprise, and to his horror, the sound echoed and echoed. It bounced first from the heavy line of trees that surrounded the lake, then from the stone face of his brother. Again and again, the sound of his fear came back to haunt him, and then there was silence for a long time. He was too afraid to move, to even breathe. Up on top of his brother's head, forty feet high, a small stone fell. Michael watched its journey down, paralysed at the sight of it, thirty feet, twenty feet. The last thing he wanted was for anything else to make another sound, ten feet. 'Please, no.'

When the stone hit the water, the lake erupted and threatened to break its banks. White foam frothed at the tips of its watery teeth that gnashed and clawed in their flail to snare anything that was stupid enough to come within its grasp. The ground began to tremble beneath Michael, and he shrieked. He rocked back to his ass and began to squirm and work his leg free. The mud's suction was so tight that he felt his foot slip in his boot until finally, it let go and he fell backward as his bare foot appeared from the surface.

Michael didn't waste a second; he turned and ran for the maze. The faces that were carved into the hedge were all dead; the mouths hung open. One's skull was deformed, completely beat in, while another was a scramble of leaves and mess with one hating eye. The lake broke its banks behind him, and he heard a crash as something immensely heavy fell into the water.

Michael did not look back; he couldn't.

'Left then right. No, right then right again, then left.'

The hedge rushed past him as he ran. Behind him, he heard waves crash against the muddy half tiled surface and still he ran. 'Right then left then left again then, maybe right?' Michael swore. The hedges had begun to tremble; the ground still shook but not constantly. There were two seconds, maybe three, before each tremor.

At last, he turned right and saw a long stretch of marble tiles in front of him; and finally, an opening. He ran and ran. He burst through the opening and didn't even pause to look at the hedge faces. Instead, he was struck by the sight of another statue that had appeared in this first lake. A twenty-foot likeness of himself stood there, his face kind, but there was something about the statue he hated. It wasn't right, it wasn't him. Behind him, the hedges parted and Michael scrambled only just fast enough to escape the weight of the stone Jack's footfall.

Everything fell around him, large clumps of hedge and stone shards from the joints of his brother's likeness. He scrambled and crawled and narrowly avoided a falling chunk of stone that was large enough to crush him. The question of whether or not he could be harmed in this dream or nightmare was gone; he was frightened for his life. As he made for the iron gates, he turned to watch the progress of the giant. Jack's statue was now mostly through the maze; behind it was a trail of destruction. Black water poured through the hole it created like a tidal wave, ready to suck him back to the lake and drown him forever. The giant Jack roared at the sight of its stone brother and charged. As in real life, the eerie quickness of it was startling. Stone fell, water rushed and was thrown into the air by the statue's momentum. The ground shook like it was about to collapse, and finally, they met, the ferocious Jack and the placid, fake Michael. As soon as the two stone likenesses touched, they exploded.

Chunks of stone flew through the air, large trees were uprooted, and the ground fractured beneath Michael's feet. Below the whole catastrophe, the iron gates rattled so hard that sheets of iron had begun to fall. Michael turned and fled his sanctuary; as water gushed at his heels and threatened to trip him, while trees fell in front of him to block his path. The pebble path was a sea of moving slippery stones; his muddy foot slid each time he placed it.

By the time he reached the gates, they were barely standing. The iron chair and the television screen, were completely gone. Part of the chassis on the side had collapsed, taking with it most of the corrugated iron. Beyond it, were swirls of smoke and although he couldn't see it, his body lay on the side of some track. Michael caught the cross bolt as its handle rattled tremendously. He lifted it and pulled with all of his strength while the ground behind him was falling away. The world was full of rushing water, cracking timber and stone.

Finally, the steel rod slid out of its rusting sheath. He pressed his hands against the pipe of the boiler and shoved while the panels of the Whippet fell around him. Slowly but surely, the door began to move, and he leapt through into the smoke and the reality that lay beyond.

RANKIN

'Long as I remember
The rain been coming' down
Clouds of mystery pourin'
Confusion on the ground.
Good men through the ages,
Trying to find the sun.'

Creedence Clearwater Revival – *Who'll Stop the Rain* (1970)

The International's engine groaned and fought through the uneven road. Its tyres ground with traction and surged with power one minute, only to succumb to loose dirt and chunks of bitumen the next. Rankin was at a loss for words about how Brisbane had changed. The scene from the rear opening of the truck's canvas canopy painted a scene that could have been from France in the forties. He watched the driver of the truck behind his own as he fought to keep the truck upright. Its rear tyres slid into a crater which swallowed half of the road and most of the structure of the shop front adjacent. The frame of the truck shuddered as its tyres hooked the road, then slipped, and finally hooked once more as its engine laboured to haul its weight out of the hole.

A bank of helicopters bored through the air above them, their black hulls only just visible through the heavy clouds of smoke and dust. Hunters and killers sent to roam the air and look for any signs of Chinese movement. The M134 Gatlings that were bolted to their side were ready to fill the air with walls of lead. Rankin had only ever heard the rip tearing effect of M134's once in his life. A person could not tell one shot from another; they just screamed their fury as metal churned and the fire erupted from its many muzzles. He saw six Hueys in that first bank; he didn't know how many more roamed the skies above. All the air power that the Australian Defence Force could muster was concentrated in Brisbane. All that power, yet still, he didn't feel as safe as he had when the Black Dread flew above him.

As the smaller convoy of trucks passed through the destroyed streets of Brisbane, Rankin caught glimpses of other streets through the haze of alleyways. He caught a glimpse of a Centurion that ground its way over a burned out hull of either a Ford or Holden while its escort detail of foot soldiers trotted alongside. The shelling had destroyed the façade of Brisbane, many buildings were on fire, and most roads were undrivable hence the issue the truck drivers faced. A layer of smoke and dust had settled over the streets, which gave each corner a blurred effect, where shadows lurked just beyond the line of sight.

The trucks had no sooner dragged their sorry hulls out of the fortified gates of Enoggera when the problems had started. Their trucks were to cut north to resupply and rearm a scattered company of 6 RAR. The shelling had affected them the worst, and elements of the Chinese vanguard had begun to test their borders. They all knew it wouldn't be long before everything turned to shit. Hell, it already had. Their progress was halted by a civilian vehicle; an EH Holden had dropped a tyre into the edge of a crater, which blocked the only route through. A young man was the owner of the car, he along with his bride and their newborn, stood around the propped EH like sheep with no direction. The International halted, and the men piled out to pry the car from the gaping mouth below it. If the power from the Holden's plant wasn't enough to free it, the strength of six men was, and once it started rolling, it never stopped. The occupants never looked back, never waved. Somewhat insulted, the men piled back into the truck, as their scowls turned to grumbles of dissent.

Rankin was amused by this; didn't they all come home from war? Didn't they all know what it was like to get no thanks, no respect? Nothing apart from looks of mistrust and discomfort from these people they had fought and died for. He left his thoughts to himself; he needed to look after himself and Sam, his adopted friend. His Enfield stood upright in front of him, the magazine loaded and one in the breech. The length of the rifle made it feel cumbersome, but he didn't think he'd be waiting long before he traded. Somehow, he felt the sergeant back at Enoggera was right.

The truck hitched and weaved along the road and then the hull jerked to a halt, the sound of steel on stone ripped through the canopy. Some of the men almost fell from their seats at the sudden impact. Then they started to laugh. They laughed as they heard the differential whine below them. They laughed as the engine's revs climbed to a roar and the tyres below them ground away to try to shift the dead weight. As small holes peppered the canvas canopy, the men still laughed while they looked around in confusion, wondering where the streams of light had come from. Rankin felt warmth as something splashed across his face, and he jumped as it hit him. It was in his eyes, and he blinked rapidly to clear them; his hands were a red blur as they pawed at his face. The laughs turned to screams as the man opposite Rankin began to convulse. The canopy then became lost to panic.

Rankin dropped to the deck and tried to huddle behind the crates of supplies. He heard the heavy 'thuds' as bullets hit steel and timber, then the unmistakable noise of flesh being torn apart. His eyes had begun to clear and he looked up to see Sam, who still sat upright, his eyes wide in shock.

'Sam!' he screamed as he reached up and clutched him by the front of his shirt. More holes in the canvas appeared around them as he dragged Sam down on top of him. The eyes were still wide open but barely in focus. As men struggled to leave the canopy, he heard the rifle fire of the men that had first left. Some slow and awkward, others fast and inaccurate. Rankin rolled himself atop Sam; as he raised himself, he looked his friend over and couldn't see any wounds. Satisfied that he was frozen from shock, he left him to fight for the trucks.

Another volley of bullets hammered into the side of the truck as he leapt from its rear. Chunks of timber flew into the air as the side braces fractured under the barrage. His feet slipped as he leapt, and he hit the ground hard. His Enfield slid away from him. Partially winded, he lunged for the rifle and swore as rocks and dirt kicked up around him from the unrelenting fire. He acted quicker than he ever had. He snatched the rifle as he looked to his right, noticing a shattered section of road that jutted out from the ground in a jagged rise. Bullets ricocheted off the ground around him as he slunk in behind the outcrop; the smell of oil and fuel filled the air.

He lay there as he tried to ascertain the situation while he watched the side of the truck get withered by volley after volley of fire. A soldier fell backwards into Rankin's line of sight, his chest torn open, his face pale. The bolt of his Enfield was stuck open on a round that jammed in the magazine. The soldier and his rifle fell heavily to the ground and didn't move. He could hear the rattle of AK fire to his front. Rankin turned to look at the second International in the convoy and saw the clean face of an Australian man who looked out from behind the truck's front end, their eyes locked. Rankin could see other men's feet that worked their way behind the heavy steel of the truck's frame to his position. He held out his hand in a stop motion. The shoulder of the Australian jerked and they all stopped.

'Where the fuck are they?' Rankin questioned as a single round ricocheted off the bitumen above his head. Rankin pulled his hand in quick and curled his legs up.

The soldier raised his eyes above Rankin's position; he gestured with his head and shuffled in his crouched position.

'They're in the shops over there, we think. They hammered you lot before we came out from behind this wall.'

Rankin shuffled himself around and peered out over the rubble. Where his International had stopped left it exposed on the left by a small plaza, a shopfront mostly collapsed lay about fifty yards beyond his position. The frontage stretched a hundred feet cross. The entire left section had been destroyed by artillery fire and lay in ruins of brick and steel reinforcement. The centre section was in better condition; only the windows had been blown out. Whereas the right section remained mostly solid, only for a few large holes that had been punched through its structure. Even in the dust that riddled the air, he saw movement among the rubble and broken windows. The puffs of the muzzle flash as an automatic rifle sent a flurry of bullets to skitter around him. He quickly brought his head back under cover.

To his left lay the second truck, sheltered from the shop front by a large sandstone wall. Three men crouched by its edge, the first of which fumbled with the weight of the Bren in his hands.

'Oi,' Rankin roared at him, 'Bren gunner.' The soldier looked up at him with a shocked look of 'who me?' The man was middle-aged, still a bull in size, but the dead weight of the forty-odd-year-old machine gun made him slow. 'I heard the Japs didn't like the sound of those; what do you reckon they'd think?'

The middle-aged soldier looked down at the Bren in his hands, his eyebrows furrowed and then he looked back to Rankin. 'Where?'

Rankin gestured to the shop front that the gunner couldn't see.

'Directly twelve on me. Focus on the centre and put as many low in through the windows as you can.'

Rankin readied himself as the Bren gunner shifted into position, his head low to the sights which sat at the side of the vertical magazine. He looked back to the first soldier behind the truck, who had likewise begun to ready himself, his SLR raised and ready.

The slow thunderous fire of the Bren was awe-inspiring. The frame jostled in the soldier's hands, and chunks of stone and brick were thrown to cascade through the air as the old heavies pounded into the structure of the shops. Dust erupted from the impacts around the shop's window. Rankin leapt to his feet, his Enfield in hand and ran to the sandstone wall. The rattle of firing continued to come from the shops, but it was blind and directed at the International. Rankin threw himself behind the wall and quickly checked himself and his rifle for damage.

'We need to flank them,' he barked at the men. 'Keep that Bren on them; we will jump this wall and get up to that broken side.'

Rankin slung his rifle and rolled his sleeves up his arm. Whenever he got into conflict, he felt hot, and already the sweat had begun to soak into the cloth of his shirt around his armpits. The sandstone wall was over seven ft in height, and there was no way he would be able to clear it in a jump. As he looked around, the Chinese in the shop front lit up the section of the stone wall where the Bren gunner had leaned out, forcing him back to safety. Rankin lowered his head to listen to the pattern of fire, the chorus of volleys.

'There are at least six of them,' he said to his fellow soldiers cowering behind the wall. 'Does anyone have grenades?'

'There are crates full of supplies in the back of our truck.' A man who sat on his ass piped up, his back to the wall as he clutched his Enfield.

'Go see what you can find; get those others from behind the truck while you're there. I need two to follow me.' He looked to the others.

'Are you the Bren's support?' he asked the third soldier, who sat between the others. Another older soldier whose hair was iced steel beneath his helmet. The man nodded. 'Good, you stay with your gunner; you need to keep their heads down for us.'

As he spoke to the three behind the wall, his eyes fell back to the battered remains of the International he was in. He could see soldiers under the canopy piled on top of each other. Feet and arms, all tangled, and none of them moved. It was impossible for him to tell which limb belonged to which body from where he stood. All he knew was that in there, hopefully still alive, Sam Halfpenny lay with his eyes open while they registered nothing. The few men that had made it out of the truck had attempted to storm the shop front and had made it into the plaza. From where he stood, he could see the legs of a soldier who lay face down; blood stained his uniform and had begun to seep onto the concrete beneath him.

The smell of fuel from the destroyed International had become even heavier. It was time they attacked before the Chinese had half the thought to ignite the punctured tanks. Another four men joined them from the second truck, one of them with his SLR slung as he held a crate with ammunition and grenades. As he jogged, the crate bounced in his hands, loose rounds of ammunition spilled, while he kicked a grenade that he had already dropped along with him. Rankin helped himself to two grenades, giving another two each to the men with SLRs.

'What are your names?' he asked the men as he handed them the grenades. The one who had held the crate placed it to the ground and took his grenades, while the other man slung his SLR and held out his hands.

'Mason, sir,' the one who placed the crate down replied.

'Reynolds, sir.'

'Don't call me that; I'm no officer.' Rankin looked the two men over.

Of the ones that stood around him, these men were the fittest. 'Mason, Reynolds, we will throw one grenade each to the centre line of the shops; I will try and get mine into the rubble on the left. Do you know where I'm talking about?'

They both nodded.

'Alright,' he addressed all the men now as the Chinese started with another volley of fire. He pointed at a younger Enfield carrier. 'You will need to give us a boost over the wall; we will go as soon as the Bren starts firing.' He looked to the Bren gunner, 'As soon as the grenades go. Okay?'

'Okay.' This was echoed by a few of the men.

'Get yourselves ready, fresh magazines, no fucking around.' He looked back at Mason and Reynolds. 'Straight to the left side.'

The sound of bolts slid to engage rounds of ammunition filled his ears. The Bren's bolt reciprocated, and the slide returned and locked; the gunner readied himself near the wall, as the support gunner and another soldier readied themselves to boost the others over.

'Grenades!' Rankin roared as he pulled the pin on his and lobbed it over the wall; the release tab clinked as the casing left his hand. Soon after, two more clinks were heard as the others let theirs go. Rankin listened as the weighty grenades thudded to the ground.

'Ready!' he yelled as he ran towards the Bren's support man. The three explosions came within a second of each other, and they rung through the air as small stones and silt were thrown upward. The Bren started its slow, methodical fire; it ran in chains of four to five rounds before he eased on the trigger for half a second and started over again. Rankin placed his foot in the hands of the support man, and he felt himself rise as he pushed down hard with his foot. He placed his right hand on the wall and hoisted himself over; his legs didn't even touch the sandstone in the hoist. Then he was over and falling. He saw the silt and residue of the three explosions. Likewise, he saw the hint of the men that cowered behind brick walls as the Bren thundered into them. As he fell, he lost sight of the Chinese, and he stumbled as his feet connected with the ground.

He ran into his stumble and headed directly for the left flank of the shops. Below the bellows of the Bren, he heard two more thuds behind him, but he never looked back. He dove as he reached the crumbled wall and looked back to Mason and Reynolds. Mason, being shorter and heavier set, had fallen slightly behind, whereas Reynolds had powered ahead. When Reynolds slid in next to Rankin, Mason still had twenty ft to travel. Rankin urged him silently on from his position when the Bren stopped. Mason laboured as he ran; only ten feet remained when the clatter of automatic fire erupted from inside the shop, and the brute force of four rifles hammered Mason. His body crumpled as he ran. Chunks were torn from him, and blood filled the air. A bullet slammed him in the face to snap his head back and leave him collapsed rearward over his shins. Mason's SLR clattered to the ground beside him, only ten feet away, but it may as well have been a hundred for the amount of good it was going to do Rankin at that moment.

Rankin swore as he clambered to his knees; he raised his Enfield and threw the safety off. He lifted his head and saw one Chinese soldier already headed for their corner. The two raised their rifles at the same time, Rankins long and cumbersome, whereas the Chinese's AK short and solid. The Chinese began to fire before the rifle was on his shoulder, and the rounds all went wild as the assault rifle bucked like a crazed bull in his hands. Rankin lowered his head quickly in a flinch to the blast in his face, then snapped up the Enfield and laid the sights on the soldier's chest. The rifle thundered in his hands. The recoil was savage and the Chinese collapsed, his chest caved in. Rankin worked the bolt rapidly as he stood and kept the rifle in a ready position. Reynolds followed him through the broken wall and came up along his right, his SLR raised.

The three shops had once been separate entities, with no entrance between structures inside. However, parts of the interior brick walls had collapsed, and from where they stood, they could partially see into the next centre shop through a large hole. A large portion of the rear had totally collapsed and would allow them to pass through.

The Bren fired up again and thundered into the centre shop. Rankin could hear the Chinese shout to each other in their guttural tongue as he moved closer, his head low. Rankin headed for the hole in the wall while Reynolds headed for the rearward collapsed section. Rankin pulled a grenade and removed the pin but held onto its release tab. Reynolds saw and nodded; he readied his rifle. Rankin peered through the hole and saw at a quick glance four of them just on the other side of the wall, their attention focused on the Bren, their heads down.

He flicked the grenade through the hole and ran for the back. He heard the clink of the tab release, the thud as the casing hit the ground, shouts of alarm and then the explosion. The thud was deafening inside. Another part of the wall collapsed, and dust filled the air. Rankin's ears erupted in a horrible pitch of outroar, but he yelled for Reynolds to move up. His voice sounded as though every orifice in his head was blocked, and he was trying to talk underwater. He heard the thud of Reynold's SLR, and he saw the flash of its muzzle through the dust, silt and the failing light. Rankin rounded the corner; Reynolds had taken the two on the right. They had attempted to throw the grenade to the rear of the store and, in doing so, had escaped most of its blast but were left incapacitated by the explosion. To the far side of the centre store, a soldier covered in dust from head to toe stood up and raised his rifle. Rankin threw the Enfield into his shoulder and fired into the mass of his body; he fell to the ground lifeless. He had seen four and looked for the final one, but there was no body to be seen.

The Bren had moved its fire over to the final store when the grenade had detonated. Rankin mentally praised the gunner, whom he had never stopped to ask his name, for his quick thinking and understanding of the situation. Together with Reynolds, he moved to the final wall. As they approached the collapsed centre, both of their rifles raised, dust flowed out in plumes. They stood side by side and approached the hole in the wall directly, as they held onto the belief that the blistering fire of the Bren would keep the heads of the enemy down. Not five ft away from them, an AK rattled in automatic fire. Rankin instinctually dropped backwards as he lifted his Enfield. Reynolds dropped his SLR, and his hands went to his throat as blood poured down his chest and from his mouth. The rattling fire continued to pound into Reynolds as Rankin returned fire into the cloud of dust. He worked the bolt again, fired, then again and fired. Reynolds had fallen to his side and barely clung to life in blood filled gurgles and groans. Rankin rolled over and grabbed Reynolds' SLR as he did and regained his feet. He fired it now with semi-automatic power and charged into the blinding dust.

He fired blindly in the hope of killing the bastard that hid within. He tripped over something almost instantly as he charged in; whatever it was, it was heavy and unmoving. Automatically his mind went back to the tunnel in Vietnam, tripping over bodies while fighting blind. He had had his fair share of this and wanted no taste of more. He rolled to his back, the SLR partly raised and waited. Outside, the Bren's assault had stopped, and he could hear the Australians in discussion. One screamed for help in a high-pitched cry of panic and fear.

'Sam,' Rankin said and he raised himself to sit.

Behind him, he heard a shuffle, and he rolled as he ducked his head. The Chinese man screamed as he swung his rifle butt downwards to graze Rankin's head as he rolled away. Rankin shot up, sunk his shoulder in the man's waist and drove him backwards in a tackle. As the two men fell, the back of the Chinese landed on a pile of rubble, and they both rolled off it as they came to the ground. With the Chinaman on top, he pressed the weight of his rifle down onto Rankin's throat while he screamed wildly. The sudden weight of the soldier landing on him had pushed most of the air out of Rankin, and he desperately needed to gain more. He grunted as he got his hands under the rifle and began to lift it, combined with the soldier's weight on top of him from his neck. As the air came back into him, so did his strength, and he could have easily lifted him to arms-length, but he wanted him close. He pushed the man up and then let him fall as he drove his fist upward. The naked fist connected with the soldier's jaw and sent him sprawling.

Rankin moved atop the soldier and scrambled to grab the barrel of his attacker's rifle as he brought it up. The room was filled with the roar of automatic fire as the AK clattered near his face. They fought against each other; the Chinaman tried to drag the course of fire across Rankin while he held it away. He felt the heat on his skin, and the thunder close to his face made everything else go into a deep silence. Finally, the rifle fell silent while the horrible pitch in his ears drove a head-splitting wedge down the centre of his brain. Rankin pulled at the AK and tried to take it from him, his anger unsurmountable at the pain he felt, along with the deaths of his fellow men the Chinese had ambushed. The soldier's grip lapsed on the stock of the AK, Rankin raised it above his head, and he roared in primitive victory.

He brought the butt down on the soldier's body. He felt the blow and the clatter of the mechanism as the butt drove into his side. Then he brought it down again on his chest while the soldier fought to shield himself. Again, on his chest, then on his face. All the fight went out of the Chinaman, yet Rankin kept on the attack. Again and again, he brought the steel plate of the butt down on his foe to crush his skull blow by blow. His features changed with every strike. The soldier's mouth opened and gasped for air in a shocked state, like a fish that had been brained by a spear. With each further blow, he saw the life in the man's eyes disappear and vanish into nothing while the rifle's weight crashed down on him.

Rankin collapsed, exhausted by his surge of anger. He rolled off the fallen soldier and lay on his back, while his lungs sucked in air still laced with dust and silt. He coughed as his eyes watered and he forced himself to his feet. He was met at the entrance to the centre shop by other soldiers, the Bren gunner being one. They parted to let the unarmed Rankin through. He stood there in the small plaza and looked at the International that had carried him only minutes before. Only now did he notice the driver, his body slumped over the wheel, the glass of the cabin either shattered or lined with blood, the passenger door riddled with bullet holes, as was the canopy. The contents of the fuel tanks had been exhausted and now the only thing that ran from the back of the truck's frame was the blood of the men that didn't make it out.

He pulled a cigarette from the crushed packet in his pocket and straightened it as best as he could before he lit it. His lungs, still filled with dust, choked as he took his first drag, and he was sent into another coughing fit as he walked to the street. He settled himself as he approached the few men that crouched around the soldier who lay trembling in their centre.

'Sam, are you alright?' Rankin asked as he crouched and took another drag on his cigarette. Still wide eyed, Sam's eyes met his own, and he saw the young soldier relax some.

'Oh, thank God,' Sam sighed. 'I didn't remember anything much of the truck; I thought you might be in there.'

Rankin uttered a soft laugh and he pushed the cigarette into Sam's mouth for him to finish. 'No one's that lucky.' He tussled Sam's hair and stood up again.

The Bren gunner came around the side of the sandstone wall he hid behind moments ago, his face sullen as he hung his head low. He sank to his ass, his back against the wall as he broke into tears. Rankin went to him; his hand went around the back of the machine gunner's neck. 'Hey, that was all you, man. We would have all died if not for you.'

'There was only fucking six of them,' he sobbed, 'I didn't even hit one of them.'

'You did your job; you kept their heads down while we took their flank. You drew their fire.'

The gunner looked at Rankin, his old eyes bloodshot from the tears that ran from his eyes to be caught in the wrinkles of his face and became rivers of their own. 'Six of them did all of this.' He pointed to the destroyed truck, the bodies still at the foot of the plaza. The men dead in the street or tangled together in the back of the truck. Rankin knew what he meant. There was nothing he could say to that. He stood up and started to walk away, then he turned and asked the gunner what his name was. The older man met his gaze once more, his eyes still a bleary red. 'Kelleher.'

'Thanks, Kelleher,' he said in a soft voice and left him. The other soldiers gathered their dead. They pulled the men out of the trucks and laid them on the ground. They collected their tags, their weapons, ammunition and gear and piled as much as the remaining International would carry, into the rear. They also took the rifles of the Chinese and everything else they could of theirs and left their bodies to rot in the store. Rankin picked up Mason's SLR and took his webbing for himself. The feel of the same rifle he carried in Vietnam was somewhat soothing, how he had survived all of that with a bolt action he never knew, but he wouldn't tempt the fates again.

Once they set out, it took no more than five minutes before they had come across another Centurion with a M113 armoured carrier behind it, headed in the opposite direction. The foot soldier escort approached the lone International.

'You boys alright? We heard that there was a squad back here pinned down.'

Rankin laughed. A Centurion would have shat that whole thing in without having to fire a shot.

Another foot soldier came around the rear and took one look at soldiers all crammed into the rear of the truck around the supplies, the dead and live alike.

'Welcome to the front boys, and you're not even there yet.'

RANKIN

'Children of tomorrow,
Live in the tears that fall today
Will the sun rise up tomorrow?
Bringing peace in any way?'

Black Sabbath – *Children of the Grave* (1971)

A lonely, gentle breeze worked its way down the quiet street as it attempted to rouse movement in the debris that lined the cracked blacktop. It tried to poke its nose into the shops that bordered the quiet stretch. Tried to sneak under the cracks of doors that were locked and rapped gently on the glass panes of windows that remained intact. It howled as it ran under dormant vehicles, their engines still and cold. It passed alleys and streets, powerless to turn, to choose its own path in life. Once the rails of its path had been laid, it was helpless but to follow. It clawed through the holes punched in brick walls and called deep inside for anyone to come. It caressed the hairs on the heads of those that lay in the street. Tugged at their clothes and tickled their lips, but they wouldn't acknowledge it. They didn't turn around and smile or complain in annoyance; they only continued to lay there, their eyes open in a fierce stare.

A lone smouldering shadow stood defeated in the centre of the street; the red star painted on its hull slowly bubbled from the fire beneath the steel. Large holes had been torn through the armour on the sides and rear from the sixty-six-millimetre rockets that had descended from the apartments above. Rubble had scoured the road from the tank's retaliatory fire. Wounded, blind and near death, the tank had sprayed the street with its coaxial machine gun and hammered into the brick structures with its main gun. It managed two devastating blows into walls, which collapsed fascia's and sent roof supports crashing down when another sixty-six-millimetre strike silenced it. The small detail that scurried behind the armour as it had rumbled down the street were taken without incident shortly after the first rocket strike. A shower of Bren and M60 fire from covered positions on ground level. They had all succumbed to the crossed lines of fire from the two positions before the tank's coaxial had started its monotonous thud.

When the tank had fallen silent, the Australians cheered from their cover. Men were crouched in craters in the road formed by Chinese artillery. The two gunners squatted behind partial walls and in the shop fronts on opposite sides of the street. Each gun had three men; the gunner, his support man and a rear guard. It was the gunner's job to pepper the Chinese on the street. The support man needed to supply the gun with the ammunition and change the barrels when they needed it, while the rear guard basically sat there with his back to the fighting and made sure no one flanked the crew.

Rankin sat with his back to Kelleher throughout the whole encounter. The thud of the Bren behind him rattled his spine. The calls of success from the support man as each contact fell was like a stain to his resolve. Every man played their part and every man needed to know his position if a battle were to be won, he knew that. The machine guns were vital to their survival and to ensure the position held was one thing, but to sit and do nothing while his fellow soldiers fought and died around him was another. He wanted to get into the action. He needed to, but in thirty seconds the action was over and enemy had been overwhelmed.

Rankin had gotten to his feet as the cheering began. He moved behind Kelleher's prone position and peered out to the street. The road looked clear.

'You two stay here; I'm going to take a look,' he said to the gun crew, who nodded in agreement, smiles on their face over the small victory they had secured for their country. As Rankin walked out through the back of the hairdressers, he heard the support gunner joke.

'Hell, if they all just keep walking down this street the war will be over in no time.'

'One could only hope,' Rankin muttered as he walked out into the open air. The two squads had positioned themselves along the street and waited to ambush any Chinese that tried to make their way south. They had headed north as the shells sporadically fell around them, all of them lucky enough to have been missed by the falling hell. The skies above had fallen silent; the Huey's had retreated to airs less volatile. The planes refuelled and re-armed while the men below crawled through the dust and concrete hail stones that pelted them as the city crumbled around them. Rankin, Kelleher and his support gunner Michaels, another aging veteran of the Korean conflict, had taken shelter in a barber shop while the other gun squad moved across the street into a partially destroyed pub. The plaques that once lined the front of the structure were gone. Destroyed by the brick and concrete as the walls that held them fell beneath the storm of shells that ravaged the street. Only a small square of gold could be seen shining proudly from the depths of the chaos and one red X; the remaining three were buried and forgotten.

As Rankin approached the crippled tank, others emerged from the rubble around him. Smiles plastered across their faces as they casually approached the burning hull, their rifles low to their sides. He watched as they surrounded the tank and laughed at a few barely surviving Chinese who were trying to crawl their escape from the death that surrounded them. One such soldier groaned in agony as his entrails dragged across the bitumen behind him. His bloodied hands grasped the broken road and pulled his body along. With each inch his body was pulled, it seemed that two inches of intestines were pulled from his gut. The groans turned to screams and grew harsher and ragged with each tug until an Australian placed the barrel of his Enfield to the back of his head and fired. The shot echoed through the streets and resonated off the tank's crackling steel. The screams were cut short, and soon, other shots rang out as other Australians had started to fire their rifles into the wounded and the dead alike. Some of them were men that had survived the shop front; others were men that had met the Chinese onslaught in Brisbane from the beginning. All of them had seen loss, and all of them wanted a taste of revenge. They were encouraged by their senior, a Sergeant with eyes as grey as fog and a boxer's jaw, 'Take no prisoners, men. Australian doctors will work on our own men and women; our food is for our stomachs. Put them down like the dogs they are.'

Some men had mounted the tank and started to lift the hatch open while the two men that stood below lit the wicks of their Molotov cocktails. The glass bottles of VAT-69 shimmered under the fire which spouted from their lips. They called to Rankin as they descended into the depths of the tank's belly, called out for him to join them and to taste their cleansing fire. Then the flames burst upward through the manhole, and the soldiers jerked their heads back and laughed at their deeds. The pub, although mostly destroyed, had contained a few cases of whiskey and bourbon, spirits and beer. Whatever the men drank, the bottles had been saved and filled with petrol or spirits or whatever they could find. Metal didn't burn very well, but the people behind the metal burned just fine if they were touched by the liquid fire. However, no moans or screams of pain came from within the tank, and one young soldier took offence. He removed his Hi-Power from his hip and began to fire it into the open cupola as the flames clawed their way out into the open air.

'Suffer you bastards! Burn in Hell,' he spat as the Hi-Power bucked in his hands. Ten men stood in the streets, they laughed, smoked and shouted at the tops of their voices, while they stood tall over the fallen soldiers. The young soldier that fired into the tank drew all the attention. Rankin turned away from him and shook his head. His eyes widened as he watched the smile vanish from one of the soldier's face. His hands went to his chest as part of it was torn out. He opened his mouth in a silent howl of horror and pain, only to vomit blood over the back of the man in front of him. His face went pale as his knees gave way and his eyes rolled back into his head. The soldier in front of him turned, his hand wiped at the wet sensation he felt on the back of his neck.

'Sniper!' Rankin screamed as the faint roll of the gunshot washed over them. The soldier in front of him dragged his hand away from his neck and held it in front of his face, frozen in shock. Sam Halfpenny's eyes were open wide in the fear that existed in his mind. He looked at Rankin and held his hand out to him to show him the blood on his palm. 'Sam!' Rankin shouted as he ran to him, 'Get down!' Everything moved as though it took years to take a step, a decade to say the words. In his mind, he screamed at the young man that was panicked at the sight of blood. 'It's not your blood,' he repeated, but he knew if the idiot didn't move, then it soon would be. The soles of his boots slammed against the torn road, the air hot in his lungs. As he reached him, he felt the air rush out of Sam, only a second before their bodies crashed together. Sam's SLR crashed to the ground as Rankin slammed down on top of him and dragged them both behind a pile of broken bricks and concrete while the sound of the second gunshot rolled over them.

He heard the other soldiers run and scramble for cover behind him. He felt wet and was astounded by how much he could be sweating, but when he looked down at Sam's eyes, he blinked, looked away, and then lowered his head.

Sam no longer had the look of fear in his face. Both of his hands were pressed to the centre of his chest. His eyes were still trained on Rankin, although they didn't see him anymore. Men had begun to fire their rifles into buildings at random, others just fired down the street where the tank had first appeared.

'Enough!' he heard the sergeant yell. 'Enough!' The shots petered out, and eventually, the street was thrown into silence once more. Rankin rested his forehead on Sam's, his eyes tightly shut while the sergeant barked at them all from behind the tank.

'Stay where you are. Do not move.' The sergeant's voice was calm, but assertive. The Bren's support gunner had rushed to the edge of the hairdresser's crumbled fascia. 'Michaels, if you take one more step out here, I'll shoot you myself!' The sergeant roared at him. 'Everyone stay where you are. Don't move and stay calm.'

'Johnny?' a soldier called. 'Johnny? Hey man, you need to get out of there.'

Rankin opened his eyes, and the soft faint stare of Sam greeted him. Rankin ran a hand down Sam's face to close his eyes while he rested him down on the bricks.

'Johnny, you need to come to me.' Small chunks of brick skittered across the road. A soldier on the other side of the street had noticed the soldier, Johnny, who lay in the middle of the road with his hands over his chest. Rankin watched as the soldier threw another brick toward his friend in an attempt to wake him up.

'Hey... Hey,' Rankin started at him, softly at first then louder. The soldier from across the street looked at him, a blank look on his face. 'You need to stop man, don't draw attention to yourself.'

'But Johnny's there. He's going to get hit.'

Rankin looked back at the collapsed body of Johnny. 'What is going on?' he muttered to himself.

'Johnny!' The soldier had started to get to his feet. 'Johnny, I'm coming man.'

'Soldier, stay where you are!' The sergeant's voice from behind the tank now.

'I'm coming, man.' The bewildered soldier lifted himself up and broke cover.

'God damn it, get—' That was all the sergeant managed to get out before the familiar thud sounded from the middle of the street and a red mist floated into the air. Rankin watched the whole thing happen. He saw the bullet catch him mid-stride. He saw the look of surprise on his face, his mouth gape open, and his legs crumble beneath him. He was hit lower than the others, probably due to his movement, and the shot failed to kill him. Now the screams of a dying man on the road were coming from an Australian, but no other shot of mercy came.

The body of Johnny lay ten feet to Rankin's right; the screaming mess of a soldier was fifteen. He rolled on the ground, his hands to his gut as blood and bile ran through his fingers. 'Help me!' He screamed continuously while the other soldiers shifted behind their cover.

'God damn it everyone, stay where you are,' the sergeant roared again. 'He is trying to draw us out, don't move.'

Rankin had his hands to the ground, his heart was in his throat. He felt as though his hands had started to shake again and he quickly held them up as he took a deep breath. Steady as a rock. His eyebrow furrowed, as he turned his hand overlooking for any sign of a tremble, but there was nothing. Behind him, the sergeant continued to scream at his men to stay behind cover; to his right, the dying man cried for help while he bled out. Rankin turned his head quickly as a small piece of brick fell from high on the pile he hid behind. It bounced its way down the heap and vanished among the other thousands that littered the streets. Rankin focused his hearing, but his attempts were fruitless over the contending pleas for men to either break cover or keep it.

'Shut the fuck up!' Rankin yelled, unsure who he was addressing, but no one listened. He placed his hand on the ground again, as he peered down the street.

'Sarge!' he called back, over the cries of pain. The sergeant's voice fell silent. 'We aren't going to have a choice for very long.'

'You stay where you are, soldier,' their leader barked back.

Rankin peered over the rubble; he stretched his head as far as he felt comfortable outside of his cover. His fist clenched and pounded the dirt.

'Fuck,' he muttered as another chunk of rock rattled loose from its hold on the pile in front of him. The sound of rushing air filled his ears, and Rankin ducked his head as a round ricocheted off his rock pile and sent more chunks of brick tumbling to the ground.

'We've got enemy armour, maybe thirty plus infantry,' he yelled as his back slid down the rubble. He grabbed his SLR and checked the breech. Other soldiers swore from their places of cover. The sound of panic in the voices of pinned down Australians was apparent.

'Gunners, get ready; how many sixty-sixes do we have left?' the sergeant called and the sounds of rifles being checked and the racks of machine guns being pulled echoed around the street while the men muttered.

'Two on right side,' a voice echoed from above.

'One on left.'

'I need .303,' Kelleher called from behind them.

'And I need a fuckin holiday,' the sergeant roared. 'No one move until the rockets hit that tank.' There was silence as the sergeant desperately scrambled around the rear of the tank. 'There's enough room for the armour to come past. Everyone keep your heads down until it's next to the wreck and light it up, use it to block the street.'

Rankin's position was terrible. The soldier to his right still screamed. He was furthest forward of all the remaining Australians. The machine gun positions were now to their rear. His position was undefendable.

'What about the screamer?' Rankin asked, his eyes on the delirious soldier whose screams for help had all merged into one inaudible groan.

'Leave him; it needs to look like we've abandoned our post.'

Rankin looked back to the wrecked tank, its main gun aimed left and high, everything silent apart the flames that still burned within its hull.

The soldiers sat in wait. They felt the ground begin to tremble beneath them as the enemy armour rattled its way down the street toward them. Sickness came over Rankin, he felt like he needed to piss, shit and vomit all at the same time. The sensation of his entire body being rattled by the slow progress of the tank was worse than any hand tremble he had ever suffered.

It wasn't long before the sounds of the diesel engine began to overpower the groans of pain and suffering from the soldier to his right. Soon he could hear the short, sharp exchanges of the Chinese soldiers that walked alongside and behind the tank as it came down on them.

The pile of rubble that Rankin lay behind chattered furiously with the vibrations of the tank's tracks. Bit by bit, the pile became smaller as chunks clattered to the ground and tumbled into the street. Rankin hunched over his rifle and shuffled to his left. He needed to stay hidden as they would come right past him, but then when it all started, he would be in the line of the M60 and the Bren fire. As he moved around, he saw a small brick alcove in the book store to his left that was used for rubbish bins. When the shit hit the fan, he would need to run for it.

In the meantime, he slunk himself low in a section of cracked road and dragged Sam's body partially over him. He needed his cover to look genuine; he ran his hand over Sam's chest and smeared his friends' blood over his own face. He positioned his SLR so it lay flat to the ground. His hand wrapped around its grip and tried to relax his muscles.

The ground shook under him, and stones shook; it felt like the tank would roll right over him. His heart hammered in his chest like the fast-paced fire of the M134 Gatling. He could now hear the squeaks of the metal cogs that drove the tank's tracks and the hydraulic hum of the turret as it pivoted slightly on its axis. Slowly, the main gun barrel became visible; the tank was mere feet from the wounded man in the street. His groans had either fallen completely silent, or they were now so weak that they couldn't be heard over the racket of the armour.

A boot slid down the rock embankment right next to his head, kicking dust into his eyes. Rankin tried not to move; he couldn't blink, he couldn't breathe. He hoped the soldier above him didn't even consider him. His eyes watered and went out of focus as he tried to hold his dead stare. He saw another boot swing past, then another set and another set. He heard them talk, almost bark at each other. He couldn't hear what had happened, but the soldiers laughed as the tank ground the road up next to him as it stopped and readjusted its position. There were clunks and a slight grind from within its hull, all under the rumble of its diesel. Then it screeched as the tracks began to churn again. Under it all, he heard screams of pain, horrific in their desperation and panic. Rankin had no idea what was happening until the screams finally stopped as the tank continued its progress. They had run the wounded Australian over. Rankin hoped as he lay there that they didn't bother with the bodies. To his relief, the soldiers continued to laugh as they spat and turned to continue down the street.

Boots passed his head to his right, others to his left as they followed behind the tank. He closed his eyes and took in a rather shallow breath as he tried to keep everything together. The tank's body hitched, and grinding came from within its hull once more. *It's turning,* he said to himself in his mind, *it is turning to go around the wreck.* He heard the hum of the hydraulics again. With his eyes still closed, he imagined the long barrel of the main gun rising into the air to clear the wreck of its fallen brother as its hull edged closer to the brick walls of the shops. It wouldn't be long before it all started, and the death and fire were all around him.

He heard more barks of their dog language around him and he felt Sam's body jerk. He kept his eyes closed, his grip loose on his SLR but firm enough. Sam's body continued to twitch as he stole a quick breath. Right above him, a man spoke, but no one answered so he didn't know how many stood around. He felt Sam move slightly and then his whole weight came off him. The soldier continued to talk, as Rankin felt hands grope him, undo his shirt buttons and reach down inside. He felt a dirty hand brush around his neck, flick his dog tags, then vanish. Pockets were tugged, as the Chinaman above him fumbled with the buttons and pulled what was inside out for inspection. He felt his packet of cigarettes get pulled from his pants, the inflection of the soldier's voice rose at this but the digging continued.

Below the rumble of the diesel and the voice of the looter above him, Rankin heard the rush of a rocket in its descent. The explosion was immense; Rankin's ears erupted in a screaming pitch, and his face was showered with debris and dust. Men yelled around him. He opened his eyes. The looter stood above him; his attention was on the tank. Rankin raised his SLR and rested the barrel on the man's chest. There was a split second when the looter turned his head back to look down at what touched him. Then Rankin squeezed his trigger and felt the rifle jostle in his hand. The looter collapsed backwards, and the cigarettes flew into the air, then the street exploded in blistering machine gun and rifle fire.

He heard the steady thud of the Bren and the rapid spitting of the M60; neither of them focused on bursts but laid down heavy continuous sprays of leaden fire. Rankin raised himself and turned his SLR on two more soldiers to his right that blocked his path. He fired rapidly but accurate enough and spent five rounds on taking the two of them down. To his left, men fell and screamed as the machine guns ripped through them.

Another sixty-six slammed into the tank's right side, and he heard the tracks splinter and fall from their cogs. As he ran to his pre-planned cover in the alcove, he saw the sergeant mount the crippled tank, a Molotov in hand. He fumbled with the catch but was hit hard in the chest by infantry AK fire. Rankin watched as the glass slipped from his hand and burst against the roof of the tank. He turned his head and moved fast and low while the gunfire and screams as the sergeant burned alive filled his mind.

Other Australians forward of the tanks were also up and moving back to their fighting positions behind the machine guns. Rankin needed to get to the Bren, but there were people everywhere. No line existed between Chinese and Australian. He watched one of his fellow soldiers get sprayed up the back as he broke cover and ran to pass the tanks. Those that made it in front of the crippled tank left themselves open to coaxial machine gun fire, and he knew many that went forward would be lost to their own failure to consider this.

The road was blocked by the two tanks, and Rankin needed to get off the road. The barber shop was four doors down on his side; he dared not risk the street. A Chinaman charged him with the bayonet on his rifle extended out in front of him. Rankin fired twice into his chest and brought him to his knees. The AK clattered to the ground, and Rankin put another one into his face while he kneeled there, his mouth agape. He moved on; bullets skittered off the walls around him and more kissed the ground only to ricochet and slam into brick and mortar.

Rankin burst through the doors of the shop in front of him and raised his rifle. Chinese had fled inside before him in an attempt to flank the Bren's position. He moved through the shop, jumped the glass counter and entered the back. With the sounds of the fighting in the street behind him, he found the Chinese as they struggled with a steel grate door toward the rear of the storage area. There were three men, two were focused on the door, and one faced him; his eyes widened as he raised his rifle. Luckily, Rankin had his SLR up already and rapidly pressed the trigger. The SLR rocked and bucked as it fired again and again. He hit the threatening soldier first, low and poorly, but it was enough to send his aim off, and the AK in his hands fired far right, continuing to spray wildly in its owners' hands. He shot the other two in the back countless times before he returned to finish off the first.

The men all collapsed, those he shot in the back were crumpled in horrible positions with their legs out behind them and their backs bent up as their torsos became hung up on the steel grate door. Rankin dragged them off and steadied himself as the building shook with immense force as the tank's main gun fired outside. Dust fell from the roof and listed down to the concrete as Rankin reloaded his SLR. He fired three times into the lock to break the internals, then he grasped the door and heaved. At first, there was resistance, then the remainder of the lock broke and the door swung inwards.

He burst into the alleyway behind the shops. Chinese had entered from the shop down from him, and once more, he fired rapidly into their backs and sides as they tried to break into the Barbers. There were five of them in the alleyway; the rest turned after he shot the first man, a look of shock and panic in their eyes as they reached for their rifles. The last one had his rifle trained on Rankin, but the AK wouldn't fire. He screamed as he slammed his hand against the assault rifle's breech over and over until Rankin shot him through the face and silenced him.

The Bren still thudded; it only stopped for magazine changes. Rankin ran past the door the Chinese had attempted to break down and entered the unlocked rear entrance to the tool shop next door. As he ran, he caught the glimpse of a muzzle trained on him as he burst through the door and he dropped instinctually. He heard the singular shot of an SLR, his eyes widened in shock, 'Friendly, friendly, Fuck me dead.'

'Took you long enough,' Michaels' drawl came back.

Rankin stood and looked at the holes in the plaster where he had been only moments before; he shook his head. He joined the Bren's support gunner and grabbed a crate of .303. They both rushed back to the side office of the Barbers; the room was thick with gun smoke, the smell of oil and sweat. The floor was covered in shell casings and empty magazines. The barrel of the Bren was white with heat, yet it kept firing.

Kelleher noticed something move behind him, jerked around quickly as if to defend himself, but then relaxed and turned back to the outside street once he saw them. Rankin broke the crate of ammunition open and began to load Bren magazines, his SLR next to him, his eyes on the door to their rear.

'Barrel! Barrel change!' Kelleher roared.

Michaels left Rankin and rushed to the gunner's side. Rankin continued to load; he tossed each loaded mag back behind him as he heard them thud and clatter to a stop over the countless casings. Then screams of horror and pain broke out behind him. Rankin spun quickly. Michaels was on the floor and held his hands in front of his face; the glazed Bren barrel was on the floor next to him. The flesh of his hands had been peeled and melted away by the heat of the barrel he had clutched with no hand protection. Kelleher gaped at his support gunner until Rankin threw a magazine at him.

'Leave him; if that fucking thing stops, we're all dead.'

Kelleher looked at him, his eyes wide with panic. He nodded and snapped the replacement barrel in place. He loaded the magazine Rankin had thrown at him into the breech, and the thudding continued.

Rankin pulled Michaels away from the Bren; his hands were in a terrible state, and Michaels was in and out of consciousness. He was out of the fight, one way or another. He couldn't be relied on anymore. Rankin continued to load magazines and toss them to Kelleher's side, but the gunner used them up quicker than Rankin could load them. Soon they would be out of .303 altogether.

The stream of Chinese seemed endless; they piled over the bodies of the tanks like an endless wave of water spilling from the floodgates of a dam. The ones that fell in front were trampled by the men in the rear. They all tried to push forward; the M60 and the Bren, with the help of the few men left on the street, were barely enough to hold them. The only thought that continued to rush through his mind was how far off his original estimate of thirty infantry had been.

Rankin heard the hum of the hydraulics once more, and raised his head.

'Where's it going?' he called to Kelleher, but he never replied.

Rankin stood, tossed the last magazine to the depleted pile at the gunner's side, and looked through the murder hole. The tank's turret was moving away from them, toward the M60s position. At the same time, the increase of pressure from the Chinese infantry tripled, and bullets flew in through their murder hole, shattered their edges and threatened to kill the men inside. The M60 fell silent; Rankin hoped they were in retreat.

Smoke and dust erupted in the street as the main gun fired into the wall that hid the M60 crew. Brick and mortar collapsed inward to spill dust into the street and cover the advances of the Chinese. The barber shop rocked with the percussion, and Rankin fell backwards. Kelleher continued to fire into the smoke and dust, not relenting. The replacement barrel was smoking and had already begun to turn white from heat; Rankin knew it wouldn't hold for much longer.

A clatter of gunfire came from behind him as he regained his feet. He felt a sear of pain in his leg, and he collapsed. As he fell, he saw Michaels' head reel backwards. Blood splattered up the wall behind him. Rankin rolled over the empty ammunition crate and gained his SLR. He tumbled as he raised himself. All the while, he fought the pain in his leg and fired back. Every time he pulled the trigger, it seemed that another soldier had entered the shop. More and more flooded in. Some had broken through the front; others came in through the tool shop.

Rankin fired and fired; when his SLR emptied, he grabbed Michael's and continued the fight. A small black cylinder came through the murder hole and thudded against the wall behind Kelleher.

'Fuck, grenade!' Kelleher called, leaned back to grasp it, and threw it out the murder hole. It exploded on the street and screams followed. The gunfire on the streets had diminished to some extent;

Rankin didn't think there were many 'Aussies' left alive at their position. If there were any left, they had moved back, and he didn't see how they could have managed even that. As the Bren took up fire again, more men entered the shop, and Rankin put the first two down. Automatic rifle fire racked through the office, and Kelleher screamed.

Rankin saw the fingers on Kelleher's left hand were gone; all that remained was a bloody stump of a palm and his thumb. Rankin shuffled over to him and handed him the SLR.

'You need to watch our rear; Michaels is gone. I'll run the Bren.'

Kelleher tried to stifle his screams. With his one good hand, he clasped the SLR and propped the rifle up on his knee while he gasped with pain. Rankin turned his back on him; the sight through the murder hole was horrific. There were dead men everywhere, Australians and Chinese. He could see the bodies that still smouldered from the failed Molotov. He heard a rush of air again as the final rocket slammed into the tank's frontal armour and barely penetrated through its thickest point. Dust filled the air again, and Rankin hoped that the final rocket had knocked the tank out. He took up the Bren and began to fire into the dust. The slow, methodical movement of the bolt was encouraging, and it was easier to pick targets through the offset sights than he had first thought.

The bolt slammed forward and clicked automatically. Rankin reached forward, pulled the charging handle to the rear, then moved it forward again and flipped the handle. He pushed the old mag out and inserted another; he lowered his cheek to the stock, and the thudding continued. The sea of soldiers kept coming, and Rankin hammered them as they came. He didn't understand how there could be so many; his first thought at the sight of the mass was thirty, but there were hundreds of dead on the ground, and still, they came. The Bren continued to thud; it only stopped when ammunition ran out. Even with its barrel a gleaming red and white, it never even misfed once. A grenade was thrown in through the murder hole and narrowly missed Rankin's head. It tumbled across the ground and landed next to Kelleher; he reached for it with his destroyed hand as if he had forgotten that he had lost his fingers. Rankin watched as he desperately tried to pick it up as the milliseconds went past and their time ran out.

Just when he thought they were both dead, Kelleher rolled himself over and onto the grenade and was thrown into the air by the explosion. His body came down heavy and lifeless. Blood was thrown through the air and splattered over Rankin's already blood covered face. He was alone. There was nothing left for him to do; he turned and continued to fire into the rushing masses, his back unprotected, almost out of ammunition. It was almost a godsend when he heard the hum of the tank's hydraulics once more, and he watched through his peripheral vision the barrel of the main gun come across to him.

'Fuck you, you big steel slut. I'm right here!' he shouted as he hammered the Bren's final magazine into the tank's hull. Not even sure why he was doing it; he had nothing left. The enormous barrel rocked slightly as the turret stopped on its axis. He was left to look down the muzzle of the main gun, and he had never seen a blacker hole than that. He didn't hear it fire, and he didn't see the cloud of smoke. He felt as though his whole body had been hit by a freight train. The smoke, dust and soot whirled over him, the world crumbled around him, and he slipped into the black depths of nothingness.

MICHAEL

The boy panted as he clung to a small sapling, his small child's hands still not quite large enough to fully wrap themselves around the trunk that waned under his weight. The straps of his brothers' old school backpack dug into his shoulders. At first, he had held the weight with no trouble, then the immensity of canned foods, powdered milk and salt beef that Jack had crammed into the dusty old pack, had started to ebb away at his lower back. Soon enough it didn't matter which way he tried to shift it, the pack rubbed at his shoulders and pained him with each step he took. But he would not complain, not to Jack anyway.

The brothers had not spoken a word in conversation since Michael had resurfaced from the depths of his mind. The odd bark of a command from Jack and Michael wordlessly went about his task. Whether that was to sit still, wait there, hurry up, walk quieter or stop crying. Although he hadn't necessarily been watching, he would've bet money that Jack had not even looked at him since he had woken. He supposed that when he had surfaced, they had at least still had the Whippet; the broken spokes had been either wired together with old fencing wire or completely replaced with shards of the hardwood which lined the bed of the truck section. When Jack had placed the heavy weight of the axels back down from its perch on the small boulder, everything seemed to groan, and Michael moaned with it. His eyes had begun to blink rapidly, and his hands went to his face to try and console the pounding that had erupted. As he had pushed the two great iron doors of his mind open, everything had come rushing out. He felt a wave of emotions, aches and pains pick him up and suck him forward. He remembered the doors disappearing into the darkness. A small light shone through for only a moment until the world behind completely collapsed in on itself, and there was nothing. The rushing still came, the pains grew worse, and suddenly, he was there, sitting on the side of a chopped out track that ran directly up a hill and into the thick shrub.

He watched Jack's face as once more he took the weight of the Whippet's front end in his hands. The vein on the side of his head pulsed and his neck seemed to swell to twice its original size. The front leaves of the Whippet's suspension held, as did the makeshift spokes, and Jack wasted no further time. He rolled the boulder he had placed on the track to the side and fired the old truck up once more.

The next problem had come only forty feet further up the trail. The thin rubber tyres, although fine at low speeds along a fire trail, were not suited to mountain climbing or traversing mud. Along a particular sketchy piece of track, the road had begun to slope toward the edge of a drop off. A large iron bark tempted fate as it towered to the sky, its roots partially exposed over the drop. In other places, large shards of shale and sandstone sat in contrast to the skyline from the earth. The ground at first had felt like hard soil, yet as the old Whippet bumped and howled its way over rock scrap and wheel rut, the thin rubber soles broke through to find the soft clay beneath, and the back end began to slide toward the drop off. In true nature, Jack punched it. The old engine roared a rattled wheeze of tired power, and the slide slowed somewhat. The iron frame kept surging forward, but the back end ever so gently kept its course to the edge.

Michael closed his eyes. One hand clutched to the soft fabric of the seat while his other clasped to the top of the windscreen to try to steady himself. He wished that he had been able to stay inside of his mind; he would have enjoyed sending those white pebbles skipping across the cool lake to nestle at Susan's stone feet. Yet that was gone. He was here, and soon enough, he would be at the bottom of that drop off if something didn't happen soon. The rear wheels fell into a small rut, and the chassis screamed beneath them as steel ground on stone but the old car kept rolling. As the weight hitched from side to side, chunks of clay and earth were thrown into the air behind them each wheel lost traction. As they fell into the rut, the back end stopped its slide to edge, but now they had lost all steering. The Whippet hitched and swayed as it kept its monotonous lumber up the hill; while the iron bark loomed closer and closer. Jack had the steering wheel all the way over to the left, he tried to get the old truck's front end to swing, but it held its course. Just as they were about to hit the trunk, Jack punched it once more in a desperate attempt to keep the momentum they had. The engine surged once more, and the body lunged forward in a hungry swipe at the trunk. There was a crunch as metal bit into timber. The engine strained for a split second, and then they bounced.

Suspension howled as the truck bounced its way back onto the track, Jack's foot still pressed to the floor pan, it picked up speed once more until earth turned completely to clay and the engine revs climbed higher and higher as the body of the truck sank lower and lower, then finally stopped. Jack rested his head on the knuckles of his hand, which still clasped the wheel. He took in a deep breath as if to compose himself.

As he swung himself out of the cabin, he barked his first order of the trip, 'When I say it, punch it.' There was never a look, question, or care; just do it.

As Jack lifted each end of the car up out of the clay, he sank deeper. Michael felt the odd sensation as the front end climbed slowly, as if on a hoist. Jack then shifted it to the side and settled it back down on the unbroken section of the road. As Jack moved to the rear end, Michael settled himself in behind the steering wheel. He could see Jack's face through the specks of mud and grime on the driver's side mirror, the only mirror that still existed on this poor old car. Once more, the vein pumped, his eyes narrowed, and the rear, this time, slowly lifted into the air. The engine mumbled in front of him, his hands clasped around the steering wheel. He had never driven completely off-road before; the grass paddocks and grated dirt fire trails were one thing, but the side of a mountain in clay was another. He felt the back end settle slowly onto the soft ground. He watched as Jack struggled to remove his feet from the pits they had sunk into, and then he lowered himself. Two hands closed over the back of the tailgate, he felt a thump and the truck's body lurched as his shoulders pushed into the rear bar.

'DRIVE!'

He didn't know which was louder, his brother's booming command or the roar of the Whippets motor and clutch. A smell cut through the air as something burned, not timber but a mix between plastic and oil. At first, the tyres repeatedly spun, while mud and clay were thrown into the air like the tail of a rooster; Michael just held his foot down. The motor continued to churn, and the smell of burned oil continued to fill the air. Finally, with a heave and a bounce, Jack started the Whippet moving. It began to surge its way up the mound, but then it's back began to slide, and the momentum was sucked from it. All at once, it began to slide back again, but two meaty hands stopped its progress. Beneath the sound of the tyres as they skipped on small stones and cut through clay, he heard the roar of his brother as he strained to push the truck up the hill. Once more, the Whippet bounced and hitched as the tyres gained purchase, and then a massive shove from behind sent it barrelling forward at a high rate of knots. After the last lapse of traction, the track started to level out, the tyres held their own, and the speed of the old Whippet began to climb. He pressed the clutch, felt how soggy it was and shifted into second. His speed continued to climb as he looked in the mirror and saw the final glimpse of Jack as he struggled up the hill, covered in mud, clay and shit. Then, as the track flattened out, he vanished beneath the rise.

Michael hesitated, his foot poised above the accelerator. His hands were clasped around the wheel, and the whites of his knuckles gleamed under the dirt. What would happen if he left him, punched it again and took off into the scrub? Fled the brother that had taken him from his home, when Michael wasn't even aware of anything and brought him up here for reasons unknown.

Probably to kill you.

The voice in the back of his mind was small, but it sent a shiver up his spine. He knew Jack had killed the fat man and the ugly, smelly one; but for whose benefit was that? He killed Tony, but that was because the old man was going to hurt him, wasn't it? Or was it because of Mum? Who else was there? He thought of the faces in the hedges; he knew the Trackers were dead, and he knew Tony was too. But why was Susan's face in the hedge, but his mother's wasn't?

'Is he going to kill me?' he whispered, but as he did, he pushed the clutch and took his foot from the throttle. The weight of the car and the soft ground it rode on sucked the speed from the frame in no time. Small stones ground their way into the earth as the narrow tyres rolled over them. Michael shuffled himself over along the bench seat and allowed the engine to continue its motion of rattle and clank below the sheet metal bonnet. He sat patiently and listened, as he didn't want to look back and see his brother's face. As Jack wordlessly entered the cabin of the Whippet and urged its tired powertrain into motion once more, Michael remembered the words he had snarled in the kitchen after it all happened.

'Your life belongs to me.'

What did it mean? Was he taking him into the forest to play mind games with him, or was it to escape the kind old man with the lined face? He doubted that Jack would be afraid of a man like that, especially when he thought of the men he had broken in the past weeks. Nonetheless, here they were, running, hiding, or just moving; Michael didn't know which, and it probably didn't matter. He was here, and his home was just a memory. He wanted to ask if they would ever go home again. He wanted to ask about the man with the lined face, the car that had shone its lights through the kitchen that night, so many things. But he never did. The words would never formulate, and even if they did, he doubted that Jack would answer him. He never answered that night when he was in his room, and when Michael had sought him out. The white plaster dust was on his hands and under his fingernails, which had raised another question: What was he doing that night? What was he going to do now?

His decision to pull over and allow Jack to take command of the Whippet once more ended up paying for itself only twenty minutes later. Jack had attempted to traverse a rocky section; the wheels groaned at the odd angles, and rusty steel screamed as it dragged itself along the jagged rock. Finally, all at once, two more of the rattly timber spoked wheels gave way. Michael gasped as he heard the hardwood crack and the rapidity in which the weight shifted in the truck. He froze in the cabin and saw Jack leap from the rising cab.

The loss of Jack's immense weight seemed to seal the Whippet's fate. As the driver's side wheels lifted into the air to the height of Jack's head, Michael found the courage to leap. His foot slipped on the metal running board, and he felt the power of his jump fade into the air behind him. The rest happened in an instant; his body hit the ground and drove the air out of him. He felt his teeth come together in a clatter and the pain as the tip of his tongue was caught in between. A hot fire was in his mouth, and the taste of blood flooded his mouth. He managed a quick breath before the shadow of the Whippet came over him, and then he was trapped beneath its bench seat.

Michael knew he had used every ounce of luck he ever had at that moment. Glass shattered as the windscreen crumbled to his left, while the headboard and the back support of the bench seat sank into the ground to his right. Only the gear shift had caught him as it grazed the inside of his leg on the way through. The world was filled with an unruly clatter as metal, timber, and packs hit the ground in force. There was a cough and one final wheeze as the engine died, and now the smell of fuel and oil was in the air. Michael didn't want to stay under the truck for a moment longer. In front of him, there was a small slit of light where the foot well of the cabin had not yet touched the ground. He struggled forward, breathing heavily in shock, but each breath made him sick with the smell of the Whippet's draining fuel and oil reserves.

'Only a few more inches,' he said, but he barely heard it. 'Only a few more in...'

The small amount of light that peered through the gap in front of him was cut, and the Whippets frame shook and jolted as the cab sunk lower. He felt the bench seat push into his back and begin to suffocate him. His breaths became shallower and shallower; the car's weight didn't allow his chest to rise. Then, with a roar and a scream of rust and steel, he was free. As he lifted his head, the Whippet pitched upward and away from him. The cabin and the chassis warped out of true by the impact. As it rolled onto its side, the only mirror left in the vehicle smashed, crushed under the weight of the iron it was bolted to. When it rolled back onto its wheels, the remaining two rims shattered under the impact. It continued to roll over; its back end freely slid on the soft ground as it tumbled dangerously close to the edge of the track. Then with a final complaint from its tired suspension, it vanished over the edge. The sound as the frame slid and rolled end over end down that hill is something that Michael would never forget. The last look as the battered front end vanished behind the drop off. The sound of the frame as it crashed against gums and ironbarks on its descent, the leaves of the silent giants' rustled in fury as the metal intruder cascaded downward. And then, like most things, the sound, the smell and its memory faded into nothing.

Michael had rolled over to see that Jack stood behind him. His brother's chest heaved. There was an odd look on his face, almost of fear; his eyes were focused on the drop off where the Whippet had vanished. He stood there for some time while he caught his breath as Michael lay there in front of him. Michael sat up and rubbed at the place the gear stick had grazed him. *I'm okay*, he thought to himself, honestly surprised that he had not been more shaken by the experience. Still, with everything that had happened to him over the last months, he could understand. Did this mean he was becoming a man? He looked up to his brother once more, who had begun to move over to the gear that had been dumped from the truck when it had rolled. Chunks of hardwood and iron, Jack's old school backpack, which he hadn't used since his expulsion, another pack that Michael had never seen before and what looked like the trench coat from the Tracker's place rolled up.

Jack grabbed the rolled up package. His fingers worked furiously; he untied the makeshift bundle and revealed the rifle that had taken Tony's life. Jack held it in the air to examine it. His eyes ran over the timber and metal work, and Michael saw the full rifle in the light for the first time. Its timber was dark, almost black, while the metal was lighter but still a dark shade of grey and knurled from years of use. Even from this distance, he could see the scratches all over its frame. There was an oddly shaped handle on the side closest to Jack, which he pulled. As he did, the funny shaped handle slid on a rail until it hung out from behind the dark frame; once it reached its most rearward position, it stopped, and Jack pushed it forward once more. His brother stood up and grunted, and he let the rifle fall to rest on the green pack. Jack rummaged through the other wreckage and finally tossed the pack to Michael as he snarled, 'Get up.'

They had walked for hours, and at first, they struggled with the slippery slopes of the tracks. Each step needed a full entry and exit plan, while the ones that followed became harder and harder. Once the ground hardened and their footing became easier, only the weight and discomfort of his pack hindered him. Jack had put on the greenish larger pack that Michael didn't recognise. It looked old and even though it had been jostled around in the back of the Whippet's tray for God know's how long, dust and mould still clung to it in most places. On the side, a name had been embroidered, which was mostly rotted, but Michael could still see the outlines of the 'B' 'K' and 'E' of his last name. Jack held the rifle in his right hand; his fist closed around the foregrip forward of the dark frame. It hung there by his side the whole time they walked; not once did he use it to prop himself or assist him, not once did he need to. Michael, on the other hand, was hopeless. The heavy pack unbalanced him, and more often than not, he had slipped and fallen forward. The worst time was when he had fallen backward. He felt his spine arch around the unforgiving pack and its contents, his head smacked into the ground, and he hadn't the strength to upright himself. After a short, silent wait, Jack had angrily climbed back down to his position and had righted him while he snarled at Michael to be more mindful.

He had tried to follow that command, but his mind always wandered. He thought about the Whippet and imagined what would have happened if he had left his brother back on that hill and he had rolled it. If the Whippet's weight on him didn't kill him, Jack would've when he caught up. He tried to imagine his brother's face, as red as his father's, whenever he beat him, but somehow, he couldn't quite picture it. To be honest, he couldn't even remember the last time Jack had hurt him. It was more scowls and anger, retorts and silence. When had that stopped? He knew he was hit from time to time for one thing or another when he was younger, but Tony did that enough for the both of them. Jack was so bloody big by the time he was twelve; it was hard to tell the difference between Tony and Jack in the dark anyway.

Far into the scrub on his right, a shrub rustled, and he heard something scamper. Michael turned and looked to where he thought the sound had come from. He stopped in his tracks to peer through the leaves and the low branches of the silent giants to see what it was. The track they were on ran along a semi-peak. There was more level land on the right side than there was on the left. Directly behind where he stood now was only twenty feet of flat land, which led to a drop off similar to that which had claimed the Whippet. The rustling came again, closer but further down the track than his position. His brow creased, and he continued to peer. He knew the sounds that wallabies and kangaroos made in the scrub, there were enough of those mongrel things around Chinchilla, but this was something else. The rustling came from further up the track this time, forward of his position, and Michael took a step backwards; his heart pounded in his chest.

'Hurry up, fuck ya,' Jack boomed from in front; Michael jumped at the sound but whatever it was in the scrub did not. Michael glanced toward his brother, who still trudged in front, some fifteen feet ahead. He offered the scrub another wary look and moved on.

They had seen the deer once they had begun their descent. A mob of does were feeding along the fringe country further down the side of the slope. The direction they headed as they slowly grazed along the tree line looked like it would intersect where Jack and Michael had intended to move. Jack squatted, his eyes narrow. Slowly, he began to unloop his pack from his arms. He placed the rifle on the ground in front of him. Michael's eyes were fixed on the open hole in the rifle's breech. He could see the dull brass of the cartridge that lay in wait, the gleam of the metal bullet, and the darkness that sat in front. The gaping hole that just wanted to be fed. He didn't know how he knew it, but he did. Something about it made him want to touch it; he needed to touch it.

Jack's hand clasped over the breech, and he took it with him as he stood. 'Sit down and wait here. When you hear a shot, come down.' Michael hated the sound of that, to sit up here by himself while Jack went off. He was about to ask if he could come, but by the time he had moved his eyes from the rifle's position, Jack was well away.

He sat once more and fiddled with the straps on his pack. He rummaged through the innards to see what canned food there was. The further he delved into the pack, the more depressed he became. Apart from corned beef, it looked as though his own shit was about the only choice of sides he was apt to get. He unravelled the cloth that held the salt beef and worked away at a chunk until it broke off. The meat was cool in his hands, which was a nice change from how the rest of his body felt on this Autumn afternoon. Although the brutality of the summer had passed, the days were still fairly long, and the peak heat of the day still let the mercury rise to over thirty. His back was wet from where his pack had pressed up against him, and his armpits were soaked through. On days like this, his first thought of solace would be a bath or a shower, but up in the hills, he doubted he would have any chance of this. Their limited water supply was confined to what Jack had packed in his green pack. He could only imagine what Jack would do to him if he found out that he had wasted any on hygiene.

He bit into the chunk of salt beef; the dried meat filled his mouth with the taste of salt. This was a nice replacement from the lingering taste of blood from his throbbing tongue, which stung at the introduction of the food. Michael chewed through the pain; he didn't realise how hungry he had become from the walk. The chunk was gone in moments, and he needed to fight his desire to go back for more. Instead, he went to Jack's pack and strained as he lifted it upright. His own pack was heavy, but this was filled to the brim with metal flasks and old thermoses, and finally, a large green metal can which rattled as it moved. All of this was packed into the old army pack. Michael grasped an old thermos and undid the lid.

As he sat and sipped at the water, he heard the rustling once more. He tried to ignore it as he sloshed the water around in his mouth to get the salt out from around his gums as he tongued a piece of meat that had become stuck in his teeth. The worst part about salt beef was the hangers, he reflected as he let his mind wander away from the rustling bush. Each time he had a sandwich or a soup his mother had made, he would spend the rest of the evening trying to pick the hangers from his teeth; sometimes, he even made his gums bleed with the effort.

Another bush rustled, and he heard the skitter of an animal move its paws across the ground. He stopped. This time, the rustle had come from behind him.

'What is it?!' he exclaimed, more panic in his voice than anger. More rustling this time to his right, closer now too. He looked hard at the area; he couldn't see any shapes through the bushes. Another rustle from his left, then one from in front again. He turned his head to the bushes on the right again and froze. He could see eyes. Two golden, brown eyes in the darkness, two triangular ears and a mouth that looked as though it was full of razors. It watched, but there was no movement. A plethora of ideas ran into his head, *throw the beef, throw a can, yell, try to scare whatever it* was.

A shot rang out; it was closer than he thought. The roar of its power echoed through the hills, and the bushes around Michael came alive. He screamed and rolled over onto his brother's pack as it happened. There were so many he couldn't count, but they all seemed to run away. The scrub around him was alive for seconds, and then everything delved back into the peaceful scene it had been a moment ago; the sounds as twigs broke and the shrubbery was disturbed echoed off into the distance. Michael lifted his head and peered around, the thermos clutched in his hand like some weapon. The rolling sound of the gunshot had dissipated into the hills, and the memory of Jack's command came to mind. He clambered back to his feet and took a final sip of water as a cold shiver ran up his spine. He took a final distrustful look at the scrub behind him. Then, in fear of his brother's wrath, he struggled with both the packs and descended.

The doe was large and in good shape. By the time Michael had arrived, Jack had mostly completed the butchering. His rifle lay to his side, its mouth closed for the moment, its hunger satisfied. Michael looked at the pile of meat cuts which Jack had laid on a section of deer hide; Michael's stomach growled as his own hunger flared in his belly.

With the thoughts of the creatures in the scrub far from Michael's mind, they set up camp in a small clearing, a short distance from the place where the doe had been harvested. By the time Jack had wrapped the meat in rags soaked in salted water and had stowed them in his pack, the sun had already begun to set. Jack had set up a fire and sat by its side. He had skewered an entire cut of meat from the animal's spine on a stick and was slowly roasting it over the coals. He had never seen his brother cook, and he imagined that the meal ahead would be chewier than the salt beef in his pack, but he knew better than to complain. The smell that came from the charred flesh was making him salivate, yet he didn't see grease dripping into the fire, only remnants of blood.

The two sat silently around the fire as they watched the meat turn from red to pink to black. Then Jack would turn the skewer, and they would sit and watch again. It was on the third rotation that the rustling started again. At first, the rustle came from behind Michael; he didn't turn to look; he just raised his eyes from the meat to look at Jack's face. His brother hadn't reacted to it either; his eyes were fixed on the fire. He seemed to be lost in it; as he looked deep into the black coals and the fire that licked up the sticks he had jammed into the ground to support the roasting spit.

The second rustle came to Michael's left, but Jack still did not react. Michael looked at the rifle which lay at Jack's side. The mouth was closed; he knew that meant it wasn't ready; that's all he knew. His mind went chaotic once more. *What should I do? Should I tell him about the eyes and the teeth? Should I run?* As his mind ran overtime, he too started to look into the fire, his hand came up to his mouth, and he chewed on his fingernails. At first, he didn't notice his brother rise; he didn't even notice him pick his rifle up. He was stuck in the fire and his own panic, almost as though he had closed the iron doors once more.

As Jack pulled the handle to the rear, the receiver made a clunk. The noise was enough to wake Michael from his internal nightmare and face reality. A large brown dog had entered the clearing on Michael's right; its lip was curled into a snarl which terrified Michael to his bones. A low grumble emitted from its throat, and its eyes darted from Michael to his brother. The eyes were a golden-brown, the look of anger and ferociousness clear on its face, yet each time its eyes met Michael's, they quickly darted back to Jack. From the corner of his vision, he watched Jack raise the rifle to his shoulder. He watched as he lowered his head to rest his cheek on the dark timber. Michael heard more rustling, as did Jack, but too late. The rifle in his brother's hand roared a fraction of a second after another dog had leapt from the bushes to latch itself onto Jack's shoulder. The rifle fired three shots in fast succession, and they all missed their target.

The black dog had latched itself to Jack's flesh. His large left hand reached over and latched onto the beast's skull. There was a yelp and the sound of crushing bone; then, he flung the beast into the scrub. More had entered the fray, and all of them attacked Jack. One leapt at him, its two huge paws planted on his chest. Michael sat frozen as he watched all of it play out.

He saw the rifle fall from Jack's hands, and it clattered on the ground a foot from the fire and the forgotten roast. Its mouth was open, and the fire glinted off the dull brass on the inside. He watched as Jack's two hands went to the dog's throat and wrapped themselves around the scruff of its neck. He took steps backwards away from the rifle, placed off balance by the dog on his chest. Another dog leapt at his side and latched onto his left wrist. Yet another came in hard from his right and attacked his ankle. Michael watched as Jack went down; he watched as others closed in on him. He heard his brother roar in either pain, fear or anger; he didn't know. He glanced back to the fire, and his mind raced back to the kitchen.

'Your life belongs to me.'

Was it a good thing if these dogs killed his brother? Once they had finished gorging themselves on Jack, they would surely be too full to bother with him.

Jack writhed on the ground. He grabbed at the dogs and pulled them from him, but as soon as he did, another took its place. Michael saw that the large brown dog that had first entered the clearing was not interested in his brother; its large golden eyes were focused on him. Its lip was curled, and its head was low; it approached him slowly but cautiously. Michael fell backward off the log he was perched on and began to push himself away from the approaching beast. A roar of pain came from Jack, and Michael took a look over at his brother. A large tri-coloured beast had latched onto his face. His arms were busy in the fight against the pack and he had left his face open. He turned his face away, but the large bitch was still on him. Through the pile of beasts and Jack's immense struggling size, Michael could see one of his brother's eyes. It was focused on something, but it was hard to see whether it was Michael, the brown hound that approached him, or the rifle by the fire. Michael had stopped propelling himself backward. Something touched his stomach, and he turned his face to stare straight into the golden-brown eyes of the Alpha.

JACK

'Burn away the goodness,
You and I remain.
Did you see the last war?
Well, here I am again.'

Creedence Clearwater Revival – *Sinister Purpose* (1969)

Hot rivers of pain ran up and down his body, which made his chest, arms, and legs convulse under the writhing agony of the surface. His old boots scraped uselessly at the dirt beneath as if trying to drag his weight closer to the fire that was only a few feet away. Beneath his head, which was lost to a cloud of anger, pain and what could have been fear, he felt a wetness. In the chaos, he wondered whether the damp was his own blood or just dew from the cold. As the big tri-coloured bitch advanced up his chest, the other smaller dogs parted like the ocean in one of those bullshit religious stories he had heard one place or another. The smaller, darker hounds, still ravenous in their desire or their rage, had their muzzles buried into Jack's body. Although he held one dog by its throat, he couldn't get the grip he needed to kill it. He felt like a general of a failing army; each limb was like a company that had become overwhelmed. His left arm held, but needed support that would never come. His right arm, his most valuable asset, had lost all fighting capability and only strained against certain death. While his legs had been overrun and for all intents and purposes, were a lost cause. As the general, he was helpless but to let each company fight its own fight as the big bitch descended on his position and threatened to end it all.

As the yellowed fangs of the tri-coloured bitch tore at his cheek, he roared. The scream was a mixture of fury and agony, yet he felt that deep down inside, there was a sadness. Perhaps; he didn't know and didn't care. His eyes were closed to the fury of the pack that was on him. He thought back to the room in the Tracker's yard when he had stepped back into his own mind. He could still see, and he knew what had happened, but he couldn't feel anything, nor did he feel he had any control. He wished that he could do that now. Where was 'it'?

'The boy,' a voice in the depths of his mind whispered. A voice that was not his own.

Jack opened the eye that was not in danger from the bitch. The first sight that came to him through the streaks of blood and glistening fire, was the Browning. It lay to his left and waited for him to be man enough to pick it back up. He doubted that would ever happen. The bolt was rearward as it lay in wait, its mouth was open in its own starvation. His eye ran up its barrel, which came dangerously close to the fire where it rested. His streaked vision fell on the fire, the venison burned on its spit. The flames danced around its prize and leapt from one end of the blackened stick to the other, somewhat like the dogs that walked all over him, as they bounded from one morsel to the next.

Movement behind the fire caught his attention. It was the boy. He slid backwards on his ass, away from the fire, away from him. What had he gotten himself into this time? The look on his face was that of shock and fear, but that didn't mean anything; he had looked that way ever since that night. Jack dismissed the thought, he didn't want to think about that just now. His eye narrowed when he saw the alpha advance on his brother. The one dog he had forgotten about was now the only one that mattered. With a renewed strength, Jack fought. His left hand managed the strength to pull the black dog at his gut away, then assist his right hand in a push to remove the brown dog to his right back a step or two. Then the big bitch on his chest closed her jaw over the top of his brow and the world reeled. Everything started to sway and move in distorted images, the sounds became surreal and the pain subsided.

In the back of his mind there was no voice, just tutting. The sound someone made when they were disappointed. His thoughts went to Tony Baker, his huge arms crossed as he shook his head. Then to Tony as he decomposed in the boot of his Fairlane, his face stripped of features. All the strength he once possessed, drained from him like a creek in drought.

'I expected more from you.'

The disappointment in the tone was obvious; the voice was low and eerie in pitch. *'So big, so strong and stopped by a pack of fucking hounds.'* As the voice came to the last words of this sentence, the voice became harsh; the soft tutting that had started the monologue had turned into a roar of disgust.

Jack's body bunched up in a ball of rage; his eye fell on Michael once more. He had stopped moving backwards. The brown Alpha was only two feet away, its head low, its lip curled.

'What is it about that fuckin' boy anyway?' The voice maintained its low growl now, close to his father's but not quite. *'So weak and pathetic, he's not even worth saving.'*

In the chaos of their peril, Michael looked at him. Their eyes held contact for a moment; everything seemed redundant. Nothing else mattered, just him. Jack felt the rage inside of him build more and more. Everything he had done, every life he had taken, every scar on the base of his soul. Everything was for him.

'You are about to lose it all,' the voice said, cold and uncaring.

He watched the Alpha place a paw on Michael's stomach, its curled lip opened in a snarl. A line of drool ran from the depths of its jowls and gleamed in the fire as it ran a line to Michael's chest.

'I can help you.' Jack's temper snapped.

He felt as though he was the Hyster back at the mill. He weighed twenty tonnes and he could lift forty; the dogs that tore at him seemed insignificant now to what had overpowered him before. Yet, at the same time, he felt himself slip. He felt his consciousness abandon him, and like in the office at the Tracker's, like in the Darcy's house, he was not in control.

A roar came from deep within him, full of anger and disgust. His muscles swelled and a fire erupted inside of him. No longer a general but a bystander, he watched as his left hand clasped the jaw of the beast once more at his gut. His right latched onto the brown dog, which was now at his chest. The hounds squirmed in his grip, powerless to stop what he did to them. Their tails shot down between their legs, and he felt the piss run down their fur and soak into his already ruined clothes. The two hands clapped the skulls together; there were whines and yelps of pain from the beasts in his hands, but that wasn't enough; it wasn't even close. His palms clenched tighter still, veins stood out from the flesh on his arms, and he roared as he pressed his hands together. The two skulls pressed against one another slowly but surely began to give way. The thin legs scrambled desperately to escape the death grip, but none of it mattered. Jack roared as the dog's skulls crushed in his hands; their bodies twitched and became limp. Their remains collapsed onto his chest as his hands moved away in search of more victims. He saw the disfigured snouts, broken in odd angles, their small skulls crushed inwards. One of the eyes of the dog on the left had bulged out of its socket, and it hung there like a blob of snot while the chaos erupted once more.

Both hands latched onto the big bitch on his face, and as he rose to a sitting position, he held the dog in front of him as if to inspect it. He could feel the strength in its body as the paws pressed against his torn chest. The hind legs scrambled for purchase as it bared its teeth; his blood coated the white fur around its snout. Jack brought the dog toward him at a vicious pace, and to his horror, he felt the fur of its jowls in between his teeth. The dog whined and snapped as it tried to bring its snout around to sink into him once more, but he was too strong. His eyes were still open; everything that happened around him went from being exasperatingly slow to lightning-fast, then back to the slow crawl once more. The Alpha had continued its approach to Michael; the boy's eyes were closed. Even at this distance, he could still see the tears streaming down his face. He felt his teeth clench, and he pulled the bitch away from him, he saw the flesh tear, the meat and sinew stretch from the frame of the dog's face to his mouth, and then it broke. The bitch was still alive, a chunk taken from the side of its face, its snout now in a perpetual snarl.

He was back on his feet in an instant, the bitch still in his hands, he brought her down with all of his strength. The world slowed once more; he watched the dirt explode around the body as it hit the ground with a bone-shattering force. He saw a leaf fly from its perch on the ground, disturbed by the sudden rush of air, only to land on the edge of the fire. The green slowly turned to brown as its edges began to curl up and blacken. Finally, it caught, and it took only mere moments for something that was once full of life to be reduced to a blackened, twisted shadow of itself.

The bitch was still alive. However, its strength had left it. It rolled onto its back as if to accept its new alpha; blood still ran from its torn jowl, trickling down its throat to stain the white on its chest. Jack felt one of his boots raise behind him and the power of his leg as his foot was brought forward in a tremendous kick that he felt would have rolled the Whippet. He watched as the dog's body moulded around his boot. As it followed through, the dog went with it. Then it was in the air, tumbling over and over. Its body brushed the coals and the remains of the ironbark log that smouldered away in the fire, sending a shower of sparks through the air. Through the embers that had taken flight like birds to the sky, he saw that the life had left the bitch at some point. Yet still, it's body travelled and rolled through the smoke and embers that it had scattered, and ploughed into the Alpha with enough force to topple the big brown bastard from Michael's lap.

Jack wanted to keep his eyes on the Alpha. He wanted to move over to Michael, to protect him, but he wasn't the one in control. As more dogs spread out in the clearing encircling him, it became obvious that Michael wasn't "it's" focus. A wiry grey, hound with a long snout and black paws latched onto his leg, while another came bounding from the tree line at full speed. He sensed the anticipation of the inbound dog, and felt within him as if something had shifted gears. As if his body were just a machine, acting as any truck, forklift or tank would act, when the ones at the controls sets their eyes on a target.

The inbound dog leapt into the air while the wiry one at his leg continued to harass the fabric of his jeans, but Jack felt no pain. His two hands caught the inbound dog in the air and deflected its momentum to the left. The hound barrelled off into the darkness of the scrub, a mess of legs and tail. All the while, it growled and snapped at the sticks that bit at its sides as it tumbled past. In a fluid movement, his right hand curled into a fist in front of his face and clenched hard, the vision went to the dog at his leg, and he felt the power swell up inside of him. His body jerked its leg from the mouth of the hound as a fist came down like the hammer of Thor. The dog collapsed at his feet, its eyes open, and its snout was driven halfway into the ground. Its legs had shot out at odd angles from the impact and didn't as much as twitch from that moment.

He heard something scramble in front of him and felt his body set into motion. In front of him was the tree line; the fire was now to his back and forgotten, along with his brother. With each step, he felt power surge in him; he felt stronger than he ever had before in his life. His shoulders were as wide as the Fairlane and made of harder stuff. His hands were the pistons run by the power of the boiler in his gut and the best part was that he didn't even have to think about it. It all just happened while he sat as a witness. The dog he had thrown into the scrub came into vision once more. It tried to pounce up onto him, and his hands came up to meet it. This time his body did not throw it but slammed its back up against a ghost gum that bordered the clearing. He felt the air leave the animal, yet his body didn't stop. His left hand held the beast by its throat, its scruff bunched up around its jowls as its eyes glared at him, and it waited for its end. His heavy fist repeatedly came down on its chest, bones crunched each time, and its chest cavity sank deeper with every blow. The life left the dog on the second hit, yet his body kept going and going. With a tremendous roar, his fist was thrown into the pits of its chest again, and this time, he felt its spine splinter under his power. Behind him, he heard the snarl of the Alpha; only then did his left hand relax.

As the crushed body of the newcomer fell to the ground at Jack's boots, he felt his body turn. His fists went low to his sides, and his head lowered like the Alpha that approached him. This dog was smarter. He assumed it knew the man it faced had ripped through most of its pack, and it didn't plan to become one of the fallen. It walked slowly, its head low, its neck seemed twice the size of its companions, and its teeth shone a yellowed death. The fire glistened in the saliva which coated them. It turned its flank to Jack and stalked around him, its golden-brown eyes focused on him, but he knew that it searched for weakness; he wondered if his body knew as much. Around and around the Alpha went, its head low, its growl a constant engine burbling like the V8 of the Fairlane. Jack's body lunged at the Alpha, and it backed off; he felt his body then turn for the Browning, which still lay near the fire.

The Alpha approached and bounded at his body while it was occupied by the rifle. Faster than he knew he could move, his hands were around the beast's jaws that had started this whole thing. His left clamped down hard on the top jaw while his right held the lower. His fingers pressed into the fur of its jaw while his thumb pushed harder into the hollow in the bottom of its mouth. The Alpha hung there, helpless to do anything. Its eyes were large as it watched. Jack looked on, as his left hand pushed up while the right pulled down hard. As the time slowed again, he watched the jaw of the Alpha dislocate, then break. He watched as his hands continued to separate the top from the bottom. The joints gave in altogether, and its lower jaw jerked down even further so that it was hard against its chest, yet his body kept pulling. He watched the skin at the corners of its lips stretch and then split. The lines where the skin broke ran downward as his body pulled the entire lower jaw away, along with its tongue, its larynx and half of its throat. The Alpha's lifeless body fell to the earth; in his right hand, he still held the lower jaw. His body held it up to his eyes and let it hang there.

'That is strength; that is what we have together. That boy is nothing to us.'

Slowly, his head turned. Michael still laid on the ground, his eyes open as he looked up at Jack. His breaths were shallow; fear was on his face. His eyes darted from the face of Jack's body to the jaw that hung in his right hand. Jack took a step toward his brother as he cowered on the ground.

'We will be stronger without him.'

His body took another step. The jaw of the Alpha fell to the ground in a wet slop. His hands came up in front of him as he bent down. Michael closed his eyes.

'NO!' Jack bellowed. He thought at first this was only in his mind, but the vision of the boy in front of him jumped at the sound of it. Jack felt like he had gained control, but not enough. His hands still reached for Michael, yet they had begun to tremble. 'You won't touch him!' His voice the low boom as it always was yet with the sense that he was tired, worn out. Sensations from his body flooded back over him. The pain, the wounds he had received, the pounding in his head. Yet his hands still reached for Michael.

A laugh sounded from the back of his mind, the low cackle. His hands clasped around the cuff of Michael's shirt and lifted him into the air. *You killed your father. You killed two entire families. One full of rodents and the other your family's friends. You killed the old man, and you're telling me you won't kill this piece of shit?'* The cackle rang out again. *'Don't tell me bullshit; when I'm in your head. I can feel your lies.'*

Jack felt something happen to him; he felt his grip on his body begin to slip once more. The laugh in the back of his mind got louder and louder. He braced himself as he tried to hold on to any nook or rivet which held his pounding head together. But he slipped further and further into darkness. He heard rifle fire, people screamed, some in pain, some in a furious battle cry. Then everything went dark, and all he could hear was the cackle. It lasted what seemed hours, it continued on and on, and finally stopped. He opened his eyes.

The moment he did, he knew he wasn't with Michael in the clearing any longer. There were men everywhere. He was still in the bush, but this was more jungle than the shit Northern Australian scrub. He was on his back once more, the fire all around him as people fought hand to hand. Some with rifles, but the lines were too blurred to use them. Somehow, he knew the small men were Japanese, the larger men Americans. The man with the sword stood above him, the blade raised above his head. When he brought the blade down, Jack raised his hands, but something was in them. There was a crunch of steel and the high pitch twang as metal chipped, and the thin blade of the Japanese officer's sword crashed into the heavy metal receiver of the Browning in his hands. The officer raised the sword again, and Jack felt bewildered. He didn't know what was happening, but he knew he needed to kill the man above him. In a defensive manner, he raised the Browning again, but the officer anticipated and slashed to the right this time. Pain ripped up his body as steel sliced through the cloth and flesh of his side, the blade whipped back again, and he felt the sting across his chest. Jack howled in pain, but somewhere deep inside of him, he felt the anger brew. He felt the rage of all the years of poverty, the laughing, the crying, the death. As the blade bit into his stomach, he felt his hands wrap around the steel and hold it. The pain in his gut was horrible; he felt like everything in him was about to explode outward, but the pain only drove his anger, only made him more dangerous.

The officer above him struggled to free his blade as Jack pulled himself upwards and drove the sword deeper into his own stomach and out the small of his back. When he exhaled, he felt the blood run down the sides of his mouth, but that didn't matter; only the officer did. Soon the officer's face was right in front of his; at almost the same time, both men let go of the sword. Jack's hands went to the man's face, and the officer tried to beat him off. Jack overpowered him easily, and the officer folded under his weight and the power of his first blow. Now Jack was on him, as he pounded him over and over again and watched as his face collapsed inward. He watched the eyes burst from their sockets, only to be crushed under the weight of his next blow. He watched the officer's mouth twist open as it gasped for air, but his lungs couldn't lift the weight on his chest.

As men died around him, both Japanese and Americans, Jack pounded the man's face into the earth until there were no features, and he couldn't tell the difference between the dirt and the man's hair. When he regained his feet, there were maybe thirty people left alive, Americans using their bayonets to stab the Japanese that held them down as if to crush them with their rifles. Japanese men shot Americans in the back as they fought other men. More and more men died by the second. Jack once again felt powerless; he didn't know what he needed to do; he knew he was dead from the sword in his gut. He felt odd. This wasn't his own body; this wasn't even his life to lose. He watched as a passenger in this body that felt so much like his own as two gnarled hands picked the Browning up again, cocked it and trained it on the mass of men.

No guns fired anymore; they didn't have to. It was the Browning that mattered; that was the reason why they were here; he knew it was. Somewhere in the back of his mind, he heard an order, 'Do not fire a damned shot.' The voice was distant and old, weak, insignificant. The order hadn't even finished completely when a voice spoke out; it was cold and crackly, low and harsh. 'Use me. Kill them.' It was all the convincing he needed. The Browning Automatic Rifle erupted in a volley of fire and metal. The men were all so close that it didn't matter; one bullet cut through a man only to find another on the other side. It kept going and going. Men fell as others screamed in pain; all of them tried to turn to see what was happening but got cut down before they could react. Americans fell with the Japanese, all of them.

The Browning stopped, twenty rounds all gone. Like instinct, the magazine fell to the ground like one of the fallen soldiers, and another stepped up to take its place, and it started all over again. The men were all on the ground by this stage, but it didn't matter; bullets ripped over the fallen, the wounded and the dead alike. Blood shot up in the air each time the bolt flew forward; its hunger never fulfilled. It fell silent again, and then, a moment later, it started once more. It kept going, and Jack felt his eyes grow black, his mouth full of this vessel's blood, his hands stuck to the metal that he held. He needed to kill. He needed to kill. He needed to kill every single one of these mother fuckers. He needed them dead, and he needed to be the one to do it. Even when they were dead, he would fucking kill them again and tear their limbs from their sockets and beat their fucking heads in with them!

'NO!' he bellowed once more, as he closed his eyes. Everything changed in that instant, he felt ill. He felt weak, he held something but it wasn't the Browning. His breath was short, and hot. His stomach burned as did his face and his arms. He opened his eyes slowly and saw two more staring back at him.

'Jack?' Michael spoke softly. His eyes were dinner plates; the light of the fire behind him shone in the brown iris. The eyes that were alive. Deep inside the back of Jack's mind, the cackling began. It was distant, but the low cackle rang in his ears.

Then Jack did something he had not done since the photo that hung in his father's office was taken. He embraced his brother.

RANKIN

*'Who says the earth is crumbling
And no sky is falling through?
Sometimes, I just can't die.'*

Alice Cooper – *Still No Air* (1970)

In the state he was in, Rankin didn't know whether he was conscious and dying or dead and remembering. His entire body throbbed in a head-splitting agony one second, and the next subsided into numbness to drag his thoughts kicking and screaming into the flat silence of pure survival.

'Breathe.'

The weight crushed down on him on all sides. His head was stuck at an odd angle; the right cheek pressed up against the shattered stock of the Bren while the rest of him was covered by chunks of brick and mortar. The world around him had subsided into darkness, and he felt lost. He had once read an article in the Telegraph about a mountain climber that had been caught in an avalanche. He had tumbled over like a surfer thrown by a freak wave and had been buried twenty foot below by walls of snow. The expeditioner explained the sensation as like being in the crushing jaws of a king tide wave break, either that or he imagined that he could have been an astronaut that had felt the sense of zero gravity for the first time. He remembered reading that when the snow had settled, and he had become encased in his tomb of ice, he had become disorientated.

The writer compared it to being blindfolded as a child and spun around by his parents and then left to roam; he didn't know which way was up or which was down. At the time, Rankin didn't understand how a man couldn't tell up from down. Yet now that his world was dark, stone and metal pressed into him from all sides with equal force, he didn't even know if he remained among the living.

In the article, the trapped mountaineer had spat. The saliva didn't even make it an inch past his face before it hit the snow. The saliva had run up the snow, filled his nostrils, and seeped into his eyes. In the end, no matter how messed up someone was, no matter what they had been through, gravity only worked one way. Rankin's mouth was dry. In an attempt to breathe, all he could manage was a dry gasp that only sucked more dust down his throat and sent him into a haggard cough. His eyes began to water, and he laughed through his coughs; the tears ran along his cheeks and down the bridge of his nose. He couldn't see for shit, but he could feel the clean tracks on his face that the tears cut through the dirt, grime and blood. Then they pooled at the tip of his nose and dripped into the mess below him.

He fought with all the strength he had left in him to get free. He shifted first his arms to create a gap below him. Then his legs, which felt as though they had been shattered by the rubble on top. But the more he moved, the more the blood flowed to etch away at the pins and needles that stabbed him from all angles. Eventually, he placed his hands on the rubble below and pushed as if he were back in his cell. His chest rippled, his shoulders bulged, and small rocks and chunks of brick, unsettled by the upheaval, lost their footing and rolled away. Each pebble that shifted felt like a boulder to Rankin. With each push, less rubble stood between him and freedom. Jagged stone and clay tore into his back and his neck with each shove; he had never felt more alive when fresh blood started to run down his chin.

He knew he was close when the air began to freshen; there was still no light and the beginnings of fear soaked into him. Had his sight been lost in the firefight? Had something so traumatic occurred that the flag-waver inside his brain had finally had enough and thrown down his poles? It didn't matter. He continued to push and heave his way from the depths of the destruction, and finally, he emerged.

His uniform was torn to shreds around his body, and blood ran down his face from a gash on the back of his scalp. His leg still throbbed from the flesh wound, but the cool air kissed his filthy skin, and it could have been as though he had plunged into the springs of Elysium itself. He opened his eyes, and bright circles whirled around his vision. He fell forward on his hands and knees to settle himself. His chest heaved with each breath; the blood and tears still stained his face. He was alive.

The barbershop was destroyed, the room he was in when the tank had brought down the walls of his safety was unrecognisable. Michaels and Kelleher were nowhere to be seen and Rankin had the thought that maybe they had made it out, but the vision of their deaths came back to him and he didn't even bother to look. No one would have given him that courtesy. In the darkness of the night, he could see the looming bulk of the crippled tanks in the street. The bodies that surrounded them, Australians and Chinese alike, a swarm of flies on the faces of every man. He couldn't believe how there could be so many flies, how at one point the skies were clear and the next a plague of those filthy rotten flying scum were everywhere. *Welcome to Brisbane,* he thought, *the land of the flies.*

As he stood, his feet shifted on the loose rubble below him, and the broken frame of the Bren exposed itself as the rubble settled. He glanced toward the tank and was left unsettled as the main gun barrel was still trained on his position. He stood there, his eyes locked on the gaping hole of the abyss, as he waited to see if there was anyone left inside. Had they waited for him, the last Australian, to rise, so they could just bring him down along with the rest? A breeze rolled gently down the destroyed street and whistled around the tank's hull. On its crest, he saw the open cupola; the tattered remnants of a man's shirt clung to it as it shifted slightly in the breeze, and he relaxed. He descended the rubble unarmed and carefully placed his feet as he didn't want to step on the dead, but they were piled so thick that he had no other option in some places. He climbed the silent tank, the power of its engine long since cut, and he peered into the belly of the beast.

Two Chinese soldiers lay dead and twisted in the depths. Their eyes were open yet unseeing; their bodies were burned and distorted by the impact of the sixty-six-millimetre rockets that had struck them. They had crippled the tank, stopped it dead in its tracks, but they hadn't disabled its turret. A tank that couldn't move was still dangerous as long as it could fire; they had all learned that lesson. Still perched atop the turret, he peered down the street where he thought the Australians had retreated, and his heart sunk. The lines of bodies seemed to stretch on and on. The sheer mass of them was based around the focal point of the Bren and M60 fire, yet the fighting had continued past their destroyed positions. He saw bayonets on SLRs as they gleamed in the starlight, blood slowly drained from their fullers. He saw men with faces caved in from the butts of rifles, broken noses, and rocks in dead men's hands. The fighting had gone down to the last man, and then it had moved on.

In the distance, he heard sporadic rifle fire; the sky past the broken line of the Australians was red from fire. He remembered the old Colonel's words about the Chinese, 'They had used tactics comparable to that of Nazi Germany.' Blitzkrieg, or lightning warfare. They hit hard and fast and kept moving past the lines, burning as they went. To stand where he stood, he now understood what he had meant.

Long jets streaked through the air above him and tore through the semi-silence surrounding him. Two abreast, they cut through the air on their way south. As they went out of sight, he heard the sounds of rockets leaving their wings and then explosions. Then another wave came, and another.

He needed to get off the streets. He needed to get away.

His right hand went to the pouch on his belt as he clambered off the tank, as if he had only just remembered it. The leather was firm beneath his touch and the cool brass beneath a reassuring presence. He sighed. At least Max had made it through with him; for the moment, that was all that mattered.

He moved down the road and left the silent barrel of the tanks behind him. He passed the body of an Australian man, shot to pieces. His legs were completely cut at the knees, presumably by one of the tank's coax guns, and a single bullet hole was in the nape of his throat. His eyes were open, and he had this strange look of serenity on his face. The SLR to his side was empty, but it had its bayonet attached. Rankin claimed it for his own, then took his time to rummage through the legless soldier's bandolier for any fresh magazines. There were none.

He slipped the bayonet through a loop on the back of his belt and continued down the street, armed with no more than a club, a knife and a piece of brass. He moved past the broken line. Bodies of Australians that had tried to retreat lay face down in the cracked street. He checked each man for magazines and found none. He was at least lucky enough to find some cigarettes to replace those that the looter had taken and thought to himself, 'fuck it' as he lit one and continued body to body.

He found a soldier that had been blown through a shop front, either by a grenade or a rocket of some sort. His features were blackened and mostly destroyed, yet most of his gear was fine. The coolness of the night had started to sink deeper into his flesh, so Rankin took the opportunity to take the man's shirt to replace his own rags. The same man had a half-spent magazine still in his SLR, so Rankin helped himself. A short while later, he found another magazine completely unused. He now had thirty rounds of 7.62 to his name and only all of Brisbane to walk through.

As he moved further south, the sporadic fire continued through the streets. Jets continued to scream past overhead, but in the darkness, he had no idea whether they were Chinese or friendly. He eventually found the wrecked hull of a Huey half-buried in a building, its twisted tail broken from its frame. Bullet holes covered almost every inch of the blackened steel. He couldn't see the name that was painted on the side as the nose of the Huey was buried in brick, and Rankin had the sad feeling that it was his old friend, the Black Dread. But the Dread was still probably in Vietnam, lifting Americans out of the Silver City as the doom from the North came down on them. He moved on and walked almost casually as he smoked and limped from his wounds. The SLR in one hand and the cigarette in the other, he looked at each body he passed; street after street, more of them. Jeeps and Internationals destroyed. Chinese dead seemed to outnumber the Australians by far, but the overwhelming fact was there were just too many bodies.

The sound of an engine broke through the night, a small truck or a jeep, he figured from the sound of it. Rankin slunk down behind the frame of a destroyed truck and waited. First, he saw the pencil beams of the headlights as they cut through the darkness. Rankin watched as the line of light cast immense shadows over the crumbled walls to his left; the line jumped up and down as the vehicle bumped over the uneven surface. A flat green jeep of an odd shape bounced through the intersection in front of him, the Chinese inside easily identifiable at the speed and distance by their helmets and the red stars painted on them as proud as could be. Neither of the two even glanced in Rankin's direction as they drove through the intersection, and the wheels bounced through potholes and leapt over the dead. Neither of them even spoke a word as they went; their eyes were focused on the view through the windshield.

Rankin remained crouched behind the truck's chassis for a little while as he listened to the engine increase its pitch and then fall as the jeep wound its way through the obstacles that littered the streets. As the sound of the jeep faded, Rankin found it safe enough to leave cover. Beyond the wrecked truck, there was only one more car, a Ford sedan which had mostly escaped the ruin of the street around it. Rankin made a line for it; he kept himself low and moved quickly. Now that he had seen elements of the Chinese force, he needed to be careful. He crouched behind the Ford and considered his next move. Across the intersection, the road split in two. The median was raised concrete with a garden that remained mostly intact. The garden consisted of light shrubbery with palm trees spaced every twenty feet or so. The cover of the foliage appealed to Rankin, as he could hear the breeze rustle the leaves from where he squatted. If he managed to be heard by anyone, they would hopefully not suspect a survivor.

His eyes darted to windows above him and across the street in the abandoned pub which took up the corner. Snipers, like the one who pinned down the entire section, could be anywhere. Rankin doubted they'd stay so far behind the line of advancement, but he didn't know exactly where that was. He had woken up to nothing, yet if Chinese jeeps were three blocks beyond his final stand with the Bren, then who knows what could've happened. Just as he finally pushed himself beyond the Ford, the sounds of another engine came from down the street. Rankin paused and slinked back behind cover.

The sound was deep and throaty, and it remained low as the vehicle traversed the roads. No headlights marked its coming, only the deep throaty burble becoming louder and louder. Rankin peered over the Ford's guard as the vehicle entered the intersection, and its exhaust resonated off the walls of the street. A sleek pale ute cruised through the intersection. It was marked down the entirety of its side; its chunky tyres made short work of the potholes and bodies. The way it sat on its tyres gave it a slinking demeanour like it was stalking through the streets after the Jeep, not unlike a cat that stalked a bird. The driver sat in darkness; it was impossible to see the man's face, but Rankin was certain he did not look his way.

The utility moved on, its pace slow, likewise the mutters of its exhaust. As it exited the intersection, the smell of fuel and hot exhaust filled the air. 'Nothing like a V8,' Rankin mumbled as he left cover once more.

He crossed the intersection at a full run, as he didn't want to give a sniper an easy shot. He leapt into the foliage; the bushes caught on his clothes and whipped playfully at his face as he crawled through. He waited to hear a shot from one of the buildings surrounding him, but it never came. As he continued down the median, his back maintained the same level as the shrubs that concealed him. He passed another intersection which left him open as he crossed before he dove back into the cover of the garden on the other side. He did so quickly and without hesitation, his SLR in his hands the whole time.

As he neared the end of his garden path, he heard movement toward the end of the street. He slowed his pace, as he tried to maintain his concealment in the shrubs. He heard the sound of a Chinaman bark at something. He repeated the same words over again. Then he heard a man speak in English.

'I'm unarmed! I'm unarmed!'

The Chinese continued to shout as they repeated their harsh statement. Rankin tried to speed up. He crawled along on his stomach; his SLR slung over his back. He reached the edge of the median to see an Australian soldier on his knees, his hands in the air. A Jeep that was identical to the one which had passed him earlier sat across the lanes to his right. The Australian had been caught trying to cross the road just as Rankin would need to.

'I'm unarmed!' he called once more as they approached him. The two Chinese were both armed with AKs, and they had them shouldered and trained on the surrendering Australian. They were only thirty feet away. Rankin could easily take them both out, even with the little ammunition he had, but he couldn't afford to give away his position. As the Chinese edged closer to the Australian, Rankin saw the Australian's arm reach behind his back. The soldiers barked at him again as they brandished their rifles.

'Fucking idiot.' Ranking moaned, as he watched his countryman pull a pistol from behind his back and attempt to bring it onto the first soldier. There was a rattle of automatic fire and the Australian collapsed. 'Fucking idiot,' he repeated under his breath. The Chinese continued to bark, either in anger or surprise, at each other. One of them flapped his hands at the man they had just killed, while the other just shook his head. Rankin watched as they argued, their bodies exposed from the cover of their Jeep, its headlights still shone, and lit up the road opposite Rankin's position.

If he was going to move, this moment would be as good a time as any. Their attention was still drawn by the man they felled. Although the lights lit up the street Rankin meant to enter, he had a mind to enter the hotel partway down the road. He readied the SLR as he pulled it from his back. He shuffled into a crouched position while watching the soldiers to his right.

When he took his first step from the concrete median, he was hit by a brilliant light from his left. Instantly he turned his head to look at what it was but the light was too intense, he was forced to close his eyes and turn his head. Through his closed lids, he could see the twin circles burned into his retina, as they danced across black fields. He heard sounds of confusion to his right and then everything was muffled by the enormous roar of a V8 engine.

It was coming. He felt the ground shudder beneath his feet. He heard it rush toward him as a cat would lunge after its prey. With his eyes still closed, he threw himself back into the shrubs. His back thudded into the soft soil of the garden, and his feet flew up into the air as the utility roared past. It all happened so quickly; he felt the heat of the exhaust and smelled the fuel as it whipped by. Rankin lifted his head from the shrubs in time to see the white utility run up the gutter and slam into the soldier on the left. Being illuminated by the high beams, Rankin saw everything. He saw him crumple as the front end hit him; he saw the look of shock on the man's face, which he held until the moment he was sucked under.

The other soldier was defeated as soon as the engine roared the first time. He had turned his back and fled down the street away from his ambusher. Rankin watched the body of the utility, which now looked to be an older Holden, barely even hitch as the crumpled body spilled out from its undercarriage. The ruined body rolled and bounced in positions that the human body could not physically take until it vanished out of sight behind the Jeep.

The roar of the engine continued as the utility powered after the runner. Rankin saw his arms and legs pumping for dear life as the lights bore him down. Just when Rankin thought he had him, the Chinaman flung himself off to the right and out of Rankin's line of sight. He heard the brakes of the Holden and the tyres scream as they tried to pull the iron to a halt. Rankin got to his feet and clambered out of the garden with his SLR in tow.

He saw the Holden come to a halt; its brake lights red as the napalm fire in the dark. There was a soft 'clunk, clunk' from the transmission, and the engine roared into life again. Smoke poured from the tyres as the Holden reversed savagely back down the road. The front end scraped on the ground by the force of the wheels that pushed it back. Rankin could see where the Chinaman had gone off the street; he looked to have entered a partly collapsed apartment block. The Holden screamed to a halt outside, and the engine died as the driver's door opened.

'Hey, where you going? I just want to ask you a question.'

There was a jovial note to his voice, but nothing about the way he moved. Rankin caught a glimpse of the revolver in his hand as he vanished into the apartments in chase of his victim.

'Jesus Christ,' Rankin mumbled. 'What the fuck is going on?'

He was at a complete loss; should he stay and help? Or leave and take the man's Holden? The Holden looked fast enough, but it would draw attention. He opted to head toward the utility and decide once he had reached it. As he edged down the road, he heard the driver yell from the apartments. He seemed higher now. Perhaps his chase had led him up the stairs.

Rankin reached the utility. Its driver's door was still open while its engine ticked slowly as it cooled. He took a quick glimpse at the registration plate and saw that it had Northern Territory plates on it. His eyebrows furrowed at this, and he thought to himself that maybe this poor bastard was stuck in Brisbane like the rest of them.

He heard automatic rifle fire above him and he raised his head. He heard the driver bellow above him but the words weren't clear. Rankin took another look at the cooling utility and decided he would follow the driver. In the end, an Australian was an Australian. He entered the apartment block, the front door was smashed inward and shattered glass littered the ruined carpet, it ground under his boots as he stepped over it. In the night's silence, he heard the thunder of footsteps and the occasional shout from above. As he gazed up the cavity of the staircase that spiralled up on right angles about him, dust sprinkled down from a disturbed light hanger. He watched as it swayed all that distanced above him.

Rifle fire clattered again, and he saw some of the projectile's impact against the banisters. Three stories high, he checked the chamber of the SLR and let the bolt slam home as he mounted the stairs. His feet thundered as he climbed, heavy boots on carpeted hardwood. The SLR was high on his shoulder, and his cheek hovered over the butt. As he climbed, the words became clearer, but they made no sense to him.

'I think we got off on the wrong foot. I only want to ask you something.' The driver's voice was oddly calm for the booming he heard from the streets. 'Come now. Shhh shhhhh.' The sounds a mother made to calm her child.

Rankin heard light footsteps as he presumed the Chinaman ran from room to room. The only sound that came from the driver was his voice. When he did speak, each sound came from a different place than before, almost as if he played a game of cat and mouse. Wherever the voice seemed to come from the Chinaman sent a shower of rifle fire in that direction to hammer through horsehair plaster and crash into brick.

As Rankin rounded the third story, he waited at the crest of the landing. His ears strained to hear the sound of footsteps or breaths, anything. Another shower of fire came from down the hall, and Rankin ducked his head as a sheet of plaster gave way and crashed down the stairs behind him; it cast a cloud of white dust and dirt into the air. Then there was a series of thundering footsteps and an almighty crash from way down the hall. Rankin heard the Chinaman yell in his own tongue, and below all of it, he heard the driver.

The door at the end of the hall swung on its hinges. Most of the others in the hallway were open, which allowed the little light that was available from the street to trickle in. As Rankin passed one of the open doors, he saw that most of the floor on the street side apartments had collapsed. Sheets of concrete lay on angles to give the entire street side wing the look of a labyrinth. He saw the footprints where either the driver or the soldier had tracked upward then down again, the lines visible in the dust. Light shades and couches were thrown here and there in the chaos. In one place, he could see a woman's body, partially crushed by a bedroom suite that had slid down the collapsed concrete and pinned her to the wall.

He continued down the hallway, his eyes focused on the room at the end. As the door swung open, he saw the shadows of figures, one man on top of the other.

He heard the driver scream, 'Look at her face!' Then the door swung shut. Rankin moved up as the door bounced off the broken frame and swung open once more.

The two figures were gone. He stopped and took a knee as he raised the SLR to his shoulder. He had a bad feeling about this place, and the hairs on the back of his neck had raised on end. The apartment door began to swing shut once more, and he saw movement just as the gap closed. He waited and let it bounce off its frame again. As the gap increased, he saw the two men in a struggle, locked in a grapple as the driver pushed the soldier across the room and out of sight. Just as the door was to the end of its opening swing, it was struck and slammed shut.

Rankin took his opportunity and moved forward. He kept himself low and his rifle ready. The door shook in its broken frame and dust spilled from the edges. Beyond, Rankin could hear the struggle, the heavy breathing and the swearing. He was only ten feet away now, most of the open doors to his back, only one on the left remained to him now, and he headed to the door jamb to give himself some sort of cover.

'I told you, fucking look at her!' The driver roared from the other side, and the door shook violently. There was more struggle; Rankin trained the muzzle of his rifle to the door and waited. He didn't want to shoot the driver, but if the AK started again, he didn't have much choice. His plan ran through his head. 'Three through the door, then breach. Whoever gets hit, gets hit.'

He waited; his finger twitched slightly on the trigger. Gently, more and more pressure was placed on its mechanism. He heard the Chinaman scream, and then the tip of a blade was driven through the door. Rankin watched as it pushed further through the splintered timber. Inch by inch, it grew longer. As its spine pushed through, blood flowed from the fullers on either side of the blade. It ran down the timber and followed the lines of the routed pattern cut into its face. He watched as the blood levelled out on the vertical section, then broke its bank and slowly trickled down to the dusty, cracked floor.

The blade protruded by about eight inches at the end. Rankin shuffled and settled himself in the door jamb as he released the pressure on the trigger. The tip of the blade jerked down, then up and rapidly slid backward through the timber. Rankin heard a body slide down the door and collapse at its foot. He tried to see movement through the crack at the base of the door, but the thickness of the blood had somewhat sealed it. He heard something shuffle once more as someone breathed heavily. Then the door swung open, and Rankin stood as he raised his rifle, its muzzle only inches away from the face of the man in front of him.

His beard was shaggy and with filthy patches of brown and silver. His greasy brown hair had fallen over his eyes, and a horribly burned hand moved up to brush it away. At first glance, his eyes were grey and lifeless, yet when the night's faint light washed over his grubby face, Rankin saw the hint of hazel in them and a sadness.

They stood there in the hallway for a moment, Rankin still with the SLR in the other's face. The driver with the bloody bayonet in his hand and the revolver tucked down the front of his jeans. Then Rankin lowered the muzzle slightly. 'You almost ran me over back there.'

The driver cocked his head slightly as he considered Rankin. A ghost of a smile came from under his ragged beard.

'Almost.'

CHRIS

'Hey, let him follow you down
Way underground wind, and he's bound
Bound to follow you down
Just a dead-beat right off the street
He's bound to follow you down.'

The Rolling Stones – *Torn and Frayed* (1972)

Red tears streaked the night sky. It looked as though the surface of the sky was only the skin of a celestial being. The scales of a colour shifting chameleon cut to ruin by the fine edge of a dagger that dragged against its hide. Wounds that worked their way across the darkness to expose the red flesh beneath, and the pigments of the scales that lined the edges flickered in their death from red to yellow and finally black. The stars had retreated behind a veil of smoke, even the brightest being drowned out of the sky by the reign of fire beneath. All the while, the moon wept tears of stone and ice, its never-ending cycle of silent orbit along the path that only it could see, with nothing more to do but watch as the beings below feasted on each other's young, weak and helpless. It abandoned its post at the last scene of horror, not caring for the tides or the charts that it had set out a millennia before. The lonely giant had shaken its head for the final time and turned its back on the lands and oceans below, never to show its gleam again.

The city was in turmoil. Streets lined with bricks all smashed to pieces, glass, blood and flesh. Nothing seemed to move but the shadows cast from the headlamps of the pale utility. Figures that stood twenty-feet-tall as they slinked across the broken walls of buildings. Their claws wrapped around the crumbled edges as they peered at the rumbling Holden. The light that poured from its front end blinded them and sent them back to the safety of the dark. Chris passed each wrecked home, each filled with a thousand stories from a few people. The mothers, fathers, and children who cowered beneath their covers in their concern for the monster in the night, found that the magic that possessed the quilts of the children only worked for the shadows. He wondered how many had died as they cowered in their warm fortress of cotton, only to be crushed by the walls that had protected them. Then pounded through the floor by the artillery that came and went and the boots of the men that followed.

A brilliant flash of light sparked in the seat next to him. Chris turned his head from the wreckage surrounding them and watched as his passenger lit a cigarette. The young soldier sat back on the bench seat, his filthy head rolled on his neck as the Holden bounced over the bumps of the destroyed road. He stared out through the windscreen, his eyes as blank as the corpses they drove around. The cigarette between the fingers of his right hand lay across the leg of his trousers. Chris watched as the Holden's suspension took the main brunt of a pothole, and as the body rolled soggily, a short stem of ash broke from the shaft and fell to the carpet below.

Silently, Chris leaned across, snatched the cigarette from his passenger's hand, and tossed it from his window. The young soldier jumped as Chris's burned fingers rasped against his skin. His eyes were now alert and angry.

'The fuck you do that for?' he complained. His eyebrows hung low over his eyes, but the eyes were those of soldiers that had seen so much death. Chris had seen eyes like that in Africa, the eyes of men in their holes, those that crawled through the hot baking sand.

Eyes that didn't just look at you, but into you and through your back as if they could never focus on the surface. In the end, when a man had seen enough death, there was no point to face value; everything lay hidden beneath. Everyone always lied and hid their true intentions. Everyone, except her.

'You know how much that shit stinks when it gets into fabric?' Chris replied, his expression serious. The two men's eyes locked while the Holden rumbled down the street. His passenger continued to stare at him with a look of disbelief, then he broke his gaze to look down at the grubby seats, stained with grease, blood and dirt. While the carpet wasn't far off being a clot of matted strands.

'Yeah, righto mate, the interior's only 'A' grade after all,' the soldier said as he slunk back into his seat and lowered his head, as if he were pretending to go to sleep. As if he was tired. Who could be tired as they wound their way through the endless scenes of death and carnage? Who could ever feel tired again while they hadn't found what they were looking for? Who could ever sleep?

'What's your name, soldier?' Chris asked him while he still neglected the view through the windscreen.

The young man remained slouched, his eyes closed in pretend slumber. Young blokes were always fit; it seemed that no matter what they put into their bodies, shit always turned to gold when a man was young. This soldier was built like a mallee bull, broad and muscular but still only average in height. His biceps bulged through the torn rags that hung around his arms, and through the holes on his service shirt, there was a set of chiselled abs below. Chris thought to himself that he had picked up a hitch-hiking pretty boy, more concerned about his body than anything else. Still, if he survived what he had seen of Brisbane, perhaps he could be of some use.

'Rankin,' he grumbled. He never opened his eyes nor stirred from his slouch.

'Ran? Rang?' Chris tried to replicate.

'Ran-Kin,' his passenger opened his eyes to glare. There was an anger in this man, but there was an anger in every man, and in war, the bastard would always come out.

He smiled. 'Chris Lowe,' he extended his hand and Rankin shook it. 'How did you survive that?' Chris asked, his eyes back on the broken streets in front. A fire had raged in this part of town. It looked as though the Chinese had tried to burn their tracks as they had achieved in Katherine and multiple other towns in his venture South East. The smoke was so thick on the road that Chris had to squint to cut through the glare that the headlights cast.

'Who said I survived?' his passenger grumbled.

Chris barked with laughter, 'Well, the fact that you're sitting here talking to me sort of suggests it.' He tried to keep his mood high, to soar above the smoke that dragged his spirit down with it.

'Humph.' Rankin had subsided into a brooding sulk once more. 'An old friend of mine would disagree with you.'

Chris nodded and gave another small chuckle as he wound Pestilence through the remains of a smouldering fuel station. 'Yeah. Old friends always do.'

Rankin didn't reply. However, he had raised his head at the smell of the smoke, and his eyes peered at white walls like those of a hound baying at a rustling bush. From the corner of his eye, he saw the young man's SLR barrel shift as he pulled it from its position jammed up between the seat and the door. Chris felt safer having the brooding soldier with him, even if he had a weird name. With Pestilence's tray filled with jerry cans that looked just the same full when they were empty, he knew how much of a target one single man was by himself. But two men, one armed with a battle rifle, the other with a revolver and an old bayonet from a world war long forgotten. Maybe, just maybe, that would be enough to quell any ambusher's thoughts.

The smoke at this stage was so thick that he could not even see the crest of the Holden's bonnet; thick plumes rolled and swirled in through the open driver's window. Yet beyond that wall of white and grey was a brightness from the headlamps that could only suggest a hint that they still worked. The rumble of the engine seemed to cut through everything. It bounced back against the crumbled bricks and mortar and thudded into Chris' ear with each stroke.

'Let's get out of this place,' Rankin muttered beside him.

Chris shot him a look. He didn't know the plan; that was fine. He would know when the time came, and that time wasn't now. The smoke had begun to clear, yet it still spun in thickets as if caught by a listing breeze. Chris strained his eyes even further, and something familiar caught them.

He slammed his foot on the brake, and the utility propped at such a slow speed the tyres didn't even scream their protest. Rankin, on the other hand, slipped forward on his seat; the barrel of the SLR clashed against the dashboard.

'Fuck, man, give a guy some notice.' But Chris didn't respond; he never even heard him. He saw the wisp of a blonde tail of hair vanish into the smoke in front of them. He sat and stared into the haze. The body of the Holden shuddered beneath him with the power of the engine; it quivered as if it felt the same exhilaration as its master. They sat there, all of them quiet except for the car. Chris' mouth was dry, and his scarred hands death gripped the wheel. Both he and Rankin leaned close to the windscreen as if it would make a difference to how far into the shit they could see.

'Angie!' he called out the window, and Rankin looked at him.

'Angie?' the soldier whispered, his eyebrows furrowed.

Something moved in front of them, a figure. Slim, slender as it moved out of the smoke. Everything went quiet in Chris' head.

It was her; he had found her. As she walked calmly out of the abyss toward him, her arms were held out in front, and tears streamed down her beautiful face. She screamed something, but he couldn't make out what she said. The light blue summer dress she wore flowed from her body like an aura; it seemed to float through the smoke as she walked toward him. He saw Rankin move beside him. He shouted while shifting his body around and away from the door.

'Angie!' Chris screamed at the top of his voice, and tears streamed down from his eyes. There was no way to describe the feeling of relief and tiredness that washed over him. His whole body and mind gave way to the sleepless torment that he had gone through. The sights that he had seen on the Chinese trail of death. All to find her, and he had done it.

Gunshots rang out to his left, and he saw Angie stop. She held her hands to the flat of her stomach; the light blue slowly stained red, and it flowed outward like a cancer. She coughed, and blood sprayed from her mouth and ran like the tears before, down her beautiful face, and she began to fall.

The world came crashing in around him.

With the sound of rifle fire from all directions, Rankin roared at him to drive the car while he leaned out the window and fired his rifle sporadically.

Chris looked back at her. The body continued in its fall, the hands still pressed to the gut. But it wasn't her. It was a Chinese officer, and he wasn't alone. More and more of them emerged from the smoke. Muzzle flashed through the veil, and he heard the snicker of bullets on steel and the windscreen cracked.

He punched the throttle. Pestilence's back end dropped low, and it roared the sound of a predator. The front end lifted as the tyres powered through the rubble, while smoke poured anew from the churning rubber. He felt the steering go light as the front wheels lifted, all the while chunks of metal were taken from her hull by the spray of leaden fire. As it surged forward like a shot out of a barrel, he heard the bodies crunch beneath her and faintly below it, he could hear someone scream, but all he could see was the grey veil.

The front end came down hard, just in time for Chris to see more men. He kept his foot pressed flat while the 327 continued to surge. The tyres now locked with traction, Chris threw the speeding hull forward into the soldiers. They both watched as the men were sucked up, their bodies already broken by the railway track that slammed into their chests. The frame jolted and rose as they tumbled underneath, but Chris never let off, not once.

Through it all, Chris had not realised that he was crying. He still heard distant screams, and it wasn't for some time until he realised that it was him. He stopped to take a breath as Pestilence shot out of the smoke. They were well and truly above sixty by this stage, and the world around them became clear. Only for a second before the high-speed impact of another soldier covered the windscreen with the blood and gore of his former self.

'Tank!' Rankin roared as he tore the rags of his shirt from his body and leaned forward. His left arm out the window as he wiped at the blood covered glass with the rag and managed to just smear it everywhere. Chris pulled back on his wiper lever, and two piss poor jets of water spat onto the windscreen, but it was enough. He could see the green hull, rounded at the edges. Not a hundred foot down the road, the same style of tank that he had watched burn in Darwin all those miles ago.

He pushed down hard on the brake and the tyres locked. The front end twitched, then lumbered to the left. Chris looked out of his window as he took his foot from the brake while the main gun belted the air. Chris saw the billows of smoke jet from the end of its muzzle brake, and he felt a wall of air hit them as the projectile rushed over the top of the Holden's tub. Pestilence shuddered fiercely under the power of the shell, then he slammed his foot down on the gas once more, and the tyres erupted in smoke as he felt himself sink into the seat.

'Shit, shit, shit!' Rankin screamed as one of his hands pressed against the dash while the other death gripped the frame through his window. The SLR clattered against Chris' leg as the rear end of the utility swung savagely around. Chris glanced down and felt his stomach sink as he looked directly down the barrel. He kicked it back at Rankin while his eyes returned to the windscreen. He would've liked to have seen a road or a large, open highway. Instead, the patterns of blocks and mortar rapidly revealed themselves to him as they hurtled toward the wall of brick.

'It's a boundary wall, it's thin, it's thin!' he screamed to Rankin as he steered into the slide he was in and pushed the front end of the ute back into a controllable direction.

'It's fuckin' brick! I was safer with the Chinese!' Rankin screamed back as he grabbed the SLR as the Holden came out of its slide. Rankin dumped rounds of ammunition into a beaten pattern on the wall. Already he could see how weak it was with complete bricks being punched out by the 7.62, and Chris committed with everything he had.

He looked in the rear-view and saw the tank's body bounce as it accelerated after them. The barrel swivelled on its turret, then stabilised as the tank hit a smoother road. There was another puff behind them, a deep thud. The body rocked once more as the shell buzzed straight past them and hammered into the boundary wall. Brick, dust and part of the road exploded thirty feet in front of them. Chris smiled and turned the car into the dust.

'Jesus Christ!' Rankin let his rifle clatter to the floor and covered his face with his hands as the front end disappeared into the dust cloud. As the tyres hit the small curb, the front end soared into the air, and shortly after, the engine's revs screamed beyond the red line as the rear end followed the arc. There was a grind, and the sound of crumbled stone below the roar of the engine and Chris began to laugh.

The weight of the railway track pulled the front end down. There was a horrific sound as metal ground into concrete. The suspension groaned in complaint as Pestilence bounced, and its front lifted into the air again. Through the lower half of the windscreen, the blood was mostly washed away by the weak jets of water, and Chris made out a parked Landcruiser on the other side of the road. He pumped the brake hard, but the utility was still mostly in the air. When the tyres hit the ground, they howled horribly as the overweight Pestilence slid helplessly. There was a sickening crunch as metal bent, warped and tore as the heavy iron bar drove into the Landcruiser's flank. Rankin flew forward into the dashboard, his side impacted hard, and his head kissed the glass. He sagged into the foot well and groaned as he clutched his head.

Chris heard him mumble, 'Fuck me drunk.'

'Walk it off, you pussy,' Chris mumbled as he threw the shifter into reverse and pegged the throttle again. The tyres howled over the engine's roar, and the car shifted back and then came to a screaming halt. Chris looked forward as he pegged it again and watched the whole Landcruiser come with him as he backed up. The railway track had become wedged in the metalwork of the crippled four-wheel drive. Chris threw the shifter back into drive and hammered the Landcruiser again as he tried to break the pinch. He let the vehicles come to a soft stop and then selected reverse once more. As he turned, he saw Chinese infantry breach the hole they had created in the brick wall.

'Fuck, Rantang, we have more company!' he bellowed as Pestilence shot backwards again. Metal ground and Pestilence's tyres screamed, and the Landcruiser's hollered, as the heavy vehicle was dragged sideways. The glass windows of the four-wheel-drive exploded in a hail of gunfire as Rankin finally lifted himself from the footwell.

He pushed the barrel of the SLR out of the window just as Chris selected drive and hammered the utility forward again. Rankin was thrown into the seat face first, and he shot wildly out the side.

'Fuck, man! We need to work together here!' Rankin shouted as Chris pushed the Landcruiser to the curb. Behind them, the Chinese had begun to form a firing line, and automatic fire hammered into the back of Pestilence.

'We are going to get overwhelmed in a minute!' he roared as he slammed it into reverse again and pushed the 327 as hard as he could.

'Yeah, well, say my fuckin' name right, and I'll listen!' Rankin roared as he trained his SLR out the window again; he braced his back against the dashboard and his knees under the seat. He fired, quickly yet calmly. As Chris continued to pull his way out of Landcruiser, he watched the Chinese fall behind him while packets of food and water exploded in the back of Pestilence's tub.

'One more, and we've got it!' he yelled as he pushed into the Landcruiser one more time.

'Make it quick,' Rankin replied through gritted teeth as he continued to fire into the enemy infantry.

He threw it into reverse, 'Here we go!' As he watched their path, the brick wall behind them crumbled twenty foot to the right of the hole Pestilence had created. The light tank pushed through at such speed that large chunks of brick were thrown into the air and cascaded across the road. They smashed into the hard structures as if they were coordinated artillery strikes. He pressed hard on the throttle, there was a scream of metal and then the brilliant sound as a panel gave way and Pestilence was freed.

'Tank!' Rankin roared again as he shifted himself in his seat and continued to fire.

'Thanks, mate. I didn't see the fucking thing.'

'Just move!'

Chris slammed the transmission into drive again and hammered it down the street. The exhaust bellowed off the buildings surrounding them, and the Holden rocketed away. As the 327 surged, they narrowly avoided coaxial fire from the turret as the tank slid on its tracks.

'That light tank can move,' Rankin warned as he kneeled backwards on the seat and peered out over the lip of the rear window. Chris saw him brace himself once more against the dash and the door as Chris threw the car into a high-speed slide to try to cut a close corner.

'We just need to keep buildings between us; she ain't that quick.' Chris groaned through clenched teeth. His arms crossed up as the Holden roared its way sideways toward the intersection. Way back, he could hear the rapid thudding of the coax and then the horrible ground shattering thud of the main cannon. The shopfront on the corner exploded in a shower of glass and concrete, and once more, Chris pushed Pestilence into the dust cloud.

The engine stammered as its tyres skipped over the rough ground, and then it bit in and hammered its tone through the night. Its headlights split the dark as if it was the Red Sea. The back end fishtailed slightly outside of the corner, but the wide tyres hooked in and drove them out. The revs climbed as they sped down the road, two hundred feet to the next corner. They needed to clear it before the tank reached the intersection; they needed to stay a street in front.

'Come on girl, come on,' Chris urged his second love as it hurtled down the road. He steered it far to the right and tried to give them as much time in cover as possible before the tank could see them. Also, it gave him the wider line to the left-hander he was about to attempt.

'Come on girl!' he roared just as the nose of a Chinese jeep edged out from the right entrance of the intersection in front. Chris hammered the brakes, and he felt the front end dip. The railway track ground against the bitumen. As he began to swing, he punched the throttle once more and Pestilence came about. The Chinese soldier who sat as a passenger in the jeep peppered them with automatic fire as they sailed through the corner. Chris paid them no mind; he was concerned about the tank. He stretched his head back and tried to hold his vision of the road they had just traversed until it was cut off by brickwork.

'I think we've lost that tank, but you need to do something about the jeep,' Chris yelled to Rankin, who leaned the muzzle of his rifle out of the window once more. Chris heard the definitive clack of an empty chamber and looked to his passenger as they were racked by fire once more. 'At this rate, I'll need to make an insurance claim, mate.'

Rankin shook his head and tossed the rifle to the seat. 'Out. You got anything else in here?'

Chris drove his hand down beside his seat while he swerved the Holden over the road in an attempt to make a harder target. His hand closed around something timber and oily, and he pulled, but it was his bayonet, so he let it fall back. He swerved the car again, and cool metal bumped his hand, and he latched onto it. He pulled the revolver out and handed it to Rankin. 'I've only got what's in it.'

The Jeep had powered up to them and had gained ground on Chris's sloppy line. Chris watched Rankin flip open the revolver's cylinder, turn it slightly and close it again. He steadied himself. 'Alright, brake hard when I say. Let him get closer.' Chris eased on the throttle, and he heard the engine whine as gears meshed as the engine pulled back and began to slow the car. 'Almost. Almost.' Rankin said as he cocked the hammer on the revolver. 'Now!'

Chris hammered the brakes once more, and the tyres howled again as they attempted to pull the car up. The Jeep came up hard on the passenger side, and Rankin aimed the revolver out of the window and fired. A flash of yellow flame erupted around the cylinder as the Jeep droned past. As it flashed by, it listed to the right, and Chris hammered the accelerator again. Pestilence squatted and shot forward; he saw the blood caked windows of the driver's side and the passenger that frantically tried to gain control of the jeep when Pestilence slammed into its side. Another horrible grind of steel and rubber screamed as the Jeep was pushed sideways. Then the far side tyres caught, and it yawed up into the air and rolled.

Chris gassed the throttle again and pushed Pestilence passed on the right side. They had lost only a little time, but little was enough to have him worried about the tank once more. He pushed the Holden down the main road as hard as it would go. The speedometer stopped at one hundred and twenty miles per hour, and the needle had well surpassed that marker by the time Chris let off on the revs.

The exhaust crackled and spat hot breath into the night air as the revs fell along with the speed. Rankin shifted himself around on the seat and sat down. Chris held out his hand for a handshake, but Rankin just slapped the butt of the revolver into his palm. Chris smiled as he pushed the revolver back behind his seat. They drove in silence for some time as they passed a billboard that was still new in contrast to the world around it that had burned: *Thanks for visiting Brisbane.*

They pushed on and found that they only had to pull into back streets at one point or another to avoid further conflict with Chinese convoys and patrols. Finally, on a quiet highway that stretched straight for over a mile either way, Rankin spoke.

'Pull in here.'

Chris let the utility purr down to an idle. He pulled the battered

Holden off the highway and onto the widened dirt shoulder. Rankin opened the door and had exited the cabin before Pestilence had even come to a halt. Chris watched him as he lit a cigarette, smoked it, flicked it and lit another. He got out to assess the damage. As he expected, the front was pretty well fine; the heavy steel bracing to support the weight and reinforce the railway track was all still in fine form despite the heavy blows. The back, however, was shot up pretty bad. He had been thankful for his own idea to place jerry cans full of water along the outer edge of the tray. Many of which had holes punched through one side but not the other. He had lost maybe fifty per cent of his water; that was fine, he could always get more of that. Minimal food loss and only one jerry can of fuel had copped a stray shot, but the shot hit high and very little fuel had escaped. While he let Rankin smoke, he used the punctured jerry can to fill at least some of Pestilence's tank and tossed the steel can to the ground once he was finished.

'We will need to resupply,' Chris said aloud, not necessarily to Rankin.

'For what?' Rankin stood right behind him. Chris turned, almost surprised to hear an answer to his statement. He looked at Rankin as if it was the first time they had met.

Chris shrugged his shoulders as if there could be no other answer. 'To follow them.'

'Who?' Rankin shot back instantly. 'The Chinese?' Chris could tell the young soldier had started to get his back up. He didn't know how to reply, so he remained silent. The two men stood there for a moment. Rankin lit another cigarette as he paced back and forth. The hunch in his back and the way he paced made Chris think of an Alpha in a pack of dogs, one that put on a show of dominance, to try and force his subordinate to break its ranks.

The smoke listed from Rankin's lips and curled up in front of his face. Chris looked him over, blood was coursed over his face, his skin was black from dust and grime, his bare chest bled from scratches. His scalp bled also from the impact to the windscreen and finally Chris saw a bullet wound in his leg. Blood darkened the fabric that surrounded the wound.

'You're shot,' Chris pointed to his leg.

'Flesh wound,' Rankin muttered. He took another drag on his cigarette. 'Chris, right?' Chris nodded. Rankin nodded as well and took the cigarette from his lips. Then he bellowed, 'Who the fuck is Angie?!'

MICHAEL

'When I find myself in times of trouble
Mother Mary comes to me.
Speaking words of wisdom, let it be.
And in my hour of darkness,
She is standing right in front of me.
Speaking words of wisdom, let it be.'

The Beatles – *Let it Be* (1970)

The rain pattered down on the mountainside to drench the leaves and wet the exposed roots of the old iron barks and gums, the soil and the two brothers. Some shelter was found under the great boughs of the silent giants. The sound of the water against the timber growth and the earth almost put the boy in a slumber as he sat and rested his aching feet. Jack was twenty feet in front of him, his back barely visible in the light fog of the early morning and the mist created by the downpour. His face was turned upward to the clouds, as if confused by the substance that fell from the sky. His enormous body swayed slightly in the fog. Still, he stood there as he either contemplated, wondered, or just slowly died.

After the fight with the dogs, Jack had held him. He didn't know what to think of that, as only a moment before, his brother's hands had been wrapped around his throat. He could still feel the life being crushed out of him by Jack's immense grip. His face had been another thing. Jack's features were blurred, either by the mess the tri-coloured bitch had made of its right side or something else. Michael shook his head and brought his hands up to his face to wipe the water from his eyes and tried to dismiss the thought of that whole night from memory. He just kept going back to Jack's eyes.

You're going crazy. It was a dark night, he told himself over and over again. Now that Jack had fallen back into silence, his mind was his only source of conversation and boy that thing just didn't shut up. 'They were black, the whites of his eyes were black, everything was.' In the end, everything was what it was. His memory was flawed and that's all there was to it. But still, every time he dwelled in the semi-conscious state of a daydream when he walked slowly along behind the waning strength of his brother, it would start again. 'They were as black as the ace of spades.'

His mind went back to the night of the dogs; Jack's hands fell from his throat to his shoulders. When Jack's eyes opened once more, he remembered seeing the whites; maybe the moon had peeked its nose out from behind some low-lying cloud cover. Michael remembered the way Jack's eyes looked him over, head to toe, then his huge arms pulled him close to his chest and squeezed him. Never before, had he felt his brothers embrace. He could smell the musk of his clothes, which were cold now from the dew that had soaked into them. The sweat and blood that covered Jacks neck stuck to him, as the heat radiated out of him his battered body, almost too unbearable for Michael to stand. Jack held him there, Michael's left arm was trapped between both of their chests, but his right arm lay by his side, unsure whether he should hug back, never sure of what he was supposed to do. He felt the hint of tears begin to well in his eyes, and he blinked rapidly. Those days needed to be behind him now; those days were done. Then, as suddenly as the embrace had occurred, it was over. Jack stood and let Michael fall to his knees in front of him. His brother turned his wrecked body and headed to the fire to sit by its side once more. He retrieved the blackened mess of venison that had fallen to the ground in the struggle. He brushed some dirt away, pulled the skewer from its middle, tore it in half and threw the considerably smaller section to Michael.

Michael remembered the way he sat there. His face was half torn, his right cheek almost non-existent, and blood ran down his neck to stain the torn shirt. The cuts and chunks taken from his arm were as bright red as the fire he sat in front of. The worst was the chunk taken out of his side. The fabric had been torn away, and the flesh underneath had been ripped from his brother's hide in strips. Clots of dirt and bits of his shirt were stuck into the flesh, yet Jack just sat there, his jaw working as he pushed blackened meat into his mouth. His eyes vacantly stared into the fire; the rifle that had been no use in the conflict remained active at his side. Once the meat was gone, he continued to stare into the flames. His jaw still worked as if he chewed, his torn cheek rippled, and the muscles curled as he did. Michael looked down at the untouched venison on his lap. The burned flesh and the dirt that was stuck to its sides. He stood up and approached his brother. Jack's eyes never left the fire, and his jaw never stopped. Michael placed the meat into his brother's hands; Jack never reacted.

'You can have it, I'm… I'm not hungry.' For some time, Jack never responded, then his eyes flickered and he blinked. His jaw ceased its grind and he shifted slightly on the earth.

'You'll need strength for tomorrow,' Jack extended the meat out toward Michael, his eyes never leaving the flames. 'Eat.'

Never one to question, Michael had sat down and tried his best to stomach the venison. The meat had gone cold and the little juice under the charcoaled flesh had congealed. Still, he tore small strips off and chewed and chewed until his jaw became sore, and his mouth and throat were left completely dry. When he threw the rest of the meat into the scrub beside him, he made sure that Jack wasn't focused on him. The last thing he needed was to anger him.

Jack had saved his life, but there was still that moment of uncertainty after the fight. Michael still didn't know what to do. Was he a prisoner? Was he being led along a trail just to be put down at its end like a lame horse? What did Jack want from him? There were so many questions that he had that had remained unasked and unanswered. He was afraid of his brother; after all, he had seen him do horrific things. But there Jack sat, bloody and half dead, yet still with so much power in him. To help him seemed like the only thing he could do. Michael went to the green pack and pulled an old metal, military canteen from the main pouch. He shook it to feel the weight of the liquid inside. He placed it on the outskirts of the fire, on a small pile of the remains of a burned out log. In no time, the water hissed as it boiled; steam escaped the cracked rubber seal under the cap and whistled slightly. Michael wrapped the old strips of cloth that had been used to cart the venison to this bloody clearing around his hands and retrieved the canister.

Jack seemed dead to the world; his eyes were unfocused.

Michael leaned in close. 'This will hurt, but we need to do something.'

No reply. Michael unhooked the lid. The steam rushed upwards to heat his face and forced him to close his eyes against its onrush. He wanted to leave the worst to last and decided that he may as well start from the top. He held the top close to his brother's face and let the water splash onto his cheek.

He didn't know whether it was the flesh or water that hissed on contact, but the sound of it made him want to bring the small amount of venison he had eaten, straight back up. The flesh darkened at first, then lightened. Jack's eyes remained out of focus, lost in the fire; he didn't even flinch. However, under the steam, he could see the tendrils of his muscles as they contracted and relaxed repeatedly. Michael used most of the reservoir on Jack's face and needed to refill multiple times before reaching the gore on his side. He said he wanted to leave the worst to last, and the wound did not let him down by any stretch of the imagination. While the canteen heated for the fourth time, Michael started to pick at the specks of dirt and blackened cloth, which were stuck almost inside of Jack. Cloth tore and stuck to anything it touched as he pulled each strand out. The beast that had torn into Jack had done a good number, and he didn't know if pouring boiled water onto this was a good idea, but he figured it was better than nothing. Once more, he retrieved the hissing canteen from the embers and took a deep breath before he splashed out the innards on the wound. The howl that came from Jack on this last was blood-curdling; it started low then built in his diaphragm to a roar that took Michael's mind back to his book and the mountain troll of Khazad Dum. When it subsided, the scrub had come alive around them, sounds from far off as dogs howled to the moon. Branches cracked as birds took to the air in the night out of fear of being attacked in their roost, and under it, all were heavy breaths as Jack tried to contain the pain at his side.

Michael proceeded to do a very poor job of wrapping his brother's wounds in strips of torn, clean fabric. They had no medical supplies, only what Jack had brought. He dared not use any more of the water as a good portion of their drinking water was now on the ground or ran down Jack's body. He wished his mother were there to tend to Jack. While he wrapped long strands of fabric around his brother's face, he looked to the mark where Matt Tracker had tried to cave his head in; there was barely anything there anymore. Grace always knew what to do, but she was gone now, along with the rest.

Michael didn't think he would get a wink of sleep that night. Jack kicked and rolled throughout the night; he swore and muttered to himself in his sleep. There was one point where he was sure he had heard his brother say, 'Fucking Japs,' but that couldn't have been right; Jack had never met a Japanese man in his life. The tossing and turning became contagious. Soon enough, he felt a twitch in his own leg or an ache in his back that was only remedied when he rolled onto his side. The cold ache would work back into him every minute or so, and he would be back to page one. Sometime before he fell asleep, he lifted his head to check on Jack's bandages, only to see that most of his work had come undone. He dropped his head in defeat; he wished once more that his mother had been there to care for them, himself mostly and shortly after, he had drifted into darkness.

That was days ago now. How long, he couldn't remember. Each day on the mountainside had drifted into one. They had no salt and no other way to keep meat, so Jack had shot a new animal every day. Deer mostly, when they were lucky enough to find one, but a dog had been their dinner one of those nights and a kangaroo another. When it was burned within an inch of itself, all meat tasted the same, like charcoal. Water to wash it down and cold, burned offerings the next morning to break their fast. Michael had begun to feel weak. He had never just gorged himself on meat when he was at home; he had milk and cereal in the morning, vegetables with bread and meat at night and generally always something different. His jaw hurt, and his teeth felt loose and gritty with all the strands of meat caught between them. Everything seemed to hurt more and more as each day went on. He didn't know how long they could survive.

The worst part was Jack. Michael's efforts may have worked to some degree, but in others, they had failed. Even through the rain, Michael could see the sweat running from him. He could see the redness in his skin. The blackness of the open wounds left to fester as they lacked the provisions to cover them. At first, he thought his brother would shrug it off, as he had most everything in life, but Jack walked slower as the days went on. He took more rests after they climbed hills or carved meat out of the animal that had given itself up for them. He saw dark lines on his neck, and his veins seemed to stand out on his arms like rivers that were threatened to break their banks. Some days ago, Jack had fallen, his legs had given out underneath him, and he went down in a heap. The rifle he held skittered across the ground and stopped at Michael's feet. He looked down and into the open mouth of its breech. He saw the brass gleam, the hungry emptiness of its chamber. He bent down slowly and stretched his hands out to touch it, just a bit closer, almost there.

'No!'

Michael stepped back, his hands snapped back up to his chest. Jack stared at him as he struggled. The veins on his neck pulsed and bulged out of his skin.

'Don't... touch...' He groaned, as he pulled himself along the ground over to the rifle. His breaths were short and rapid, which made it hard for the big man to talk.

Michael left the rifle where it lay and instead went to his brother and tried to help him. He felt the heat coming from his flesh before he even got close enough to touch him. Once more, he held his hands out to reach.

'Don't... fucking... touch...' his brother growled as he pulled himself along the dirt and tussock to his rifle until finally, he reached it. He lay there for a while, his head pressed into the ground with his right arm outstretched and his hand clasped around the frame. His knuckles stood out, white bone pressed through red, sweaty flesh.

'Jack, we need help.' Michael tried.

'I just... need... to rest,' Jack said. He didn't even lift his head; his booming voice flattened and feeble as he panted into the dirt.

Sometime later, Jack arose. He used the rifle heavily to support his weight as he first clambered to his knees, then to one foot and finally the other. Long pauses of heavy breathing came before each step of progress and then when Jack was ready, they continued to walk.

Now, instead of miles, they travelled feet. Hundreds at first, if not thousands, but less and less every day. Jack had begun to lead them down the mountain now, defeated in his resolve to stay high, defeated in everything. They had used up most of their water. The canned food was gone and although their packs were considerably lighter, Jack only carried his rifle and ammunition now. The small amount of supplies that Michael could fit in his pack had begun to scare him. They had seen a town through the fog a day or two ago and it was hard for Michael to trust in Jack's directions, but he thought at least that was their heading.

Sometime later, they'd reached a road. The feeling as he stepped from the soft grass of a paddock onto a hard-packed dirt road was tremendous. Each step felt lighter. The wind blew through his hair and it had even stopped raining. As they walked along the flat earth, they covered more ground, even more than what they covered when they walked downhill. He would never have believed it, but he had come to hate walking down a hill more than walking up. His toes felt as though they were beaten and swollen against the hard tips of his engineer boots, like the battered heads of nails that refused to sink into the solid base of hardwood below them. Now that they walked on flat ground, he felt like he could trudge for days; Jack, on the other hand, couldn't. His boots scraped at the earth beneath him as he swayed on the road. Each step was more a stagger than the last, and his line was far from what you would call a straight one. They continued to take rests until they saw the town in the distance. Michael had begun to question why they hadn't seen any cars. As usual, every time he raised a question, his brain quelled it.

It was probably just a small town and not many people travelled to it.
There will be cars and people when we get there and then we will be fine.
What about the rifle...? Heaps of people have rifles, they won't care.'

As they neared the town, which had indeed turned out to be smaller than he first expected, the dirt became the hard blacktop that he associated with civilisation. His knees and his aching back near sung for joy when his rubber sole's skittered across the bitumen for the first time since he didn't know how long.

It wasn't until they reached the town that Michael understood just how long they had been in the mountains. The world had changed while they had played at hide and seek. They had changed themselves, and he thought nothing had changed for the better. He looked to his brother, who had collapsed on the outskirts of the town against an FJ Holden that had been parked at an odd angle, half on the bitumen and half on the dirt shoulder. There was a metal sign only a few feet past the battered Holden; the base was a reflective green with bold white letters that read 'Kootingal.' Below the town's name, smaller white letters listed the population, which numbered four hundred and thirty-seven. Red paint had been smeared over the number, and jagged words were poorly written across the metal sign to its right. The paint had run from the letters' peaks and trickled down the metal in droops and sloppy lines that resembled blood smears: *The lambs have gone to slaughter. The Shepherd has come.*

Michael stood as he read the scrawling letters, confused at what they meant. Behind him, Jack sagged to the ground, his back pressed up against the side of the Holden. The bags under his eyes were the black of night. Sweat coursed down his face, and his body had begun to shake. Michael didn't know what sight bothered him more, the writing on the sign or the state his brother was in. A gust of wind tickled the back of his neck, and a scrap of paper was swept from the earth to slap against the windscreen of the Holden. As if it was the first time he had seen it, Michael looked at the Holden. The side of its body was caved in. The light blue paint was scraped back to bare metal in places, and streaks of red were imposed over the top. It had two flat tyres, and some of the windows had been smashed in. Shards of glass littered the interior, and there was a pool of what looked like mud in the floor pan. As his eyes ran over the car, he noticed bullet holes speckled here and there. One particular small one he found was on the outside of the car's door, but on the inside, the material that lined the panel was blown outwards in a tangle of metal and vinyl.

'Jack, I don't like this place.' He said it almost in a whisper; his heart had begun to hammer in his chest. He had a bad feeling, and he didn't want to walk another step into the town. He turned to his brother. Jack's eyes were closed; his head hung down so that his chin rested on his chest. His head lifted slowly and then sunk a few inches with every breath he took.

Michael swore; he had no choice. He couldn't carry Jack; he didn't even have a hope of getting him into the smashed up FJ. He looked at the rifle that lay at his feet. Jack's hand was still clasped around the timber stock; his grip tightened and then slackened with each breath. Michael thought about taking it, but the rifle was near as tall as he was, and there was no way he would be able to use it; there was no safety there for him. He turned his back to his brother and made his way into the town. The streets were littered with papers, cars were parked crookedly along the curb, and it was an odd sight for him to see kangaroos in the main street.

As he walked down the quiet main street, the wind blew in his face, and a door clapped against its frame. The sound made Michael jump, and a cold shiver ran up his spine, but as he looked, he saw the door bounce off the frame and swing open, unmanned to hit against the inside wall. He walked slowly as if in a sneak; he needed the help of someone, but he wasn't about to call out. He thought about the old man's lined face that had come to him when he had retreated into his sanctuary. He wished that nice old man was here, but his face was on the hedge now; he didn't think that was a good thing.

As he continued down the street, he came to a line of shops that had glass frontages. Most of them had been smashed in; one building still had a park bench that protruded from its fascia and shattered glass lay all over the sidewalk that glittered in the afternoon sun. One window was left untouched, apart from more poorly written words. From what Michael could tell, it was written by the same hand that had scrawled on the town sign.

'The Shepard has come for his flock,' Michael mouthed the words as he read them. Something bad had happened in this town, he didn't want to know who the Shepherd was, he didn't want to know what had happened to the people here, he needed to find something to help Jack and get out.

As he continued down the empty, littered street, he passed numerous cars whose doors stood open. Water sat in the floor pans from the recent rains, and small bugs bred in the now stagnant puddles. The smell was sickening, but perhaps one thing sickened him more: a child's doll on the ground, only a few feet from the car door. Part of the plastic had been crushed by a man's boot, yet the face still smiled as its arms were outstretched, waiting for its owner to pick it up and play with it once more. Michael turned his head away and continued down the lonely street.

Eventually, he found a small brick house with a timber sign out the front that read 'Doctor.' If there was going to be anything in this odd town to help Jack, it would be in there. He walked across the lawn, which had grown substantially in the rain and was well in need of a good trim. Each step he took across the lawn almost swallowed his boots. He looked at the house as he approached; the thought of entering the place seemed more daunting with each step he took. Spiderwebs had accumulated around the small ornate metal brackets which sat under the squat eves. No light came from inside the house, no windows were broken due to the bars across each one, and almost everything was painted mission brown. The house looked like one dark brown, squat piece of shit with a freshly painted green roof. A screen door that looked like it was once mounted to the front of the structure lay across the lawn. The grass had grown up through the latticework and had punched holes in the fly screen; only a portion of its rusted metal frame was still visible. When he reached the front door, a brilliant white hardwood monstrosity, he hesitated. He was about to turn the door handle when he saw the pry marks on the frame. Michael placed a trembling hand on the enamel paint and pushed.

The door whined as it swung open slowly on its hinges. Darkness met him in the hallway, but he could still see the mess inside from where he stood. The place had been ransacked, chairs lay on their sides, porcelain lamps lay shattered on the ground, their shades lay lonely only inches away from their broken perch. Books and magazines lay scattered from end to end of the waiting room. Michael went to one of the windows and pulled the curtains aside to allow the outside sunlight to flood in through the clean window. These things didn't add up to Michael. This was a nice house, it looked bad by the colour but it was looked after. What ever happened didn't happen long ago. He turned back to the waiting room to see the jagged red letters scrawled once more by the same hand on the off white-wall. *Only by the grace of the Lord shall you be healed.*

Michael was beyond scared now. He walked through the waiting room; he stepped over books and magazines and the belongings of people that had been in the room when whatever this was happened. He saw women's handbags, men's coats and hats as they lay around, the contents of their pockets spread out over the ground. The plaque on the adjoining door read 'examination room.' He felt like he was getting close. He pushed the door open and stepped inside to be hit by a foul smell of rot. Michael clapped his hands to his mouth, and his eyes instantly watered.

In the corner of the room, a man lay sprawled. His back partially up against the wall, his glasses hung crooked over his discoloured face. His stomach looked bloated to the point that the fabric stood taught on his skin; each button hung on for dear life as the shirt pulled outwards in between each fastener to reveal the milky skin beneath. In the middle of his forehead, there was a similar-sized hole to the one in the body of the beat-up Holden on the outskirts of town. Michael thought about the other side of the door and decided he didn't want to look at the other side of the man's head. With his hand still over his mouth and his breaths reduced to shallow skips, he went straight to the cupboards and started to look for anything. Yet, the more he searched, the more he found that every cupboard was stripped bare. Each time he threw a white chipboard door open, nothing lay behind. As he struggled to cope with his shallow breaths, he grew more and more frantic, nothing, nothing, nothing!

Out on the streets, he heard a woman's scream. Michael stopped breathing and froze. His ears rung slightly in the silence, his heart hammered in his chest.

'No, no, no!' He could hear the shrill voice from the streets. He left the examination room and kept his head low as he slinked over to the window that he had cleared, thankful to be away from the smell of the man behind him. From this view, he saw an older woman shrieking as she ran down the street. She wore blue jeans with leather work boots and a red and black plaid shirt. Her black hair was streaming behind her while tears ran from her eyes. He could hear the roar of an engine but didn't dare swing his head out from behind the brick frame of the house any more than it was.

In the end, he didn't have to change his position to look any further as a battered red Toyota hurtled down the street at the woman. Michael gasped as he closed his eyes; the car was right on top of her; there was no way she could get away. He heard a crunch of metal, and the screams came again, full of pain and fear. He heard the tyres of the Toyota lock and howl as the red truck came to a crooked halt. The driver blew the horn in a flurry as he sang his triumph out of the open window. Michael lifted his head once more; he saw a lanky man throw the Landcruiser's door open and slink out. He had a big shit-eating grin on his face as he approached the screaming woman who writhed in the street. The passenger door of the red Toyota opened, and a shorter squat man rushed over, his left hand holding the Akubra to his head as he did so.

'Ahh shit, Johnny, you messed her up,' the squat man said to the laughing lanky driver.

Johnny tilted his head back and laughed while the woman screamed and clutched at her twisted leg. She looked up at the two approaching men and started to back away from them. His hands were in the pockets of his jeans. His silky green dress shirt had pulled out at the back and was barely buttoned at the front to reveal his hairless chest. 'Aww, come on, she's okay.'

'You know the Shephard likes them clean, man. He won't be happy with a leg and her face all marked up like that.' The squat man was dressed in triple denim, dark jeans, light blue shirt and a black jacket. Michael imagined if he could get his Akubra fashioned from denim, he would have jumped at the chance. 'I ain't cleaning another one up for you man, this ones on you.'

'Billy, my friend, you worry too much,' the slick driver said as he walked up to the woman. He cut the distance she had made in a heartbeat. 'Look, she's still pretty nimble. I bet she ain't even hurt so bad.' As he said this, he pressed the sole of his leather boots onto the twisted leg of the woman and she howled in pain and strained under his boot. 'Come to think of it, maybe I hit her harder than I thought.'

'Aww shit, Johnny.' Billy shook his head as he turned away. He fixed his Akubra as he needed something to take his mind off the scene before him.

'Naww shit nothing, you grab her arms and I'll grab the good leg and well get her in the back, ready to go.'

As Michael watched the two men wrestle with the woman, he saw another ute drive past. The men inside laughed at Billy and Johnny as they struggled, but they didn't stop. The ute kept on up the lonely street to where Jack was lying unconscious. Michael swore and let his back slide up against the waiting room wall.

'Jack.' His heart pounded at the nape of his neck and threatened to leap right out of him. 'I need to get to Jack.'

JACK

'Pack my bag, and let's get moving
Cause I'm bound to drift awhile
Though I'm gone, gone
You don't have to worry
Long as I can see the light.'

Creedence Clearwater Revival – *Long as I can see the Light* (1970)

Everything ached his arms, neck, feet, and worst of all, his head. With every movement, his right cheek ate away at him as it tried to exact revenge on his body. The fire was in his blood, and though he never thought it possible, he could feel every ounce of blood move around his body as though it were an acid that was eating at him from the inside out. His eyes felt like stone, weathered and pitted by the years of wind and water that had coursed over its smooth façade. Their lids were sandpaper, moved by a craftsman who had worked tirelessly throughout his life to try and give the unforgiving substance some sort of shape. Each blink was the motion of his arm as it moved the sanding block back and forth. He felt that with each movement, more and more of him fell away to be collected and washed away through the night.

The only escape he had from the aches and pains of his body was to fall back inside of himself, to be alone. However, ever since he had pulled that damned rifle out of the wall, he had never been alone, not quite. He imagined he still sat in the cabin of his father's

Ford Fairlane; the vinyl leather interior smelled as new as it always had. Yet underneath the plush carpet and its glistening hide, there was a smell of rot. He knew what it was, what he had done, but part of him refused to believe it had been him. Where had he been when that had happened? Had he been at the forefront, the man behind the switches? Or had he been in the cockpit of that bloody car, his hands wrapped around the moulded and wrapped wheel while his forehead rested against the backs of his hands? His eyes shut to what happened through the windscreen.

He looked over to the glistening chrome of the radio and turned the volume knob. The light behind the channel listings began to glow and the speakers in the door crackled. He reached for the other knob yet it began to turn on its own. It scrolled and switched back, over and over again until finally the voice of Eric Bogle began to flow through, clearer than it should ever have been.

'So, they gave me a tin hat, and they gave me a gun.'

'And they marched me away to the war,' Jack mumbled to himself. A scowl spread across his face, the half-eaten waste of what it once was. He turned the rear-view mirror to himself and just stared while the song replayed over and over. He didn't know how long he had looked at his own reflection, but he had heard that same line four times by the time he blinked.

With each replaying of that damned song, he saw changes in himself. He saw the skin around the edges of the wound on his face turn red, then black. Then the darkness spread through his veins, it stretched up his face to his eyes, down his neck and across his chest. Like a spider's web, the lines traced across his flesh, the sickness coursed through his veins and gained ground with each heartbeat. But the thing that fascinated him more was his eyes. With each replaying, the whites became awash with specks of black, his pupils began to dilate, until finally there was nothing but black holes to stare back at him until he turned his head to look at something else.

He had wound the window down but had lasted only minutes before he was forced to wind the glass back up. It seemed when he sat inside the cab of the Fairlane, the words of the 'other' couldn't reach him. If it was that son of a bitch that had infected him when he picked up that Browning, then 'it' must have been driven mad in that wall for God knows how long because it itched for conversation. No matter how long the windows of the Fairlane remained tight in their rubber channels, the minute the seal was broken, it let slip to a nonstop barrage of questions and put-downs. But this time, he needed air, the smell of the rot overpowered him, but the worst part was he didn't know if the smell was from him or the three decaying corpses in the boot

'What is it with the boy?' Was the first question to hit his ears, almost a sneer as the words flowed in through the otherwise silent depths of his mind. No sooner had the first question ended than another and another were slung at him. *'Where are you taking us?'* Slightly louder this time. Then, *'How did it feel when you saw their bodies?'* Louder again, the voice rose from almost a whisper; with each step in volume, the words flowed faster and faster to keep pace.

Then the insults started. *'Fucking, pathetic weak piece of shit.'* Louder, faster. *'Kin slayer.' 'Bastard! Waste of time. You could be so much more.'* Faster and faster, the pitch was peaking now as the other roared the words at him. *'Should have squeezed the life out of that faggot brother of yours, that useless fucking scum that you're obsessed with!'*

The glass inside the frame of the door began to rattle on its runners, Jack had begun to have had enough of the insults and the threats.

'Next time I'm in control, I'll gut the fucking piglet and let you wake up just enough to see the blood drying on your hands.'

The window crawled upward, as if the 'other' sensed the time to be heard was close to an end, the words sped up again and rose to a higher pitch. The shrill tremor of the incessant hammering at his ears near drove him over the edge. His head throbbed and he couldn't bear to remain where he was. His hands went to his head as if there was a worm in there, that just crawled and grasped, each twitch was an agony that drove him closer to the brink.

With the Fairlane's window mere inches from the top, it rose to its final peak. *'You gutless fucking waste, such a strong man, but you can't protect him, in the end, I'll—'*

The window sealed finally to cut the words mid-sentence. Jack took a deep breath, then another. His hands still clamped to his face his eyes shut tight. The worm that writhed inside of his mind had finally stopped, as had the pain, the smell, everything.

'Thank fuck for peace and quiet,' he mumbled, as he let his hands fall to his lap. He allowed his shoulders to slump and the rear of his head to rest against the plush headrests. As he exhaled, he opened his eyes and his body clenched. His hands rose to his face, his knees slammed into the underside of the dash and the steering wheel.

His stomach turned into a knot as the corpse of his father drove his rotting fist through the windscreen in front of him.

The sound of flesh against glass, filled his world and then he felt shards of his protective barrier fall into his lap. The instant the status quo of the interior was broken, wind gust inside to throw shards of glass mixed with water, salt, shrubbery anything and everything into his face. He tried to take a breath, if only to scream but the rotting fingers, mostly bones closed around his throat. Again, the sense of being powerless that he associated with his father washed over him. He felt small, he felt insignificant. He felt as though Michael could lift him, push him, bully him and he could do nothing about it.

The thoughts all rushed through his mind as Tony Baker dragged his eldest son single-handed through the windscreen of his pride and joy.

Jack still struggled for air; the strength he had once possessed had now left him. It was his life or his sanity that would leave him next. Tony dragged him closer and closer. The flesh of his lips had rotted mostly away to expose the yellowed teeth and the receding gums. His body reflected the wounds that the Browning had given him. Racked from knee to neck, parts of him were gone altogether, like his entire right arm, which was reduced to a stump that came to a jagged end only inches past the armpit. His work clothes remained, mostly holey rags now that had been the first thing to be eaten by the bugs that had infiltrated his tomb. Bile and organs oozed from the holes in his chest, stomach and throat, but his eyes were perfect.

Jack expected them to be shrunken, or the sockets to be empty, but the eyes were that of a live man. The whites were brilliant, the pupils pinpricks of rage.

As his father's left hand lifted him upward the figure swelled, the rags tore away from the chest as it doubled in size. Jack was lifted higher and further away, as the girth of the arm grew at the same rate of the length. The head swelled, dried skin split to expose the skull beneath, old blood and puss ran down his forehead. Tony's jaw clacked as he tried to speak. The eyes darkened, the left hand dragged him closer. He tried to squirm to get out of the grip but he couldn't. The eyes were completely black now and were only inches from him, the smell of old guts and bloat consumed him. His father's forehead touched his own, the eyes level.

The voice shook through him like an earthquake.

'Choose your fucking weapon, you can't hide forever!'

Jack opened his eyes; he gasped and slammed the back of his head against the FJ to his back. The pain washed over him, the heaviness, the weakness. His heart pounded inside of him, and his head throbbed tremendously. He raised his hands, and the Browning came into his sight. The weight of it, the power of it. He spun his head around in both directions, but there was nothing. He fell to his side; he watched as the Browning's barrel stretched out and out and then clapped to the ground in a heavier heap than himself. He rolled onto it; the cool metal kissed his flaming cheek as he did so. He could smell the dirt and oil as one, the old rubber in the bitumen to his right and the fever inside of him. As he lifted himself off the ground, his arms trembled in the strain to hold his weight. His gut felt as though it was about to break loose, as if to spill everything inside of him out on the shoulder of the road. His heart slowed but near drove him insane with the constant thud, thud, thud which he heard in his ears and felt in his acidic veins.

When he got to his knees, he lifted the Browning from the roadside and placed the butt in the dirt. He put all of his weight on it as he gained his first foot, then the second. As he straightened up, a feeling of light-headedness came over him, and he reeled; his feet took short skipped steps as he tried to regain his balance. To his luck, he stumbled into the FJ to his side. The suspension groaned under his weight, and he clung to the car for dear life. He stood there for some time; he breathed heavily as he peered over its rust pitted roof. Even in the afternoon sun, the metal felt cool to his touch. Sweat poured out of every inch of him, and the hand that rested in front of his vision shook with every thud of his heart. In the distance, down the main road, he saw a red Landcruiser turn off and disappear down a side street.

'Michael,' he managed to say between rasped breaths. Where had he disappeared to? How long had it been? It didn't matter. He could tell from the look of the street something was wrong here and something in his gut reassured him. He was thankful at least he had so far earned a reprieve from the 'other' in the back of his head.

The last thing he needed was for that bastard to criticise every move he made.

He steadied himself on both legs, closed his eyes and took a deep breath. He welled up the strength in him, the little he had left. He felt his hands that twitched with each thud of his heart slowly settle and finally sit still. They became calm as they held the weight of the Browning easily across them. His pack was lighter on his shoulders and barely even touched his back. The straps still felt heavy, yet with each breath, the strain lightened as his chest swelled and his heart slowed. Jack opened his eyes; he felt four tonnes lighter and felt as though he could at least make it halfway down the road. His mind was on the Landcruiser, who was in it and could he overpower them to take the car off their hands. He took his first step, shaky, still too shaky. With more effort, he took in another barrel full of air and held it as he took his second step. Stronger, harder, he exhaled and felt phlegm rise from his lungs to catch in his throat. A cough racked him hard, but didn't slow his pace; his eyes were focused on the road ahead. As the coughs thundered through him, his vision waned slightly; he saw one road, then two, then three that swayed hard in front of him. He closed his eyes. Each leg mechanically stretched to lift his body, then thudded back to the earth below. He didn't know if it was his heart or the impact of his boot, but in his mind, each footstep was thunderous in the quiet town

His eyes were still shut, his mind on fire, yet it maintained its resolve.

'I don't need to choose my weapon,' he growled at no one as he picked up his pace. He felt lighter and each movement became easier. He opened his eyes, only one road; his vision seemed improved. The clarity, his ability to focus, everything came flooding back, even if it was for only a short time; that was all he needed. 'I am a fucking weapon.'

The streets were quiet, but not quiet enough. A four-wheel-drive droned its way down a street to his right, but he knew the Landcruiser was to his left. At first glance, the town looked abandoned. Houses that were fairly new stood silent, their doors opened either by force or left that way by careless tenants. Most cars sat quietly on the street, but the drone of the vehicle to his right unsettled him. To his left, he heard a shout and then laughter. There was more than one; he heard knocking like someone rapped their knuckles hard on the glass, then he heard glass break and a roar of anger.

This was his mark; they were to the left of him. If he could hear them, they couldn't be too far. He made his way to the house on his left. The lawn was overgrown, and even though he felt stronger, the grass weighed his feet down even further as he struggled to pull his weight through the green tangles. As he neared the side of the structure, he saw some things that concerned him. The household bins had been tipped over, and their contents were spilled over the concrete drive. Someone's hat jostled in the slight breeze; the looks of heavy use were evident in the sweat-stained felt lining. His foot landed on a small pamphlet; an image of a cross and a man nailed to it was printed as the letterhead. He lifted his foot. His footprint had marked the paper, but he could still read the message through the dirt:

'People Rejoice, The Lord has come again.
The Shephard is calling for his flock.
Be born again.
Join your brothers and sisters
In Tamworth.'

The breeze toyed with the edge of the pamphlet and then caught it. The paper was whisked from sight as the wind took it into the air. Jack scowled. He hated religious people. The only ones that sought help from the divine were the ones that weren't strong enough to help themselves. He had sat silently and pretended to pray while his mother made the family hold hands to say grace before dinner; he did that to survive. Tony's wrath came for a multitude of reasons. Honestly, he thought that any given excuse for Tony to hit either of his sons was more than enough. Michael at least, didn't need help to learn the lesson about being quiet during grace.

He continued around the side of the house, more belongings were scattered around the yard. A large gum stood in the corner of the small plot and towered into the sky, one large branch hung out over the yard. Jack stopped and looked at the sight before him.

In the yard was a ten foot crudely made cross that had been planted into the ground. From this distance, Jack could see the rough edges and the burs that waited to spear themselves into a man's flesh. A man had been nailed to it. Flies covered his face, the palms of his hands and his bare feet where the railway spikes had been driven through his flesh and into the hardwood below. His head was low to his chest; he was dead. A woman and her two children hung from the large bough of the gum only a few feet in front of him. Their faces were black, their hands bound behind their backs and their feet tied together. As the wind blew behind him, the children swayed slightly, and the branch groaned. From the looks on their faces, although they were all covered in flies, the people hung had died first. The man on the cross looked to have only died recently.

Red letters were painted on the side of the house, the paint ran in most places as if it were someone's blood splashed on the cladding: *I have been crucified with Christ and I no longer live. Christ lives within me.*

Jack stared at the bodies for some time. Sometimes, monsters don't need to be big or in danger to do atrocities. He thought perhaps every man had a devil inside of him. At the sight of these people, the children that hung from their throats, he became worried for

Michael. Who were these people that had destroyed this town?

'Now, son, it's okay. I ain't going to hurt you.'

Jack's hand tightened around the Browning's grip. The voice had come from the other side of the fence. Jack lowered himself, mindful of his own height and that of the timber mission brown fence. He took a few steps closer, the Browning high on his shoulder, at the ready.

'We just want you to come with us. You'll be safer with all of us.'

Jack peered through the cracks of the timber fence, being once more careful not to get too close if the man happened to see movement behind it. There was a balding man beyond the threshold, he had one hand outstretched to someone, while his other hand held his hat.

'That woman that kicked the glass out of the back of your car didn't seem too safe.' That was Michael's voice. Jack's breath caught in his chest, and his eyes widened. He wanted to sigh in relief, but he held his silence. His raw cheek twisted in on itself as the exposed muscles clenched.

'Aww, now that woman is a wanted criminal,' the man said with an all-knowing smile. 'You see, I'm a police officer.'

'You tried to run her over.' Michael's voice again. Jack needed to get over that fence, but he couldn't do it while the so-called police officer looked straight at it. Michael had his back to the fence while the lawman advanced toward him inch by inch. The Browning was out of the question; the sound of it would bring everyone down on him.

Fuck it, kill him. Let them come, let them all come. The voice started. *You don't know what happens when you don't use it. They come anyway. Kill the bald fuck.*

Jack shifted the rifle into his left hand and readied himself. Out on the street, he could hear another man yelling at the woman that

Michael had spoken about. On and on, he bitched about the glass.

Jack's brow furrowed, and the thought seared across his mind, *If that fucker doesn't shut up, I'll give him something to complain about.* The fever had started to flare up once more, and the sweat had started to course down his back. The aches and pains never left him, and they had begun to ebb away at his strength once more. He settled himself and watched the man take another step toward Michael; they were only a few feet to his left, not far from him now at all.

'That was only an accident, son.' The man took another step closer. Jack braced himself and prepared to rush when the man shrieked in pain and doubled over.

'Sorry, it was an accident,' Michael panted at him as he darted past. The lawman swore under his breath at the boy who had just sunk his boot into his groin. Jack raised his head so that his eyes breached the top of the fence; he saw Michael dart around the side of the house. Jack swelled with pride. The boy had grown up since they had left Chinchilla. A ghost of a smile came over his disfigured face, then vanished. About time.

The lawman still reeled in pain as he worked at something in the back of his pants.

'I'm going kill that little fucker.'

Jack's eyebrows raised, his fist clenched, and he lowered his head. In an explosion of timber fence palings, Jack went through the fence. He hadn't broken out into a run, yet the timber cracked around him and flew outwards as the dried planks gave way. The lawman spun, his eyes wide; the revolver in his hand came up but not fast enough. Jack came down on him with the butt of the Browning, all the force of the heavy rifle and Jack's force behind it was directed into the bridge of his nose. It cracked heavily as the steel butt plate drove through it. More than that, the plate kept going, driving the lawman's head backward with it as it went. When he hit the ground, he did so as a heap of lifeless meat. The butt of the rifle had driven the man's nose back into his face, and blood had exploded out of each nostril under the impact, leaving a mess of gore all over the front of the bald man's shirt. The explosion of force took everything that Jack had, and he stumbled forward with the blow. His feet became hooked under the fallen man's body, and he felt himself drop. He hit the ground with all the force that it had taken from him to explode through the fence. The air rushed out of him, and all of his strength went with it.

He tried to lift himself, but his arms had begun to fail him once more. He had managed to bring himself to his knees when the commotion had started on the street. Jack heard more glass break and another roar of anger from the man on the street. Except this time, his anger wasn't toward the woman they had apparently captured.

'Come here, you little shit,' he heard the man say as the sound of boots slapping on concrete drifted from up the street.

Jack tried to summon his strength again, but the walk into town and the king hit he had dealt the lawman had exhausted him. He used the Browning to help him clamber to his feet and ambled his way to the street. He heard the first gunshot by the time he had reached the curb. The shot echoed through the silent street.

The red Landcruiser was parked directly in front of the yard he had just left. It was parked with one wheel mounted on the curb; the others sat comfortably on the blacktop. Its rear window had been kicked out along with one of the rear side fixtures. There was a woman in the back whose eyes widened when she saw him. She had been gagged and bound, and she writhed against her restraints when she saw the badly battered Jack Baker. Jack left her without a word, his breathing heavy and his pace hastened with the echoing gunshot. Before he passed the front of the cab, he saw a chunk of concrete tile that had smashed the passenger's window. Shattered glass lay all over the passenger seat, and the chunk of concrete had marked the truck's centre console, only to come to rest in the driver's footwell.

Jack continued down the street in the direction of the gunshot. His footsteps felt heavy once more and every now and then his strength would flag and send him stumbling dangerously to the curb.

The voice in his head spoke up, *'Use it, kill with it, own it,'* and the idea didn't sound like a bad one to Jack.

As the second gunshot ripped through the silence of the street, Jack hoisted the butt of the Browning up. Another shot, and then another shot, then the distinct sound as a ricochet whirred through the air. He was getting close now. All he hoped for was that the boy hadn't worn one of those shots. Forty feet further down the street, a white four-wheel-drive took a wide turn into Jack's path; the tall tyres rolled on their rims as the speeding vehicle over steered poorly into the street. There was no hope for him to hide, and he was beyond it. With all of his strength being used to either walk or hold the heavy rifle up, the simple idea of squeezing the trigger sounded divine.

The driver of the four-wheel-drive locked up all four wheels at the sight of him and went into a slide. Jack remembered the whites of the passenger's eyes as he lifted his hands above his face to shield himself from what was coming. None of it mattered. The Browning cut through the light steel panels like the mills twelve foot saw through ironbark. Glass shattered, steam rose from the radiator, all the while the bolt worked tirelessly to feed the everlasting hunger of its open breech. Again and again, with each new round came the muzzle blast, the slight recoil and the fire-driven bullet ripping through chrome, metal, glass and flesh. Somewhere through the magazine, he was too tired to know exactly; he saw a splash of blood erupt onto the remains of the windscreen. As the four-wheel-drive still slid, it turned uncontrollably and clipped a parked car. The chassis groaned as the driver's tyres lifted. It continued to rise slowly as if time was suspended while the Browning continued to send fire and metal into the cabin. Finally, the momentum too great, the heavy car tipped onto its side and came to a grinding halt in the street. The Browning fell silent at about the same time; the echoes of its hellfire still rolled all around him. He let the empty magazine fall to the bitumen. It skittered across like a blade across ice as he fumbled with the rifle's weight and inserted a new magazine in its place.

The passenger of the car tried to crawl out through the shattered windscreen. Jack continued to advance as he did. He was more of a boy than a man, younger than Jack, but not by much. Blood coursed down his face from a gash, and when he coughed, blood sprayed on the bitumen underneath him. His hands were shredded, and he had lost one of his ears in the chaos. He looked up at Jack as he approached, he held one hand out once more as if to try and stop the inevitable. The Browning started up once more, the slow and methodical thump, thump, thump. The street was filled with fire and spitting metal as the wounded young man's body was sent into a fit of convulsions as his nervous system failed him. The Browning fell silent, only half of its magazine used in the last flurry of fire.

'JACK!' he heard Michael scream. He whirled around, too late. A man with long hair and a green shirt was on him. The heel of the man's revolver connected with his forehead and drove him back two steps. He could see the man's hooked nose and his thin lips twisted in a sneer. Jack tried to bring the Browning around, but it was too long for combat this close. The barrel slapped the man harmlessly in his side as he brought the revolver down once more. Jack tried to jerk his head at the last minute, but the hard handle glanced off his brow and continued. As the man's hand, the steel frame of the revolver, and a jewel-encrusted ring slid down Jack's face and across his disfigured cheek, pain exploded inside of him. He lost all of his strength at once and began to collapse, his head reeled as he went.

He saw Michael on the street, a look of horror on his face as his brother fell. He saw that Michael had a rock in his hand, and he ran toward them. Jack tried to tell him to stop, to run, to let him handle it but by the time he had hit the bitumen, he had already felt himself start to slide backwards in his mind.

The vision in front of him had become further away, with each blink, further and further. Still, Michael came for him. Finally, the vision went black. He felt soft vinyl leather underneath his back. The smell of freshly shampooed carpet. He heard a soft clunk as the Fairlane's door shut him inside and the thump as the locking indicator on the crest of the door shot down.

Deep inside of himself, deeper than he had ever been, he heard the raspy cackle of the other.

CHRIS

'You can listen to the engine
Moaning' out his one-note song.
You can think about the woman
Or the girl you knew the night before
But your thoughts will still be wandering
The way they always do.'

Bob Sega – *Turn the Page* (1973)

Dawn. Slithers of silver etched their way across the blackness. They worked through the perpetuity of existence like the veins of precious metal through rock. Although some loved to sit back and watch the splendour unfold before their own eyes, Chris hated this time of day. Especially in this instance. As the darkness faded and the glow of life and light surged from the east, tears ran down his dirty face like the rains of the north. The rest of the stars glinted, free to sparkle in the smoke-free sky of far southern Queensland. He yearned for her. All he had to remember her by were the stars in the sky and the rolling iron to his back. As he drove the straight roads through day and night, he always searched the skies and looked for the constellation in her eyes. He searched tirelessly for the faintest hint, the dream of being together, the dream of being alive.

The weariness of the past week had started to overcome him. Sleepless nights, the insanity that came with the lack of sleep, the constant straight roads, and the loss of her. With not a wink of sleep, the world looked different, felt different. Shades of light seemed to break in the air to reveal their crux; shadows twisted and intertwined their way through all. Their smothering cloaks shrouded the world. At times, he had sworn he had even seen the arms of the dead drag the darkness over the world in places. To claim their own rift in the world of the living, as long as the sun didn't touch them, they were free to corrupt, to spoil, to thrive.

But this had all been madness, the results of his desire. He couldn't afford to stop; he couldn't afford to fall asleep. With sleep brought the courtyard and the road past the gate. He couldn't bear to watch the people pass him any longer as he lay trapped in his sanctuary behind the veil and waited to see her hair as she walked on the road.

He opened his eyes. They burned from the tears and the weariness, and his head ached from the strain. She wasn't dead; she couldn't be. He had seen her in the smoke of Brisbane, at least at first. He had seen the gold behind the grey and knew he was close. The only question stood. Would the young soldier help him find her or not?

'Who the fuck is Angie?' Rankin had asked. Such a simple question, but how could a man such as him even begin to answer it? Below the tears that ensued after the question, he began to laugh. While Rankin stood by smoking, his anger was whittled away by Chris' response. Chris sat there and laughed into his ravaged hands while the tears poured from their reservoirs.

'Why do you think art exists?' Chris asked him as he raised his face from his damp palms. He took a deep breath to settle himself. 'Why do you think the first brush of paint was ever put to canvas or the first key ever struck of a symphony?'

Rankin was visibly at a loss. Chris gave him a moment as the ground around them slowly became clearer. The young soldier, still half-naked in the coolness of the morning, approached him and slowly, with a considerable ache in his battered body, slunk to the ground beside him. Even in the faint light, his flesh erupted in ripples and lumps as his back touched the cool steel of the Holden.

The two men sat there and watched as the sky's colour shifted to a bronze. Rankin lit another cigarette; the burning ember reflected the power of the sky. 'I've never been much for words.' He sighed as he exhaled his first drag.

'Neither were the artists,' Chris groaned as he fought the tears and sobs in his throat. 'How can I describe to you what she is to me? Words don't do enough.' He placed his face into his palms again, the rough skin scratched at his face, and they pained as the raw skin dragged across the steel wool of his beard.

'She's your wife?' Rankin asked as his head thudded softly against Pestilence's side.

'That,' he sobbed and lifted his face to look at the horizon, 'And so much more.' The tears in his eyes refracted the light and it looked as though beams shone through the sky. They reached outward as if to warn the arms of the dead that the cover of darkness and grief was at an end. The day was here and the time for stargazing was gone.

Rankin gave a soft laugh beside him as he took another drag of his cigarette and let the smoke list out of his mouth. It rolled around his face then slowly faded as it was sucked below the chassis rails of the Holden. 'It's got territory plates,' he said, gesturing to Pestilence.

Chris nodded. 'That's where we live.' He paused, then corrected himself. 'Lived.'

He didn't like to think back on the events of the past weeks, especially the events in Darwin. Yet he had dragged this boy into his problems, and he figured that he owed him an explanation.

'I was there when they landed.' He spoke softly, his eyes unfocused as he stared at the dirt on the shoulder. He watched as each pebble, each piece of grit, cast its own shadow as the sun finally peeked its head above the horizon. 'I was in town; it all happened so fast. But when I got back, she was gone, and the house was burning.' He lifted his arms to reflect this statement. 'Everything burned. Everything.'

He remained silent for a while, trying to settle himself once more as the thoughts had put rise to another well of tears. His face contorted as he tried to fight them back, but the tears began to flow just as hard as before, and he was racked by sobs of pain and weariness.

Rankin sat silently by his side. Chris somewhat appreciated this. No words could fix anything; no words ever could. He didn't need sympathy or the false pity offered by people he didn't even know. He just needed her.

'They took her, those sons of bitches. They took her.' He spoke through sobs and sniffs. Even his nose had begun to run, not wanting to be outdone by his eyes. Rankin had turned his gaze from the horizon and now looked at him. Was he judging him?

'You've followed them all the way from Darwin?' he asked, his eyes narrowed.

Chris nodded and patted the front tyre of Pestilence. 'We have. Pestilence and I, that is.'

'Pestilence?'

Chris laughed, the sound choked by his sob again. 'Yeah, that was her name for it. The Holden.' His face screwed up again, but the tears had run dry. 'She said that the amount of money I put into this thing would make it a pestilence on the household. So, it's kind of stuck.'

Rankin laughed. 'Yeah, wheels and women. They always give you trouble.' He had turned to watch the sun's progress again, his face solemn and dark in its own right. The sun's progress had cast shadows over his eyes, shielded by his brow and the angle of his head.

'We followed them as they butchered their way through town after town, killing and burning, then moving on. They're fast, too, unresting. Always moving on as soon as the destruction is finished. But in each town, they would leave behind a contingent to strip all the supplies and fuel they could find unburned while the column moved on. We ambush these contingents.'

'Yeah, that much I know,' Rankin mumbled.

'And I question them.'

Rankin looked at him again, his eyes squinted once more. 'Do you get anything out of them?'

'Well, they led me here.' Chris sighed. He pulled his wallet out from under his ass and opened the worn, cracked leather, revealing her photo. 'I show them this and demand to know where she is, but not many speak English; I kill those that don't. The ones that make the mistake of speaking the odd word, I persuade.'

He felt Rankin lean across to look at the photo behind the dirty plastic sleeve. He whistled as he saw her in all her beauty. Even behind the shit yellowing plastic, she was everything.

'So, you think they have her, that they've brought her down with them from Darwin?' Rankin asked. Chris could feel eyes burn into the side of his head while he continued to look at her likeness.

Chris turned his face so that they were eye to eye. The soldier's thousand-yard stare into the red bleariness of his own. 'I know. I don't think.'

The two men held eye contact for some time. Rankin's face twisted as the blankness of his eyes was encapsulated by the shadows that they were cast under. He seemed to look into Chris; he could feel his breath on his face. They were that close. Finally, Rankin spoke. 'You'll follow them south each day?'

'Each day. I'll follow them, and I'll run them down until I get back to her. Each night I'll drive closer and get closer.'

Rankin turned away. His cigarette had burned down to the butt, and it smouldered there in his hand, dangerously close to his fingers. He flicked the butt and chuckled as he raised himself from the ground. 'And I thought I had woman problems.' He began to walk toward the horizon as he stretched his arms out to allow the sun to soak into his exposed skin. He began to laugh again. 'Fuck me drunk. Out of the frying pan, into the fucking fridge. Then into the fire, then thrown under the coals. What next?' he complained. He turned back to Chris as he shook his head. 'How long do you think you're going to last riding on these bastards' coat-tails?' He gestured with his thumb over his shoulder.

Chris continued to look up at him; the increasing daylight burned into his tired eyes. He was just so tired, but it didn't matter. None of it did. 'As long as I have to.'

Rankin sneered. 'Yeah, how did I know you'd say that?' His hands went to his hips, and he looked down on Chris like a disappointed parent.

Chris stood up. He was an old man to the soldier. He wasn't anywhere near as strong, but he had something that everyone wanted. Chris took a step toward him. Rankin didn't flinch, although Chris had tried to make himself intimidating. 'I'm not asking for sympathy from you; I'm heading south to kill Chinese and find my wife. If you want to come, then come; if not,' Chris hardened his face and gestured his thumb over his shoulder. 'Then fuck off back to Brisbane and go back under the rock you crawled out from.'

Rankin held his sneer; his hands were still on his hips as the men of similar height stood toe to toe. He never broke his eye contact as he spoke back calmly. 'Three shots left in a revolver, a knife from last century and Frankenstein's ute. Forgive me if I have my doubts.'

Chris continued his stare into the blank eyes of the younger man. His eyes had finally cleared, and he was beginning to feel like his old self once more. He shook his head and tutted. 'Negativity, negativity. Just pop into the next town, and we'll find something. Although I'm strapped for cash, what's the credit rating like for Aussie soldiers these days?'

He kept his face straight as long as he could. Then his lips began to work, and then the silent highway was filled with the sound of his laughter. Through his laughter, he saw Rankin look at him. The sneer on his face vanished, then as he started to shake his head, he began to laugh as well. Chris watched as Rankin turned his back on him; he walked partway down the Highway and spat. His laughter had ended when he had turned. He stood there, overlooking the road in front, the hills that rolled away in front of them. The town was only just visible in the early light, but Rankin's eyes weren't on the town; his attention was down and off the shoulder. His eyes were fixed on something below that Chris couldn't see.

Chris stopped laughing and moved to his side. He felt older with each step he took as the sound of the dirt grinding beneath his boots filled his ears. He reached Rankin's side and saw the hatred on his face. His eyes never changed from that blank stare, but all the expression came from his mouth. Chris turned and followed his gaze. 'Each day,' he said while his own face twisted at the sight below him, 'Is another day to find her. I have to find her.'

His gut turned, and his heart sunk.

Below the highway was a river that ran inland. The shoulder dropped off beyond their feet and rolled down a rocky hill to the bank. A bus had been run off the road and its body lay twisted and torn, partially submerged in the river. Chris could see bodies of the poor people that had never made it out of the bus. Through one of the broken side windows, he watched as the water's current tugged at the arm of such a person. The skin was pale and lifeless as the gushes of water encouraged it to rise and fall. Just beyond it in the shallows was the face of a girl. Her face shone white as the water rushed over her. Her eyes were wide, unblinking, but they seemed to stare at him. Angry, yet distorted by the shallow water that covered them. Her hair flowed with the current; it swished back and forth with the water as it coursed through the destroyed body of the bus.

Outside of the vehicle were the bodies of twenty or so people. Men, women and children were spread sporadically across the bank. Some were clumped together; their arms covered each other as they tried to climb the bank or escape down the river. The water ran red, stained by the blood of the people that littered its bank. It lapped at their heels as if to beckon them to become lost in its rills. Chris looked just beyond where he stood and saw a glint of brass. The shell casings had rolled down the bank as they had been fired and one that had caught on a small pebble was visible before him. They had fired from where he and Rankin stood. Rained bullets down on them as they tried to escape, the women and children alike.

They stood there for some time, silent. A small surge from the river lapped higher than usual and washed over a cluster of people low on the bank. They watched as a toy bear was pulled from a girl's arms, its brown fur matted with the life of its owner that had held it so close. The bear sunk slightly under the power of the current, then rose to the surface once more; its face bobbed as if it tried to gasp a final breath. The blood from its owner washed out of its fur as it travelled, and it left its own trail of memory in each of their minds as it was carried down the river and out of their sight.

'I'll help you,' Rankin said low next to him. His face was sullen, his eyes covered in shadow. 'I'll help you find her.'

Chris nodded and lowered his head once more. He closed his eyes and thought of her face. *We're coming babe,* he thought to himself. *Even if I have to gut my way through the whole army. Nothing will stop me from getting to you.*

He felt a hand clamp down on the back of his neck and squeeze. 'Come on,' Rankin said to him softly. 'Let them be.'

The two men turned and headed back to Pestilence; they walked in silence, their heads hung low. Chris watched as his boots scuffed at the dirt shoulder and sent small puffs of dust into the air as he walked. What he wouldn't give to be back in Darwin, to be back in the heat and for this to have never happened. He fell into his thoughts, and his mind rolled on. What anyone would give. He imagined the people in the ditch behind him would have had similar thoughts. What did anyone think when they saw it coming? Would they know that this breath, whatever they just saw, whatever they smelt or felt, would be it for them? Would they appreciate it more? Would they be awed by how the leaves broke from the branches and floated through the air? As they worked their final flight to the ground, where they would decompose and begin again. Would the movement of the insects below their feet, the ones that would eventually feast on their flesh, have any significance to them at that point?

Birds sang in the trees behind him, and the river continued to flow. The world never stopped turning at the death of a man, nor a woman or child. Even in the exact proximity, the earth and nature did not mourn. Everything in this world fed on each other. The humans killed each other and everything else, either to conquer, brag, feed or survive. The scavengers eat whatever is left, and the earth takes the rest. In the end, the earth will claim everything and survive those that walk it.

The chrome that was left of Pestilence's front end glinted in the morning sun. It, too, looked hungry. Blood caked the railway iron and the bonnet. Streaks made by the hands of those pulled under it in the skirmish's past ran snakes of red across the pale white of its paint. One smeared hand print stood proudly on the driver's side, each digit visible over the dirt and road grime that caked the guard. Then, as the owner's body was pulled under, it smeared faintly toward the front end and the death that awaited it.

'We will need to resupply and rearm before long.' Rankin's voice was factual and back to business. He was along the back of the tray and rummaged through the odds and ends that Chris had stored there. Chris opened the driver's door and turned the key in the ignition to 'ON'. The pump whirred below the chassis; it free spooled at first, then groaned as the pressure built up. He turned the key. The engine turned over once, twice, then fired with a roar of power and idled humbly.

'We will find everything we need further down the road,' Chris shouted over the sound of the exhaust. Rankin looked at him over the flask of water he emptied. The water ran down his throat and chest; it pooled in his naval before it continued to his belt. 'And for Christ's sake, we need to find you some clothes while we are at it.'

EPILOGUE

EDGAR

"The time and the tears went by, and I collected dust
For there were many things I didn't know.
When Daddy went away, he said "Try to be a man
And someday you'll understand."

Creedence Clearwater Revival – *Someday Never Comes* (1972)

Darkness. Pure and utter darkness. Well, mostly. The large thunderstorm front swelled over the mountain ranges in the distance and although Edgar couldn't see its progress, the rolling thunder was a precursor for what was to surely come. Large streaks of lightning etched their way across the mountain peaks, illuminated their bulk as they stood guardian over the Peel Valley and the damned city which he had come to hate. He sighed as he strained his ears to listen for any activity, anything, anywhere, that might foil his plan but there was nothing. As far as the old nursery rhyme was concerned for Tamworth at least, there was not a creature stirring, not even a mouse. If there was ever going to be a time, it was going to be now. He swallowed even though his mouth was dry and his Adam's apple lurched in his throat. He took one last glimpse at the wondrous, toxic landscape and turned his back on it, for what he hoped was the final time.

Lucy stirred as he walked into their bedroom, sound asleep after her days labour. It felt cruel to wake her, but hopefully one day she would understand. When he placed his hand on her cheek, her eyes opened. Those beautiful brown droplets, that reflected her concern the second she looked at him.

'It's time.' He breathed with certainty. 'Get Joe and don't turn on any lights.'

'I know,' she replied, 'but... are you sure?' Questioning him, again.

He clenched his jaw as he removed his hand from her cheek, frightened he might not be able to restrain himself. 'Yes, I'm sure,' he whispered in the harshest tone he could muster. 'Now, would you just get your act together?'

She looked hurt at that. Of course she did. It didn't take long for the pangs of regret to soak into his spine. He'd apologise when they were moving, when he knew they were safe, but not before.

It took her five minutes; time that he had allowed for, but it felt like it passed in hours. Every second he seemed to check his watch, and glance over the mountain peak that loomed through the window, as if expecting the sun to illuminate their peaks. But it didn't happen, only the odd streak of lightning coursed across the sky. Exactly what he needed.

'I'm ready,' she said and he hushed her.

'We need to be quiet,' he grumbled, fighting to soften the sharp edge in his tone. 'Is Joe asleep?'

'For now,' she said after a quick inspection. The hurt now showing in her voice as well as her eyes.

Edgar sighed again. 'Okay. Quickly and quietly. If we see anyone, do not talk to them.'

'Okay Eddy.'

Edgar took his wife by the hand and led her into the night, leaving everything they had made behind.

Everything they had made, he thought as their shoes softly padded the cold grass and Joe stirred in his wife's arms, *all based on the bullshit of a deranged man.* When they had first come to Tamworth, it had seemed like a godsend. A free society operating outside of the Chinese oppressors and the Australians. At first, the idea seemed a little too communist for his own tastes, but one couldn't argue with the results. Everyone worked if they were able, which was okay. Everyone ate and was given the same rationing. That was even better, as there was ample crop and boundless cattle to be slaughtered. There was organisation and there was structure, something that Edgar had always excelled with. He wasn't proud enough to say that he didn't like being told what to do; in his opinion, it was a relief. Someone had already done the hard thinking, and he had no problem being a pawn on the chessboard. Especially when it looked as though he was on the winning side. But now? Only time would tell.

The day the Chinese marched into Tamworth was a day he would never forget. However, "march" seemed like the wrong word. Half-starved, weary and for all intents and purposes, cut off from their main battle group, this "Western contingent" as Shepherd had dubbed them, had barely crawled into town. Even the only remaining vehicle they had managed to muster, a lone assault tank, didn't even make it past the city limits before it had drawn a final breath and quit, lacking the fuel to drag itself forward. The Chinese had fought for barely ten minutes before, the sheer numbers of Shepherd's district of Tamworth, overpowered them.

Even Edgar had played his part, like any good pawn could. He had lain in wait, as the Chinese ambled past. Some of the stronger few helped the others, who looked as though they didn't even have the strength to walk on their own anymore. Nothing about them struck Edgar as intimidating. Maybe that was why he had managed the courage to stand up to them at that point. He sure as the hell didn't have the spine to stand against them at Brisbane, and good thing too. If he was seeing Chinese in Tamworth, it meant that any Brisbane defensive was long gone, he figured most of the men along with it.

When enough of them had made it into the city, the bell in the old St Andrews Church began to chime. As if calling the parishioners to sermon, the tolling was the queue for the rout to begin. At its sound, Edgar, along with the twenty-odd men and women he had lain in wait with, had picked up his weapon and headed out to the street. In Edgar's case, his weapon had been a pick axe, meant for working fields, not breaking skulls. He had liked the weight of it in his hands as he ran to break the ground between his hiding place and the horde of Chinese.

Bunched together like they were, the already broken men failed to bring up a firing line. The odd soldier in the mass fired into the rushing nationals and people fell, but not enough. Once the nationals were in pick swinging distance of the soldiers, it was over. They just didn't realise it. Edgar still remembered the first man he had hit. The man had stood, leaning heavily on the solider next to him, his arm around the shoulders of the man. He stood there looking at Edgar as he ran, his mouth open in exhaustion rather than disbelief. He didn't even raise his hand to defend himself when the pick spike came down on him. The blow tore him from the arms of the man who had been helping him and was enough to topple both. The spike had driven itself down through the top of his skull through the roof of his mouth and had broken the yellowed teeth at the forefront of his lower jaw. Edgar remembered the way his eyes had bulged out of their sockets with the impact. Worse yet, the spike had become jammed and the dead weight of the man at the end of the implement, although not considerable, had taken seconds to dislodge. Seconds that had passed like hours as the carnage spread around him.

These weren't soldiers, he remembered thinking after the battle was won. *They were closer to refugees.* That hadn't stopped him stoving in the heads of six of them. The scene had been gruesome and the smell of the mass graves that had come later had been worse, like a living nightmare. One that had made the days just as unbearable as the nights. But none of it mattered now, none of it even mattered back then, it had just been another fresh wound. Like a child who had skinned their knee, they never thought about the times they had done it before, or in his case, what he had seen and what he had known before that day. This was the freshest of all horrors and that was what kept him up at nights. Perhaps it was that, that had led him to where he stood now, with his family ready to flee.

The work continued after their victory; there was barely even a day's respite before Shepherd's men had started to gather his herd, or his "flock" as Shepherd liked to call them. Except now there were more workers than there had been before the fighting, or the slaughter. Although many Chinese had fallen victim to the farm implements of the flock, many more surrendered. Those that were able enough, worked. Those that weren't, weren't. As far as Edgar knew, they may as well have ceased being altogether, but talk like that never got a man far, so he kept it to himself. If it hadn't been the smell of the mass graves of the Chinese refugees, that had sparked this man into action. The suggestion of them being slaughtered for the amusement of the flock had been more than enough. Further insult was inflicted as Edgar had silently laboured under the watchful eye of the armed few. He witnessed crucifixes being made in plain sight. Not small, wall hanging signs of devotion, but heavy, hardwood crosses that stood fifteen feet tall with bracings to ensure they could hold weight. Edgar had never seen them put on display, but men had a way of talking when the guards were not around. If the sights and the suggestions were not enough, the ache in his heart for the mock blasphemy that was occurring made him sick to his soul.

Whether he liked it or not, Edgar had more and more to do with the Chinese survivors, prisoners, condemned, he didn't know the word to use for them. It seemed to change from day to day as more of Shepherd's plan was unfolded. At first prisoners, now at this stage in his plan, they were labourers, if there was a difference. Edgar seemed to remember stories of how Polish prisoners of war were put to work to feed the ever-starving Nazi war machine, and that was barely thirty years ago.

'How history repeats,' he had laughed a dry, humourless cough when it had occurred. 'How history repeats.'

If there was ever fate in this life, it had led every man to their role. Before the conflict, Edgar had been one of the most devout. He had done what had been expected of him, and when a sudden lapse in his faith and tradition had led Lucy to become pregnant, he had done his duty and had wedded her, without a shotgun being needed. Whether duty and fate knew each other was to be considered, or perhaps they were opposing blades of the same sword. The thought had crossed his mind more than once. It had been duty that had led him to marry Lucy, to be a doting father to Joe and when it had all gone to hell in a handbasket, it had been duty to his family that had led him to Tamworth. Fleeing their home in Brisbane as the many trucks and the fewer tanks rolled the other way. If it was duty that had landed him in this mess, it was fate that put him to work on Shepherd's grand design.

Of all the things to build, in all the times of the world and a nation under invasion, what looked to be an arena was being constructed. Men talked as they worked, Edgar wasn't one of them, but if he didn't talk, he listened. Some talked of it being the flocks reward for defending the free state of Tamworth. Others told stories about a giant of a man that was felled in Kootingal, a town not unlike the place where Edgar and his family were "liberated," once again the word choice seemed shaky. In fact, a lot of talk had been about that giant in one way or another. Many talked about the rifle he carried, and what had become of the man who had tried to claim it. But more importantly, to Edgar's life at least, they had talked about another pair, two that had come into town in a shaky state, in a hotted-up Holden Ute.

'The thing was in bad nick, but you could see it had some good power,' one of the countless workers had said. 'I helped fat Billy take it to the lock up down off Calala.' This pricked at Edgar's ears. 'Never knew they had so many cars there, good ones too, runners mostly.' The ever so courteous worker had elaborated. Sure enough, the lock up had contained many runners, including one such car that he was relieved of upon his liberation.

The washed out bluey green EH sat exactly where it had sat the few times he had taken the long way home from the worksite out on the Sydney road. The lock up was placed far enough out of town so not be easily watched and the route South to Sydney, to what Edgar thought of as Australia, led away from the city centre, not toward. Although the lock up did have a guard, Edgar felt sure enough of himself after the events with the Chinese, to deal with the old blighter that had been left to watch over Shephard's rag tag fleet. In the few times that Edgar had walked past the lock up and had seen his old EH wagon sitting almost forgotten among the other family sedans, the yard had been lively with working men. Not interested in the old EH, the men focused their attention on the large, squared body Internationals that looked as though they had been likewise liberated, not from civilians but from the lacklustre mobilisation of the Australian Military.

Work-hours for the liberated Australians on the arena had been long slogs, until the Chinese prisoners had bolstered their numbers. Day after day, Edgar found himself being able to leave earlier and earlier, to take the long walk home rather than the organised truck shuttles to and from the town centre. The same wasn't so for the mechanics, and one day when Edgar dragged his feet past the mesh wire that made up the boundary of the lock up, he heard one of the mechanics complaining from beneath a battered Landcruiser.

'It's alright for Jonathon to tell us what to do, being one of the top dog's boys and all. But Christ, I am sick to tears of that bastard.'

There was apparently general consensus on this.

'Now Tommy,' the fat, balding man Edgar had pegged to be the one night guard had said, 'You can grumble your bitterness all you like here; you know I don't care. But you better watch your tongue in that bar that you boys frequent, or you're apt to lose it.'

'Wish you'd lose your tongue, you fat bastard,' Tommy snarled back from beneath the Landcruiser, to the laughter of the other mechanics. 'The way you flap your gums I thought it might fall right out.'

The old man had gone red in the face and had walked off muttering something about the young men of today not respecting their elders. Edgar didn't care. The fat man had said enough for him. Sure enough, a further walk, one well after dark, had taken him past the doors of the Tamworth Hotel. Not being one of Shepherd's top working men, he wasn't allowed in but nevertheless, he could see through the windows well enough to spot grease covered men, well into their drink. Night after night, this was the case and although Edgar had no reason to believe that the lock up was apt to be unmanned this particular night, he was desperate and willing to take a gamble.

Sure enough, as the rain started to patter down and Joe stirred again restlessly in his mother's arms, the lock up looked as dormant as could be. The only problem was that the large main gates were chained shut.

'God damn it,' he muttered as he gave the gate a shake.

'What's wrong?' Lucy questioned him as she shifted Joe in her arms.

'Shut your mouth woman!' he snapped, too loud and then swore again at his slip in temper. There was another thing he would have to apologise for later. He clenched his fists and jammed them into his pockets so that they wouldn't wander anywhere they shouldn't and looked around. There was no way he could get her over the fence, not with the child. He could leave her out here while he took care of business, but if someone drove past and saw a woman holding a child in her hands, questions were sure to be asked.

'There.' He pointed to a shrub. 'You take Joe and go sit behind that bush. If a car comes, you duck down real low and don't be seen, okay?'

'Where are you going?'

He quickly jammed his hands back into his pocket. 'To get our car back. You just go wait and when I bring the car around, be ready to get in. Don't mess about.'

When she was on her way, he turned back to the gate. Fate and duty petered through his mind again as he wondered which to blame, if not for bad luck, for him to have wound up with such a half-wit for a wife. He took off his coat and threw it over the barbed wire upper, muttering to himself as he proceeded. The weeks of labour had kept him fit enough and clearing the gate came easily enough for him, although the coat tore as he retrieved it. More bad luck. Despite the racket he had thought them to have made, the lock up remained quiet.

He slunk over to the EH, popped the driver's door and hopped inside. His hands went straight to the ignition. From years of having owned the Holden, he didn't need to look. When his hand groped for the key, it didn't find it. When he flipped down the visor, nothing fell into his lap. His jaw clenched as his fists closed around the steering wheel. More bad luck.

He sat in the car for a minute, at least. The time that he had wanted to be on the road had come and gone. The rain had come in heavier and heavier over the passing seconds as he thought about what to do.

His thick-skulled wife was sitting on the road shoulder, in the rain, no doubt dreaming up all the different ways in which she was going to berate him about his decisions. Meanwhile, he sat in his old trusty car, with no god beloved key to start the son of a whore. He took a deep breath and stepped back out into the rain.

It wasn't far to the office, the building itself sat dark and quiet. He turned the knob to the heavy, metal lined door and breathed a sigh of relief when it turned. If it hadn't, then that would've been the end of it, for better or worse. He stepped inside and closed the door quietly behind him. The sound of the heavy rain took on a new noise in the solid structure, as it panged off the iron roof. The sound of his footfalls were easily hidden beneath the sound of it. He poked his head around, trying to make heads or tails of the layout of the building. The old, iron roof, allowed a few beams of light to penetrate through old screw holes and they cast themselves down over the floor, like beams of light from the heavens. A few cars, a beat-up Holden utility and a truck that had half of its front end removed, loomed in the darkness off to his left. Smells of oils and old grease affronted his senses as he gently pawed his feet forward in the dark. The office, where he assumed the keys to his trusty old station wagon were, lay to his right, the door closed against the pungent aroma of the workshop. Once again, he tried the door handle and found that it was unlocked.

The door groaned as he pushed it open. Being a building inside a structure, no further light penetrated into its depths and Edgar had to pause in the open doorway to allow his eyes to further adjust to the darkness. Eventually, as he made his way in, the layout of the office became clear to him. The fat night watchman, ever vigilant in his duty, lay asleep in the cot across from the door. He snorted and scratched at his crotch as Edgar edged further in. He paused in anticipation of the fat man waking, with his fists poised above his head, ready to pummel the man if need be. The guard snorted again, tossed in his cot and continued to snore heavily.

Edgar sighed in relief as he cast his eyes around the office again. Papers and rubbish littered the desk, among other things. He slipped open draw after draw, to find nothing but more papers and old receipt books while behind him, the fat man continued to snore heartily. The stress pounded away at Edgar, as his heart fluttered a tremolo in his chest, space after space left him searching for the next place a key could be. In his frustration, he pulled a draw open too vigorously and some of the papers spilled over onto the floor. The small hairs on the back of his neck stood up on end as the guard snorted behind him again and Edgar froze as he turned his attention away from the desk, but the guard didn't wake.

Again, Edgar sighed as he turned back to the desk and spied a small metal cabinet positioned up on the wall near the office door. Quickly and quietly, he went to it. When he opened it, countless keys glinted out at him, all of them hanging neatly from small pegs. One small win. The challenge he now faced was to find the key he needed in the dark. Row after row, he strained to look at keys and the small tags that were attached to them, registration numbers barely visible in the low light.

AE:1949, BF:186, CH:202; he made out the initials and the numbers. Knowing his own rego number and what it meant, he could only imagine the story behind the plates. 1949, was no doubt the birthyear of whoever AE was. 186 and 202 were probably engine models, some of his own friends had selected their initials and the engine numbers of whatever rod they were driving at that time. Not being so imaginative, Edgar had selected his initials and the numbers that represented his favourite bible verse. *Proverbs 3:5, Trust in the LORD with all your heart and lean not on your own understanding.* Unfortunately, with the addition of 35, there were still not enough digits for the clerk, so he added some zeros to either side.

Eventually, after endless squinting and a pause to rub at his weary eyes, he found the key. ER:0350. He blinked and stared down at the key in his hand again, as if in disbelief that he had actually found it. ER:0350, he read it again, so focused on the key in his hand that he hadn't realised that the guard had stopped snoring until his hands fell down on his shoulders.

Edgar roared in his fright as he flung his arms up in the air, spilling keys from the cabinet everywhere.

'Who the fuck?' the old man panted in his ear as he tried to overpower Edgar in a rapid takedown. The fat man did catch Edgar off-guard, but it mattered little. He failed to bring Edgar down in his rapid assault and the two ended up locked in a struggle in the doorway of the dark office. It didn't take long for the overweight guard to begin panting and soon the strength in his struggle began to fail. When one of his arms was freed, Edgar lashed out with the only thing he had in his hand, the car key.

The fat man wailed as Edgar raked the key across the place he thought his eyes to be. The fight went out of the man as he gasped, clutched at his chest and promptly fell heavily to the floor.

'It's fate!' Edgar gasped as he fought to regain his own breath. 'God hasn't left me.' As if there was God in the heart attack of a fat old man, but Edgar was too elated to see anything but. He trusted not in his own understanding, but the knowledge and actions of his God. His eyes fully adjusted to the darkness now, he left the office at a run, to burst out into the fresh open air and the hammering rain.

Edgar didn't even notice the wet seat of the Holden as he threw his weight behind the wheel, not even caring that he had left the door open in the pouring rain. He rammed the key into the ignition as he pushed the clutch and pumped the throttle. The sound the red motor made as it turned over, wasn't audible over the pounding of the rain and Edgar only knew it had caught by the vibrations it made as it came to life. Elated again in small victories, he slammed his door closed as he pushed the car forward. Cold, and after obviously sitting for some time, the EH stalled. However, as he knew it would, with God looking out for him, it started again first go and this time he gave it more love as he urged it forward.

There wasn't much ground in the yard, and he had barely picked up enough speed to outpace a walking man when he crashed into the gate. The speed washed out of the Holdens crawl and again the motor stalled. The smile never faltered on his face as Edgar turned the key again and the Holden started once more. This time he reversed, giving the throttle plenty of love as he first brought the Holden back and then surged it forward to hammer at the gate. This time, when the bull nosed EH hit the gate, the chain broke and both sides swung open freely in the night. He screamed in joy as the nose of the Holden bucked and came around to where he knew Lucy was waiting for him. He changed into second as the old station wagon lurched and bucked with his sloppy gear change.

Lightning erupted over the town centre and cast light down over the land below, illuminating his wife as she stood next to the shrub. The thought crossed his mind, with a slight pang of anger, that he had told her to stay hidden. But he was just too damned happy for something small like that to get him down. Even when he opened the door and the wailing of little Joe drifted in, the smile only half faltered on his face. Hell, it didn't matter. The kid could bawl all he liked in the car; no one would hear anything over this storm.

Lucy slammed her door shut and Edgar revved the sewing machine motor, bringing the old girl up to speed. He dared not turn on his lights until they were at least beyond the arena work site, and so travel remained slow enough. The rain offered excellent cover for the bluey green wagon, but was horrifically detrimental to his vision. Even when the heavenly father cast lightning down across the land again, it offered barely a fraction of a second worth of respite, but Edgar didn't care. He leaned over the steering wheel, smiling an almost psychotic grin as he motioned the old car through its paces. It wasn't long before they passed the looming site of the new arena, the big shipping container doors that marked its entry and the looming concrete pillars that sat like Stone Henge in its centre. A shiver ran up Edgar's spine as they passed, but he remained silent as he shifted the EH into third and let the car pick up some more speed.

It wasn't until lightning struck again that Lucy spoke. Joe had calmed down enough by then so that she didn't have to yell to be heard.

'What is that on your hands?'

'What?' he asked as he glanced away from the road. His hands were clenched in a white knuckled grip on the steering wheel. A red smear traced across the back of his fists and ran down his wrist, to disappear beneath the cuffs of his shirt. 'Oh,' he said as he wiped them one by one across the breast of his coat. 'I must have cut myself climbing the fence.' For all he knew, that was the truth. He didn't think the Holden key could have cut the guards face, nor in the end did he care. He was doing God's work.

Now that he had escaped Tamworth, he thumbed the light switch and felt the strain on his eyes dissipate somewhat as his visibility improved. He allowed himself to sit back in his chair as the Holden did its work and he thought back to how they had managed to get themselves into this mess in the first place. Leaving Brisbane had been an easy choice. With the Army moving in, it was time for the civilians to move out. Hell, the Chinese shelling was enough to make his mind up. He remembered getting the rear wheel of the Holden stuck in a shell crater in the middle of the street as some big damned Army truck was coming the other way. It was nice enough for the soldiers to have helped him free the EH, but he was so damned occupied with the kid bawling and Lucy standing there doing absolutely nothing, as always, that he had forgotten to thank them. Of all the things he looked back on, he regretted that. That wasn't the Christian thing to do but when Lucy had brought it up, it had angered him, so he had told her to shut her mouth.

It had been his idea to leave Brisbane, as had it been his idea to go west, down through inland New South Wales, rather than the coastal road. No doubt many people would take the most direct road to Sydney and no doubt the traffic would be horrendous. Finding himself intelligent, as the EH had cruised along northern New South Wales country roads, at speeds unheard of on coastal roads, he had allowed himself to smile then too. Fuel had been hard to find, but once again the genius forethought of Edgar had meant that he had brought cans full of fuel. It wasn't until Armidale where the situation had become desperate and he had really needed to search. Being so confident in his own successes, he hadn't realised the town was deserted until he had stopped at the main service station in town.

It took him a few minutes to realise that no one was going to attend him and fill his vehicle up for him. The smile had more than faltered by then, and was replaced with a scowl. *So much for country hospitality,* he had thought as he had clambered out of the EH, stiff backed. He walked to the bowser, the type with the glass bowl that you primed to whatever measurement you wanted and then drained the fuel into your tank, and gave the priming handle a pump. Nothing came up. Again, he pumped. Nothing. He tried the next bowser along to find the same thing. Frustrated, and essentially running on empty, he turned to the office and paused.

Written on the frontal glass panels in large, red letters was a bible verse he was familiar with: *He will appear a second time, not to bear sin—*

Edgar finished the line aloud, 'But to bring salvation to those who are waiting for him.' With the line completed, it sounded right, but something felt ominous about its omission in this sense. It was only then that he turned and saw really for the first time, how empty the town was.

No one was in the street, no one looked out at him from windows and only the howl of the wind as it rushed past vacant buildings offered him any sort of sound. He saw elsewhere more writing, this one not related to scripture, but written in the same cast: *Shepherd has called his flock to Tamworth. Come and be one'*

Edgar had frowned at this, but didn't have the forethought to see the harm in anything he had read so far. After sometime, he had clambered back into the EH and decided to try for Tamworth. He didn't even get out of Armidale before they had found him. His story, he imagined, had been like most. He wasn't greeted with open arms, but by a surly, bushy bearded man and a slick looking long haired feller, who couldn't keep his eyes of Lucy. When Edgar had brought attention to this, the slick feller had just smiled and offered her a compliment, while bushy beard pulled a can of fuel from the back of the Landcruiser and offered it to Edgar to fill the EH. To look back on it, there wasn't anything really obvious about the state of affairs in Tamworth, but there had been no question about them joining the "flock" either. In Edgar's mind, he had thought they might stop over a night or two, get their road readiness back in hand and move right along. Yet, not twenty minutes had passed since their entry into Tamworth's city district, that they were relieved of all their belongings. Apparently 'being one' meant all your shit became someone else's. Edgar had spoken up about this and had wound up with a sore jaw and a headache to thank for it. Work detail and rationing replaced any sort of freedom and as if in thanks, they were upgraded from communal bunks, where men and women slept and fornicated in front of everyone else, to having their own quarters granted to them. They were still not granted money, belongings, nor permission to leave.

A frown had crept over Edgar's face as he reminisced. A small town had come and gone as he looked back on his time in Tamworth, rather than ahead. He didn't think twice about the town that he had driven through, nor the fact that cars had been left uninhabited in the middle of the road. Almost as if on auto-pilot, he steered around them and continued to dwell on the past. Nor did he take notice that there was no traffic South of Tamworth, like there had been none in Armidale. He didn't look out at the walls of structures to see if Shepherd's men had cast their net in this direction as well. It didn't even cross his mind until he reached the next town.

With the headlights blaring on high beam, a small sign reflected brilliantly: *Murrurundi.* Just another small country town. Likewise, with the last small town Edgar had absent-mindedly driven through, Murrurundi had parked traffic scattered along the street. The difference was the Chinese tank that sat among them and the men that all turned to the lights of the EH as it came around the small bend and into the main street.

'Oh, Christ,' Edgar said softly as he saw the men turn and he jammed on the Holdens brakes.

'Who are they?' Lucy, wide eyed beside him, shifted as the EH came to a crooked halt.

'Oh Jesus.' Edgar gasped as all elation evaporated from him.

'They can't be *his* men,' Lucy said.

'That's the tank.' He pointed as the men approached the car, automatic weapons likewise liberated from the Chinese, raised toward the small Holden.

'The… tank…' Lucy could not argue. The damned thing had sat just outside of town for weeks, until the surly, bushy bearded feller had fuelled it up. It was all the talk for a day or two.

'Oh Jesus,' was all Edgar repeat as he tried to find reverse. The men shouted as they brandished their rifles, obviously seeing what the runner intended.

Shots rang out as the EH hurtled backwards. The red motor wailed as the revs climbed. The windscreen cracked as a bullet slammed into it and Lucy screamed. The EH bucked as the rear wheels left the road and Joe added his wails. Before, the cries didn't worry him, but now as the EH's rear bumper slammed into the dirt culvert and the engine died, all Edgar could do was lash out. 'Would you shut that damned thing up!'

Lucy cowered as he turned the key and the motor whirred. More bullets panged off the guard and steam erupted out from under the bonnet. The whirring took on another note and for the first time since he had owned it, the EH did not start. As Lucy whimpered and the kid bawled unconsolably, Edgar sat there cranking the engine that refused to fire.

As the men surrounded the car, Edgar looked around confused. 'But God was with me?' he questioned as the passenger door was pulled open and Lucy was dragged out screaming and kicking, Joe still bundled in her arms.

Edgar was still trying to turn the engine over as one of the men pulled Joe from her hands while another held her in place. She screamed and tried to claw at the baby snatcher as her child was dragged from her grasp. Either the baby snatcher didn't have the grasp on his temper that Edgar did, or he was the lowest of the lows that existed among men, because he struck Lucy—hard. Hard enough to silence her. Edgar didn't get out of the car. He still just sat there confused trying to crank the engine over as he looked from the slumped Lucy to the man that held the wailing child.

'That one is good enough for Shephard,' a man said as he pointed to the unconscious Lucy. 'Shut that fucking thing up, would you?' he barked to the other man who held the kid, as he rounded the car to where Edgar sat.

The baby snatcher exchanged a glance with one of the other men, who stood with rifle raised at Edgar. He then shrugged his shoulders, as if to push away any ownership he might have had in the crimes that were about to be committed. The man bent down and placed the child on the ground, still wailing. Edgar looked up as the order giver finally arrived at his door. Edgar was still turning the red motor over as a rifle shot rang out and suddenly, Joe wasn't crying anymore. He looked up confused as his door opened. The order giver stood there and finally, some recognition came into Edgar's broken mind. It was the same man who had given him the fuel in Armidale. The bushy bearded feller.

Edgar nodded as the recognition came over him, and still he turned the red motor over. The man with the bushy beard pulled a pistol from his hip and raised it. Edgar looked up to him, as he gave the red motor one last try and said, 'I just don't understand. He was on our side.'

The hammer on the Colt auto fell, and then there was only darkness. Darkness... Darkness...